Anne Ousby lives on the No~~r~~ have been published in antholog~~ies and broadcast on Radio~~ Her stage plays have been performed in the North East and a half hour made-for-television drama, *Wait Till the Summer Comes*, was broadcast on ITV.

Patterson's Curse is her first novel and has been inspired by South Africa's rural Western Cape where she has stayed many times with her family.

Patterson's Curse

ANNE OUSBY

To Margaret
love from
Anne

23-11-10

Published by Room To Write

www.roomtowrite.co.uk

ISBN 978-0-9564823-1-0

Designed and produced by HPM Group. Tel 0191 3006941
www.hpm.uk.com

For my husband, John, a man who was always there for me, nurturing my self-belief. His love of South Africa and its plants inspired Patterson's Curse.

Let us be grateful to people who make us happy, they are the charming gardeners who make our souls blossom.

Marcel Proust

Acknowledgements

I want to thank all my family and friends for their encouragement in the long process of writing this novel. Special thanks to the *Room To Write* team for their incredible support and practical help, without which, I and my fellow writer Erica, would have given up years ago. To Wendy Robertson for her insight and seemingly unending patience and sound advice. To Gillian Wales for reading the book and offering such warm encouragement and to Avril Joy for sharing some of the joy - no pun intended - she felt when her book was published. To Brenda for line editing the book and to Juliet for trying her darndest to get this published. And a special thank you to Craig and Catherine and the children in South Africa, for sharing their wonderful life with John and myself.

Endings

I can get my little finger through the burn-hole in Pete's fleece. I'm always telling him not to wear it when he lights the bonfire but he takes no notice. I'm wearing his fleece tonight. African nights can be cold. The jacket is too big and, when I zip it up, it comes right over my nose. I breathe in his smell. However much he sweats he never stinks of sweat – not like me. His scent is warm and salty like the summer sea.

Leaning back against the water tower I watch the stars. The children lie at my feet wrapped in duvets. Lilah snuffles in her sleep, one small hand curled around a bag of sweets. Jeth's eyes are closed but he isn't sleeping. His dog, Spider, lies pressed up against him, their bodies breathe as one...

The moon is huge, deep and wide enough to plunge into, and the constellations pulse about my head. I am wrapped around by the throbbing of cicadas and I feel the wind-rush as hunting owls sweep low over my head. Later I watch as the ghostly shapes of porcupine and bok step warily through the dark damp grass.

I wish this night to last forever.

But all too soon the sun heaves itself above the mist-shrouded mountains, covering them in a purplish haze. Steppe eagles labour upwards through the leaden morning air. A new day. The day I bury my husband.

As the first shafts of sunlight strike the green corrugated roof of our house I see Vantonde *bakkies* winding up the track towards Blue Gum. Taking Lilah in my arms I lead the way back down the path. Jeth trails wearily behind - one hand resting on Spider's head. We walk slowly, heads bowed, while jewelled birds call and flicker through the trees and the garden is drenched in the impossibly sweet smell of frangipani.

The Vantonde women are there before me, treading softly, filling each room with their suffering, bearing their loads solemnly. There are boxes of cutlery, china, glass, tablecloths, *potjie pots*, casseroles and cool-boxes. The mingled smells of *wors,* pickled fish and chicken fill the air and Spider's nostrils flare. Outside in the garden the men-folk crash about, gratefully unloading folding chairs and trestle tables and setting them up under the oak tree.

My mother-in-law, Ma Vantonde, has organised everything, the funeral service, the burial, the gathering – everything. There is only one thing I insist on.

'But a funeral's no place for children, Katie,' she pleads, her doughy cheeks flushed, tears threatening to spill. 'Their Auntie Miriam will look after them, ja? Poor babies.'

But she sees the look in my eyes and backs off. If I am to survive this day I need my children beside me.

While they work I take Lilah and Jeth up the track and give them a small basket each, woven from restios reeds. 'Let's pick some flowers for dad, hey?' That "dad" is too much for me and I sit down heavily on a tree trunk.

Lilah rushes off. She needs no encouragement to make petal

'potions'. Normally I don't let her trash the plants but today she can take whatever she wants. I light up a cigarette and watch the flotilla of cars coming up and down our track like ants after the honey. In the corner of my eye I see Jeth kicking at the earth and occasionally bending down and tearing at the vegetation.

Lilah jumps up beside me. She has filled her basket and is tossing petals high into the air, watching as the wind catches them and spins them away. I wrap my arms around her chubby legs to stop her from falling and press my face into the sun-drenched material of her dress.

Someone is shouting. Shielding my eyes against the now fierce rising sun I see Ma. She is standing on the path waving a white hanky. The sun sends her black shadow rushing towards us.

Back at the house the children are swooped on and 'made decent'. They would like to do the same to me but there is a limit to my tolerance. It's only when we're squashed together in the car that I see what the children have filled their baskets with. Lilah has a mixture of rose petals, agapanthus flowers, protea sprinklings and quaking-grass heads. I kiss her blond head and she presses herself into me, sucking furiously on a sweet.

Jeth clutches his container against his chest, small hands shielding the contents. When I pull them away I see that his basket is full of red soil, planted with gaudy sprigs of a plant covered with violet-blue flowers - Patterson's Curse. A wave of nausea hits me. I wind the window down and stick my head out. I know Jeth is watching me. When I can I turn to face him.

'Why did you do this?' I whisper.

He gives me a look so full of hatred it takes my breath away.

Later, when their baskets disappear into the grave the last thing I see is that purple plant. I will always see it. .

'I promise you, Kate. I'm gonna kill every last germ of this bloody alien, or die in the attempt.'

The white, Dutch Reformed church is full of black cloth and the smell of clothes from the back of the wardrobe. I hold Lilah in my arms and she winds her sticky fingers in my hair. Jeth stands beside me, stiff-backed - as far away from me as he can get - his eyes never leaving the coffin. The Vantonde fill the front bench and when I look along the narrow pew I see everyone's shiny black shoes, forced apart by the kneelers, absurd like penguin's feet. Ma had insisted the children had black shoes too. They never wear shoes.

Pete's sisters, Gloria and Antoinette, are at the far end of the bench. Antoinette erect, legs crossed at the ankles, smart in her black straight skirt. Gloria slumps beside her, crumpled and weeping, a handkerchief pressed against her mouth. Pete's stepfather, Lionel, is uneasy and sweating in his shirt and tie. His chubby fingers ceaselessly pulling at the tight collar. His neck a fiery red from all the scraping. Maarten, Pete's brother, sits hunched beside Jeth, head down, eyes squeezed tight shut, as if he's in pain. Ma is wedged between her two men, in blackcurrant glossy hat and shiny black skirt and jacket. She cries silently but violently, her large frame jerking to the spasms. Hankies pass along the line of Vantonde women like a white linen lifeline.

I don't cry.

The service is in Afrikaans so I don't know what Pastor Billy says about my beautiful Pete, but I know what these people are thinking.

Going too fast they say.

Straight over at the four way stop.

Always such a careful driver.

Things on his mind, hey? Worries.

Something must have happened between the funeral and the end of that day but I can't remember any of it, except Lilah was sick and the dog licked it up.

And when at last the people leave, taking the funeral with them, miraculously, I am still standing. The men sit in their *bakkies* waiting for their womenfolk, relieved to be escaping back to their beer and telly, while the women linger, covering the children with kisses. They clasp my hands and pat my shoulder. I swear that if anyone else touches me I will do something terrible.

Ma wants to stay but just for once Lionel is assertive and leads his weeping wife away. Her parting words linger in the air, like dust specks in the shafts of light, filling me with dread.

'Remember, Katie, you are not on your own. I am here for you. You are my beloved Peer's wife.'

His name is Pete, I want to scream. *Call him Pete.*

I sit alone on the *stoep* as the sun ploughs down behind the eucalyptus trees, catching fire to the leaves. Blue cranes fly homeward and guinea fowl settle noisily on their roosts. The Hadida ibis squabble overhead and frogs begin their night song from the vlei. Each creature with purpose. Each in its proper place.

At last I drag myself upstairs and lie down fully dressed beside the children. Lilah sleeps noisily, a tidemark of sugar around her mouth. Jeth lies still, his breath a butterfly-wing shudder. I lean closer to make sure his chest is moving. Spider is curled up against him, one anxious eye fixed on me, but I let him stay. Then I screw my eyes tight shut against the dying sun, praying for oblivion.

Bird Table

The sickly smell of glue will always remind me of the day that it happened. When the phone rang Jeth was holding two pieces of glued wood together, while he counted slowly to sixty and Lilah was snipping happily away at bits of material, making fairy clothes. So, for once, I got to the phone first.

'Hi, Pete,' I said, before he had chance to say anything. 'I'm sorry about...'

'...Is that 603?'

I didn't recognise the voice. 'Yeh. Who is this?'

'Katie? Is that you?'

Only one person I knew called me Katie. 'Oh hi, Ma.' I said, trying to hide my disappointment. 'What's the matter? Got a cold?'

'Can we come over?'

'Of course.' Since when did my mother-in-law ever ask permission to visit? As long as Pete was at work she could come and go as she pleased. 'It's just me and the kids as usual...'

But she'd gone.

'Mum? Can I let go now?'

I knew Jeth hadn't forgiven me, but at least he was talking to me. He was making a new bird table. The old one had been broken for months and each time he put food out for the weaver birds it blew straight back inside the house. The wind blew most of the time here. Actually the bird table was a peace offering. Jeth hated it when Pete and I quarrelled and we'd had an awful row that morning. Thank God Lilah didn't get upset like Jeth. She had seemed oblivious as the storm raged around her. She just kept shovelling corn flakes into her mouth, spreading cereal around her like crunchy ectoplasm.

We'd had Blue Gum for nearly seven years then and we still hadn't got the plant nursery running properly. Pete was doing a job he hated to bide us over while I battled to look after us all and do the gardening. There was never enough time or money and we were always tired and irritable.

While I waited for Ma and Lionel I dialled Pete's number again. It was still engaged. I'd been trying all morning.

Today's fight had been so petty. The milk was off because one of us had forgotten to put it back in the fridge and someone had left the top off the sugar and the ants had moved in. Pete blamed me but I knew it was him and the injustice of it all got to me. I was always asking him to put things away but he refused to own up and it turned into a slanging match. Usually one of us would have laughed and we would have made up before he left for work, but not this morning. He stormed out without saying goodbye to any of us.

I followed him, determined to have the last word. Jeth came out and stood at the door. Pete was kneeling down beside the bakkie yanking out fistfuls of Patterson's Curse. He glared at me. 'You're letting this bloody stuff take a hold again.'

'Forgive me, baas, I will work harder.'

He swung up into the driver's seat, slamming the door shut behind him, and turned the key. It wouldn't start; it never does first time. He waited and tried again.

'I won't be here when you get back.' I shouted. It was the day I took the kids to the Vantonde house for their tea.

He leant out of the bakkie window. 'Ever thought you've got your priorities wrong, Kate? Blue Gum is more important than tea parties with my mother.'

'D'you think I want to go?'

He shrugged. 'It's your choice.'

'No, it isn't. She's their grandma, for God's sake.'

And there we were again, rowing about Ma. It seemed like every argument we had always ended up about her.

The engine spluttered into life and Pete reversed onto the track.

'I won't be back until late. You'll have to get your own meal.' Gloria was going to take the children to see the ponies at the animal rescue centre where she helped out.

'Don't come back on my account,' he yelled.

I ran to the bakkie, scooped up the pile of Patterson's Curse and lashed it through the open window. 'D'you know something, Pete Vantonde. I wish I'd never come to this bloody awful country. I hate it and I hate you.'

He turned an angry, shocked face to me and I saw an ugly red welt down his cheek, where a woody stem had caught his skin. I was horrified but as I stepped towards him he accelerated away, leaving me stranded in a tidal wave of exhaust fumes and dust.

Back inside the house Lilah was in the fridge with her fingers in the apricot jam. Jeth followed me and sat down, pushing his toast around the plate. He was crying. I should have told him then that I hadn't meant it. That Pete and I were just tired and of course we loved each other. But I didn't. And when I dropped him off at

9

nursery he turned his face away so that I couldn't kiss him.

When Lionel's bakkie pulled up outside the children rushed to greet them - bird boxes and bits of material forgotten. Where their Ouma went, so did treats.

The moment Ma was out of the car she grabbed Jeth and pulled him into her arms. He tried to wriggle free – he was like me, didn't like too much handling - but she clamped him against her chest, staring at me over his head and then she burst into tears. I could feel my heart thumping and clutched the door handle for support.

Lilah was hanging onto her granddad's hand. The big man stood motionless, his free hand fluttering, as if he didn't quite know what to do with it.

'Maarten got a message,' he mumbled, not looking at me. 'From the traffic cops in Hermanus?'

'You poor little darlings. ' Ma was sobbing into Jeth's hair. 'You must be the man of the house now, Jethro…now he's…now your…daddy's gone.'

Jethro struggled to get away from her. 'Where's he gone?'

And then she said the words and he went totally crazy, punching and lashing out at her. Lionel tried to grab him but Jeth head-butted him in the stomach. I managed to get hold of him and dragged him into the back garden. He was screaming and kicked me hard on the shins. I managed to pin his arms to his sides and then he bit me. 'You killed my daddy, you killed my daddy,' he shrieked. He was crying and I was crying and we were both so angry. I wanted to smack him - to really hurt him - but I managed to hold onto myself.

Eventually he calmed down enough for me to take him into the house. Lionel was working on the bird table, a stream of white glue oozing out from between his large fingers. He looked at me and shrugged hopelessly. Jeth ran upstairs. Lilah was sitting on Ma's lap cutting up a new T-shirt.

Later, when Lionel managed to get Ma to go home, I sat with Lilah on the *stoep* and she snuggled up against me and fell asleep. We stayed there until the sun disappeared and then I carried her upstairs. Jeth was spread-eagled across the bed, his dirty little face channelled with tears. I kissed his sad little face and then lay down beside them.

First Days

Time plays weird games on me. I have no chronological memory of that terrible time. It might be days, weeks or hours since he died. Ma and Lionel are a constant presence, they look after the children. I don't - I can't. Gloria is in the house too, clutching her latest angel for Lilah, her fingers, sticky-bright with sequins and glitter. She is crying. Antoinette stands watching, saying nothing, but sometimes I catch something in her expression that is so like Pete that I feel a knife twisting in my gut. I don't understand her seething resentment but I welcome her anger. It gives some reality to this waking nightmare I've found myself in.

'Where's Uncle Maarten?' I hear Lilah ask repeatedly.

'He's busy at work, hey?' Lionel's voice.

Ma makes the decisions and deals with callers. Gloria cooks and fusses and Lionel answers the phone. I managed to ring mum the day it happened but when the phone goes now I can't speak to her or anyone.

'It's Maggie again, Kate.' Lionel says softly, offering me the phone, but I back away, shaking my head.

'What shall I say?' he whispers.

I shrug helplessly.

'She says she's getting the next flight, Kate. She could stay with us if you…'

'No, no, please.' My voice is shrill now, panicky. 'Tell her I don't want her to come. Please. Not yet.'

And I hear his kind voice, reassuring, calming, and trying to explain the impossible. What sort of a monster am I? I try not to think of the look on mum's face, the rejection she'll feel. 'Thanks, Lionel.' I say, as he puts the phone down.

'She's very upset, Kate...'

And I stumble from the room. '...Sorry, Lionel, sorry...' And I find that small place in the myrtle hedge, just wide enough for me to crawl into, and I lay there, eyes tight shut, hand pressed across my mouth so they won't hear the scream.

Maggie didn't recognise her daughter's voice. It was late and Kate never rang unless she had to. She hated the phone. 'Kate? Is that you?'

'Were you asleep? Sorry.'

'It doesn't matter. What is it, Kate?'

Silence.

'Kate? You still there? Has something happened? Is it one of the children? Is it Jeth? Tell me.'

'It's Pete, Mum. He's dead.'

And that's when a thousand miles becomes a million - a hundred million. Kate was talking fast now, firing the words at Maggie. 'I can't speak now. I'll ring you when I can. Don't ring back. I'm not answering the phone. And, Mum? Please don't come. I'm coping...'

'...But, Kate...'

'...Please. Promise you won't come till I ask you?'

'Yes okay but...'

'...Love you.' And then the phone went dead.

And Maggie somehow kept her word and waited and waited for her daughter to ring.

Some part of me knows that Ma shouldn't be here still but I'm not strong enough to see her off and the children need family.   I'm no use to them. If it's left to me they go unwashed. I forget the time and they sleep where they drop. Some days I don't get up at all. On days like these I sometimes forget and my fingers touch a cold space, a smooth acre of emptiness beside me and I roll over and bury myself in the place where he has lain, hoping to feel him there. But there is nothing, not even the memory of his body in the mattress.

Ma wants to wash the sheets, to tidy the bedroom, but I won't let her. His clothes are still on the chair, his half-read book open on the bedside table, a partly-drunk cup of tea beside it – the orange scum studded with flies. I lie there listening to Jeth commanding and Lilah demanding. I say *'go away'* or *'ask Jeth,'* or *'wait till Ouma comes.'* I hear the bakkie come and go and Ma's high-pitched voice. Lionel takes the children to nursery for me. Lilah clings to my legs on the first day, refusing to move. She seems okay now. Jeth goes without a murmur. I smell frying food and hear the television. There are loud voices speaking in Afrikaans, the dog barks and then it is night again.

Night becomes day for me. While they sleep I creep downstairs and sit at the kitchen table eating banana sandwiches. I watch the frenzied moths as they dive-bomb the light bulb and hear the *thuds* as larger flying insects crash against the windowpanes. There's another sound too, a faint, yet persistent electrical hum. In the stillness of night this noise gets louder and louder until it fills my brain, the room, the universe. One night, I can take no more. It's the sound that drives men mad and I know what it is.

Beside our kitchen is a small room - one table, a chair, computer, printer and futon. All the surfaces are covered with neatly stacked piles of books and alphabetically-labelled files. Bookshelves clad the walls from floor to ceiling. This is Pete's room.

As I am untidy and haphazard so Pete is neat and methodical. Jeth could ask his dad about the most insignificant little bug and within minutes Pete would find the appropriate reference book for him. And when we got the second-hand computer and access to the World Wide Web Pete's joy was complete.

All his letters and emails are in this room; the correspondence from a hundred environmental agencies and NGO's; information on government schemes for conservation; bills from years back; all his school books and reports; drawings from the children – each dated. His entire life was in that room.

I push the door open. Blue and white light pulses across the ceiling and down the walls. I steel myself. Maybe one day I'll be able to deal with Pete's room but not now. I reach across for the mouse trying not to think that he was the last one to use this computer. The imprint of his bottom is on the leather chair.

I know nothing about computers except how to turn them off. As I switch off my arm catches some loose papers and they shiver to the floor. Gathering them up I thrust them back on the pile but I've missed one. I pick it up and leave the room, meaning to throw it away, but I recognise the writing. It belongs to me.

'What are you accusing me of exactly, Katie?' Ma asks indignantly. Her back is to me. She is dusting the piano, making a huge show of cleaning between each key. I say nothing and finally she turns to face me.

'And I certainly wouldn't read my son's private correspondence, if that's what you're implying.' Her blue eyes are wide and innocent.

'You know I don't want anyone going in Pete's room.'

I'd stayed up all night reading my letters to Pete and I'm dizzy with tiredness. After I read them I burnt them. All that loving and longing - such private things - and I know that this woman has read every word. My mouth begins to water, as if I'm going to throw up. I get a drink and sit at the kitchen table. My hand shakes as I hold the glass.

'Are you ill, Katie?' Her voice says *concern,* her eyes say *whore*.

'I think it's time you went back home, Ma.'

'What?'

'I appreciate what you've done.' I hurry on, 'but I have to manage on my own.'

She flaps the duster at me. 'Nonsense, you need me. It's my duty to be here, to look after Peer's family.'

'No, it's my job.'

'You?' she says, barely able to conceal her contempt. 'You can't look after yourself, Katie, let alone my grandchildren.'

I don't know where I found the strength but this was one argument I wasn't going to lose. I wanted her out of my house before the children got back from school.

After they'd gone, with Lionel promising to continue with the school run and Ma refusing to look at me, I went back to bed and floated in that blissful unknowing state of consciousness, halfway between wakefulness and sleep. But then I felt his eyes on me and there he stood, my son Jeth, hands on hips watching me. Always that same expression - the one he gave me the morning Pete left and never came back.

'Where's Ouma,' he demands.

When I don't answer he turns his back on me and walks away. .

Miriam and Rob

I know it will be difficult without the Vantondes but I hear Pete's voice whispering. 'Promise you'll never trust her, Kate. Promise.'

Word gets round that I'm on my own now and strangers descend on Blue Gum like flies on a cowpat. *We're not stopping. We don't want to intrude.* Vantonde relatives and Pete's friends, bringing sweets and toys for the children and beautifully wrapped packages for me. Dainty fancy goods, beaded jam pot covers, crocheted toilet roll holders and embroidered place mats… why? Is it someone's birthday? *We're so sorry, Kate. If there's anything we can do to help, you only have to say the word.* Some bring alcohol. *Better off without a man,* one confides. *You'll be fine, Kate. Enjoy your freedom, hey? God! No man? I wish.*

Gifts of food line our kitchen table. We eat from one dish; then move on to the next. What is left is fed to Spider, or the feral cats which have become sleek and fat. I haven't been into Kleinsdorp. I can't face the 'kindness' stalking the streets, waiting to pounce.

Miriam is the only person I can tolerate in these early days. She and Rob live in a rondavel down the track. Rondavels are round, thatched little dwellings with rooms radiating off from a central point. They remind me of the mushrooms I used to pick when I was a kid. You had to search for their perfect white bonnets in the early-morning, dew-wet grass. I always felt mean wrenching them away from their marks.

Jeth was having a major strop the day Miriam and I first met. I was attempting to slap some paint on the kitchen walls and we were fighting for the one large paintbrush.

'Hi,' she said, peering around the open door. 'I'm Miriam, from down the lane? Bad timing?'

'No please, come in. I'm Kate and this is…'

'…And this is the lovely Jethro.' She swung the little boy high in the air and kissed him on his nose. 'Sweet boy.' Then she sat down with him on her knee and gave him a beautifully wrapped present. It was a picture book about animals and insects – perfect for him. She turned the pages, while I boiled the kettle. Jeth was wearing grubby shorts and his legs and feet were dirty. I searched around for something to cover her immaculate white trousers with, but she was okay about it.

As we talked I couldn't take my eyes off her feet. Her toenails were painted a peachy pink and her feet were brown and smooth. I was wearing shorts as usual, so I couldn't hide my legs. Sod it. I hadn't shaved my legs since I was fourteen. I didn't believe in any of that crap. However, in South Africa, not shaving your legs meant you were gay.

Miriam put down her cup and searched for something in her expensive handbag. 'Oh hell. I've forgotten my ciggies. Can I borrow one, Kate? Everyone smoked in South Africa.

I gave her a roll-up. She held the weedy thing between her long fingers and took a suspicious drag, widening her eyes in horror as she picked wisps of tobacco off her pink tongue. 'My God, Kate, does everyone eat tobacco in the UK?'

She was funny. I knew I should hate her on principle, but I'd found a friend. It was a great feeling. She was the first real friend I made in Africa.

Now, she comes most nights after work. She doesn't ask questions or give advice or try to cheer me up. We have a smoke and sit outside, watching the sky darkening, while her little white poodle, Fluffy, nestles beside the pathetically grateful Spider.

As Miriam is great so Rob, her husband, is a nightmare. He and my Pete go back a long way. He breeds horses on the farm and, when Miriam's at work, he often drops by "for a chat." I never had much to do with him before but now he's always here, leaning against the back door, offering me a beer. *'Just passing, Kate. Thought you'd like some company.'*

He's British South African so in theory we should have a lot in common, but he's what my mum would call an *unquiet spirit*. He's always on the move, changing the subject mid-sentence, jumping up suddenly and pacing about or grabbing one of the kids and swinging them around. He doesn't talk normally, he shouts. Jeth disappears as soon as Rob arrives and Lilah sticks close by me.

One day he squeezed my knee. He must have seen the look on my face because he was immediately on his feet apologising. 'Hey. Sorry, Kate. Just being friendly. Old Pete wouldn't want to see you like this. He was always full of life. Great mate. Bloody great mate.'

'Look Rob,' I said. 'No offence but I…'

'…Did he tell you we were called up together?'

'Yes,' I said, 'Please, Rob…' But there was no stopping him.

'A lot of our mates buggered off abroad rather than join up but we stayed put. Bloody stupid but it turned out okay. Told the bastards from the start we didn't want to fight, so they put us on patrol on the Angolan border, fighting SWAPO guerrillas? We had bushmen trackers – amazing little yellow guys. Nothing they didn't know about the bush. Stop me if I've told you this before but Pete was our driver and one of the little fellas would sit up on the bonnet and track through the bush. Never knew which side they were on but we never caught any of the bad guys - thank God! Trapped us some good bush meat, though. Had some great brais, our platoon.'

The day Rob tried to kiss me I lashed out and my fist crunched into his beer paunch. It must have hurt a lot but d'you know what? I didn't give a shit.

After that Miriam didn't come so often. Maybe Rob had told her I punched him but whatever, on the few occasions she comes now there's a definite coolness between us.

One particular day she brought a bag of rusks for the kids. South African rusks are crunchy little biscuits and Lilah loves them. Miriam was on her way to work and as always looked amazing - slim, immaculately dressed, short blond hair beautifully cut.

'Are the kids okay?' she asked, breaking a long silence.

I shrugged. Jeth and Lilah were outside somewhere. If she wanted to see them she'd have to go find them. I didn't ask her to sit down.

She sighed. 'See you then, Kate.'

I grunted a goodbye and waited for her to leave but when I looked up she was standing there staring at me. She looked very serious.

'There's something I've got to tell you, Kate.'

I waited.

'There are a lot of rumours flying around Kleinsdorp.'

'So what's new?' Kleinsdorp was a typical small community, seething with gossip and misinformation. Pete and I had always stayed well clear.

Miriam took a deep breath. 'Your mother-in-law's telling people you're not fit to look after Jeth and Lilah.'

I was so shocked I laughed. 'She's probably right. What's she going to do?' Get me arrested?'

Miriam said something under her breath.

'What?'

'This is serious, Kate. She could take them away from you.'

I stared at her. 'No she can't. I'm their mother, for God's sake.'

'If she could prove you were negligent she might get custody.'

'Over my dead body,' I shrieked. 'The bitch, the two-faced bitch.'
I jumped up, grabbing my car keys.

Miriam put her hand on my arm. 'What are you going to do?'

'I'm going to rip her head off!'

Miriam held on tighter but I shook her off. 'Look after the kids for me?'

Her face was stony. 'I can't, I'm on my way to work.'

'Well thanks a bunch, pal.'

'You've got to stay calm, Kate. You go down there now ranting and raving and she'll use it against you. Believe me I know what she's like.'

I sank back into the chair. 'What am I going to do?'

She sat down opposite me. 'You've got to prove her wrong.'

I followed her gaze as her eyes slid around the kitchen. I saw the piles of dirty dishes in the sink and Spider's bowl crawling with ants and flies. I saw the mud and food detritus under the table and the mountain of children's dirty clothes hurled by the washing machine, waiting to be washed. Finally Miriam looked at me.

'I know it must be terrible for you Kate, losing Pete but…it's not just about you, is it? There's Lilah and Jeth. You've got to get it together for their sakes. That's what Pete would want.'

I don't know where it came from but I was suddenly so angry I felt as if my head was going to explode. If I'd had a knife I would have stuck it in her. I swept the bag of rusks off the table and lunged at her, fists flailing. She jumped away from me.

'Who d'you think you are?' I screeched. 'Coming here, lecturing me. I don't want your help or your kindness or your bloody advice. I'll deal with Ma in my own way; now get out of my house.'

Miriam stood her ground. 'Okay, okay. I'm sorry.'

I marched past her and flung the door open, waiting for her to go.

'Kate, please, don't be like this…'

'…Get lost, Miriam. D'you think I need some self-centred bitch telling me what my children need? You want kids, Miriam? You have them. What's the matter? Afraid your man won't fancy you with droopy boobs and baby's puke down your designer clothes, um…?'

Her hand came out of nowhere and struck me hard across the side of my face. The force drove me back against the door. Her fury fuelled mine. '…Scared he'll ditch you for some "coo" girl, younger and prettier than you? We all know what an old lecher he is.'

That stopped her.

'He even tried it on with me…Yes me, with the dirty hair and smelly clothes.' I was enjoying myself now. 'God! Shows how desperate the poor sod is.'

Her eyes were bright with tears. 'You're lying.'

I shrugged. 'Am I?'

She seemed to shrink before my eyes. Her shoulders hunched and she stared down at the ground. 'I know what he's like but I love him…' Then she looked up at me. Tears were streaming down her face and her nose was running. I looked away. I couldn't be responsible for this. When she spoke again I could hardly hear her. 'I can't have kiddies, Kate. Didn't you know? Or maybe you do and you don't care. Rob? He can't handle it.' And with that she stumbled out of the house.

I shut the door and stood with my back to it, eyes closed. When I opened them again Lilah was on the floor, under the table, picking up pieces of rusk and jamming them into her mouth as if her life depended on it. Her curly blond hair stood up in ratty spikes and her little bottom stuck out through the seat of her torn shorts.

Jeth stood by the door, his mouth set in a hard disapproving line. His face was smeared with dirt and his shirt was ripped. Spider leant up against his legs and when he saw me looking his ears flattened and his tail disappeared between his legs.

The Coral Tree

Whatever I thought about Miriam, she was no liar. I knew enough about Ma to know she was dangerous, so I took Miriam's advice and stayed away from my mother-in-law. There was only one way to fight Ma Vantonde. I had to do what Miriam said, get off my backside, or I might lose my children. That terrible thought drove me on. The first thing I did was to phone my mum and ask her to come out. It was a quick, business-like phone call. That was the only way I could handle it. She was so grateful I could have wept. The children were delighted of course they love their Grandma. Even Jeth was in a good mood and I heard him shouting and playing with Spider in the garden - the first time since Pete's death.

I toured the house, picking up discarded dirty clothes; ripped off all the bedding, mine included, and had a massive wash. Afterwards I took us all out to the shower by the water tower and we spent an hour in there getting very clean. We always use this shower in the summer when the water's hot from the sun. Pete and I and the children love it. I held my face under the shower-head, letting the warm water clear my head.

It wasn't just the children I'd neglected. Pete's trees were crowding my dreams, reaching out to me, their dead, desiccated leaves crumbling like dust about my head. I vowed that from now on I would set myself a mission each day and today I would water the Coral tree.

Fiery red blossoms, Pete had promised. *For our children and grandchildren.* And he'd kissed me and traced his fingers down my arm and across my pregnant bump. *One day, Kate, you'll wake up and it will be the most beautiful thing you've ever seen.* And I'd believed him. Like I believed everything he said. We would grow old together on Blue Gum and the children would marry and we would build houses for them nearby. And black, white and Cape-coloureds would be taught side by side in the school we built. And we would farm the land in a sustainable, ecological way. The African philosophy of humanism or *ubantu* would exist here on Blue Gum and it would be the most wonderful place in the world to be. It would be bloody Shangri-La.

I called the children and lathered them with sunscreen. Lilah wailed when I got it in her eyes but I persisted. Then, I filled two watering cans and we set off. I could see the tree's puny outline shimmering in the killing heat. It was only a five-minute walk away. All I had to do was get there and back before the sun skewered me into the red-baked earth. I could do that.

I hadn't gone more than a few paces before Lilah screamed. I looked back to where she lay in a golden heap on the path, her plump brown arms waving forlornly, like some upended dung beetle. 'Marmy! Lilah got thorn.'

Why was it always her? 'Where's your brother?' I shouted. 'He'll get it out for you.' I looked for Jeth and was just in time to see his blond head disappearing over the lip of the reservoir. 'Jethro! One more step and you're in big trouble.'

The fynbos was dense up that bank and Jeth wouldn't be able to see where he was putting his bare feet. He knew the rules. There were certain places on Blue Gum where snakes lived - the giant aloe behind the chicken coop; the hollow log by the washing line; our woodpile and this side of the reservoir.

'Jethro?' My heart was hammering. 'Come down now or...'

He heard my fear and his face appeared over the top of the bank. The sun was behind him and a huge orange and red king protea stood erect beside him. For a moment I didn't know which of the golden faces was his.

'Mum. I found the tortoise.' His voice broke with excitement. 'The biggest one in the world? The great great granddaddy tortoise? The one Dad told me about...'

'...Did you hear what I said, Jethro? I want you down here now...'

'...But Mum, he lives in this big hole in the side of the dam and I...'

'...I'm not listening. Do as you're told...'

'...You can't make me. You're not my boss.'

Lilah's voice cut across her brother's. 'Marmy, Marmy. Come get.'

I dropped the cans and marched back towards her, machine-gunning words at Jethro as I went. 'Don't make me come up there for you. I'm counting to ten and you know what happens if you don't do as you're told...one ...two... Jethro? I mean it. Four...five... six...seven...eight...' And then, thank God, I saw the tree-heathers lashing from side to side as my son slashed his furious way down the bank.

My daughter made no attempt to get up when I reached her and

I had to crouch down to search her foot. Devil thorns are innocuous looking little brown prickles but they're very painful if you get one in your foot. I was gentle but she still yelped when it came out and clamped her arms around my waist. I struggled to my feet with Lilah straddling me like a straightjacket. She was crying loudly and snottily into my neck and I breathed in her warm biscuity smell.

As I re-traced my steps to where I'd dumped the watering cans my son fell in behind us. 'Thanks, Jeth. I'll take you up there tonight, promise...'

A clod of earth whistled past my ear and exploded in a dust bomb, directly in front of us. The fine red dirt blew up into my eyes and mouth and Lilah screeched again. I faced the defiant boy, spitting out grit. 'What did you do that for? You were good and now you're bad so you won't be going to the reservoir tonight or any night. Jethro? Where are you going? Come back here now.'

But he was already halfway back to the house and there was nothing I could do about it. Spider was lying in the shade of the blue gum tree, his front paws crossed, deep worry lines etched into his forehead. I watched as Jeth threw himself down beside the dog and buried his face in the animal's flank. I would have to be quick. Jeth does stupid things when he's in one of his moods.

I grabbed the cans and stumbled towards the welcoming shade of the halfway pomegranate tree. Once beneath the canopy I dropped the cans and some of the precious liquid slopped out onto the parched earth. I watched as it evaporated in one tiny hiss, like the drops of moisture on a boiling kettle. The shade was an illusion. It was almost as hot in there as it was outside.

Lilah sat on the ground making necklaces out of seed heads while

I checked under the tree for spiders. I made my mouth smile. 'I know, Lilah. Why don't you stay here? Make me a lovely bracelet, um? I'll only be two minutes. See? You can watch me all the way.'

'No, come with.' Lilah leapt at me, gripping my legs, her little fingers digging painfully into my flesh. It would have been so easy to give up and go back to the house but I wouldn't be beaten. I swung Lilah into my arms and stepped out onto the orange path that flared away like a line of fire. That's when I noticed a shape, drifting towards me, buoyed up on the crackling heat-haze. I watched as the shimmering form ebbed and flowed in size and substance until it coalesced into one distinct silhouette, a person, with something large and black floating overhead.

There was something hypnotic about the way the figure moved. Advancing slowly, then stopping and sinking to the ground before bobbing up and moving on again. Dip, rise, dip, rise, like the pelicans on the pond in St James's Park in London - all lined up in a stately row, bending and stretching in the water, synchronised to some telepathic beat.

Whoever it was had seen me now and raised a hand in greeting, palm flat, fingers spread. It was a woman, a black woman, carrying a large umbrella. I turned for home. I didn't have cash for casual labourers and I couldn't speak Afrikaans or Xhosa, so I wouldn't be able to explain. I couldn't face the awkwardness.

'Oi! Wait!'

The authority in her voice stopped me dead. When she reached me she upended the umbrella on the path, dropped the bag she was carrying and mopped at her face with a bright orange and green bandanna. She was short and stocky and dressed in a black skirt and white T-shirt emblazoned with a 'Working for Water' logo. She wore headphones, which she took off and stuffed in her bag and then she turned her full attention on me. She was grinning.

'That Brian Van de Bull? He makes me laugh so much. SAFM? You listen to him?'

I shook my head, thanking God that she could speak English.

Her smile was generous but her eyes missed nothing. I felt as if I was being scanned and was relieved I'd had a shower and change of clothes. But the woman wasn't looking at me. She was staring at the watering cans. I waved towards the tree. 'Coral trees are very...special,' I explained. 'They have lovely vivid red blossoms...I have to water it each day or it will die.' It sounded pathetic, even to me.

'It's dead already. I see it, just now. I think why is this dead twig here?' She wagged a finger at me. 'You want to get black like me? Where is your brolly?'

Her mouth had the same childish downward curve as Jeth's and I glanced apprehensively back to the house. I'm sorry that you've come all this way for nothing but we...I don't need any help at the moment...'

'...No time for sorree. Come.' And she pointed to the house.

'No,' my voice was firm. 'I have to water the tree first.'

Lilah was staring open-mouthed at the woman, sore foot forgotten. She loved umbrellas. She had filled my last one with water and used it as a paddling pool. Wriggling out of my arms she stood beside the woman and stared longingly up into the black bubble. Up close I saw that it wasn't really black at all, but a bloomy green, peppered by a tracery of tiny pinpricks.

'Silver fish.' The woman explained, seeing what I was looking at. 'Everywhere you go silver fish.' She grinned at Lilah and raked her fingers through the child's curly hair. Then she bent down and whispered something in her ear. Lilah hated strangers and I waited for her to react but she nodded happily. The woman took out her transistor and let Lilah listen on the headphones then they disappeared together under the brolly.

'Are you looking for someone?' I asked.

The voice came back strong and assertive. 'No, I found who I look for.'

'There must be some mistake.'

She poked her head out from under the umbrella. 'Your name please?'

'Kate, Kate Vantonde. '

'Hi, Kate. I'm coming to work for you and Pete.'

I turned my head away so she couldn't see my face but she was fishing in her bag for something. Finally she produced a piece of paper. 'See? Official documentation. Our beautiful government pay for me to work for you. I am opening a store on the RDP as soon as I have enough rand but now I am working for you.'

The writing was in Afrikaans and, while I stared uncomprehendingly at it, she emptied her bag on the track. A tangled mass of wilting weeds tumbled out. Of course, that was what she'd been doing as she walked towards me. Pulling up aliens. There was Port Jackson willow, rock Hakie and Patterson's Curse and others I didn't recognise.

The woman piled the vegetation in a heap. 'I show you what South Africa thinks about aliens, mummy.' She began to stamp on

31

the weeds and after a moment Lilah joined in. They held hands and jumped up and down, as if it were some game - my daughter's injury totally forgotten. They pounded and ground the weeds until all that remained was a smear of green slime on the red earth. Then the woman wiped her laughing, sweating face and turned to me.

'I start the big clear up, Kate. You know?' And she made her voice loud and important. 'Get rid of aliens. 'Work for water project.' ' She thumped her chest. 'Only nice kind African plants allowed, aye? Only little drinkers. Not greedy guzzlers like spider gum and willow. Each time I see one of those little bastards, I kill them.'

Then she picked Lilah up and her voice echoed back to me as she hurried down the track to the house. 'We go now, Kate.'

'But the water,' I stammered, 'I must do the watering...'

'...Okay but we go for shade before we are burnt like chops.' She didn't look back to see if I was following.

I hesitated for a moment and then I dropped the cans and turned for home. I would do it later when it was cooler. 'Excuse me?' I shouted, suddenly remembering Spider, 'Our dog? I'm afraid he doesn't like...'

She didn't alter her stride but flapped one hand to show she had heard me. '...No worree, Kate. Dogs like Nomatuli. Even bastard Boer dogs.'

When I got back Lilah and the black woman were in the shade of the blue gum. Lilah was dancing to the music on the woman's transistor, waggling her little bottom to the beat and shrieking with laughter. Spider was barking excitedly and jumping up, first at

Lilah, and then the woman. I opened my mouth to yell. He could be quite rough when he was over-excited. But the woman raised her finger at the dog and said, 'No', in a deep strong voice. Spider backed off, ears flat, tail wagging apologetically.

Jeth was perched high up in the tree. I didn't say anything, but the tops of my legs were tingling. I hated it when he climbed so high but if I made an issue of it, he might climb higher still. He was shouting something at the woman. When he's excited he gets louder and shriller, almost hysterical. Pete was the only one who could calm him down when he got like that.

'…I saw it up by the reservoir,' he was shouting. 'It's the great, great granddaddy tortoise. My dad told me about him. He lives in a big hole. D'you want to come see?' He'd been working his way down the tree and now he dropped out of the branches and ran to the woman, pulling at her skirt.

`Jethro? Enough.' My voice sounded harsh, even to me, and I saw the woman's surprise. I grabbed Jeth's arm, harder than I meant to, and yanked him away from her. 'I've told you, Jethro. You are not going up there again. Do you understand?'

There were tears in his eyes. 'I hate you. You always spoil things.' Then he grabbed the woman's arm and tried to drag her away.

She loosened his fingers and turned a friendly yet firm expression on him 'No, rather you stay here, like mummy says.' She rested her hand briefly on the sulking boy's head. He moved away so that her hand fell loosely on his shoulder. 'Hey? Big boy, aye? Your daddy will take you to see the tortoise some time, for sure.'

Jeth jammed his hands over his ears and shouted 'la, la, la' at the top of his voice, before running off behind the house.

The black woman turned off her music and Lilah slipped her hand into mine, sucking the thumb of the other.

'Your husband Pete? He is not here?' The woman was frowning.

Someone said, *'He was killed. In an accident.'* It must have been me.

'My turn to be sorry, Kate.'

The woman bent down and took Lilah's other hand. 'And who is this angel child? Tell auntie.'

Lilah dimpled. 'Lilah.'

She smiled at Lilah 'Hello, Lilah.'

I scrubbed at my eyes with the back of my hand. 'Would you like something to drink before you start work Notamu…'

'Nomatuli,' she corrected me, holding out her hand. Her grasp was firm and her skin warm and dry. 'Nomatuli Izhaki.'

'Nomatuli,' I repeated. 'Would you like something to drink? It's so hot today.'

She shook her head. 'I bring my break time food and drink, thank you.'

'Nommy,' Lilah said suddenly and grinned.

The woman patted Lilah on the head and then glanced at the large watch on her wrist. 'I start work at two a.m. Hours for working in documentation?' Then she swept out towards the shade of the oak tree. She stopped halfway and looked back. 'Maybe Nomatuli pull up that greedy guzzler?' She was pointing at the oak tree. I could hear her laughter all the way up the path.

Maggie

The taxi driver caught Maggie's eye in the mirror. 'This it?'
She nodded and he swung the car onto a deeply rutted farm track.
As they bumped their way along she could see the gum tree
getting nearer, towering above the surrounding, smaller pines and
spider gums.

'It's that one,' said Maggie, pointing out a house with a sage-
green corrugated-iron roof. The taxi parked between an ancient
yellow Renault - one headlight tied on with wire - and a bakkie that
was well past its sell-by date. Maggie got out. The man grinned
encouragingly from his seat as she battled to get her cases out of the
boot. On the drive she'd attempted to work out how much to tip
the man but her tired brain refused to do the sums. She thrust a
handful of notes at the driver which he stuffed into his pocket,
before she could change her mind. Then, with a grin that threatened
to split his face in two, he accelerated away, kicking up a wall of
stifling orange dust.

Maggie closed her eyes. She had a pounding headache. The man
had played loud Cape jazz all the way from the airport. In normal
circumstances she enjoyed jazz but not after a fourteen-hour flight
packed into a sardine tin, laughingly called a plane.

When the sound of the car died away there was absolute silence,
except for the pigeons and cicadas and the wind winnowing
through the eucalyptus leaves. Maggie looked about her. Where
was everyone? Maybe they were at the top of the garden? But they

would have heard the car, surely? She dragged her cases into the shade of the blue gum and took a long drink from her water bottle. Then she sat down on her case and kicked off her shoes. She was very careful where she put her feet. Ever since she'd shoved her foot into her sandal without looking and got bitten by a scorpion she'd been extremely cautious.

It was so quiet – so different from anything she'd experienced before, but then it was different. Nothing would ever be the same again, would it? Pete was dead. She let the tears come. She couldn't have stopped them, even if she'd wanted to. She hadn't cried for Pete because it hadn't seemed real back there in a cold, dark English winter but now, now she knew it was true.

Finally she wiped her tears and forced her thoughts away. It was too hot to think. Maggie had never visited in high summer before and the flight had been worse than usual. Every seat was taken, mostly by huge Afrikaaners and she held her breath as they taxied onto the runway, convinced that a plane carrying all that weight couldn't possibly take off. She'd spent the entire journey with her shoulders hunched and her hands in her lap while the people on either side commandeered the arm rests. Her shoulders and neck ached horribly but maybe the sheer physical discomfort of the journey had been a blessing because it was only much later, when the sadistic flight attendants had ceased stalking the aisles with their lollies and juice that she thought about Pete. In that silence, when everyone else in the world was asleep, the worry and grief paddled about in Maggie's brain. She still couldn't believe it. How could someone so young and alive and full of hope be dead?

Maggie hadn't wanted or expected her daughter to meet her at the airport but it was hard to run the gauntlet of all those happy family reunions in Arrivals. She remembered the special times with Lilah hugging her and Jeth's excitement and Kate smiling, waiting patiently to step into her mother's arms, and Pete, dear Pete, with his warm smile and old-fashioned courtesy. He would kiss her on the cheek and lead her outside into the warm bath that was Cape Town. And she would have the front seat of the bakkie while the others squeezed into the back. On the drive over the mountains everyone would talk and laugh at the same time and the children would ration out sweets and water and plan the holiday with Grandma.

It was too hot in the taxi but the driver wouldn't let her open the window. 'Air conditioning, man,' he said proudly, pointing to the AC button. Trouble was the cool air didn't quite reach where Maggie sat and she was dressed for an English winter, not a South African summer. She haemorrhaged sweat as they swept past the Cape Flats - the largest informal settlement in Cape Town. Mile upon mile of tiny shacks, built on glaring white sand. If Maggie was hot, what would it be like in one of those sweatboxes? Every hundred metres or so 'mother-ship' telegraph poles sagged under weighty garlands of cables, feeding electricity into the shacks. Along the boundary fences were blocks of concrete latrines, some only a step away from the habitations. Maggie couldn't smell them or see the flies but that didn't mean she couldn't imagine what it was like.

There were people everywhere. Women with babies tied to their backs talking animatedly in groups; small children scavenging for coke bottles and anything remotely usable, piling them into home-made carts. There was a never-ending procession of people going backwards and forwards from the townships to Somerset West and Cape Town, carrying booty. Old pieces of pipe, machinery, cupboards, mattresses, bags of potatoes, boxes of mangoes, watermelons balanced on heads. Sometimes a smartly dressed young man or woman strode purposefully along as if they'd just left their bank/estate agency or office to pop home for lunch. And joggers sprang in and out of the trudging lines of people, passing young and old men sitting on their haunches on the kerb, one finger raised at passing traffic.

Maggie used to think that these men were giving the finger to the drivers but now she knew it meant they were available for hire. *One finger for work*. It was early afternoon and it seemed a forlorn hope for those not selected yet. The young, able-bodied men would have been chosen hours ago, but what else was there to do for these others but to sit and hope?

Several small fires smouldered along the wooden fences that separated the settlement from the busy motorway. People gathered around these fires cooking their midday meals, the wood from the fences adding extra heat to the blaze.

Perversely, Maggie's driver chose to lower the windows when they stopped at traffic lights and the street-sellers descended like flies on road-kill. They thrust re-cycled wire toys at her; paintings of the townships, sun hats and Zulu beadwork, while shouting out prices in Afrikaans. Wary of being ripped off she stared straight ahead, not making eye contact, hoping they'd go away. Her driver knew a lot of the traders and laughed and joked with them while

Maggie prayed for the lights to change.

She only relaxed when they started the long haul up into the Kleinsrivier mountains, via the tortuous Sir Lowry Pass, and on through the apple growing regions of the Western Cape towards Hermanus. In the mountains the tin roofs of the Cape Flats gave way to tiny concrete houses, part of the Regional Development Programme or RDP. These new houses weren't much bigger than the shacks, but they were waterproofed, had their own electricity supply and there was street lighting.

But then in a blink of the eye all the poverty and ugliness vanished and the empty mountain slopes stretched away, studded with multi-coloured rocks. Eagles spiralled overhead and jackal buzzards patrolled their borders. Turning a corner in the road, a group of baboons waited, poised to cross, anxious mothers with babies clinging beneath them and dominant males barking their commands.

Maggie checked the track again. It was comforting to see the cars there. Kate couldn't have gone far. In a way Maggie was relieved they weren't here, it meant she had a few more moments to herself, to plan what she was going to say. But she decided to go indoors. At least she'd be cooler inside and she could change into some fresh clothes.

She tried the door handle but it was stuck and she had to put her shoulder against the woodwork and push. The door swung open and she stumbled inside, almost falling over something. The door banged shut behind her and she was in darkness. All the curtains were drawn. She bent down to retrieve what she'd tripped over. It was a welly - a child's welly. She held the boot against her nose and breathed in the comforting cocktail of smells - hot rubber and feet.

Clutching the boot Maggie got her bearings. She knew this room. There was a box by the door, for old hats, sticks and shoes. Beside this was a nature table: skull of tortoise, body parts of birds, puff adder skins, guinea-fowl feather's, porcupine quills and assorted shells – abalones and sea urchins. Then, in front of her to the right were the stairs, leading up to the communal sleeping deck. To her left would be a semi-circle of chairs facing the telly - which only worked when the atmospherics were right. On the left of the telly was the door into the room where she slept and straight ahead of her was the kitchen area.

'Kate?' She called but there was no sound except the buzzing of some insect, trapped behind the curtains, frantic to escape.

Maggie took a tentative step forward and something scrunched under her foot. A shell. Shapes were beginning to loom out of the darkness now. Ghostly furniture appeared and a tiny chink of light from one window spotlighted a piece of Lego. Maggie could see enough now to be confident and went to the windows, throwing back the curtains and letting the light flood in.

She stripped off her clothes, pulled on shorts and a T-shirt, and slipped her feet into sandals. Then, she wandered out into the back garden with a glass of water and sat in the shaded courtyard watching the weaverbirds fighting for scraps from a newish-looking bird table. Their squawks and beating wings were the only sounds apart from a rhythmic banging in the distance, as if someone was knocking in fence posts.

Maggie got up and made her way up the path, passing eucalyptus, conifers, bamboo and banana trees entwined with honeysuckle. She found, as she always did, that the mixture of the exotic and the familiar was unsettling. Africa was like that. The path ended at the old oak tree and then the land opened out into flat grassland where Kate and Pete were cultivating orchards and a tree nursery. Pete loved his trees.

Further on she passed an old-fashioned pink-climbing rose that threaded its thorny way through a giant aloe. The garden was full of some long-dead European woman's memories of home. Maggie came to a small stunted tree. It had naked branches, like fingers reaching for the sky. It looked dead but Maggie knew it wasn't because there, on one branch, was a flower. In fact, now she looked closely, there were two. She was glad it had survived the move. Pete had said it would, even though she and Kate had doubted it.

'Oh ye of little faith,' he'd laughed. 'Don't believe everything you read in gardening books.'

Maggie put her nose to the bloom and inhaled the exquisite scent of the frangipani.

The swing on the oak tree creaked in the wind and its knotted wooden seat hung at a crazy angle. It had never swung true however many times Pete had shinned-up the trunk and re-tied the ropes. Maggie sat on the lop-sided seat and twisted around and around; then she lifted her feet and let go.

When the world stopped spinning Maggie noticed a movement up ahead in the orchard area. The sun glinted on a machete as someone hacked rhythmically at the vegetation. Maggie stood up to get a better view. It wasn't Kate. No, Maggie's daughter was slender and this figure was substantial.

Maggie made her way towards the figure and as she got closer she saw it was a black woman. She had her back to Maggie and was dressed in brightly coloured clothes with a scarf tied about her hair. She was attacking a copse of young saplings and every now and then she wiped her face with the back of her hand and took a deep drink from a Coca-Cola bottle.

Maggie was surprised to see a woman doing the gardening. The farm usually employed men on the land. Maggie was uncomfortable with the local blacks. Most of them spoke Afrikaans. She turned to retrace her steps but then she hesitated, maybe this woman would know where Kate was.

She cleared her throat. 'Er, excuse me...' The woman went on working. Maybe she hadn't heard her so Maggie tried again. 'Excuse me.' A bit louder this time. There was still no response. How rude! Maggie was tired and hot and emotional and this ill-mannered person was the last straw. She put her hand on the woman's back and pushed. The woman toppled forwards, only saving herself by planting her hands firmly on the ground. She sat back on her haunches, dusted her hands off, and turned to face Maggie. She was scowling and that's when Maggie saw that she was wearing headphones.

'I'm so sorry. I thought you hadn't heard me.' She held out her hand. 'Please, let me help you up.'

The woman ignored the hand and scrambled to her feet. She smoothed down her skirt and re-tied her scarf. Finally she unhooked her headphones and stuffed them into her pocket. 'Do you need help?' The voice was hostile.

Maggie hardly noticed the woman's anger. She was just pleased that she spoke English. 'I was looking for my daughter.'

The woman screwed up her eyes, examining Maggie's face and then down to her winter-pale legs. Finally she smiled broadly, as if she'd just solved some puzzle. 'You are Mummy?'

I'm Kate's mother, yes.'

'Good, good. She will be happy, now her mummy is here. I am Nomatuli, I work for the government and Kate,' she said, taking Maggie's hand in her strong grip and pumping it up and down. 'I am happy to meet you.' She was looking beyond Maggie as she spoke. 'Daddy stay in England?'

Maggie took her hand away. 'Do you know where Mrs Vantonde is? '

'Watering, mummy. That tree up by the gate? I tell her, this tree, he is making a fool of you. Coral trees are strong, like a first born son, not a weak girl child. I have a son,' she added, as if Maggie was interested. 'Thembo is smart – he is going to be a lawyer. I have to work all jobs to get money for fees but it is good. Thembo is not like his bastard daddy.' The black woman was collecting all her gear together as she spoke.

'Please, don't stop your work on my account,' Maggie interrupted. 'I'll go back inside to wait for my daughter.'

'That's okay, mummy. This is my official break time. We will have some rooibus together, after your long journey from England.'

Maggie turned on her heel.

The black woman fell into step behind her and said, 'I hope you have not had influenza, mummy.'

Maggie had no idea what the woman was talking about.

'It says on my radio,' the black woman insisted. 'There is bad flu from chickens in the UK.'

'Bird flu,' Maggie corrected. 'But, no, we don't have it yet.'

'It says on the World Service.'

At that moment Maggie heard a child's excited voice. It was Lilah. The black woman put out a hand detaining her. She spoke softly. 'I am glad you come at last.'

Maggie shook her arm free and hurried down the path. The voices were getting louder now and Maggie saw figures moving towards her through the house, silhouetted in the light from the open front door. Lilah came first like a little blond arrow. She was shouting, 'Grandma, Grandma,' and hurled herself into Maggie's arms.

Jeth followed more slowly, as if he doubted she was really there. The dog, Spider, stood against the boy's side, his tail waving gently.

Maggie smiled at the boy over Lilah's blond curls.

The boy was tall for seven and he'd lost his puppy fat. His hair was cropped short and his eyes were wary. Maggie took a step towards him but his expression gave her a clear warning. *Don't touch me. Don't...just don't.* Maggie smiled at him. 'Okay, Jeth?'

He nodded. Then he went back inside, passing his mother, who was standing in the doorway with exactly the same expression as her son.

Hitching Lilah onto her hip Maggie went to her daughter, willing herself not to cry. But all she saw was Kate's achingly thin body and piercing blue eyes, set in dark holes in her gaunt face.

Maggie reached out and pulled Kate to her. Nothing mattered now she had her in her arms. 'Why didn't you let me come, Kate?

It's been so awful, not knowing how you were.' These weren't the words she'd rehearsed over and over again. She hadn't meant to sound accusing. She held Kate tightly against her and felt her daughter's body hard and unresponsive against hers.

The girl turned her cheek to accept the kiss, but then she slipped out of her mother's arms and took Lilah off her. 'It's great to see you, Mum. You must be shattered. Come inside.'

The black woman followed them into the kitchen and sat down across from Maggie while Kate piled a plate of salad for her mum. Jeth had gone off somewhere. No one else ate and they sat around watching each forkful as it went into Maggie's mouth. No one spoke. The only sound came from the black woman as she sang along to whatever she was listening to on her transistor. Lilah sat on Maggie's knee and put her dirty fingers in her Grandma's food but Maggie didn't care. She wasn't hungry; in fact each mouthful was a battle.

'Don't eat it if you don't want to, Mum. I'm a rubbish cook.'

'It's delicious, Kate. It's just that I'm full of in-flight food. You know? '

Kate took the plate away without a word and forked the remains into the dog's dish.

Maggie refused the cup of tea the black woman offered, willing her to go so that she could talk to her daughter properly, but she stayed with them and she and Kate drank tea and ate rusks. After a moment Lilah slipped down from Maggie's lap and stood beside the black woman, opening her mouth like a baby bird to receive titbits of biscuit.

Kate was relaxed with the woman. She even smiled once or twice as they talked about the garden. Suddenly Kate looked directly at Maggie. 'I'm sorry we weren't here to meet you, Mum, but Lilah was going crazy waiting for you, so I took them for a walk.'

'To do the watering.' The woman interrupted, giving Maggie a knowing look.

Maggie looked away. She didn't want Kate to think she was siding with this stranger.

But Kate smiled. 'Have you been telling tales about me, Nomatuli?'

The black woman tapped her nose, got up and rinsed her cup.

After tea Maggie gave presents to the children. Jeth had a telescope. He went upstairs immediately to set it up. Lilah had glitter, glue and sellotape. When it was time for bed Maggie told Lilah a story and lay with her until she fell asleep. Jeth was in his bed, eyes shut, although Maggie doubted he was asleep. She bent down, and kissed his flushed cheek and briefly rested her hand on his forehead.

When Maggie got downstairs Kate and the black woman were seated opposite each other at the table and the woman was in the middle of some story. She was finishing off a plate of food. In between mouthfuls she talked animatedly to Kate.

When she saw Maggie she smiled broadly, pushed her plate away, and got up, offering Maggie her chair. 'Now mummy is here, everything is OK.'

Kate picked up her car keys. 'D'you mind if I run Nomatuli home, Mum? The kids will be fine. Won't be long.'

Maggie nodded. What else could she do?

But Kate was a long time and Maggie was almost asleep when the car's headlights swept the walls of her bedroom. By then Maggie was too exhausted to do anything about it.

Weddings and Baptisms

It was unforgiveable leaving Mum alone on her first night but when I saw her standing there, her eyes full of pity, I knew I wasn't ready for her. I'd built a flimsy barrier between myself and my grief and she was capable of destroying it with one kind word. I was so frightened of going back into that black pit. So, after I dropped Nomatuli off that night I popped in to see Miriam. I wanted to be sure Mum was asleep before I got home.

I have only recently made my peace with Miriam. I'd plucked up the courage and taken the children down one night, clutching one of our keurboom saplings. I prayed Rob was out and he was, thank God. When Miriam saw me she only hesitated for a second before she smiled and invited us in. I said "sorry" as I handed her the pretty little tree. Neither of us talked about what had happened. I think she's forgiven me. I hope so. She's such a nice woman and I owe her so much.

As I lay in bed that night I thought about all the shocks I'd given my mum over the years.

Pete and I met one summer when he was visiting the UK. He and Mum got on well but, when I told her I was planning to go travelling with him in South Africa, I knew she was worried. Me too. The press continually bombarded us with the bad stuff that was going on out there. Pete said it was media hype but I'd read Nadine Gordimer and Coetzee. Friends told us scary stories about muggings and car-hijackings. I knew about the spiralling gun crime and the horrifying Aids epidemic. Every book I read, every newsreel I saw, was the same. Cape Town, Jo'burg, Pretoria - tourists beware - everybody on the make, every black a potential rapist or thief. Little babies gang-raped in the townships; young black women fearing for their lives, let alone their virginity. Migrant workers from Zimbabwe beaten to death. Black workers treated like dirt - even after apartheid - still subjected to horrors and discrimination. Squalor, hopelessness and ignorance still part of normal life for the poor.

Pete said the truth was something else - another country - lying somewhere between what the papers said and the partisan political stand. There was only one way to find out what it was really like.

The next bombshell was when I rang to tell Mum I wasn't coming home. Her shock and disappointment hung between us like some huge cork, plugging the words. When she was able to speak, her voice was forced, bright. I didn't need to see her face to know she would be wearing that thin, brave smile of hers that drove me mad.

'And is this truly what you want?'

'Yes.' I was surprised at how confident I sounded. 'I love him, Mum. He's brilliant. I've never felt like this about anybody before.'

Silence.

Was she crying? 'Mum? You okay?'

'I only want you to be happy.'

'I know.'

'That's all I've ever wanted for you, Kate.'

'I know, and I am.'

Silence.

'You like him, don't you? Mum?'

There was the slightest of hesitations. 'Of course I do…but… but South Africa's so far away, Kate, and what if…'

'…You can visit us whenever you want.'

'But what if you…what if things don't work out for you?'

'Mum it's not gonna happen.'

I didn't tell her I was pregnant that time. Enough information, I think, for one day. But she found out soon enough and missed out on seeing her first grandchild until he was almost six months old.

She wasn't even there for our wedding. She'd been on at me for ages to sort Jeth's passport. When I eventually got the form and Pete and I read it through, we realised how much easier it would be if we were married. Sure, we were as committed as any couple could be. Our love was beyond bureaucracy, religion or pandering to relations. But we had to re-think our decision now.

Up to then we'd stood up to Vantonde pressure. Pete's mum was big in Kleinsdorp's Dutch Reformed Church and in her eyes we were living in sin. This didn't bother us. Pete wasn't religious. In fact he was positively anti-religious. He placed the white supremacists doctrine of racial bigotry directly at the church's door. I didn't have strong views either way. I'd been brought up a lukewarm C of E, going to church at Easter and Christmas. I'd also had a one-year Catholic school experience, but it wasn't important in my life. We both believed in some sort of spiritual force, more to do with nature, but we didn't have a name for it.

It was typical of us, how it happened. We just got up one morning and the sun was shining. Pete kissed me and said. 'How about getting married today?'

I laughed and pretended to think. 'Okay. It's either that or do the nappies.'

There was a registry office up on the RDP. The only people we told were Miriam and Maarten – who we asked to be our witness. While Pete rang his brother I popped over to see if Miriam could have Jeth for an hour or two.

She was so excited. 'Oh my God, that's brilliant. What are you wearing?'

I hadn't even thought about that.

'Is there anything I've got you'd like to borrow?'

I smiled. 'Thanks, Miriam, but no.' She and I were probably the same size but I couldn't imagine wearing her designer clothes. I was just happy that I'd washed my hair recently and my after-baby-belly was beginning to shrink. Shame it looked like a puckered deflated balloon, but you couldn't have everything.

I was still breast-feeding but I'd be back before Jeth needed another feed. I left her some boiled water in a bottle and a piece of dried kudu. Jeth loved biltong. I wasn't a great meat eater and the idea of air-dried flesh made my stomach heave but he was wild about it.

When I got back to the camper-van Pete was in the wilderness at the back of the house. We hadn't had time to do anything in the formal garden yet. The bamboo grove, climbing roses and banana plants had fused into a Frankenstein wall of vegetation. Pink roses sprouted from banana leaves and small green bananas hung on

51

bamboo shoots. When Pete came back he was waving something at me - a pink frangipani blossom. He knelt down and offered me the flower. 'Will you marry me?'

'I will,' I said, breathing in the incredible fragrance of the star-like flower. I tucked it behind my ear and we set off, hand in hand, like two little kids.

Maarten was waiting for us outside the registry office, wearing a broad grin and a smart formal suit.

Pete had warned me that the registry office might be packed out but nothing could have prepared me for that small airless room filled to capacity with prospective 'happy couples' and their families. The heat and noise were over-powering. The only source of moving air came from an ancient ceiling fan that would suddenly burst into a few moments of frantic whirring, before rasping to a rusty halt. In the periods of stillness the hot, stale air descended on us, like leaden confetti. Pete sat between Maarten and me. Where Pete's arm touched mine we were welded together with sweat. Was this what they meant by 'Joined together as man and wife'?

I was so sorry for Maarten. At least Pete and I were dressed casually, but he was a ball of sweat in his hot suit. He sat still, staring straight ahead. We left him alone in his misery.

I kept looking at my watch and shaking it, convinced it had stopped. Our details had been lost – twice. All I wanted was to be outside, breathing my own air again. I was squashed beside a young girl in the frothiest meringue wedding dress ever invented. The oceans of scratchy petticoats threatened to suffocate me. I looked down at my once smart trousers and T-shirt. They were fairly new but now they looked like rags. And my frangipani had died. I clutched the pathetic petals in my hand. I was a very poor relation at this particular wedding spectacular.

Everybody was shouting and eating and drinking. I wished we'd thought of bringing refreshments. One couple had a spectacular row and the man marched out, chased by older women, hurling abuse, while another relation comforted his weeping woman. I hoped Jeth was behaving for Miriam. It was getting late and he'd need a feed soon. The thought of Jeth made my milk come and I held the thin fabric of my shirt away from my leaking nipples, hoping the dark stain wouldn't show.

At last the registrar's assistant poked his head around the door. There was an imperceptible intake of breath as everyone waited to see who would be chosen. The young man was dressed in a formal, black suit with collar and tie. Sweat flew from his hair. Sensing his power the man took one majestic step into the room, keeping the door open with the other highly polished shoe, looked slowly around the room until his gaze rested on me. He said something in Afrikaans. Pete had a hurried conversation with him, which everybody understood except for me. The only word I recognised was Vantonde. My neighbour was smiling and pushing me out of my chair. Pete led the way into the office. The people all clapped and the children shouted excitedly as I followed the men inside.

'Oh, and before I go, I've got something to tell you. We got married today.' I was on the phone to mum. I hadn't meant it to come out quite like that. I'd intended making her laugh but then I remembered that I was her only child and I'd got married without her in a foreign country thousands of miles away. She didn't speak for a long time.

'Mum, you there?'

.'Did you say married?' her voice quavered.

'Yeah.' I replied. 'It seemed a good idea at the time.' My voice was too loud, too flippant. Neither of us liked the phone - there was a slight time-lapse that made fluent conversation difficult. It was like one of those *Two Ronny's* sketch shows from years back when I was a kid, where one guy asked questions and the other is always one answer behind.

'There's no need to shout, Kate, I'm not deaf.' There was another uncomfortable silence before she spoke again. This time her voice was brighter. I knew how much it was costing her. 'So? Tell me all the details.'

'It was just a registry office, Mum. No big deal.'

'Was his mother there?'

'No. Just me and Pete and Maarten – you know? Pete's brother. He was our witness. He's a great bloke…'

'…Yes I know Maarten, Kate. What did you wear?'

'I don't know. A top and trousers? It was just a formality, Mum.'

'Get Pete to e-mail the photos.'

'We didn't take any, Mum. Sorry.'

Another silence.

'So? What will you be called?'

I hadn't thought about that one. Weird. My name was going to change. 'Mrs Vantonde, I suppose.'

'You could keep your maiden name.'

'Why?'

Mum sniffed.

'Mum?'

'Take no notice. I'm being silly.' Her voice was husky. 'Vantonde is Pete's name… And it makes everything so…final. I thought – well, I hoped actually - that you'd come back here to live, you and Pete and Jeth. Bring up your family here, live down the road. Come for Sunday lunch. Stupid umm? But that's what kept me going and now…it's all over. You belong there, in Africa, with… them. I miss you so much, Kate. And I haven't even seen Jethro yet and now he's a Vantonde baby. He won't know me.'

'You're coming next month, Mum. He'll love you.'

Pete refused to tell his mother, so I had to.

'Well of course,' she said, 'if you want to run off and get married in secret, Katie, that's entirely up to you. But we're hurt. Aren't we, Lionel?'

'Look, I'm sorry,' I said. 'I know you're disappointed, Ma, but it was a spur of the moment thing.'

'I suppose we should be grateful for small mercies. At least the child's got a name now…'

'…He had a name before.'

'Not in the eyes of the Lord, Katie. But you've made your vows now so we'll say no more about it.'

Had we? I couldn't remember much, except for the embarrassment of leaky nipples and poor suffering Maarten. While the registrar fired words at us in Afrikaans and Pete whispered the translation in my ear, Maarten started to sway dangerously. We both thought he was going to faint.

Ma was still talking. '…And you can't expect any wedding gifts if people haven't been invited to the wedding.'

I managed not to laugh. 'That's fine, we don't want presents.'

'But we could combine the two. That way you wouldn't miss out'

'The two what?'

'Celebrations of course, Katie, your marriage and Jethro's baptism. Now he's a Vantonde we'll be able to get him christened. You needn't worry about the arrangements. I'll organise it all with Pastor Billy. He does a lovely baptismal ceremony. We'll have the party here afterwards. I'm sure we could arrange it for the Sunday after next.'

'I don't think we'll be getting Jeth christened,' I stuttered. 'Pete and I don't believe in things like that...'

'...But it's not you we're talking about is it? This is about Jethro and his immortal soul.'

'You'll have to speak to Pete.'

But she wasn't listening. 'Peer was brought up in a god-fearing, Christian household and I presume you have some sort of grounding in the scriptures?'

'Yes, but we've chosen not to go to church, Ma...'

'...Bah! You're still Christians.'

'That's not necessarily true...'

At that moment Pete came in and I pushed the phone at him. 'It's your mother. She's organising Jeth's christening.'

I picked Jeth up and took him down to the oak tree. I could hear Pete's angry voice as Jeth and I watched the shimmering sunlight filtering through the canopy of dense glossy leaves and lighting up the new lime-green acorn buds. Jeth reached out to touch the flickering dancing sunbeams and I kissed the back of his neck and made him giggle.

'Hello, Jethro Vantonde.' I said and he looked at me. 'D'you see this tree? Daddy is going to hang a swing for you, right here on this branch. And it will be Jeth's swing.' And the little boy smiled and said, 'Da da' for the first time.

Pete stuck to his guns and we didn't get Jeth christened but Ma wasn't beaten. Gloria visited us regularly now we had Jeth. She was so sweet with him, carrying him around with her, showing him the garden, the flowers and birds. Anyway, one day she brought a note from Ma, offering to put us up until the house was ready. They had all that room, she said. It seemed a genuine offer and I tried to talk to Pete about it but he wouldn't even discuss it. The van had been cosy while it was just the two of us but now it was cramped and claustrophobic. Jeth didn't sleep much and I couldn't wait to move. Pete's enthusiasm for the house and land never wavered, not even when things went wrong – and they often did. Like when we paid some guy up front to do our roof and he never came back. We needed a proper plumber and electrician. I did what I could to help but I wasn't particularly skilled. A bit of plastering - pathetic - and most of the decorating and wood staining. Pete and Maarten did all the hard graft. Maarten was fantastic. I don't know how we'd have managed without him. My Pete was very volatile but Maarten was always calm and reasonable whatever happened. He was the only one who could make Pete laugh when he was in one of his moods.

When I rang Ma to tell her we wouldn't be taking up her offer I could tell she was furious. She had this way of clipping the ends off her words when she was mad. 'Well, of course,' she said. 'If you want to keep my grandson in damp, dirty conditions that's up to you. I wouldn't dream of interfering.'

'We appreciate it, Ma' I lied, 'but you know how it is.'

'Oh yes, Katie, I know exactly how it is.'

I thought she'd give up on us after that but I soon discovered that Ma never gave up on anything. Several days later Gloria brought us another invitation, this time to a family brai to introduce Jeth to the extended Vantonde and Groos clans.

Amazingly Pete agreed. Apparently he liked some of his cousins. I think he was just a proud dad wanting to show off his son but I was pleased we were going. And it might be fun. I come from a very small family. My mum was an only child and Dad never had much to do with his sisters and their families, so it was just the three of us. Now the two of us, since Mum and Dad had split up.

The Vantonde garden was crowded when we arrived. I saw Ma kiss Pete. He smiled at something she said and I relaxed. I know it's a national stereotype but Boer men are very big. The older ones wore full beards and had no necks. They talked loudly and ate huge amounts of meat. The women were well-built too and dressed in floral prints and hats. The younger men and women were fashionable - just like kids everywhere. The girls wore moon boots with very short sundresses, and the boys jeans and baseball caps. Antoinette was drinking with a group of Pete's younger cousins. She wore a white micro skirt and halter-necked top and she nearly carried it off. But who am I to criticise anyone's style? I looked down at my crumpled shirt and cleanest trousers.

It was all a bit daunting but Gloria and Maarten looked after me, while Pete took Jeth to meet his relations. On the whole they seemed a friendly bunch and spoke to me in English but there was a group of men and women standing on their own, speaking in Afrikaans.

'The Groos clan', Maarten whispered, when he saw where I was looking. 'Watch out for that one.'

He pointed out a beefy, florid-faced man in a check shirt. He was talking into a mobile. He saw me looking and turned his back. When I caught Maarten's eye he pulled a face.

'Rude bugger. Johannes Groos. A mate of Eugene Terr'Blanche? The maniac who runs the AWB? The Afrikaner Weerstands Beewigging.'

'The resistance movement?' I said. 'The ones with a swastika on their flag?'

'Three sevens,' Maarten corrected me and winked. 'Three sevens signify Yahweh apparently.'

'I thought the AWB was banned?'

Pete shrugged. 'So they say.'

'Is Ma a member?'

Maarten shook his head. 'Believe it or not, she's a moderate compared to them. This lot believe that the blacks are the *animals of the veldt* and need to be treated as such. No, Ma's racism is based on what it teaches in the bible – well, her version of the bible. She believes that King David was directly descended from Adam. And everyone knows that King David had red hair and white skin, don't they? She's genuinely sorry for anyone who doesn't share her beliefs because they will go to hell. They are as lost to salvation as were the whores of Sodom and Gomorrah.'

'You know a lot about it.'

'Got it with my mammy's milk, Kate. Pappie saw to that. '

'Was he really so terrible?'

'Oh yes, Kate. A mad, bad man.'

Halfway through the afternoon most of the men went missing, including Pete. Gloria was changing Jeth for me, surrounded by women, all wanting to help. Ma was keeping a critical eye on her daughter's performance.

'Where have the men gone?' I asked.

She pointed over the road to the pub. 'Watching the rugby and having a beer.'

She saw my look.

'You'll have to get used to that now you're married to a Vantonde, Katie. Boer men are real men.'

I smiled. 'It's the same in England, just swap football for rugger.'

'Not too tight, girl!' Ma suddenly shouted at Gloria. 'You'll cut off his circulation.'

She hurried off to supervise while I got some food and a beer, found a spot in the shade of a tree and stretched out on the grass, closing my eyes. This was the life.

Someone was screaming in my dream, but then I woke up and it was real. The men were back and Ma and Pete were facing each other in the middle of the lawn, yelling. Ma's face was bright pink but Pete was deathly pale. Everybody pretended not to be watching them.

'...But that doesn't mean the poor child has to suffer, does it?'

'I told you,' Pete was fighting to control himself. 'The house is almost ready.'

'Rubbish. You've been saying that for months. You can't take a young baby into a dusty damp building, Peer. It's not…hygienic. He'll get ill. Is that what you want? You stay there if you want, but let them come here, the baby and mother.'

'For God sake, woman. Don't you ever give up? We're staying at Blue Gum – all of us.'

I looked for Jeth. Gloria came towards me - reading my mind. She had collected all the baby's stuff together. I took Jeth from her and kissed her on the cheek. 'Thanks, Gloria. It's been a lovely day. See you soon?'

Ma's lips were thin as she said goodbye. She patted Pete on the cheek and he flinched as if she'd slapped him. 'We'll say no more about it for now. I was thinking of Katie that's all. It must be hard to keep the child clean with no running water or …amenities.' She looked meaningfully at Jeth. I'd dressed him in a T-shirt and realised too late that it had a stain on it.

Pete didn't speak as we drove. I had gut's ache. I wasn't used to all that protein. Fingers crossed Jeth was due for a sleep when we got home and I would try to persuade Pete to have a siesta with me. He needed to calm down. Back at Blue Gum I settled Jeth in the van, and then I went to find Pete. He was standing with his back to me in the kitchen working on the sink. I crept up behind him and tickled him around the waist. He swung around and shoved me away as hard as he could. I staggered backwards and almost fell. 'Keep you bloody hands to yourself,' he screamed at me. And the look on his face was terrible. It was like he really hated me.

I was so shocked I didn't know what to do.

He stared at me for a moment, breathing heavily, and then he grabbed me and pulled me into his arms. 'Sorry. I'm so sorry, Kate. Forgive me.' He buried his head in my neck.

'Why are you like this?'

'You know,' he groaned.

'She wanted to help us. What's so terrible about that?'

He took a step away from me. 'Don't you know what she's doing? She embarrassed you in front of everybody.'

'What d'you mean? About Jeth?'

'Of course. She was criticising you – us.' He hit his head with the palm of his hand. 'Why am I so bloody stupid? Well, no more, Kate. That's it.'

It was my turn to be angry. 'So, what am I supposed to do, Pete? Stop her seeing her only grandchild? What?'

'No. No. Do what you have to but leave me out of it. Okay?'

Pete and his mother never spoke again after that day. Gloria and Maarten were always welcome at Blue Gum and Lionel popped in when he could but Ma only came when Pete was at work. I hated being piggy in the middle but that's the way it was. Ma never said anything about Pete to me.

I felt sorry for her back then. All I could see was that she was a good grandma and she doted on Jeth. Sometimes he fell asleep as she rocked him in her arms and her mouth would soften into a sweet smile. I wish Pete could have seen her then.

Nomatuli

The first day Maggie arrived at Blue Gum set the pattern. Each time she attempted to talk to Kate, her daughter would find something else to do – run the black woman home, do the watering, gardening...something, anything as long as she didn't have to say how she felt or what she planned to do. In the end Maggie gave up and turned her full attention on the children.

She took over the cooking and washing and general running of the house. She made sure they had regular meals and fussed about the children's table manners. She tried to make them eat while Lilah whined, already full of Vantonde cake and sweets, and Jeth played with his food, slipping bits to Spider when he thought his grandma wasn't looking. Maggie concentrated on the children but all the time she was really watching her beautiful girl, bewildered by this stranger who had become her daughter.

I was so sorry for Mum. I saw how hurt she was by my behaviour. I wanted to let her into my life but I couldn't. What I needed was someone who hadn't known Pete and could be normal around me. It wouldn't help me forget but it should enable me to focus on what I had to do. Nomatuli was practical, non- emotional and down-to-earth. She didn't believe in wasting time feeling sorry for yourself. Maybe, when I was with her, I could pretend that everything was okay.

I think Lilah felt the same because the first thing she asked every morning was, 'Is Nommy coming today?' She had fallen under the black woman's spell. Jeth is a harder nut to crack. He avoids her. He avoids us all except for his Grandma and Spider.

Nomatuli works for us three days a week. She arrives early in the morning with the other workers from the RDP. We hear her singing long before we see the farm bakkie coming down the track. Most of the women are employed as maids and the men as gardeners or labourers. Pete and I had employed a couple of women in our plant nursery, doing the potting up and watering, but I couldn't afford them now. We had planned to give regular work to these people as soon as our business was up and running. A man called Lucky had worked on the farm. He'd helped Pete and me sometimes but he was good with horses and had spent a lot of time with Rob. Horses and women were Lucky's speciality apparently. He and Nomatuli hit it off from the start.

One brilliant thing about my mum being here is that Ma stays away. They still do the school run and have the children twice a week for tea but she barely speaks to me. She hasn't forgiven me for turfing her out. I never mentioned about her trying to get custody of the kids. I'd thought of banning her from seeing them but, when I thought about it, the only people who would suffer from that would have been Jeth and Lilah. It's better that she and the good people of Kleinsdorp see that Jeth and Lilah are being well cared for. Ma hasn't breathed a word of it to me and Miriam says the rumours have died down but I'm still on my guard.

So I was surprised one day when Ma tracked me down in the

vegetable plot. It was very unlike her to come into the garden. It was incredibly hot and I was just about to go inside out of the sun. I could hear her gasping for breath long before I saw her. She's an asthmatic and very overweight. I found a bit of shade for her by my shed and gave her a seat, and then I poured her a cup of water from the tap.

I waited until she got her breath back.

'I wanted a word, Katie, about this black woman you've hired?'

'Her name's Nomatuli and I haven't hired her. She's paid by the government'

Ma waved that bit of information away like an annoying fly. 'She's a Zulu, ja?'

I nodded.

'Zulus think they're a cut above the other blacks, Katie. They're troublemakers and have to be watched, very carefully.'

'She's a great worker.'

'Take it from one who knows, Katie. Zulus can't be trusted.'

'Really?' I said innocently. 'I know a lot of people who can't be trusted.'

She looked away and heaved herself up before lumbering away into the undergrowth. It's useless arguing with Ma about black people.

As I followed her inside I saw Nomatuli sitting in the shade of the oak tree, having her break. She waved and shouted something and I waved back. She was always cheery, God knows why. Her work was backbreaking and I knew it wasn't what she was used to. Her fingers were long and tapered and her fingernails had once been manicured. Now they were broken and her nail polish chipped.

Pete would have been thrilled by this national initiative to get rid of *aliens*. Aliens. That's what they call non-indigenous plants in South Africa. I thought it was funny back then.

Pete spent a huge amount of time bombarding local and national politicians with letters and e-mails about the problem. He was convinced that, if everyone did their bit, the Western Cape could be free of invasive aliens in a few years time. Always the optimist, my Pete.

Nomatuli was the first black woman I got to know properly. I'd met one or two coloured families at the school and in the shops, but most of the local blacks couldn't speak English and didn't mix socially with the whites. There were black customers in the Cape Town restaurant where Pete and I worked before we bought the farm. These people were confident, urbane and had money but Kleinsdorp was a rural backwater and I soon discovered that what happened in the rest of integrated South Africa had no bearing on this place. The town was almost one hundred percent white, divided between Afrikaaners and British South Africans. There were three coloured families and one black living there, and the black man was a doctor in the Hermanus hospital where Miriam worked.

On the outskirts of Kleinsdorp lay the RDP where coloured and black families lived in small uniform, concrete dwellings. The people here were mostly in work but they were still poorly paid. There was a minimum wage but one in four black men was out of work and if a man complained they weren't being paid enough there were a hundred more waiting to take his place.

A kilometre out of town, beside the rubbish tip, lie two squatter camps on either side of the road. These were full of migrant workers, the old, disabled, or women with no husbands and big families. It was these people who hung about outside the Spar in Kleinsdorp, the men squatting on their haunches drinking from bottles in brown paper bags. If you made eye contact they held out a hand as if in greeting – but they wanted rand. The women's glances slid away – half embarrassed and half something else, harder to decipher. Whatever it was it made me very uncomfortable. I might not have much compared to other whites but in relation to these people I was a millionaire. I didn't know how to behave with them. When I gave them money I felt patronising and if I ignored them I felt guilty. But the real problem was the language. Whoever said *Language is a cul-de-sac* was right. I should have learnt Afrikaans but Pete had been dead set against it. It would always be the *language of the oppressor* to him.

There was one old woman I did get to know. She wore a faded dress several sizes too large for her and her name was Elizabeth – I didn't know her Xhosa name. I always tried to give her something. Her face was a mass of wrinkles but she had a lovely smile, even with two of her front teeth missing. Although she got to know me she never approached me. She would stand at the back of the crowd in the shop doorway, waiting. You know? Like that one small duckling on the pond, that never gets the bit of bread - however much you aim for it.

Sometimes I had nothing for her and I would smile apologetically but she seemed to understand and smile back. Occasionally I'd give her some milk or bread. Food was usually the best thing to give because there was a man who stood nearby and took any rand the old lady got.

Nomatuli was the exact opposite of these people. She spoke four languages, Zulu, Khosa, Afrikaans and English and was from Kwa Zulu Natal. Employment for blacks was bad here but was even worse in Natal. Nomatuli was supporting her son through university. He was going to be a lawyer she told me. She earned money any way she could but her long-term plan was to open a general store on the RDP. She'd been promised a small grant from the government plus our farm co-op was considering giving her a loan to buy stock for the store. Apparently Nomatuli had experience of storekeeping in Natal, where she had sold paraffin and fresh produce - yams, mealies, beans and corn cakes.

Nomatuli was a great talker. Sometimes we'd meet up for our mid-morning break and chat. She was so open and there was none of the wariness or hostility that I'd encountered with the local blacks. Her eyes lit up when she talked about her homeland. One day I asked her why she'd left. She didn't speak for a moment and then she picked up her machete and slashed viciously at the nearest plant.

'Not all men good, like your Pete. Now I work.'

Later that day I caught sight of her from the house. She looked like a small sturdy rowboat, set adrift in a vast purple sea. I think that was the first time I truly acknowledged the futility of what she was doing. For each alien she destroyed six more sprang up overnight, like dragon's teeth.

Patterson's Curse

The first time I saw Patterson's Curse was the day I knew I was pregnant with Jeth.

Pete and I were living in the camper van in Cape Town at that time. We'd had our year travelling around South Africa and neighbouring countries and were working on the Waterfront. I needed cash for my return fare to England and Pete needed to add to his farm fund.

The year had been incredible, full of amazing things, like when we camped in the Okovanga Delta and woke up early one morning to find a lioness standing on a termite mound, only metres away from where we'd pitched out tent. Her breath came out in gouts of steam in the cold morning air and the rising sun caught fire to her golden fur. She was so beautiful and when she turned her head she looked straight at me - I mean really looked at me, like she could read my mind. Finally she jumped down and sauntered off without a backward glance. I'll never forget it. I know I should have been scared shitless but I wasn't, because Pete was there.

But now it was time for a reality check. Pete and I had plans – separate plans. I was returning to the UK to do a gardening course and get a proper job – my mother's favourite phrase - and Pete was looking for a small-holding in the Western Cape to grow indigenous plants and trees. He was into conservation and passionate about the Cape's unique plant and animal Kingdom.

We were both over thirty and being responsible, doing grown-up things. Having a great time – a fantastic time - but being sensible.

We knew the year would end but knowing is one thing and by then I knew I loved him. Somehow I kept quiet while he scoured the local papers each night, looking for land sales. Even when the date for my departure got closer and closer I still refused to think about the future - the future without Pete. So, when the inevitable happened I was incredibly shocked. Stupid.

'God, I can't believe this, Kate,' he yelled one night, paper in one hand the other arm wrapped around me. 'It's perfect, exactly what I've been looking for.'

He was so excited he didn't notice how quiet I went.

'It's being auctioned off in twelve separate pieces, Kate, - a community farm.'

I could see why he was excited. He would be farming alongside like-minded individuals, just what he'd always dreamt of. He insisted we went to view the land the next day.

'But what about work? 'I started to say, but he wasn't listening. He was spreading a large map on the floor of the camper van. I had to draw my legs up underneath me on the bench and hang over the edge to see where he was pointing. He read out the map references and we found it, a tiny pinprick beside a town called Kleinsdorp. The name was vaguely familiar. Pete's smile faded.

'Is there a problem?' I asked.

'No,' he said. 'It's…nothing.' He sounded as if he was trying to convince himself.

And then I remembered where I'd heard the name before. 'Isn't Kleinsdorp where your family live?'

He nodded slowly.

It was good news as far as I was concerned. I hadn't met any of his relations yet so it would give me the opportunity to say *hello* before I went back home.

'There won't be any time to see them, Kate. We've got to get back for the evening shift.'

This time it was me who was adamant. It was ridiculous being that close and not visiting his family. He agreed grudgingly.

We were on the road very early the next morning, when it was still blessedly cool. The one thing I wouldn't be sorry to leave behind was the heat. My red hair and pale skin were meant for colder climates. My face went all blotchy in the heat and my fine, long hair hung limply.

I wound the camper window right down and watched as the sky filled up with colour. Pete talked non-stop. What he would do with the land. How he'd grow his wonderful trees and farm in a holistic, sustainable way. I'd heard it all before, hundreds of times, and I closed my eyes, willing him to shut up. By the time we turned off the main road and onto the farm road I felt sick and had a thumping headache. I clung on as we lurched along the rutted track. After a kilometre or so Pete suddenly jammed on the brakes and I shot forward, jarring my shoulder.

'Shit shit shit,' he yelled, jumping out of the van.

'What happened?' I shouted, rubbing my shoulder. 'Did we hit something?' I hoped it wasn't another baby baboon. The amount of road-kill on South African roads was horrendous. I'd never get used to it.

Opening my door I stepped out, nearly falling over Pete, who was down on his hands and knees; tearing out fistfuls of a purple-flowering trailing plant. Both sides of the track were covered in the stuff and a purple haze covered the fynbos in all directions. Whatever this was it was prolific. Pete stood up and thrust one of the plants at me. It had small violet blue flowers – pretty, a bit like viper's bugloss.

'Um, nice.' I said, smelling the sweetly scented flowers. 'What is it?'

'It is not 'nice',' he lectured, scowling at me. 'This is Patterson's Curse.'

I laughed. 'You made that up.'

'It's not a joke.' He snatched the plant off me and tore it into shreds.

'So? What's the problem?'

'The problem,' he said, ticking the points off one by one, 'is that Patterson's Curse alienates all natural pollinators. It offers no protection for the specialised and threatened fynbos fauna. It sucks the subterranean water resources dry and the fynbos dies. The entire Cape's most beautiful indigenous flora, Kate, - the proteas, tree heathers, agapanthus, lilies…everything. All killed because of this "nice" plant.'

He was red in the face now and breathing hard. I touched his shoulder. 'Hey, Pete.' I'd never seen him like this before. He was silent for a moment then he touched my face gently and smiled.

'So?' I said, 'This Patterson's Curse? It's highly invasive? Like Japanese knotweed or the wild rhododendron back home?'

'Worse, much worse.'

'Shame, eh?'

He looked puzzled.

'Well, you won't be buying the land now will you? Not now you've discovered this… infestation.'

His eyes narrowed, 'I promise you, Kate. I'm gonna kill every last germ of this bloody plant, or die in the attempt.'

He wanted to put in an offer on the plot that included the footprint of an old farmhouse. This meant that he could rebuild on the same site. Pete loved the idea of settlement continuity. We parked up under a huge old blue gum tree. All that remained of the former building was a ruined chimney-stack, sticking out through a tangle of briars, bamboo, ivy and small wiry saplings.

'Pete pointed an accusing finger at the small trees. 'More bloody aliens. Port Jackson Willow.'

I was staring at the gum tree. It had been struck more than once by lightning. There were two jagged 'wounds' running down its white massive trunk. Pete rushed off to explore and suddenly, without warning, I threw up. Pete's excited voice came yipping back to me as I sat in the shade of the gum tree and attempted to clean myself up. I had no desire to meet his mother smelling of sick.

'My God, Kate. There's a banana plantation back here and a pink rose - just like your mum's? I don't believe it. You must see this. A frangipani in bloom, right in the middle of a whole grove of alien bamboo.'

When he finally came back he was grinning from ear to ear. He flopped down beside me. 'You okay, Kate? You look terrible.'

'I've been sick.' I'd been sick a lot lately.

'Hey, poor you.' He cuddled me. 'Why don't you get in the back of the van and shut your eyes while I have a nosy, hey?'

'There's no time. Your mum's expecting us.'

He looked at his watch. 'We don't have to go.'

'But I'd like to meet them. What's the matter? Ashamed of me, or something?'

He stopped my words with kisses. 'Don't ever say that. You're

73

the best thing that's ever happened to me. I don't want them to spoil it that's all.'

'How could they?'

He took a deep breath. 'Maarten and Gloria are fine and Lionel, my step-dad's, a good bloke, you'll like him.'

Pete's real dad had died when he was a baby and Pete had taken his stepfather's name.

'So? Who does that leave?'

'I suppose Antoinette's okay - in small doses. She's my full sister. But...'

I waited.

'...My mother. She's a very difficult woman, Kate, incredibly manipulative. Plus she's a racist and a bigot.'

'But apart from that she's okay?'

He didn't smile. 'If you want to see her, fine, we'll do it, but don't say I didn't warn you.'

I shrugged. 'It's not as if I'm going to see much of her, Pete.' I could feel the tears building up.

'That's the problem though, isn't it?' He took my hand and kissed it. 'I don't want you to go back to England, Kate. I want you to stay with me. I want us to buy this land together and build a house on it and have kids and live here for the rest of our lives.'

And that's when 'plans' become dust.

I didn't say anything, I just put my arms around his neck and kissed his warm, sweet mouth and breathed in the familiar scent of the man I loved.

Fortress Vantonde

Kleinsdorp was a sleepy little town with one wide main street. It was lined with sprawling white and apple-green Cape-Dutch style houses, reminding me of the set for a Spaghetti Western. All that was missing was Clint Eastwood with a half-smoked cheroot clamped between his teeth.

The street was deserted, except for some black people squatting outside the store and a little white dog chasing its tail in the middle of the road. It was blistering hot and I still felt nauseous but I was smiling inanely. Nothing mattered now that I knew Pete loved me.

As we went through the gate into the Vantonde back garden Pete squeezed my hand and hissed 'Geronimo!' at me. The family was seated in a semi-circle facing us. They were so still they could have been statues. A large woman with a pretty doll-like face was the first to move. Heaving herself out of her chair she aimed herself at Pete and clutched him to her pouter-pigeon chest.

'Peer, Peer,' she squealed. 'You're late. I thought you weren't coming. Didn't I, Lionel?'

It was weird hearing Pete being called by another name. A man got up and shook my hand, offering me a chair. This must be Lionel. He was big and had a warm, wide smile. 'Nice to meet you, Kate,' he said, before slapping Pete on the back.

Pete finally managed to escape from his mother. 'Enough, Ma.' He was smiling, despite himself. 'You're embarrassing me.'

'Well, it's your fault for abandoning us.' His mother turned her attention on me then, and wagged a plump finger. 'But I think this young lady may have something to do with that.'

Everyone laughed politely and then Pete introduced me. The sisters were total opposites. Gloria was fair-haired and round and hugged her brother tightly as if she was frightened he'd disappear, while Antoinette was slim and dark like Pete and barely gave him a second look. Maarten was blond and large, like Lionel and yet I could tell he and Pete had shared genes. Maybe it was the way they grinned and waved their arms about when they got excited. Whatever, I could see that they liked each other and there was a lot of banter between them.

As soon as I could I asked to use the bathroom. I was desperate to clean myself up properly. God knows what they must have thought of me.

When I got back there was a table laid with fragile rose patterned china on a lace tablecloth, piled with plates of cakes and sandwiches. They must have been cooking for days. We all sat down on the porch under a vine. Bunches of grapes hung over our heads and sweetly-scented jasmine scrambled up the veranda pillars. I still felt queasy and played with the cake on my plate, hoping that no one would notice.

'If only Pappie was here.' Ma sighed, and dabbed at the corner of her eye with a lace hanky. She smiled at me. 'Peer was his favourite grandson.'

It was no good. I was never going to get used to this *Peer* thing.

Gloria put her arm around her mother but she pushed her away and the younger woman got up to fetch more food. I caught her eye and smiled and she grinned back. Antoinette didn't move from her chair, which was set at a slight angle to the rest of us. She didn't talk to anyone and kept looking at her watch and yawning.

Pete went off happily with Lionel and Maarten to inspect the new brai pit. That left me with his mother and sisters. We all pretended to be busy eating and drinking.

'Do you eat a lot of venison in England?' Gloria asked suddenly, munching away on a hefty slab of cake.

I was trying to think of a sensible answer when Antoinette spoke. I saw Pete's mother stiffen. 'I've always wanted to go to the UK,' Antoinette drawled, nibbling around the edge of a biscuit. 'Do some shows, shop till I drop, you know, the usual tourist stuff, but Ma hates the Brits, don't you?'

Ma's cheeks flushed. 'Isn't it time you were off, Antoinette?' she asked. 'I thought you had important business to attend to, in Hermanus? Don't let us detain you.'

Antoinette shrugged and got to her feet. 'Have fun, hey?' She smiled wryly at me as she sauntered out of the garden.

'Have you met the Queen, Kate?' Gloria again.

Ma shooed her away. 'Go get the men folk, Gloria, before their tea gets cold.'

Gloria trotted off obediently. I forced down the last bit of cake and took a huge gulp of tea to wash it down. My stomach heaved. *Please, God, don't let me throw up - not all over Pete's mother.*

'So, Katie? You don't mind if I call you Katie do you? It's such a pretty name.' She put another large piece of cake on my plate. 'It's a shame that your trip has been so short this time. But maybe you'll come visit us again one day?'

She obviously didn't know I'd been in South Africa for a year.

'I've had a fantastic time, Mrs Vantonde…'

She held up a hand. 'Ma, my dear, everybody calls me Ma.'

I smiled my thanks, thinking that I could never imagine calling this intimidating woman anything but Mrs Vantonde. 'It's been a holiday of a lifetime. South Africa's an amazing country.'

She pursed her lips. 'It was once, Katie, but no longer.' She moved her chair closer to mine and laid a damp hand on mine. 'I'm going to tell you something that may surprise you, Katie. The blacks don't want integration any more than we do. They have their own customs and superstitions. How can a civilised Christian society like ours mix with a people who believe in shape-changers and *sangomas* – witch doctors? Who believe that a pain in the gut is *isidliso* – black poison put there by a sorcerer?'

'I suppose we all have our beliefs, Mrs Vantonde.' I said. 'Catholics believe that the wine and wafer at communion and changed into the actual body and blood of Christ.'

The woman's hand flew to her small pink mouth and her baby blue eyes widened with horror. 'There is no comparison between the one true religion and…black magic, Katie.'

Fortunately, the men returned at that moment. Gloria had her arm linked through Pete's and she was chatting away to him.

After everyone had eaten and drunk enough to satisfy Ma Vantonde she put down her cup, wiped the crumbs from her mouth with a serviette and smoothed down her skirt. 'Well, this is very pleasant, ja?' She beamed around the table at us all, her double chins trembling. 'All the family together and even Peer's little friend.'

Obviously Antoinette's departure had been forgotten.

She patted my knee. 'Katie and I have had such an interesting chat.'

Maarten pretended to groan. 'My God, Ma, have you been indoctrinating her already?'

'As it happens, Maarten, Kate agrees with me that integration will never work.'

I stared at her. What was she talking about? 'I didn't say that, Mrs Vantonde. Obviously there's a long way to go but surely anything's better than apartheid. It was evil.'

Maarten winked at me. 'Good job Pappie Groos isn't here, Kate, or he'd get the *sambok* to you…'

Ma cut in. '…A bit more respect if you don't mind, Maarten.' She turned to me. 'My father was taken from us last year, Katie. Sadly Peer wasn't able to attend the funeral. Apparently he had more important things to do.'

'You know why I wasn't here, Ma.'

I was surprised by the hard edge to Pete's voice. I tried to catch his eye but he was staring angrily at his mother.

Maarten jumped in. 'Pappie was one of the original *Voortrekkers,* Kate? Hated you Brits. Wouldn't allow any book written in English in the house. Made Ouma's life a misery.'

'Ouma?' I asked.

'Afrikaans for grandmother.' Gloria chipped in. 'She loved poetry, especially Wordsworth and Coleridge. She used to read her poems in the outhouse.'

'Brave old girl.' Lionel muttered.

'Her favourite was the one about the daffodils? We all learnt it by heart.' Gloria's eyes were shining. 'All those fluttering and dancing daffodils. D'you remember, Pete?' Gloria caught her mother's black look and shut up.

'If I may continue?' Ma said. 'Thank you. You are young, Katie and don't know our history…'

'…My God, Hannah, can't you give it a rest?' Lionel interrupted.

But Ma Vantonde wasn't going to be silenced. 'The British have a lot to answer for in this country.'

'I did the Boer wars in history, Mrs Vantonde.' I told her. 'I know about the concentration camps. I agree it was a terrible time for your people.'

'Ma won't be content until we're all living in the *Volkstaat*, Kate.' Maarten said. He was trying to keep the conversation light but I could feel the tension growing.

'Volkstaat?' I asked.

Lionel pulled a face. 'A Boer Israel on the banks of the Orange River? Full of fanatics like Hannah's old man? Not for me, dankie.'

Ma glared at her husband. 'Pappie was a saint…'

'…Your 'pappie 'was an evil old bastard.' Pete was on his feet. He pulled me out of my chair and hustled me towards the gate. As it closed behind us I glimpsed his mother. She was sitting very still; eyes heavenwards, her small hands pressed together in prayer.

Pete's knuckles were white on the steering wheel as he accelerated down the street, sending the little white dog yelping for cover.

'What was that about? Pete?'

But Pete wasn't saying anything. After several kilometres he pulled off the road and killed the engine, and then he leant forwards, resting his head on the steering wheel.

I put my hand on his arm. 'Pete? What is it? Please. Tell me.'

He groaned and shook his head.

'Was it me? Did I do something wrong?'

'No, no.'

'Then what? I thought it was going okay. Sure, your mother's a bit of a racist, like you said, but the others were okay…'

'…Why don't I ever learn? I thought it might be different now he's dead but it's just the same.'

'Your grandfather?'

'Pappie Groos was a sadistic, evil old bastard. He enjoyed beating the blacks, Kate - any excuse - men, women, children, he didn't give a shit. *'They need chastising.'* He used to say. *'It's good for them. Watch and learn, boy. Watch and learn.'* Then he'd smile at me through those piggy little eyes of his. I never hated anyone as much as I hated him, Kate. And the day I left Kleinsdorp, I vowed I'd never come back.'

'But now he's dead.'

'Thank God.'

'So?'

Nothing's changed, Kate.' He grabbed my hands and squeezed them really hard. . 'Don't be fooled by her. She's exactly like him.'

'Pete, you're hurting me.'

He let go at once. 'I know she's my mother but never, ever trust her. You've got to promise me.'

His face was grey with worry.

'Okay, okay,' I said. What else could I do?

We drove back to Cape Town in silence. I knew Pete loved me and wanted me to stay - that was brilliant - but where would we live? He wouldn't want to buy the land, not after today. And then there was the little problem of my being pregnant and, finally, how was I going to break the news that I was staying in South Africa to my mum?

Blue Gum

But Pete wasn't going to let anything get in the way of his dreams and we did buy the land. As long as he didn't have to see his mother everything would be fine, he said. And pretty soon we were living on the farm in our camper-van. All the plots had been sold and people were busy constructing their homes. They would all be *rondavels,* except for ours, which would be a Cape-Dutch style, like the original farmhouse.

We parked our van under the blue gum tree, where I'd been sick on our first visit and we named our smallholding *Blue Gum* after this tree. The irony of the situation wasn't lost on me. Eucalyptus trees are aliens, like Patterson's Curse, and the beautiful old oak tree at the back of the house and so were the roses and…me.

We couldn't afford to pay builders so we bought in outside labour when .we needed it, and did the rest ourselves. It was a huge undertaking but we were young and in love – and anything's possible then.

If we got a free day we would jump in the van and head off to the beach, or go camping, or visit one of Pete's many friends. We didn't see his mother or the rest of the family except for Maarten. He and Pete went fishing and surfing together when they could.

One thing I needn't have worried about was telling Pete I was pregnant. The morning after I told him, I woke to find him with his head resting on my belly, whispering to his baby.

Life was good but there were some worries maggoting away in

my brain. I have this guilt thing? Mum blames it on the nuns. Catholics are experts at guilt. I spent a year at a convent school when I was thirteen. I was hormones in search of a passion and Jesus seemed a good idea at the time. I soon gave up on Jesus but the guilt thing stayed. And here I was, being happy at the expense of his mother. I thought we should tell her about the baby.

Whenever I broached the subject with Pete the shutters clanged down. There was a lot of bad stuff going on around his childhood but he wasn't ready to talk about it, not yet, and I wouldn't push him. I couldn't anyway: I was beginning to see what a stubborn man he was. It had been hard enough persuading him to tell his mother about our move to *Blue Gum*.

'Why?' he asked, looking up from the detailed drawing he was making of his proposed tree nursery.

'It's the least we can do.'

'She'll find out. She's got spies everywhere.'

'But I don't want her to find out from someone else. That's cruel. *Oh and by the way, Mrs Vantonde? Your favourite son's shacked up with a skinny Brit. They're living up the road on that farm, ja?*'

Pete laughed at my pathetic attempt at a South African accent. 'I am not her favourite son.'

'I think so. I saw the way she looked at you.'

He nibbled the ends of my fingers. 'How about one of those skinny Brit kisses.'

So the summer passed and our house and my bump grew. Pete was up very early every morning walking our boundaries. In the beginning I trailed after him as he measured our land, my feet slipping about in his wellies, my eyes glued to the ground, watching out for puff adders. Pete shouted out the distances after each stride. I don't know why. Maybe he thought the fairies would make our plot bigger in the night? I loved the childish delight he got from marking his territory. He was so enthusiastic about everything and ploughed ahead of me in bare feet, ripping out aliens.

'See that bird, Kate?'

And I saw a little brown bird with a very long tail and bright yellow under-parts perched on a protea head; drinking its nectar.

'The Cape Sugar bird. Pretty, hey?' Then he waved a handful of the dreaded purple alien in my face. 'Patterson's Curse? No fynbos? No fynbos no Cape Sugar bird? Understand?'

Eventually he did his morning rounds without me while I luxuriated in the extra space his departure left in our small bed. I would spread my sweating limbs, seeking out cooler parts on the sheets. Then when I woke I would flick through one of Pete's huge collection of books on South African flora and fauna, until the stench of bonfires drove me out of the van. The smell made me sick. There was a long list of things that made me want to puke. All meat and poultry - including bacon, my one-time favourite food - plus coffee and tea and anything to do with sugar and especially cinnamon. Cinnamon made me throw up for hours.

I had asked Pete fairly politely to light his fires away from the van, but the incessant wind always delivered the smell back to me.

I never truly understood why Pete hated Patterson's Curse so much. It was only trying to survive - like the rest of us. There were worse aliens, like Port Jackson Willow, that sent suckers everywhere and was a nightmare to dig out. Patterson's Curse was easy to pull up and its tenuous grasp on life touched me. Plus I'd read some really interesting facts about it.

When the nauseating stench of smoke finally drove me out into the blinding white light of the African morning, I would find Pete pitch-forking mounds of the stuff into the flames.

One morning I made the mistake of going 'Ahh'. Did you know,' I said waving the book I'd been reading. 'That 30% – 40% of all Australian honey is made from the flowers of Patterson's Curse?'

He continued to shovel, his back eloquent with disapproval.

'And,' I added, my finger on the paragraph. 'It has another name? Salvation Jane? *"Patterson's Curse,"* I read, *"is toxic to pigs and horses. However, in times of extreme drought, when other more acceptable fodder plants die, then, as a last resort, Patterson's Curse can be fed to cows and sheep and they come to no harm."* Hence Salvation Jane I suppose.'

Pete stopped shovelling and glared at me. 'Let's get this straight, Kate. You're sad because I'm clearing our land of an incredibly invasive alien? D'you know something? Pregnancy has turned you into a lame brain.'

'Really? Well at least I'm not paranoid. You're obsessed, man. Can't you see? It's only a little weed, for God's sake, not Pappie Groos.'

Pete hurled his fork down and walked quickly away from me. Within moments he was a tiny pinprick on the track before vanishing around the bend. I was stunned. I knew I shouldn't have said that about Pappie Groos but he'd called me a lame brain.

As the day wore on I went through the gamut of emotions. Anger gave way to indignation, then to understanding, then remorse and finally and horribly-fear. What if he'd had an accident or he wasn't coming back?

When he finally did come home it was dark and I was huddled pathetically in our van, trying to decide what to do, where to go and who to contact. That was our first major row and later, when we lay in each other's arms we said we were sorry.

I truly wanted to understand about Patterson's Curse, but I doubted I ever would.

Maarten

Mum had been with us for about a week when I heard the familiar roar of a powerful motorbike coming down the track. Jeth and Lilah screeched in unison, 'Uncle Maarten! Uncle Maarten!' and rushed outside.

They love their uncle. He used to come to dinner every Friday night. He and Pete were into those stupid zombie films and he would bring the latest video and pizzas and we'd all watch. The favourite was 'Shaun of the Dead' *'It's only pretend,'* Jeth used to giggle, when I hid my eye during the zombies' feeding frenzy. *'They use loads and loads of tommy sauce, Mum. It's not real.'*

The big man was taking off his helmet when Lilah flung herself into his arms and demanded an aeroplane. He swung her around obediently while Jeth clambered up onto the bike's big plush red seat and bounced up and down, pretending to rev the engine. The bike was Maarten's pride and joy. It was a huge job with luxurious padded seats and so many gears and levers it looked like a car. I was surprised it could move when Maarten climbed aboard. All that weight on two little wheels.

Pete had loved motorbikes too and he and Maarten had often gone off for the day together. Maarten had given Jeth all the leather gear for his last birthday and took him for rides around the farm. I wouldn't let him take him on the main road. I'd always been a bit scared of these powerful machines but I trusted Maarten. Everybody did.

'Leave the man alone,' I shouted, coming out onto the *stoep*. 'Uncle Maarten's come to see me and Grandma, not you two.'

He looked up and smiled but I saw the strain in his eyes. I gave him a peck on the cheek and led the way into the house. He followed me inside, a child attached to each hand. Mum made tea and we all sat down. We talked about the weather and the UK and whether the Springboks were going to win the rugby World cup. We talked about Mum's trip out and the cost of petrol in England and the weather. We talked about everything and nothing.

Lilah was bored after a few minutes. 'Come see Stompy's chicks,' she ordered, grabbing Maarten's hand.

'For goodness sake, Lilah,' Mum said. 'Let your uncle drink his tea.'

'It's okay,' he said, following the little girl outside. 'We won't be long.'

I guessed he was grateful to escape. While they were gone Jeth ran upstairs and we could hear him pulling out drawers and banging about.

'He's so nice,' Mum said.

'Maarten? Yeah, he's lovely.'

'How's he coping?'

I shrugged. 'This is the first time I've seen him...since the funeral.'

'Ah.' Mum said and drank her tea.

Just then Jeth hopped downstairs. He had managed to get one foot into his black leather trousers but the other was stuck. When Maarten came back in Jeth was waiting, helmet on, visor down and gauntlets swamping his arms.

'I know, Uncle Maarten.' His voice was muffled. 'I can show you Uncle Rob's new foal.'

Maarten nodded. 'Okay but let me drink this tea first.'

Both children tried to climb onto his lap at once. Maarten whispered something in Jeth's ear and he immediately jumped down and pulled up a chair beside his uncle. Marten was so good with them, just like his brother. He grinned at Jeth and my chest tightened with misery. I was glad Mum was there. She made it easier. There were no awkward silences. Mum was a huge rugby fan and they argued about the Southern and Northern Hemisphere styles of rugby – whatever that was.

As they chatted I looked at my brother-in-law. He was every inch the archetypal South African policeman: a big man with blond close-cropped hair. He wasn't exactly fat, but he was going that way. He loved his grub, especially brais. I don't think he ate anything that wasn't burnt first. I bumped into him once in the Spar and his trolley was full of junk food and meat – not a green thing in sight. He regarded chicken as the vegetarian option and vegetables as the spawn of the devil.

But he wore his gun in a self-conscious way as if it was an embarrassment to him, and he couldn't do 'swagger' to save his life. He was good at his job and got along with the locals – black, coloured or white. When there were drunken fights up at the squatter camp and RDP over the weekends, Maarten was always the first guy they called for.

He was still living at home and it was obvious it was doing his head in. Ma had to know where he was going and who he was with at all times. I'd never understood the hold Ma had over her children.

'You'll never get a woman, living at home,' Pete had warned him once. But back then Maarten didn't want to upset his mother. He'd had a girlfriend once. A nice girl, Pete said, but she got fed up with waiting for him to escape Ma's clutches and finally went off to Durban, where she married and had kids. Ma had interfered in all her children's love lives.

'Lucky I grabbed you in the UK then,' I said.

Pete laughed. 'No luck about it, Kate. Once, on an island far away, I met a wild elemental being with fiery red hair and she put a spell on me. Witchcraft is the only way to escape Fortress Vantonde.'

'I seem to remember I smelt of chips and my legs were hairy.' I was working in a restaurant in Scotland when we first met.

'Umm, chips and hairy legs...sexy.'

I laughed. 'So? What about Antoinette? Three marriages under her belt?'

'But all down the pan.' He frowned. 'Look into her eyes, my darling. She's a very unhappy woman.'

'You can't blame your mother for that. No one made your sister get married. We all have free choice.'

'Yeah? Your mum never put any pressure on you? '

'All mothers put pressure on their kids. It goes with the territory. You're gonna laugh at this, Pete, but I envy you your family.'

He snorted.

'You know who you are; where you come from.'

'Yeah, unfortunately.'

After that first visit Maarten came regularly. It was lovely to have him around the place again. He'd spend time with the kids and when they were in bed we'd have a natter. He liked us to tell him about the UK and our family and stuff.

The unwritten rule was we didn't talk about Pete. And that was okay by me. It was Jeth who finally forced the issue. On Maarten's fourth visit Jeth disappeared upstairs. I thought he was getting ready for bed but he came bouncing down again with his duvet. He threw something down in front of Maarten.

'I know, Uncle Maarten. We can watch a video.'

Maarten took one look at the black plastic box and picked up his motor bike keys. I could see the panic in his eyes. 'Sorry Jeth, not tonight…I'm on nights this week.'

'…Aw, Uncle Maarten. It's your favourite. You and Dad love it.'

Maarten shook his head. 'No, I can't do it…I can't watch it tonight, okay?'

I took the video off Jeth. 'Maarten's got to go to work, Jeth.' I didn't know whether Maarten was really going to work but it didn't matter. All of us were coping in our own way.

'But…'

'…Maybe another time.' Maarten was trying his hardest to smile.

'But you love this one. And my daddy loves it.' Jeth's lip was trembling.

'Yes,' Maarten put his hand on the boy's shoulder. 'Yes, he did, he really loved it. See you soon, hey?' And then he fled.

Maarten phoned a couple of nights later.

Hi Kate, how are you?

We're fine, Maarten.

I thought I'd come around tomorrow, if that's okay? Maybe bring a pizza?

That sounds great. *There was a long pause.* **Still there, Maarten?**

Yeah I'm still here, Kate. I was thinking. There's a really good zombie vid just out. I thought maybe I'd bring it, if that's okay.

Of course it is.

Good, Maarten said. *That's good.*

Kanferbos

When Lionel picked up the kids for school today he brought three bills for me. We have a mail box at the Kleinsdorp post office. When I settle these bills I won't have much left. Mum's tried to talk money with me but up to now I've avoided it. I'm not stupid. I know I have to earn a wage somehow but what can I do? I have no skills and I can't speak Afrikaans; so the garden is my only resource. This was the day to take stock. I have no more excuses.

Ironically this was to have been the year when Pete and I launched our nursery. Pete was going to give up his day job and work full time at home. He had acquired funding from the Fynbos Unit, to establish a protea orchard. There was an international market for the cut flowers and plants. We were also specialising in herbal tea plants like rooibus and honey-bush and growing fynbos bulbous plants like freesias, gladioli and ornithogalum. None of this would happen now.

Since Pete's death I had done the minimum of watering. We had automatic irrigation in some parts of the garden but there was still a lot that had to be hand-watered, especially the poly tunnels where we grew our annuals.

It had been a particularly hot, late summer and I dreaded what I'd find. I wedged a brick against the heavy plastic doors, praying that it wouldn't be as bad as I anticipated. Inside, the air was thick and foetid and smelt of sour earth. Every tray, so carefully planted up and cared for, was full of pathetic, wispy dead stalks. I pulled up a plant and it came out on a ball of rock-solid earth.

'What were you growing?'

Mum was standing in the doorway. She had a basket of washing at her feet.

'Zantedeschias and gerberas.' I said automatically, not looking at her.

'The ones you sell in that store in Hermanus?'

I nodded.

Mum sighed and picked up the washing. 'I wanted a quick word, Kate. But maybe later?'

'What is it?' I welcomed her intrusion. I wouldn't cry in front of my mother.

'It's about Jeth,' she said. 'I'm really worried about him. The only time he smiles is when Maarten comes. And these awful nightmares he has? I know he misses his daddy terribly but he's bottling it all up, Kate. Does he talk to you about it?'

I laughed. It wasn't a nice sound. 'He never speaks to me, Mum, surely you've noticed. If I walk in one door he walks out of the other.'

'But that's not right, Kate. Maybe he should ...see someone?'

'Who? A doctor, psychiatrist...a sangoma?'

'This isn't funny.'

'Did I say it was? '

'So what are you going to do?'

I shrugged.

She shook her head slowly at me in disbelief; then picked up the washing and walked away.

Didn't she understand? I couldn't think about Jeth - not yet. I had other more important things to worry about, like how we were going to survive. Looking around at the devastation. I wanted to cry but I wouldn't allow myself the luxury. It was all my own stupid fault. I'd let Pete down – I'd let us all down.

I went to the protea orchard next. Thank God most of the plants here had survived. Our vegetable plot wasn't too bad either. This part of the garden was irrigated and I turned the tap on and watched as the parched earth soaked up the water. Soon we would be harvesting potatoes, tomatoes, beet, mealies, onions, garlic and strawberries. At least we wouldn't starve.

The berries would please my daughter. She and our bantams loved the sweet little fruits. It was a race each day to see who got to the strawberries first. Lilah had a favourite black hen called Stompy who she shared the crop with. Stompy was a good mother and the matriarch of the coop. When we let the bantams out, Stompy and her chicks were always the first after the rooster and woe betide any other hen that tried to jump the queue.

I grew herbs and lavenders amongst the vegetables, to sell at the farmer's market in Kleinsdorp. Mature plants were stacked in rows in their neat, black polythene pots waiting to be taken to market. I gave them all a good soaking.

After that I made my way down to the bottom of our land, plodging along in Pete's wellies, scything the long grass as I went. Nomatuli saw me coming and raised her hand in greeting. 'I see you, oh sister.' She was stoking a small bonfire of weeds. We were always careful with fires. She had a bucket of water within reach.

The young trees in the nursery weren't much taller than the grass. These were to have been our major source of income this year. The staggeringly beautiful coastal strip between Cape Town and Hermanus was a sprawling mass of holiday homes for wealthy city dwellers. These houses had big gardens and would need spectacular trees to plant in them.

I found two healthy yellow wood saplings – these were very slow growing but there was a good market for them. There were several sturdy little Natal Mahoganies' and a stand of Keurboom – lovely little trees with dainty pea-shaped flowers. These were suffering from drought and I dragged a hosepipe down and left it pumping water into the red earth. The Hard Pear saplings were dead but amazingly the Cape Chestnuts, with their large white and pale pink flowers, were thriving. Finally I found one tree fuchsia, with its striking brick red flowers.

I was searching for a label on some bushes I didn't recognise, when Nomatuli came and stood beside me, wiping the sweat out of her eyes. She saw what I was looking at and smiled delightedly; showing her white, even teeth. 'Kanferbos', she said, and took some leaves off a bush, crushing them between her palms, then holding them first to my nose and then to hers. The smell of camphor was strong. She bunched my hair together in one long rope and rubbed the leaves down its length. Then she did her own.

Some of these plants were ready for potting up; so I went to get the spade while Nomatuli squatted down for her break. When I came back she was singing along to her transistor.

'I've never known anyone listen to the radio as much as you do, Nomatuli.'

She switched off. 'My mother listens to *Woman's World*, all through the troubles? You hear of that programme in England?'

I shook my head. 'There's something called *Woman's Hour*.'

'Black, white and coloured women all talk together on air. Very important for us. You understand? I listen to everything, World Service, all the music stations. Brian Van de Bull, Kippie Makusi - the disc jockey on SAFM? He is my God, Kate. And I hear all news in the World. Ask me a question. Go on.'

I laughed and shook my head. 'Like what?'

'Who is the President of the United States? Who is Condoleeza Rice? I know. Who Tony Blair and the lovely Cherie? What was the score Italy against France in the last World Cup? Who scored the goal for France? Who the manager of Chelsea? Who highest paid footballer in the world. What is this Global warming? ...'

'...Okay, Okay,' I laughed. 'I surrender.'

She smoothed the shiny iridescent green casing of her transistor. 'My Thembo, he bought this for his mummy last Christmas. It cost many rand but he works in restaurant in Jo'Burg to pay. My son is good to me.'

'And I'm sure you're good to him.'

She nodded and smiled. 'Nomatuli is very good to him. And one day he promises to buy house for *manane*. I will have a kitchen with all things to make life easy. And a floor I don't have to sweep every day. The life of luxury for Nomatuli Ikhaki, but first Thembo must work hard and pass his exams. *Get good grades* I tell him, *Nothing easy in life*. But it is hard for a beautiful boy like my Thembo, aye? When all he wants is to dance with pretty women.' She laughed uneasily. 'He likes them and they like him, Kate – too much I think.'

I was in the tree nursery all morning, moving the hosepipe from tree to tree. In between I potted up the camphor bushes and helped Nomatuli with the weeding. She had a great technique. She gave the plant a quick tug, then a sharp twist, and out it came. If it proved too obstinate she sliced through the stem with her machete.

I yanked at some Port Jackson Willow but my fingers slipped painfully up the stem, leaving a tender pink mark. Nomatuli tossed the knife over to me.

The sweat rolled down Nomatuli's plump cheeks as she worked and she was breathing heavily. Every few minutes she sat up, stretched her arms above her head and rotated her neck; then she wiped her face and eyes and started again. She had great stamina.

I was struggling to dig out a particularly stubborn sapling, not really concentrating on what I was doing, when she shouted, '*Cha,*' and grabbed my wrist. We both watched as an insignificant spider legged it into the undergrowth. It was straw-coloured with a largish jet-black head. There was no red mark as far as I could see. 'Poisonous?'

She wrinkled her nose in distaste. 'Not so nice spider. It eats the flesh. Leaves big hole where it bites. The flesh, it …' she made a fluttering motion with her hands, '…it…'

'Dissolves?'

'Exactly. It dissolves.'

I was very careful after that.

At lunchtime I go to the end of the lane and wait for the children. I take two watering cans with me. Yesterday I was sure there was a flower bud coming on the Coral tree but today I see that it's a rusted-off leaf bud. There's no reason why it shouldn't flourish now that I'm watering it every day. But maybe it's lonely up here, with only the guinea fowl and the spotted flycatchers for company.

Lionel drops the children off at the end of the lane and I wave my thanks as he heads back for Kleinsdorp. Lilah's got a keen sense of smell and the minute I hug her she wants to know what I've got on my hair. After that she is always picking camphor eaves for her potions. I have to stop her in the end or the poor shrubs would be stripped bare.

Settling In

Nomatuli works with me in my nursery one day a week now. It was her idea. I can't afford to pay her but I feed her and give her any spare fruit and veg we have and then I run her home afterwards. The RDP is a couple of kilometres up the road. Black people walk everywhere, hitching lifts where they can. Nomatuli stays with her cousin, Nandhi, and her children. Nandhi's husband works away in the apple-growing region.

We soon became a regular sight up on the RDP. Kate Vantonde – *the English woman without a husband* - and Nomatuli Izhaki - *the Zulu who doesn't have a man*. The difference being that Nomatuli had chosen not to have a man. Her husband of twenty years had taken a new, young wife and she had walked out. I didn't care if the women were sorry for me but Nomatuli hated it. She despised the locals and, as much as I liked her, I could see how arrogant she was.

When Pete was alive he'd helped build the adventure playground up there and he'd started the communal kitchen garden. They all remembered Pete. When he was alive I'd been shy of going up there. It was the language thing again. So I used to make feeble excuses like I couldn't go because I had to put the kids to bed, but I didn't fool him, not for a minute. He never pressurised me but I knew he was hoping that one day I would be confident enough to get to know these people on their own terms.

'Just be yourself, Kate. They're not judging you.'

When I take Nomatuli home now, the children go with me. I don't like driving back on my own. Once or twice young men had pretended to block the lane so that I couldn't get through. If I had the kids with me they left me alone. I knew it was just fun to them but it made me uneasy. Once, when it was quite late, a man suddenly leapt out from a side alley and thumped loudly on the bonnet of my car, yelling something aggressively at me in Afrikaans and shaking his fist.

Jeth sat rigidly in the back seat on these trips, hugging his knees to his chin and refusing to get out. Lilah loved all the attention she got from the aunties. Not only did she look like a little blonde doll but also her daddy was dead. She was passed from woman to woman to be hugged and kissed and petted.

'Is it safe to take the children up there?' Mum asked once.

'I'm with them all the time,' I explained, trying to keep the irritation out of my voice. 'And Kleinsdorp's not like the Cape Flats or Jo'Burg.'

'Only you read such terrible things.'

'What about the gun and knife crime in the UK?' I snapped.

'That only happens in the inner cities.'

'Exactly!'

'Okay, okay, there's no need to get angry.' Mum's face was flushed. 'You're always yelling.'

I stared at her. Was that true?

'And it's not just at me, it's the kids too, especially Jeth.'

'Maybe he deserves it.'

Her eyes blazed at me. 'You're not too big for me to smack, you know. He's a little boy, for God's sake.'

'He's a brat.'

'I wonder who he takes after? He's seven years old, Kate, not much more than a baby. There's something bad going on in his head.'

'He'll be okay.'

'You've got the garden to distract you, Kate, he's got nothing. Spend some time with him, Kate, please.'

'I'm very busy, Mum.' I muttered.

'You've got time to talk to her.'

'Who? '

'Don't play games with me, you know who I mean.' And she went out, banging the door behind her.

Mum was right. I was treating them all terribly, especially her. If she was nice to me I was horrible. If she retaliated I would storm out. I knew it was only a matter of time before I chased her away. Is that what I wanted? I wasn't sure. Some part of me longed to step into her arms and cry like a little kid, but I couldn't, because if I did I might never be able to stop. But Jeth? Was I really so horrible to him? I thought it was him. It was like he hated me.

When I was moody Nomatuli would fix me with one of her looks and snort. 'Why you sad, Kate Vantonde? You have beautiful children, big house, land to grow crops, sexy legs... What more d'you want? The kingdom of God?'

A Lodger

I did try to talk to Jeth but it was useless. Each time I asked him a question or said something he walked away from me. In the end I had to leave it. My financial worries had to take precedence.

I'd planted up new annuals and some of the trees were ready for market but what I made from them would barely feed us, let alone provide money for clothes and pay the bills. I would have to see the bank manager. I needed an overdraft.

In the middle of all this Nomatuli lost her job. The funding for alien eradication came to an abrupt end. Maybe the government had realised that the task was impossible. I'd picked up a leaflet from the local library about alien plants. The list got longer all the time, Spanish reed, Queen of the night, pampas grass, loquat, St John's wort, jacaranda, lantana, St Joseph's lily, the New Zealand Christmas tree, oleander, prickly pear cactus, guava, weeping willow, gum trees, oak trees... I tried to imagine the scene if our oak tree had to be chopped down. Lilah was convinced that fairies called 'Oak Hats' lived in our tree. Jeth loved to climb it and its shade was the best for picnics. And where else could we hang the swing or the hammock?

Fortunately Nomatuli's funding for her store had come through, so she had already begun work on renovating an old shack up on the RDP for her store. Lucky was helping her. In the meantime I asked if she'd be willing to work for me full time in return for her keep. I was desperate for help in the nursery.

I knew Mum wouldn't like the idea.

'But where will she sleep, Kate?'

'In Pete's room.'

'But I thought...' She stopped.

'What?' I asked.

'Nothing.'

It was time I did something about Pete's room. This was the perfect excuse to clear it out.

'I'm not sure it's such a good idea, Kate, having her here.'

'Why?'

She looked away.

'I never had you down as a racist, Mum.'

'This has nothing to do with the colour of her skin, Kate, and you know it. I'm not sure it would work out that's all.'

'Who for? She'd be a great help to me and Lilah would love it. I don't think Jeth would even notice. So? Who does that leave I wonder?'

Mum sighed. 'I'm an outsider, Kate, but even I know that you'll be making trouble for yourself if you have her living with you. You know what it's like here. Blacks and whites don't mix. 'Also,' she added. 'I don't think she's a good influence on you.'

'Excuse me?'

'You heard.'

'For God's sake! I'm not a kid, Mum. I'm old enough to choose my own friends. '

'You've always been easily led.'

'What d'you think we're gonna do, for Chrissake? Smoke pot round the back of the banty coop?'

'Well. If you're going to be childish,' she said, walking away.

When I told Nomatuli my plan she pumped my hand up and down, her grin nearly splitting her face. 'Thank you, thank you, thank you, Kate. Now I can leave the hyena's house. He is back and making life very difficult for Nomatuli.'

Nandhi's husband was the *hyena*. He hated Nomatuli at the best of times but if she couldn't pay the rent he would enjoy kicking her out.

Nomatuli beamed at me. 'You are a good friend.' Her eyes were shining. 'Good times, Kate,' she said. 'Good times are coming. I feel it here.' She placed her hand on her heart. Then she took a deep breath, like a nervous child about to recite his first poem. 'You help Nomatuli I will help you. We will be partners in the Purple store.'

'Me? In a shop? I don't think so.'

Her smile faded.

'I'm …flattered, really I am, Nomatuli, but I'm no business woman.'

'But I am. All I want is your money. You pay how much you can afford.'

I didn't know what to say.

'I will make good profits for you.'

'I don't doubt it, but…'

'…You don't trust me?'

'Of course I trust you, it's just that I haven't got much money to spare.'

'I will turn your little money into big money. Nomatuli Izhaki and Kate Vantonde owners of Purple Store and Purple Shebeen.'

She winked at me. 'That is where we will make much rand. A store in the day, then a shebeen at night.'

'I'd be totally useless working in a bar.'

She was horrified, 'No, you stay away please. All those young men? They would stare at you all night with cow eyes and not drink my beer.' She took my hand in hers and shook it gently. 'Nomatuli make sacred promise. I will make money for Kate, no more worry.'

'It's very kind of you but I need time to think about this.'

'It is not kind.' She looked fierce for a moment, and then patted my arm. 'It is business. And, of course, you must have time to consider my offer.'

It was a huge decision. All I had left in the bank was R40,000 - about £4,000. But Pete had known several really good women bar owners when he lived in Cape Town. For one thing they didn't drink the profits away and they were good businesswomen.

I decided not to mention anything to Mum, not yet.

Nightmares

That night Ma and Lionel were coming for dinner at Blue Gum. Maggie didn't like Ma but she thought she owed it to her and Lionel for all they'd done for Kate and the children. She invited Gloria and Maarten too but they couldn't make it.

Maggie put a lot of effort into the evening and the Vantondes seemed to enjoy themselves, although Kate barely said a word. After they'd finished and the children were in bed they sat outside in the fading light. It was a beautiful autumn evening and the swallows swooped in the rich, insect-laden air, feeding their last broods before flying North to Europe and beyond. Kate had gone to see Miriam about something, so it was just the three of them.

They sat in companionable silence, finishing their coffee. After a few moments Ma put down her cup and sighed heavily.

Maggie looked up. 'Everything all right, Mrs Vantonde?'

Ma shook her head sadly. 'Katie's not coping. We're so worried about her.'

Maggie was immediately on the defensive. 'My daughter's had a terrible shock. Pete was her life.'

The woman leant towards Maggie, covering her hand with her own. Maggie was forced to breathe in the sickly sweet smell of Ma's stale face powder. Orange particles clogged the large pores on the woman's fleshy nose.

'It's difficult for us all, hey?' Ma dabbed at her eyes with her hanky. 'I've lost a son, my first born – my beautiful Peer. You don't

have sons, do you?' She allowed a significant pause before continuing. 'But I don't let grief swallow me up. I put my trust in the Lord. Are you a religious woman, Maggie?' she asked, not waiting for a reply. 'Peer attended church every Sunday when he was a child, but when they leave home and meet…outside influences, all you can do is pray.'

'We are all C of E in my family, Mrs Vantonde. Kate was christened and confirmed in the same church that I was christened in and…'

'…C of E?' Ma raised an eyebrow.

'The Church of England.'

'Ah,' Ma smiled. 'I'm sure it's a good enough grounding but… Can I tell you something, Maggie? You won't be offended?'

I wouldn't bet on it, Maggie thought, pouring some more coffee.

Lionel smiled apologetically at her. 'I think it's time we went, Hannah. Busy day tomorrow.'

But his wife wasn't going anywhere. 'I prayed that Peer would meet someone from his own background, someone to keep his faith alive, but…it wasn't to be. Of course we all love Katie but I think you understand what I'm saying?'

And Maggie did. For all that she had loved Pete, how much better if Kate had married someone from home.

Ma sniffed and sat up straighter. 'But what matters now are Peer's poor babies.'

At least this was something they could agree on. 'Children are very resilient…'

'…Did you see what she did this morning? That silliness? Over the koekseisters? And in front of the hired help?'

Koekseisters were plaited lengths of donut-like cake dripping in syrup and honey goo and Lilah loved them. Ma had brought a bagful that morning and Lilah had immediately ditched her breakfast and started on the cake. Kate had taken the bag and the piece her daughter was eating and dumped the whole lot in the bin. Maggie knew it was rude of Kate but Lilah would never eat properly if Ma kept filling her with rubbish.

'They've lost their daddy, Maggie. I'm just giving them a few treats. Is that so dreadful?'

'No, of course not, but Kate and Pete are…were very particular about the children's teeth.'

Ma snorted. 'What harm can a bit of cake do? I've eaten it all my life and look at me. I've never had a day's illness in my life.'

Lionel said something.

Ma turned on him. 'Asthma is not an illness, Lionel, it's a genetic condition. Pappie had it. ' Ma was working herself up. 'I was so upset this morning. Ask Lionel.'

Lionel got up, collected the coffee things and went into the kitchen. Maggie liked him. He was so nice with the children. She could see Pete in this man and he wasn't even his father. But there was nothing of Ma in Pete.

Maggie let the woman moan on about the stupid cake while her thoughts drifted to the children. She thought Lilah was okay, maybe because she was younger, but she wasn't as confident about Jeth. Most nights he woke up screaming from nightmares.

'What is it, Jeth?' Maggie asked, cooling his burning face with a flannel. 'Your mum's here, I'm here, Spider's here, there's nothing

to hurt you. Monsters don't exist.'

'They do in my dreams, Grandma,' he whispered.

And she would lie beside him breathing his breaths, stroking his hair, until at last he fell asleep.

She'd discovered what it was all about when she and Jeth were searching for a broody hen one day. They were on their hands and knees peering underneath the hedge when suddenly a reptilian head poked out. They leapt back, thinking it was a snake, but after a moment a very large tortoise staggered out with leaves sticking out of either side of its mouth.

Jeth laughed delightedly. 'You should have seen your face, Grandma. You were so frightened.'

And she was, absolutely terrified. It didn't matter that Maggie had only seen two snakes in all the years she'd been coming to Africa – and one of those was dead. Maggie was paranoid about snakes.

But it was lovely to see Jeth smile and she hugged him as they watched the tortoise lumber towards an orange-berry bush. He extended his neck and took a succulent fruit, eating slowly, eyes closed, in some sort of tortoisean ecstasy.

Afterwards, under the oak tree with his Grandma's arms safely about him, Jeth told her about his dream. 'It's a huge red snake, Grandma. It's coiled around our oak tree, crushing it so much that the tree is screaming. And it sees me, Grandma, and comes after me. It moves so fast. I can feel it breathing on my neck and I'm choking, Grandma. I can't breathe…'

Ma's shrill voice cut across Maggie's thoughts. '…We've done everything we can to help her, Maggie. If it hadn't been for us who knows what would have happened to them all. Before you came Lionel and I were considering psychiatric help.'

'A shock like that affects people in different ways, Mrs Vantonde.'

'You're her mother, tell me what we're doing wrong. She refuses to discuss the matter and I need this to be settled. I'm not a well woman.'

'Maybe we should leave it now, Hannah?' said Lionel, popping his head around the door.

'It has to be decided,' Ma insisted, ignoring him. 'I refuse to stand by and see my grandchildren suffer.'

Lionel disappeared back into the kitchen. 'I'll be in the bakkie, Hannah. Goodnight Maggie. Thanks again.'

Ma didn't even notice him go. 'No, the sooner they move in with us the better.'

Maggie was really surprised. 'Kate's never mentioned living with you.'

'Well she can't live here on her own, can she? No man, no money coming in. You must see how bad the situation is.'

Maggie wasn't about to discuss her daughter's finances with this woman. 'I'm here.'

'But you'll be going back to the UK soon.'

'Possibly.' Maggie said. 'But Kate may decide to come back with me. Anyway, even if she doesn't, she won't be on her own, not once Nomatuli moves in.'

Ma Vantonde's mouth dropped open.

'Didn't you know?' Maggie asked innocently.

'Excuse me? Are you telling me that the black is moving into Peer's house?'

Maggie nodded. 'Tomorrow, apparently.' She was enjoying herself now. 'That's her room.' She pointed to the door beside the kitchen.

'Pete's room?' Ma got unsteadily to her feet. 'This is my son's house. I won't allow it.'

'It's Kate's house now. She can do what she wants.'

'Never!' Ma began to wheeze.

Maggie went to the door and shouted for Lionel.

'That settles it,' Ma was gasping for breath. 'She will move in with us. She has no money, no breadwinner; she will make her life with us - with her family.'

Lionel hurried in and gripped Ma's arm.

Ma was bent double trying to get her breath. 'If you were a proper man,' she croaked, 'you would throw this black out.'

Lionel stared at Maggie.

'Nomatuli's moving in with Kate,' Maggie explained.

Ma glared at Lionel. 'So? What are you going to do about it?'

He shrugged and led her towards the door. 'It's time you went home, Hannah.'

'Call yourself a man?' she snarled. 'You're weak, like all your family. I will deal with it, like I deal with everything. We have ways of doing things in the Cape.' Her eyes were blazing. 'I will never shirk my duty to my grandchildren.'

Maggie followed them to the door and rested her hand on the woman's shoulder. She could afford to be kind now. 'I'm truly sorry, Mrs Vantonde, but whatever happens, Kate will never come and live with you. And the sooner you accept that the happier you will be.'

After they'd gone Maggie sat on as darkness fell. Why couldn't she like Nomatuli as her daughter did? There was a lot about the woman that Maggie admired. It must have been incredibly hard for a woman from her cultural background to walk out on her husband. Maggie was envious of Nomatuli's courage but Kate was in a vulnerable state and Maggie couldn't bear to see her daughter being used. At least, that's what she told herself. The truth was something much simpler. She was jealous. Nomatuli was Kate's confidante - the person Kate turned to, in preference to her own mother, and she couldn't bear it.

Competition

The resentment Maggie felt for Nomatuli came to a head a few days later. Nomatuli was living with them now and Maggie was feeling the strain. On the day it happened she had just arrived back from a tiring shopping trip to Hermanus and Lilah was immediately in the shopping bags, searching for goodies. Before Maggie could stop her she grabbed a packet of biscuits and ran off. Nomatuli caught the child and marched her straight back to her grandmother.

'Now say you are sorry to Ouma.' Nomatuli lectured. 'For being so greedy.'

The child threw the biscuits down and ran away.

'I can deal with her thank you, Nomatuli.' Maggie snapped, struggling past the woman with two heavy bags.

Nomatuli took one of the bags. 'Mummy have nice time shopping?'

Maggie hated being called *Mummy* and she also loathed shopping. She ordered her groceries on-line at home

The woman was helping Maggie put the groceries away when Kate came in for lunch. The black woman was reading the price on a large packet of crisps and Maggie saw the look that passed between her and her daughter. Maggie resented having to justify buying a few luxuries for her grandchildren. Of course, Nomatuli was fantastic at shopping. She knew the best butchers and fruit stalls in Hermanus. She haggled for the best price and wouldn't be fobbed off with inferior produce. The weekly grocery bill came crashing down when Nomatuli did it. It was all right for her, Maggie thought; she could speak the bloody language.

It was time to talk to Kate about the future. Nomatuli was working on her store till late that night so she and Kate would have the place to themselves. It gave Maggie the perfect opportunity.

Kate was almost her old self again that evening. Maybe it was the wine. Whatever, Kate suddenly asked Maggie if she would mind looking after the kids for a couple of days. She had decided to go away.

Maggie was thrilled. 'Of course I'd love to look after them. What are your plans? Will you stay with friends?'

'I'd like to go to Leopard's Kloof. Remember? Where Pete and I used to camp when Jeth was a baby?'

Hard to forget a name like that. Maggie had been desperately worried when Kate first told her about the place, even when Kate said there were no leopards there anymore.

"Then why call it Leopard's Kloof?"

"Because, once long ago,' Kate explained patiently, just as Pete had once explained to her. 'There used to be leopards in those hills. I'd have to be very lucky to see one now."

"'Lucky?" My God, Kate, you're mad."

"Mum. The mountains are full of vineyards and 4 by 4 trails and mansions with heli-pads for rich townies and stud farms and country hotels with mini nature reserves and rapid response alarm systems and razor wire. No self respecting leopard would show up there."

'Wouldn't it be nicer to stay with people,' Maggie asked Kate, filling her wine glass. 'You need to be somewhere beautiful and relaxing.

Kate smiled properly at Maggie for the first time in weeks and her gaunt little face was transformed. 'Believe me, Mum, Leopard's Kloof is the most beautiful place in the world.'

Maggie bit back her response and tried to show interest. 'When would you go?'

'As soon as possible.'

'Tomorrow?'

'That would be brilliant. Thanks Mum.'

After that they got to chatting about this and that and Lilah's birthday was mentioned.

'Maybe we could have a party for her?' Maggie suggested. 'What d'you think?'

Kate's hand tightened around the stem of her glass and Maggie knew she'd made a mistake. 'It's just a thought. If you're not up to it, forget it.'

'It's not that, Mum,' Kate said, 'I want Lilah to have a special day but...'

'...So why?'

'Don't you think I want her to have a nice time, like we used to? What sort of a mother d'you think I am?' Kate's voice was raw and ugly. 'Sorry, but I don't know how I feel any more. Each day's a minefield. I think I'm getting there and then something happens and...Oh, Mum.'

Maggie went to Kate, kissed her clumsily on the head, and her daughter buried her face in her skirt, sobbing uncontrollably.

Maggie didn't dare move, not until Kate raised her tear-stained face and looked at her.

Maggie was crying too. 'Look. You've made me all wet,' she said, touching her skirt.

For that one moment everything was perfect but then Maggie went and ruined it all. 'You'll see, my love. Everything will be fine once you're back where you belong.'

Kate got up and went to look out at the garden. Her back was to Maggie.

'You know you can't go on like this.' Maggie was determined not to lose her nerve. 'Of course you want to make a go of the farm, I understand that but... You could get work - maybe even do that horticultural course you wanted to do. I could look after the children for you and they'd soon make friends. Pete always said if it didn't work out, you'd come home. Africa isn't your country, Kate'

Kate turned to face Maggie. 'And England is?'

'It's where you were born.'

'So?'

'Your roots are there.'

'My roots? Okay, what are they, these precious roots? Tell me.'

'This is silly, Kate.'

'Really, Mum, I want to know.'

'Okay. There's Welsh on your dad's side. Lancashire - that was my maternal grandmother and Devonshire from my grandfather.'

'And your dad was half Italian?'

'Yes, but he was born in England.'

'And there's German on your mum's side?'

'Very distant.'

'We're racial Frankenstein's, Mum.'

'But England's your country.'

'And South Africa's my children's country. Things will get better. There's lots of ways to make money here.'

'Like what?'

'I don't know. I could sell something, just to tide us over.'

'What have you got that's worth selling?' Maggie had finished pussy-footing around her daughter. 'Your TV's broken, the furniture's old, your computer and washing machine are second-hand. Maybe you've got a secret stash of treasure buried in the garden? Some of Lilah's shinies? And what about them? Um? Jeth and Lilah? Okay, you can go around in raggy jeans but what about their school fees, doctor's bills, everything that children need on a daily basis? And I'm talking absolute basics, Kate, not luxuries. I've given up trying to work out what's going on in your head but the children don't deserve to suffer because you've got some stupid, airy-fairy idea about honouring your dead husband's wishes.'

Kate was silent for a long time but when she finally spoke her voice was strong. 'You don't have to worry about us, Mum. I've decided to go into business with Nomatuli. I'm investing in her store and shebeen.'

Maggie put a hand out to steady herself. It had been so wonderful holding Kate. She'd thought that maybe now everything would be all right, that Kate would see sense and come home. But not now…not after this.

'So? What d'you think?'

'Since when do you care what I think? You've made it perfectly clear that you don't want any advice or help from me.'

'But I am taking your advice. I'm taking positive steps to earn a living.'

'What? Sinking the last of your savings in a drinking dive for poor blacks?'

'It's a shebeen, Mum, not a...'

'...For God's sake, Kate, grow up. How much d'you think you'll make from something like that?'

'Nomatuli says...'

'... "Nomatuli says."'

'I trust her. She's a good businesswoman.'

'How d'you know? Because she told you? Don't you understand? This is what she's been waiting for.' She spat out the words. 'That woman's using you, you pathetic little bitch. It's your money she's after and when she's got everything she wants, how long d'you think she's going to hang about here?'

All the colour had drained from Kate's face. 'Why are you saying this? You don't know her, she wouldn't...'

Maggie jumped up and swept her arms across the table, scattering crockery and glasses onto the floor and then she ran upstairs.

Maggie sat on her bed and listened to Kate sweeping up the broken china. She felt no remorse. She'd done everything she could. She'd looked after the children, sorted the house, cooked, cleaned, offered her daughter a place to live and what response did she get? Nothing but this final huge insult. Kate would rather trust a stranger than her. Well, if that's the way she wanted it that was fine. It was obvious she wasn't needed here. The children wouldn't even miss her. They had the marvellous Nomatuli and Ma Vantonde. How could she possibly compete? Well, she wasn't going to be anyone's skivvy. She'd done all that with Tom. And look where it had got her. As soon as she could she would be booking her ticket home.

When she went back downstairs the house was empty. She glanced out of the window and saw Kate and Spider disappearing down the track in the fast-fading light. Maggie filled her glass to the top and took a defiant swig; then she heard the familiar sounds of the Renault.

Nomatuli breezed in. 'Hello, mummy. Where's Kate?'

'Out.'

'Is something wrong?'

'No.'

Nomatuli put on the kettle and made some toast. The woman's total ease in her daughter's house infuriated Maggie.

Nomatuli turned and caught Maggie's look. 'Do you know, mummy? Each time I see you, you look younger. The daddy was a stupid man to walk away from you.'

'I'm sorry?'

'Kate tell me. Your man walk out on you. Don't cry for him. You better off. Look at my bastard fella, married 22 years, and then he take a young, lazy skinny wife. Expect me to help new wife settle. I show her 'settle'. She'll have big bruise for long time. She will always remember Nomatuli.'

Maggie was appalled. Kate had been discussing her private affairs with this…this what? That was the whole point. She didn't know what the black woman was to Kate: a friend, a paid worker, a sponger who was using her daughter's sad situation to make a nice little life for herself? What?

Nomatuli came and sat down at the table with Maggie. 'You worry too much. Kate will be okay for sure.'

'Yes she will, as soon as she's back home in England where she belongs. She's very unhappy.'

The woman frowned, 'Of course. Her man is dead'

'Yes, but more than that, she has no money, no friends, no...prospects.'

Nomatuli yelped with laughter. 'Kate has "prospects" – for sure. She is a young, sexy woman, some lucky fella will come.'

'It's not going to work, Nomatuli.' Maggie said, her voice dangerously low. 'I know what you're up to.'

Nomatuli's smile wavered.

'You may think you've been very clever but I'm onto you. You are not getting my daughter's money. She's coming back to the UK with me.'

Nomatuli narrowed her eyes. 'She doesn't say to Nomatuli. We are business partners. Did she not tell you?'

'She is not going into business with you. The little bit of money she has is to pay the bills. She has no cash for...shebeens.' She made the word sound obscene.

'I will speak to Kate about this'

'And she can't afford to have...non-paying guests, either,' Maggie added spitefully.

Two deep frown lines appeared between Nomatuli's eyes as if she was having trouble understanding. Finally, she placed her cup carefully on the table and stood up. She spoke slowly and clearly. 'Nomatuli never take for nothing. I work hard for Kate. For Blue Gum.' And with that she went into her room, closing the door firmly behind her.

Maggie sat on in her chair, determined to wait up for Kate. She wasn't sorry for what she'd said to either of them. Her daughter was being ridiculous. "Racial Frankensteins"? Rubbish. So what? If there was a bit of German and Italian in the mix? Of course England was Kate's country. Everybody had a country, an identity – it was something to be proud of.

Her tired brain drifted to her father. Maggie's mother had died young and Maggie and her dad had moved in with a widow down the street. Maggie had to call this woman, 'Auntie.' The house was too small for the three of them and she shared the woman's bedroom. Maggie knew she was there under sufferance. This auntie-who-wasn't wanted her dad and was prepared to wait for the awkward teenager to grow up and leave home, so she could have him.

Maggie remembered the night she missed the last bus home after a dance and her dad was waiting up for her. He was a fireman and had just finished a shift. The glaring light in the hall showed up his puffy, red-rimmed eyes. He looked old. Maggie saw these things but she was young and had more important things to think about.

'You didn't have to wait up for me,' she said defiantly, knowing she was in the wrong.

'Just get to bed,' her dad said wearily.' Your Auntie's been worried.'

'She's not my auntie,' Maggie muttered, as she sidestepped her father into the hallway, trying not to breathe in. The house always stank of the fish the woman boiled for her horrible fat cat.

Her dad closed the door quietly behind her and turned the key. Maggie knew it was the woman who made him nag her.

'I couldn't help it, Dad,' she wheedled. 'The bus went early.'

'Don't lie, Maggie.'

'I'm not... Don't you trust me or something?'

'It's not you I'm worried about. You're only fifteen. Who were you with?'

'Val'

'And?'

'Just a boy.'

'Local?'

Maggie curled her lip. Tony and his friend were Londoners and wore the latest Italian suits with button-down collared shirts. They made the local 'rockers' look like swede-bashers. 'Tony's Italian,' she said. 'When I told him you were half Italian he was dead interested...'

Her dad's hand shot out and grabbed her, his fingers digging into her flesh. 'Get one thing straight, girl. You bring any dagos back here and you're in big trouble. Got that?'

'But your dad was Italian.' She stammered, frightened by his rage.

'I'm not repeating myself, Maggie. Now get to bed. And don't wake up your Auntie.'

Later in bed, her arm still hurting from where he'd grabbed her, Maggie wanted to cry. But maybe "Auntie" was listening and she didn't want to give her the satisfaction.

She lay still watching the car headlights flaring across the bedroom ceiling and tried to make sense of what had happened. Was her dad ashamed of being Italian? Maggie knew about the war but that was in the olden days. She'd always been proud she had

Italian blood. It was dead romantic. Frank Sinatra and Tony Curtis were Italian.

She liked telling people about her dad. He was different from her friend's fathers. He played boogie-woogie, drew cartoons and made spaghetti Bolognese - long before anyone else did - even if he had to use Branston pickle and tinned spaghetti instead of the real ingredients. And he had film star good looks. He had a cleft in his chin, just like Kirk Douglas.

It wasn't until she was an adult that Maggie really understood. Her father needed to fit in with the men he worked with, his neighbours, his friends. She recognised that need because it was in her too, that sense of not quite belonging; of being an outsider, of trying to find acceptance but somehow always failing. And now, she realised sadly, it was in Kate too.

Maggie must have fallen asleep then, because the next thing she knew it was dark and Spider was lying across her feet, chasing bantams in his sleep.

Spying

'She's sitting down again.'

We were on the decking veranda outside the bedroom and I was plaiting garlic bulbs. The bantams were squatting in the large birdbath on the patio below us, keeping cool. There was a lot of squawking as they jostled for pole position. For once the wind had dropped and it was absolutely still except for the droning of a far off micro-light, some doves cooing and the lazy buzzing of bees around the honeysuckle that clambered up the balcony steps.

Lilah was cutting up a cornflakes' packet and Jeth was watching Nomatuli through his telescope. I could hear Mum banging about in the kitchen. She wasn't speaking to me. My Leopard's Kloof trip looked like it wasn't going to happen.

'Now, she's watering the peach trees.'

Jeth's running commentary on Nomatuli was getting to me. I hated him being sneaky but I didn't want to spoil the mood by telling him off. It was the first time the three of us had spent time together like this for a long time – quiet and friendly – like a proper family.

'And her break was too long.' Jeth again.

Was he timing her now? I took a swig of water and thought about getting Lilah out of the sun. I could see her shoulders turning pink. 'It's very hot today, Jeth. How would you like to be out there in this heat?'

'If I was paid money to do a job, I would do it properly.'

'But she isn't getting paid, Jeth, that's the whole point.'

'She stays in our house and eats our food doesn't she? I think she should work like she did before, when she was killing the aliens. And she wasn't very good at that, either.'

'The government paid her a pittance to do that.'

'What's a spittance?' Lilah asked, snipping away at one of my finished plaits.

'It's a very low wage. Not many rand.' I said, grabbing the garlic from her. 'Why don't you go and see what Grandma's doing?' I stood up. The heat was getting to me too. 'Actually, we're all going inside now. Off you go, Lilah.'

'Does Nommy get shinies?'

'Sometimes,' I said.

'But it's not fair, Mum.' Jeth was like a dog with a bone.

'For God's sake, Jeth. Give it a rest.' I threw down the plait I was working on, watching in frustration as it unwound.

'Dad said if you do a job then you should do it properly.'

Nearly everything he said to me lately started or ended with "Dad said".

'She only waters each tree for ten seconds.'

I held up my hands. 'Okay, enough. Take that telescope downstairs and find something useful to do. What about checking Spider for ticks? That's your job isn't it? And this is your last warning, okay? If I catch you spying on Nomatuli again I will take that telescope away from you, for good.'

He muttered something under his breath.

'What?'

'Nothing.'

'Maybe you don't know how lucky we are having Nomatuli work for us.'

He turned his back on me. 'She's the lucky one. She's a lazy kaffir.'

I grabbed him and swung him around to face me. 'Never, ever use that word in this house again. It's ugly and horrible and black people hate it. D'you understand, Jeth? Well?' I shook him.

He struggled but I held on. Lilah ran downstairs and I heard Mum talking to her.

'Who said it? We're not leaving here until you tell me.'

'A boy at school,' he muttered, not looking at me.

'What's his name?'

'Dunno.'

'Right. I'm coming to school with you tomorrow and you can point him out to me.'

He wriggled out of my grasp. 'It wasn't at school.'

'Where then? Jeth? I'm waiting.'

He was packing up his telescope.

'Was it your grandmother Vantonde?'

He shrugged.

'You've got to promise me you'll never say it again.'

'But *Ouma* says...'

'...Your dad would be so ashamed if he heard you using such an ugly word. It's racist and your dad hated racism...'

He pulled away from me. '...And my dad would be double-ashamed of you.'

'What are you talking about?'

'He told me Blue Gum would be the best farm but you're going

127

to take us away and make us live in a horrible foreign country, where the sun never shines and you have to wear shoes – all the time.'

'For God's sake, Jeth!…'

'…Don't shout at me. You're always shouting.'

'OK. I'm sorry. But what you said? It's not true. Whoever told you that is telling lies. Blue Gum is our home. Your dad and I built it especially for you and Lilah, and we're going to stay here. D'you understand? Everything will be fine.'

'That's what you always say. "It will be fine." But when you say that it means that something ugly is going to happen.'

'Not this time, promise.'

'If my dad was here he'd tell Nomatuli to work harder.'

Suddenly it was all too much. 'But he isn't here, is he? That's the whole point, Jethro. Your father's dead and he's never coming back. D'you understand? He's never coming back.'

Too late I saw the pain on his little face and I held out my arms to him. 'Oh my God, Jeth, I'm so sorry. Come here…'

'…I hate you' he screamed, veins bulging in his thin little neck. Then, he pounded down the balcony stairs, two at a time, and went crashing away through the undergrowth, bantams exploding in all directions.

Leopard's Kloof

It was hunger that eventually drove Jeth inside but he wouldn't talk to me or look at me. After lunch Mum organised the children to collect my camping gear together. Surprisingly she was still expecting me to go.

'Are you sure about this, Mum?' I asked.

'I said I would didn't I?' She snapped.

While everyone was busy I got on the phone to Ma. Of course she denied saying "kaffir" in front of Jeth but I told her that if anything like that happened again I would stop her from seeing the children.

'But it's all right for that black pagan to teach them witch craft?' She hurled back at me.

'Nomatuli's a Christian.'

She slammed the phone down. We all knew the heaven Ma believed in was *White's Only*.

I guessed it was she who'd been telling Jeth we were going to England too, but I asked Mum anyway.

'Credit me with some intelligence,' she said, handing me a bag of food. 'I know how highly-strung he is. There'll be time enough when it actually happens.'

'I told you last night,' I said, keeping my voice low. 'We're staying here.'

She was holding Pete's fleece, waiting to hand it to me, but as I spoke she threw it down. 'This store and shebeen idea is a nonsense and you know it. I've already told Nomatuli it's not going to happen.'

'What?'

'Someone had to put her straight. You need that money for emergencies.'

'How dare you speak for me, Mum. It's none of your business.'

'D'you think Pete would want to see you destitute?'

'Don't…don't bring Pete into this.'

'For God's sake, Kate. I'm so worried about you.'

'You don't have to be.' I sounded more confident than I was.

She picked up Pete's fleece again and handed it to me. 'Will you be okay on your own,' she asked suddenly. 'Up there in the wilds?'

'It's not "in the wilds."'

'But it's so isolated.'

'A kilometre from the main road? And there's a campsite at the bottom of the kloof.'

'So why don't you stay there?'

'Because,' I said slowly, the words like lumpy porridge in my mouth, 'I don't want to have to speak to anyone or think about anything. I just want to…. Oh forget it!' I chucked my rucksack down. Suddenly it all seemed too much effort. 'Look, I won't go, okay? You're not up for it. Babysitting my two isn't exactly a doddle.'

'No.' She was beside me, picking up my bag and pushing it into my arms. 'You must. I'll be fine - we'll be fine. All I'm saying is wouldn't it be better to stay with friends?'

'I don't have friends.'

'There's Miriam.'

'Miriam sleeping on the ground? Get real. Look, if I'm going I have to go now. I want to get there in daylight.' I went outside and threw my gear in the bakkie. Lilah was doing what she did best, hanging onto my legs and bawling. Jeth sat in the bakkie his telescope trained on the mountains.

'She'll be home before you know it, Jeth,' Mum touched his arm gently. 'Come on, be a big boy for Grandma. Mum needs a rest and I need your help. You can show me where everything is.'

He jumped down and I extricated myself from Lilah. 'Grandma's got something special for you, when I'm gone,' I promised her, wiping away her tears with the edge of my sleeve. 'Chocolate cake with smarties? Be a good girl. Two sleeps and I'll be home.' I was such a hypocrite. I could stuff my child with sugar but no one else was allowed to. I didn't attempt to touch Jeth.

I got into the bakkie and the three of them stood close watching me, their hair on fire against the setting sun. Mum's hand was half raised, as if she'd thought of waving and changed her mind. Lilah was pressed against her legs sucking her thumb and Jeth stood aloof and stiff, his hand resting on the dog's head. As usual the bakkie wouldn't start and after a moment or two Lilah lost interest and went inside.

When at last the engine fired I reversed onto the track. Jeth and Spider ran beside me as the bakkie bucked down the track towards the road. Spider jumped into the back and I braked hard. 'Jeth? Call him.' But Jeth shook his head and walked slowly back towards the house. 'Thanks,' I shouted. 'See you soon. Love you.'

When I stopped at the farm gate I looked back and he was still there on the track shielding his eyes, watching me. I waved out of the window and then I was out onto the main road and away. Spider stuck his head through the small opening behind the driver's seat and breathed his fetid breath on me. I needed to get him to the vet – his teeth needed attention. More expense. 'Good old boy,'

I muttered and he licked my ear.

Several kilometres on I turned off the main road, unlocked the gate, and drove up into the *kloof*. As the vehicle bounced along the rutted track, the headlights picked out craters in the mud road, turning them into bottomless black pits. Then the sun disappeared behind the ridge, in one final incandescent flare of light.

Most of the land is privately owned in the Western Cape and the rights of way are very limited. Most of my childhood in England had been spent a short journey from the coast, the Yorkshire Moors, the Dales and the Lake District. I missed that freedom. I often looked out at the mountains behind Blue Gum and fantasised about walking up into their misty crags. You could see baboons galloping about up there and once I was sure I'd seen a leopard.

'I doubt it, Kate.' Pete said, taking the binoculars off me.

But I knew what I'd seen.

Someone Pete knew owned *Leopard's kloof* and we camped there with Jeth when he was only a few days old. Ma accused us of being irresponsible. *What if baboons attacked us? Or snakes bit Jeth or we fell off the edge of the world?* We swam naked in the cold, peaty water then lay under the crackling stars, with Jeth beside us, the moon reflected in his round black eyes. We watched the Southern Cross in the cavernous black sky, while shooting stars crashed to earth all about us and our heads were full of the pounding noises of an African night.

I can't say exactly when the unfamiliar became the familiar for me. At first everything in South Africa was beyond my comfort-zone: the smells, birds, vegetation, animals, people…it was all so strange. I carried a heavy brick of homesickness with me wherever I went. How long before the fiscal shrike, fork-tailed drongo and weaverbird became my starling, blackbird and sparrow? Or the pulsing cicadas as everyday as the buzzing of bees? And the noisy quarrelsome Hadeda ibis as common as rooks cawing? And the night sky? When did the Southern Cross became as everyday to me as Orion's Belt or the Plough?

That first lonely year with a young baby was my worst time. I thought I'd always miss Mum, my friends and life in England but then, one morning, I saw my first swallows. I watched transfixed as they swooped through the air, searching out likely nesting sites. Pete said they might be the same birds who nested in our garage back in England. My dad had made a small hole in the garage door allowing the birds to build their nests inside. I got Pete to do the same in our shed door and very soon we had several nests. It made me so happy to see the parent birds flying in and out all day, feeding their young. If these little creatures could endure epic migratory flights across deserts, seas and trigger-happy Europe, then surely I could survive.

There was nothing to fear in the *kloof*. I was so at ease it was like coming home. Spider sensed my mood and made a little *yip* of pleasure. When I could drive no further I cut the engine and switched off the lights. It was a clear, still night and the sky was brilliant with stars. The moon was bright and lit up the valley.

I collected my gear - one blanket, warm clothes and bread and fruit-then we set off up the track. A mountain stream tumbled down the craggy scree to the right of the path and we passed waterfalls and pulsing stretches of water – some deep enough to swim in. Halfway up I stopped beside the running water and knelt down. Spider lapped up the liquid with his spade-like tongue and I dipped my head under the water. Squeezing the moisture out of my hair I twisted it behind my ears and then I cupped my hands and took a long, long drink. I was so thirsty. I couldn't remember the last time I'd had a proper drink. It felt like a thousand cups of tea and alcohol had been pressed into my hands in the past weeks but I couldn't remember finishing any of them.

Finally I stood up and stretched my arms over my head. Every muscle ached from weeks of hunched-up grief. When I was ready we carried on. The sound of water kept me on the path and Spider trotted ahead. He knew where we were going. In the forested area the cicadas were deafening. The track was very wet and steep and my bare feet slipped on the mud.

At last Lilah fell asleep, her face and hands covered with chocolate. Maggie found her snoring away in the corner, where they kept their toys, her blond head resting on a half-deflated football. She didn't stir when Maggie carried her upstairs.

Jeth was watching a David Attenborough nature video when she came down. It was the one about the Arctic and the boy watched it incessantly. Maggie sat beside him, fighting the impulse to put her arm around him. His eyes were focussed on the screen but she knew he wasn't seeing it. A tear was inching its way down his cheek and his tongue flicked out and drank it.

'She'll be okay, Jeth,' she murmured. 'Don't worry.'

'I'm not,' his eyes never left the screen. 'I miss Spider, that's all.' And then, more quietly. 'I miss him.'

'I know you do, sweetheart, we all do.' And then, 'D'you think it's time for bed? Watch the rest tomorrow, um?' She expected an argument but he got up, pressed the remote and went upstairs without a backward glance. 'Night, Jeth, sleep tight.'

Maggie made herself a cup of tea and sat down. There was nothing interesting on the telly so she switched off, half-wishing she'd accepted Nomatuli's offer to stay at Blue Gum while Kate was away. Maggie acknowledged it was a nice gesture, especially after what she'd said to Nomatuli yesterday, but it would take more than the fear of being on her own to make her ask the black woman for anything. Nomatuli had decided to sleep at her store. She didn't trust the people up there.

Maggie had to accept that Kate wasn't coming back to England with her. She'd been kidding herself, indulging in a bit of fantasy, but Kate was like her - once she'd made up her mind nothing would shift her. She had to try this Nomatuli thing and if that didn't work out, then that would be the time to think about her other options. Maggie had already decided to go into the travel agents the next time she was in Hermanus and sort out her ticket.

When she couldn't keep her eyes open any longer she went to bed with a book. She hoped this would put her to sleep but doubted it. The African night symphony was building up to its rousing climax. How did people ever get used to it? Suddenly she was so homesick for her quiet house on the outskirts of town, with no night noises except the water gurgling in the pipes and the dog barking next door.

At last we came to the large flat rock we were aiming for. It lay beside a small, yet deep plunge of water that was fed from a foaming waterfall. I sit quietly at first letting the night wrap itself around me and then I take a scrap of paper and one of Lilah's *cokies* from my back pack. It's a pink pen, the only one I could find that still worked. Smoothing out the paper I make myself write the words. The moon is bright enough to see by but I don't need light to write. *My Pete has died*. There, I have written it down. It's real and dreadful and some sound comes from my mouth. It's raw and ugly with the terrible pain of it and Spider comes close to me, resting his paw on my leg. I hug his warm body to mine, burying my nose in his dirty, doggy fur. My Pete is dead and I am diminished.

I don't attempt to stop the tears, not this time. My nose runs and my hair flaps against my face like some dead thing. No one can see me, only the moon and Spider and they don't care what I look like. My loss is not nice or polite or reasonable. It's an ugly, smelly brute of emotion waiting to crawl away to some dark hole to die - alone.

I tear the piece of paper into tiny fragments; then I toss them away. Taking off my clothes I slip into the cold blackness, my tears mingling with the water. Spider stands guard on the rock, whining and pawing the water, breaking the moonshine into whorls of silver. The round lemon sphere of moon is reflected in his worried eyes. 'Good old boy.' I say again, 'I'll be out soon and then we'll wrap ourselves in the blanket and watch the night together.'

The Singers

Lilah was delighted to have me home from *Leopard's Kloof* and even Jeth seemed happier but I think it might be having Spider back that pleased him most.

Part of the deal was that if Mum babysat for me I'd go to see the bank manager when I got back. She had decided to go back to the UK as soon as she could get a flight. Although I'm sad about that, I think it's for the best. She knows I'm not going to change my mind about going into business with Nomatuli and she's disappointed. With me? With herself? God knows. She could be right, it might be the biggest mistake of my life but I've got to give it a go.

The next day we went into Hermanus, Mum to get her ticket sorted and do the shopping, while I went to the bank. The bank manager took an awful long time to tell me what I already knew. I had a rapidly diminishing current account and there was nothing coming in. There was no chance of another overdraft. He was very sorry but there was nothing he could do for me. I managed to get out of the bank without crying and hurried to the sea front car park. I saw a couple of people I knew on the way but I kept my head down. The jungle drums would be beating tonight. *Did you see her in town? Looked terrible, hey?*

When I got to the car, the shopping was in the boot and I spotted my mum on the sea wall. I shouted but she didn't hear me. I shouted again, louder this time and waved, but she wasn't looking in my direction. Going deaf, my mother - and suddenly I wanted to cry.

Maggie took a long drink and moved further under the shade of the oleander. Below her the little white harbour nestled beneath the cliff and brightly-painted rowboats were pulled up on a white shingle beach. The old harbour was off limits to the flotillas of whale watchers and shark-diving boats that operated elsewhere in the bay. Whales were protected and no boats were allowed within a certain distance of the spectacular animals. Sightseers ambled along the cliff tops, cameras at the ready, waiting for the whale crier's horn.

It was an unusually calm day and the water was so clear that the whales and their calves were easy to spot. The sound of the horn was continuous and tourists crowded the pinnacles of rock along the headland. When someone pointed, a hundred pairs of binoculars swept the ocean for that first glimpse of a Southern Right Whale. Maggie remembered the thrill of her first sighting. It was something you never forgot. She didn't rush to the headland now but she envied these whale 'virgins'.

Just over the wall from where she sat, aggressive little hamster like creatures called rock dassies scuttled in and out of the Hottentot figs – or Cape figs as they were now called. While the dassies squabbled in the noonday heat, black-headed gulls flocked overhead and seals oozed in and out of the Butter Churn – a circle of rocks that beat up the sea into a perpetual colander of froth, even on a calm day like today.

This was where the cold Atlantic met the tropical Indian Ocean and the resulting marine life was as diverse as it was spectacular. There were colonies of African penguins dotted along the coastline. It still made Maggie smile that Jeth had been astonished when he'd seen penguins in the arctic on the video.

'But, Grandma,' he'd said, eyes wide with concern. 'Their bottoms will be so cold, sitting on all that ice.'

Maggie loved the scenery and wild life but this wasn't why she sat on the sea wall. She came to listen to the singers. There were two boy choirs who worked the cliff path and over the years Maggie had got to love them both. There was the 'whale' group - the largest – comprised mainly of teenagers, resplendent in football shirts, jeans and baseball caps. They held the best position, directly behind the large seat shaped like a whale's tail. Tourists liked this seat from where they waited eagerly for the whale crier's horn, often unaware that one of the giant creatures and its calf were basking in the warm inshore waters, not a hundred metres from where they sat. The more whales sighted the bigger the tourists' generosity. It was as if the singing and the appearance of those incredible animals were somehow linked.

The whale group had a wide repertoire of songs, ranging from light opera, pop, rap, to English football chants. Each year they added several more to their list. They sang loudly and enthusiastically and sometimes melodiously. But their real skill lay in their choreography. For Maggie it was the Osmonds all over again – only better. They performed intricate steps, turning, clapping, never missing the beat; never forgetting the move. They must have practised for hours and hours. Maggie loved to see people's faces as they watched these routines. It was hard not to smile when the boys' enjoyment was so obvious.

They even had a little 'Donny,' no doubt chosen for his cheeky grin and angelic looks. This boy was positioned in the centre of the group attracting the,' ah isn't he cute vote.' He always gave Maggie a thumbs-up when he saw her and shouted, 'Manchester United. Ryan Giggs.' And she would shake her head and shout, 'Liverpool, Gerrard,' in return and he would screw up his face in disgust.

There was a second, slightly smaller, younger and dirtier bunch of boys who commandeered a slice of pavement beside a sign reading 'It is prohibited to feed the Whales.' This group attempted to emulate the older boys' style, but it didn't quite work for them. However, their younger voices were sweeter and truer and, although not so rigidly rehearsed, there was a quality about their singing that Maggie loved. Obviously other people felt the same, if the amount of money in their cap was anything to go by.

Usually Maggie found the singers relaxing but this year was different. This year there was a new kid on the block - a lone boy with a truly amazing voice. It was a cliché to say his voice was like a pure fluting songbird but that was exactly what it sounded like. This boy simply opened his mouth and out came this incredible sound.

But he worried her. He stood on the right-angled bend of the pavement, where Marine Drive swept around to the old harbour. Here, the pavement narrowed dangerously, allowing only one person at a time to pass. Alternatively, tourists were forced to wait until there was a gap in the traffic before stepping out into the road and while they waited they had time to get their money out.

Maggie wasn't frightened for the tourists' safety but this child had to keep his wits about him. If he was attracting too much attention, one of the older singers would charge after him hurling stones. The boy was forced to dive into the road to escape being hit, his thin legs working like pistons. The first time Maggie saw this happen she was convinced he was going to be run over but he managed to dodge the cars. He would wait for a few moments for things to settle down again before returning to his pitch.

The other groups had smart donation caps laid out on the pavement, and would smile or wink or shout something to Maggie when she gave them something. But this boy held a bowl in front of him, hands clasped tightly about it, like a priest offering up the chalice.

It was hard to tell his age, maybe ten or possibly younger. He had that pinched look around the mouth that raggy boys had the world over. He was very thin and dressed in a white shirt with the cuffs doubled back over his slender wrists. His grey baggy shorts were belted tightly at the waist.

He only sang one song - 'Nessun Dorma.' His voice was clear and strong and achingly vulnerable on the high notes, as if his vocal chords were being stretched so tightly they were in danger of snapping. The boy obviously had no idea what the words meant - there was no passion, no light or shade - but the voice was still wonderful. And as soon as he reached the end he would start all over again. Maggie came into town regularly and whatever time she came he was always there before her, whether it was early morning or late afternoon as the huge sun disappeared into the furrows of the sea.

She always gave something to the other groups first, hoping that this might protect the boy from an attack. When she dropped coins into his bowl he never made eye contact. She didn't know what to say. What did you say to a child who moved you in such a profound way? This boy had a phenomenal gift. Maggie was sure of that.

But today something was terribly wrong. He was very frightened.

Coming to the end of the song he crouched down and took a hasty gulp from his bottle of water, his eyes never leaving the other side of the road. Maggie followed his gaze to where another, older, rougher-looking boy sprawled in the shade of a tree. His legs were thrust out across the pavement, so that people were forced to step over him to get past. This boy was glaring at the younger boy and he held a stick in his hand. It was a polished length of wood with a round smooth knob on one end. A knobkerrie. He shouted something in Afrikaans at the boy and thumped the stick hard into the palm of his other hand, emphasising the point. The boy jumped up at once and the bottle slipped out of his hands, spilling his precious liquid.

That was when Maggie heard Kate calling her. She had R10 ready to give to the boy and as she dropped it into his bowl his eyes locked with hers. Neither of them saw one of the boys from the Whale group run up and hurl a rock.

Kate yelled, 'Mum! Watch out!' and Maggie ducked. The stone hit the boy squarely on the side of his head and knocked him out. He toppled forwards and would have fallen into the oncoming traffic if Maggie hadn't caught him.

Hospital

We took the injured boy to the Provincial where Miriam worked.

The child perched on the edge of the examination couch while Miriam saw to his injury. She muttered as she worked. 'Bloody little vandals. The cops should have moved them on years ago. They're nothing but trouble. I'll be filing a report Kate. Somebody's going to get killed up there one of these days. You shouldn't have got involved.'

'What were we supposed to do?' I asked. 'Leave the kid lying in the middle of the road?'

'And he sings so beautifully.' Mum said. 'It's a real shame because his voice will be ruined if he keeps on straining it.'

I turned to her. 'D'you know what, Mum? I don't think this boy has to worry about his future as an opera singer.'

She ignored my sarcasm but Miriam frowned at me.

'I'm sorry for him that's all,' Mum again. 'He looked so terrified and he isn't well. Look at him; he's all skin and bone. And there was that other boy, watching him, an older rougher type... very intimidating.'

'His minder,' Miriam said. 'The kid's on his own. Parents and family probably dead from aids or war or famine and the older kid protects him - in return for his takings.'

'Protect? Is that what you call it?' Mum looked directly at me. 'I think the boy should be put in police care, Kate. 'They'll know what to do.'

I shook my head. 'Not a good idea. I think he should come home with us. '

Miriam put her hands on her hips. 'Oh yeah, Kate, brilliant. You really need one more mouth to feed and something else to worry about.'

I patted her arm. 'Yeah, Miriam, maybe I do.' I didn't need to look at mum to know what she was thinking. But it was her fault, wasn't it?

'He'll have a nasty bruise,' Miriam said, packing up her gear. 'But I don't think there's any real damage. However,' she said, 'he needs to stay here overnight, to make sure he isn't concussed. I'll arrange that.' She spoke to the boy in Afrikaans but he didn't respond.

'I'll ring you later, Miriam. Okay? Find out how he is? And I'll pick him up when he's ready.'

'You're mad,' she said as she left the room.

'Thanks, Miriam. You're a very kind person.'

She shook her head at me but I could see she was smiling.

'I'm sorry I got you involved in all this.' Maggie said when they were on their way home.

Kate shrugged.

'Were you serious?'

'About what?'

'Taking the boy in?'

'We'll see.'

'Miriam has a point.'

Kate concentrated on accelerating past a bakkie. The men in the back cheered and waved. The driver thumped his horn. They weren't quite so pleased when the car's geriatric exhaust spat black acrid smoke at them going up the next hill. The Renault wasn't used to overtaking vehicles and coughed and spluttered to the top. Going down the other side the bakkie sped past them with the men shaking their fists and laughing.

'I got my ticket, Kate. I'm going home a week on Saturday.'

Kate glanced at her, 'Aw, Mum.'

Maggie wasn't going to cry – she'd done enough of that. She would remain calm and business-like. 'There's something I've got to say so don't interrupt. I've got my pension and money from your father. I'm well off and I'm going to share it with you. It can be a loan or a gift but you're getting it, so don't argue.'

Kate kept her voice neutral. 'I don't want your money, Mum.'

'Tough,' Maggie blew her nose hard. 'I'm writing a cheque out when we get home and you can pay it in tomorrow. There's only one condition. You're not to give it to that woman, understand? It's for you and the children.'

At that moment a sleek, red BMW surged past the Renault and disappeared in the flick of an eye. Maggie had a fleeting glimpse of a beautiful woman at the wheel - a black woman. Black men and women ran South Africa now but around here a black woman driving a car like that still raised eyebrows. Maggie could hear Ma Vantonde's voice. Must be from Cape Town or Jozy, ja? Maybe a drug dealer?

As it happened, they didn't have to worry about the boy singer because he ran away from the hospital that night.

'It's for the best, Maggie,' Miriam told her. 'Kate doesn't want to get mixed up with these people. They're trouble, ja?'

A Stranger at Blue Gum

By the time Maggie woke the next morning the sun had already burnt the dew off the eucalyptus leaves and the world had exploded into daytime. Outside the window a fiscal shrike - or Jacky Hangman - was hammering his song into her head. And somewhere nearby baboons shrieked. Even the collared doves were loud and kamikaze flies dive-bombed the windows.

The house was deserted and the car gone. Then she remembered that Kate was taking Nomatuli into Hermanus today to stock her store. The loan had come through from the farm. Kate had finally accepted the cheque from Maggie and she would be paying it in while she was in town. All of this cheered Maggie up. Even the usual mess in the kitchen didn't faze her. Toast crumbs and cereal festooned the table and floor and legions of ants were having a feast. Maggie put on her washing up gloves. She had promised herself she would get rid of the ants before she went back to England and today was the day, the perfect opportunity with no Jeth about to accuse her, 'But Grandma, ants are living creatures.' *She used the vacuum cleaner nozzle to suck up thousands of them and what she didn't get that way she zapped with a cloth. She was merciless. Afterwards, she swamped all the major ant routes with bleach, and then she captured the bull-frog that lived in the bathroom – by throwing a dish cloth over him - and deposited him in the vlei.*

Maggie loved making order out of chaos. She'd always been a bit embarrassed to admit to the pleasure she got from hanging out

*washing and seeing it flapping gently in the breeze. And even better
the folding of clean clothes and smelling the freshness and warmth
in the fabric. No need to iron anything here, when the sun and wind
did the tumble drying for you. At least that's what she'd thought
until some kind soul told her about the putzi fly, which laid its eggs
in damp clothes. When the eggs hatched into fully-grown maggots
they burrowed into the skin and left boil-like sores. Miriam had
assured her that the fly wasn't endemic in the Western Cape but
Maggie bought Kate an iron – just in case. Heat killed the eggs.*

*By the time Maggie finished her chores it was almost midday and
she heard the familiar backfiring as the Renault approached. She
got to the door just as the car drew up and waved cheerily,
determined to be nice. Kate and Nomatuli were in the front, but the
back seat was a jumble of children's heads. Obviously Kate had
picked up Jeth and Lilah from school on her way home, but there
was another child there too.*

*She could hear Jeth's voice long before the doors opened - he
was very excited about something. Spider bounded out from
between the children's legs and greeted Maggie. Everyone else was
focussed on the newcomer. Even Kate seemed animated. She lifted
a child out of the back seat. He was taller than Jeth but very thin
and his clothes hung off him. Maggie recognised him at once. It
was the boy singer from Hermanus. He held a blood- soaked hanky
to his face and Maggie could see bruises covering his thin arms
and legs. Kate carried him inside and, while she made him
comfortable on the settee, Nomatuli put some water on to boil.
Lilah climbed onto the sideboard, where she stood on tiptoe, trying
to reach the medicine box. Maggie got it down for her and the child*

emptied the contents onto the floor, searching for bandages and cotton wool. Jeth was leaping from chair to chair making Spider bark frantically. Maggie grabbed the boy and made him sit quietly beside her. Lilah handed out cotton wool buds while Kate bathed the boy's head wound. It was a nasty gash. Nomatuli sat close, smoothing his hair. 'It's okay. You fine now. No more worry.'

Fortunately the cut wasn't deep but it was still nasty and had only narrowly missed his eye. Kate looked up from what she was doing. 'Get the cream Lilah. And Jeth? Get him a glass of milk.' Both children hurried to do what their mother asked.

'What happened?'

'We were loading the car when we heard screaming. That thug was beating the boy.'

Maggie remembered that stick and shuddered.

'There was a whole crowd of stupid tourists watching and not one lifted a finger to help.'

'But before we get there the bastard, he cut boy. I cut him too if I see him.' Nomatuli's eyes were bright with vengeance. 'Then we see how brave he is.'

'My God. Did the police arrest him?'

'We didn't call the police.' Kate gave the boy the milk. 'Nomatuli thinks he's an illegal. The cops would only dump him back where he came from.'

'But isn't that for the best?'

'Why d'you think he came here in the first place?'

'But what if he was kidnapped – because of his voice - or got separated from his family?' Maggie knelt down beside the child and took one lifeless hand in hers and squeezed it gently. He kept his eyes down.

'You sing very beautifully. Did your mother teach you?'

He flinched as if she'd hit him.

'You must miss her. And your family? Do you have brothers and sisters?'

The boy murmured something. Nomatuli bent down and spoke to him in Xhosa. He shook his head, not understanding. She tried Afrikaans and then Zulu, but he shook his head each time and whispered something.

The three women looked at each other, not knowing what to do.

Suddenly Jeth spoke up. 'He says he has no mummy, or brothers or sisters, no one. They are dead.' He saw their astonished faces and sighed at their ignorance. 'He is speaking English. He says his name is Johnny Zono.'

'Jo Jo,' Lilah repeated.

Nomatuli clutched Jeth to her. 'Clever boy. Auntie give you big kiss.' The embarrassed Jeth wriggled out of her arms.

Later, when the boy was asleep with Lilah standing guard and Nomatuli had gone to her store and Jeth had lost interest, Kate and Maggie talked. Maggie was torn between pity for the boy and worry for Kate 'But won't you get into trouble if he stays here, Kate? If he's an illegal immigrant the police will arrest him.'

'You were the one who was worried about him and his beautiful voice. We can't just patch him up and send him back. His minder will be waiting for him, Mum. And he will be very angry.'

The first night Jo Jo stayed with us I put up a camp bed for him between Jeth and Lilah but the next night it was on the other side of Lilah. I knew Jeth had moved it but I didn't say anything. Lilah is pleased to have the boy all to herself.

I worried that I was doing the right thing and the only person I could ask was Maarten so I invited him to supper, later that week. I used my mum as an excuse. I knew she wanted to say *goodbye* to him before she went home.

It was hard to say who was the most surprised when Maarten arrived, the boy or my brother-in-law. Maarten had come straight from work and Jo Jo was obviously terrified when he saw the policeman's uniform.

'Don't be frightened, Jo Jo,' Lilah said, sitting close to the boy. 'It's only Uncle Maarten.'

It took some time to calm the boy and even longer to get him to say anything.

'So?' Maarten turned to the boy, after I'd explained what had happened. 'Your name is Johnny Zono? '

The boy was silent.

'He's called Jo Jo,' Lilah said.

'And where does Jo Jo come from?'

The boy whispered in Lilah's ear but she didn't understand so Jeth pushed in beside the boy.

'He is from Lesotho,' Jeth said. 'His daddy is a Zulu.'

Nomatuli nodded. 'Ayee, he has the look of a warrior.'

'He has a little sister too – but they are gone.'

Maarten was very quiet while we ate and when he was ready to leave I went outside with him.

'Well? What d'you think?' I asked.

'Take him back where you found him.'

'Oh yeah, very funny.'

'I mean it Kate. You don't want this sort of trouble. Street kids are bad news. Believe me. I know what I'm talking about.'

'But he's so gentle.'

'I'm not talking about the kid. It's the thugs who own him that worry me. They're bad boys. You don't want to get mixed up in this.'

'But they'll beat him if he goes back.'

'Probably.'

'I never had you down as callous.'

'You asked my opinion.'

'He's just a little boy, Maarten.'

'Yeah, but if it's a choice between a kid I don't know and you and the children, there's no contest.'

'I can't do it.'

Maarten touched my hand. 'Okay, Kate.' he said, quietly. 'Do what you have to, but be very careful. Oh and one more thing. We're getting a lot of illegals in the area, looking for work? And where they go the sharks go – the drug pushers, the moneylenders and the pimps? When you're up on the RDP be careful, okay? They're bad guys.'

I should have listened to him.

At least having the boy with us took our minds off Mum leaving. She had booked a night flight deliberately so that the children would be asleep by the time she left. We all said our *goodbyes* before they went to bed with Mum promising that she'd be coming back soon. There was the expected scene from Lilah but Jeth seemed to take it quite well and took himself off to bed early. However, Lilah lay awake for ages, calling down that she was too hot, that she was hungry, that she was thirsty and in the end I lost patience and yelled at her.

Nomatuli was staying at her store that night so Mum and I sat drinking and chatting together. I was very proud of us. We didn't cry and I even managed to say how sorry I was – for everything.

She shook her head at me. 'I understand. Just remember I love you. And, Kate? Good luck with everything. I mean it.'

Just then we heard the taxi draw up outside. We weren't the only ones because Jeth appeared at the top of the stairs. I wasn't prepared for the look of shock on his little face.

'No, Grandma,' he yelled, running to her. 'You mustn't go.' And he threw his arms around her legs and clung on desperately.

Mum dropped to her knees beside him and raised his face to hers. 'Shush, shush, Jeth. It's okay. I'm coming back again, really soon, for Christmas. Now be a good boy. You don't want to wake Lilah do you?'

But it was too late. She was already coming down the stairs followed by Spider. She was wailing and Spider was howling.

'Please, Jeth,' I begged, picking up Lilah. 'Grandma's got to go or she'll miss her flight.'

'But I don't want you to go, Grandma. Stay.'

Mum was crying so hard she couldn't speak. She pulled Jeth to his feet and hugged him but he struggled out of her arms and ran back upstairs, barging into Jo Jo, who was standing at the top of the stairs watching us.

I followed Mum out to the taxi; then she kissed Lilah, got in the car, waved once, and the taxi pulled away.

Next day Ma arrived with Lionel in tow. She was like an undertaker bird, insincerity dripping from her beak. '*She was so, so sad that my dear mother had gone back to England. What a lovely person she was. But I must never forget that I was like a daughter to her and there would always be a home for us with her.'* I was trying and failing to shut her words out of my head when Lilah came into the kitchen followed by Jo Jo. Ma stopped talking in mid sentence and stared at the boy, her mouth hanging slackly open.

'Who's your little...friend, Lilah?' she managed at last.

'Oh,' I said, following her gaze, 'You haven't met Jo Jo yet have you?'

'Where's he from?'

'Not sure, Ma, but he's staying with us for the moment.'

'What?' she stuttered. 'In this house? With you?'

I nodded. 'Why? Is that a problem?'

'Where does he sleep?'

'He sleeps with me, Ouma.' Lilah piped up, beaming from ear to ear. 'He's my Jo Jo.' And then she grabbed the boy's hand and pulled him outside again.

Ma felt behind her for a chair and sat down heavily. She was wheezing again. 'I'm not happy about this, Katie.'

'Sorry, but it's got nothing to do with you.' I wasn't in the mood to put up with any of Ma's nonsense today. 'Oh and there's something else you should know while you're here.' I had intended choosing my moment before telling her about my business venture with Nomatuli but her whole attitude infuriated me. 'I'm going into business with Nomatuli. In her store up on the RDP?'

Ma buried her face in her hands. 'Please, please tell me it's a joke You naughty girl, you're teasing your old Ma aren't you?'

I shook my head. 'We're calling it the Purple store and shebeen.'

153

'Shebeen? My God, Lionel, our daughter-in-law's going to work in a shebeen.'

I took pity on her. 'It's not what you think, Ma, if you'll let me explain...'

She wrung her hands. '...Thank the Lord Pappie is dead and buried. The shock would have killed him for sure. A Groos working in an ungodly, drinking den for blacks? What am I going to tell my family and friends and the congregation and Pastor Billy - my God, Lionel, what am I going to tell Pastor Billy?'

'I'm not actually going to work there, Ma. I've invested some money in the business that's all.'

I caught Lionel's worried look. So? Even he was against me. Well, to hell with him and her and the whole of Kleinsdorp and...especially Pastor Billy.

With Mum gone and Nomatuli about to open her store I was busier than ever and had no time to worry about Ma. Three children and the garden and nursery kept me occupied.

Before she left, Mum offered to pay for Jo Jo to go to school. It was very generous of her and I accepted. So, as soon as he'd recovered from his injuries, I enrolled him in the big school in Kleinsdorp – where Jeth would be going after Christmas. The Kleinsdorp nursery and primary school were adjacent so the three children went to school together.

Several days later Lionel dropped by to tell me that it wasn't convenient for them to do the school run any more - something about other commitments. He looked very uncomfortable as he delivered his message.

I patted his arm. 'It's okay, Lionel. I understand.'

'Sorry, Kate. It's difficult, ja?'

He looked so defeated I gave him a hug. 'Don't be too hard on her' he whispered. 'She's just thinking about you.'

I let that go but we both knew what the problem was. And it wasn't about me. Ma could explain Nomatuli away as my live-in maid to her cronies but not the boy.

She did me a favour, though, because it was time I got out in the real world again.

Snake

In the beginning Lilah was the only one Jo Jo trusted. He was incredibly patient with her and would sit for ages sampling her various potions. The child only had to crook her little finger and he would be there, carrying her tea set, fetching her dolly, lugging her about when she was tired. I told him not to, because she's a chunky little thing, but he seemed to like it. She certainly did.

Jo Jo was eating well and his thin little face was filling out. His arms and legs were less stick-like but his eyes still had the same dead look.

'His trouble is here,' Nomatuli said, hand on her chest. 'No medicine for heart.'

Jeth ignored Jo Jo but that was soon to change. I was busy hanging out the washing one morning while Lilah pestered me to go on the jungle gym. Pete had used a fallen tree trunk and attached ropes and swings and several planks to climb and jump from. Lilah wasn't co-ordinated like her brother and I didn't like her using it on her own, so I asked Jo Jo to keep an eye on her. Jeth was searching for bugs to look at under his microscope. Lilah went off happily with her friend and I got on with what I was doing.

I was almost finished when Lilah screamed - a real scream, not one of her put-up jobs. The last time she'd made a noise like that she'd been stung by a scorpion.

When I got there I found Jo Jo holding her in his arms, kissing and hugging her. He was laughing but she was fighting him, pummelling his chest, trying to push him away.

'Let go.' I screeched, grabbing my daughter. 'Keep your dirty hands off her!'

I kicked out at him and he went sprawling backwards into the dirt where he lay staring up at me, his eyes wide with shock.

I hugged Lilah to me. 'What did he do? Show mummy. Where did he hurt you?'

But Lilah just sobbed.

'If you've touched her I'll kill you!' I screamed at the boy.

'What's the matter?' Nomatuli was beside me now.

I jabbed a finger at the boy. 'He's done something to her.'

The child lay on the ground shaking his head from side to side and moaning. 'No, Auntie. No.'

Lilah was hysterical now and suddenly threw herself backwards. Her hard skull cracked into my nose and I tasted blood. Nomatuli took her from me and held her tight, crooning to her, smoothing her hair. 'Where are you hurt, angel child. Tell Nommy.' As she talked she ran her hands all over the little girl's body. Down her legs and over her little bottom and behind her legs. Suddenly she froze and turned a frightened face to me. She put her fingers behind one chubby knee and showed me the two red puncture marks.

'Oh my God, a snake!' I grabbed Lilah – raising her legs to stop the poison from spreading. I tried to remember what else I'd read in Pete's snake book. *Stay calm.* 'We must get her to hospital.' My mind was in free fall. 'Don't just bloody stand there. My baby's been bitten by a snake.'

Nomatuli was talking urgently to the frightened boy.

'Leave him, I need you with me. The doctor might not speak English. What are you waiting for?'

'We must know what snake it is, Kate,' Nomatuli explained. 'So they can give Lilah the correct serum.'

'It's got to be a puff adder. Just come.'

Jeth had joined us and was prodding a stick into the hollow under the tree. 'It might not be,' he said. 'It could be a boomslang or a cobra. Maybe it's still in there.'

'Leave it, Jeth. Nomatuli? Please.'

But the woman was kneeling beside Jo Jo. He was showing her something. She took one look and threw back her head, screeching with laughter.

Was she mad? Jeth joined Nomatuli and the boy and soon he was laughing too. Tears rolled down Nomatuli's cheeks. At last she came to me and hugged me, kissing Lilah's head. Lilah had stopped crying now and was staring at her friend in surprise.

'Okay, Mummy.' Nomatuli patted my head. 'Not to worree.' And she produced what the boy had given her. It was a twig and it was forked at one end, just like a snake's fangs. Nomatuli held it against Lilah's 'puncture' marks. They matched.

Jo Jo took the twig off Nomatuli and pointed it towards me going *hiss, hiss*. Soon Lilah was hissing too. She wriggled out of my arms and she and Jo Jo held hands and jumped around in a circle going *hiss hiss*. Jo Jo's foot came down hard after every fourth jump. Lilah tried to imitate him and finally Jeth couldn't resist it and broke into their circle. Jo Jo shouted *'Bayete'* each time his foot crunched down and soon all three of them were stamping in unison.

'A-yi-ze!' Nomatuli shouted. 'Zulu warrior. Johnny Zono, son of chief for sure.' Then she grabbed me and we joined in, while Spider careered around us in ever decreasing circles. We were all Zulu warriors, all bellowing *'Bayete!'* and grinding our enemies into the dust.

It was only later that I remembered what I'd accused Jo Jo of. When I went to say goodnight I whispered, 'I'm so sorry, Jo Jo, forgive me' and I kissed his sweet face. He snuggled down under the duvet and sighed. 'It's okay, Auntie. I understand. You were afraid.'

At least my nose wasn't broken but I must have looked terrible. Good job I didn't care what I looked like.

The next day Jo Jo's bed had been moved in between Jeth and Lilah's. From then on the boys were inseparable. Lilah was allowed to tag along but her slave had become her king. The Sotho boy told them stories of the great Zulu leaders, Shaka and Dingane, and they made feathered head-dresses and arm and leg ties. They carved elaborate shields from eucalyptus bark and painted them black and white, to look like cowhide. They made assagais and stabbing spears from bamboo. The Sotho boy was a great climber and stalker, with a real love of nature and creatures. He taught Jeth the Sotho and Zulu names for trees and plants and creatures and their uses. Lilah's potions became real medicines and toiletries. Any bruise or cut or tummy ache was treated by the children.

They spent hours, watching spiders spinning their webs, spotting birds and imitating their calls. One night I was at the sink when I heard a bokmakerie making its car-alarm call. I was very surprised because the sun had set and bokmakeries aren't nocturnal. Suddenly the boys' faces appeared around the backdoor. They were giggling. I waved my fist at them and they ran off.

159

The best was yet to come. One day Nomatuli called me into the garden. The black woman put her finger to her lips and pointed to her ears. I listened. Jo Jo was singing. He was a distance away from us but there was no mistaking that voice. I didn't need to look at her to know that Nomatuli was smiling. I began to think the day we rescued Jo Jo was one of the luckiest days of my life.

Purple Store Opening

At last the great day arrived and Nomatuli's store was ready. The shelves were stocked and my friend was about to begin her new life. I was driving her to the RDP with the last of her possessions. There was a small storeroom at the back of the shop, just big enough to take a small camp bed, table and stove.

Nomatuli strode out with her bag and machete and tossed them into the back of the car; then she raised her eyes heavenwards. 'Thank you, Almighty God', she shouted. Her eyes were shining. 'No more digging in the dirt for Nomatuli Ikhaki.'

Jeth and Jo Jo were up the blue gum tree and waved and shouted to Nomatuli. 'Boys? You will all come to see my Purple Store?'

. They would be okay on their own for half an hour but I lifted Lilah into the car. She'd wept buckets when I told her Nommy was leaving and she was still snivelling. Nomatuli put a finger under the child's chin and wiped her tears away with her thumbs. 'Why you cry, angel child? On this happy day. Umm? We will see each other many times. You will help Auntie in the store. Sell sweeties to all your black cousins?'

The idea of giving sweeties away made Lilah wail even louder.

'Shush, Lilah, this is crocodile tears. You know I will never leave you. Now quick a big kiss for your auntie. Come.'

The child obeyed and I got into the car with them and turned the key.

'Good luck,' yelled the boys.

'I don't need good luck, I need many customers with rand,' she said, rubbing her thumb and forefingers together.

As we drove up the dusty lane onto the RDP, children ran alongside the car. We parked under the jacaranda tree and I waved at the women who sat chatting outside their shacks in the dying sun. They returned my wave but their eyes were on my friend.

'See how they watch me?' she hissed, as we walked down the track. 'They are suspicious of this Zulu woman, but I am patient. When the owner of Purple Store gives them goods on tick they will be friendly enough then, aye?'

I hardly heard what she was saying I was staring so hard at the building in front of me. I hadn't seen the finished store. The walls were purple and the corrugated iron roof was red. Picked out in white lettering over the entrance was the slogan, *Purple Store and Shebeen. Proprietors - Nomatuli Izhaki and Kate Vantonde*. The sign was in Xhosa, Afrikaans and English. Nomatuli stood beside me. She took a deep breath and let it out slowly. 'I wish my Thembo was here to share this moment with me. Do you like it, Kate?'

'It's…amazing.'

'Lucky has done a good job, aye? He is a handy fella to have around – but not on a Friday night, I think.'

Friday nights were when the men got paid and got drunk.

Nomatuli went inside and Lilah and I followed her. The children stood at the entrance, ready to scatter if the Zulu shouted at them. Mame Nomatuli had a fierce reputation on the RDP.

Nomatuli ran her fingers along the smooth counter top 'See this,' she said. 'It is made from an old packing case from the dump, and this and this.' She pointed out the shelving running down one wall and behind the counter. There were lights slung along the shelving behind the counter and loud speakers and a sound system. This was what Nomatuli had spent my money on. She saw where I was looking. 'We have lights and music,' she said, 'very loud music. You will hear it in Blue Gum. Maybe even in Hermanus.'

There wasn't much on the shelves yet but as soon as business picked up so would Nomatuli's stock. She would sell basics like mealie flour, cooking oil, sugar, bread, beans, yams and paraffin. In Natal she had sold paraffin but the officials had closed her down because she didn't have the correct containers. 'Now I am doing everything by the book,' she said, rubbing her earth-grained fingers on her skirt. 'Nomatuli is a businesswoman now and I will paint my nails purple - to match my store...our store,' she added, winking at me.

She looked at her watch and sucked on her teeth. 'I told that woman to be here waiting for me, Kate. And where is she?'

Nomatuli knew that Nandhi was unreliable but she had her uses. Nomatuli's cousin had lived on the settlement for many years. Having Nandhi, about the place, would give people the confidence to shop at the Purple Store.

My friend didn't care what people thought of her, especially the Xhosa men. There were several husbands who had been prepared to be more than friends with this disgraced woman, but Nomatuli had soon sent them packing. One had even tried to assert his male dominance by beating her, but he would regret that for some time. She knew a thing or two about hurting a man. He walked with a limp for some time afterwards.

Nomatuli was aware of the children giggling in the doorway. She smiled and beckoned them inside and gave them a sweetie each, then patted their heads and sent them home saying, 'Tell mummy, Purple Store is open for business. Free sweeties for all children who come tonight with their mames.'

When Lilah and I went back to the car we passed lines of women and children as they sauntered down the lane towards the store. I saw the slight figure of Nandhi dodging through the women, a toddler trailing behind her. Lilah was snivelling but her cheeks were bulging with all the sweets Nomatuli had given her.

A few days later I popped into the store with some mealies from our garden. We had agreed to sell any of my surplus vegetables in the store. When I got there Nomatuli was on her own. There was a long line of women waiting. It was a Friday and everyone wanted provisions for the weekend. Nandhi's baby was ill again.

I was soon in the thick of it all. Nomatuli would shout out an order and I would get the things together, while she added up and took the money. There was no time to talk but she gave me a broad grin every now and then and I quite enjoyed myself.

From then on I helped whenever I could. There was something very satisfying about selling things. I got the same kick at the farmer's market. I sold mealies, spinach, potatoes, tomatoes and various sorts of squash to the store.

At first the women were shy with me but they soon began to talk. I even picked up a few words in Afrikaans. I asked Nomatuli to teach me some basic phrases in Xhosa but I was pathetic. It wasn't just the clicks I found difficult it was the whole concept of the language. I kept asking questions like, 'How do you say tomorrow?' and my friend would laugh and explain to the women. They thought it was funny too. There is no word for tomorrow in Xhosa because it's bad luck to talk about such things. Only Gods know about tomorrow.

Rain

My finances improved as winter came on. Several mature trees were large enough to sell and I got good prices for them in Hermanus. The new annuals would soon be ready for market and there was a steady income from the store. At 9 am sharp each Saturday morning Nomatuli would arrive with my share of the takings. She was always dressed in her best dress on these occasions and would hand the money over solemnly. Then I would sign my name in her ledger. *All legal and above board.*

The weather was much cooler now and it started to rain. I loved rain. The first black clouds sent South Africans scurrying for shelter but I was that mad Englishwoman who danced in the rain. Lilah loved it too and she'd sit on the swing in the pouring rain and sing to the oak hats. They liked it apparently, even though she was tone deaf, like me.

We'd had a very dry late summer and autumn and a large proportion of each day was spent watering but now I could get on with other more important things. It was very good at first but the rain didn't let up. It went on and on. People said it was one of the wettest winters on record. It pounded down for days, weeks and none of us slept. The sound on our corrugated iron roof was like machine gun fire. The Klein River burst its banks and flooded the low-lying land. Giant boulders 'popped' out of the rain-wicked earth and plunged down the mountainsides, gouging out huge tramways from the soil, re-routing mountain streams and tracks.

The rich topsoil was washed away leaving a sandy, gritty, boulder-strewn lunar-landscape. Fortunately our house didn't flood, but the outhouses and poly-tunnels did. I lost most of my annuals and those that survived got a fungal infection and rotted off in the pots. Most of the trees and shrubs were okay but my proteas were drowned - literally washed out of the soil.

One day I was up to my ankles in water, attempting to bail out one of the poly tunnels when Lionel's bakkie drew up. They hadn't been near us for weeks. When I got inside Ma had the kettle on. She was making a huge effort to look sympathetic but the corners of her mouth twitched and the pink tip of her tongue explored her teeth excitedly. She knew what the loss of the proteas meant to me.

'We're so sorry, Katie, aren't we, Lionel?'

The man nodded, eyes full of concern.

'We know how hard it is to farm here. Even real farmers have trouble. If it's not the sun it's the rain and if it's not the rain it's the fires and if it's not the...'

'...Yes, Hannah,' Lionel interrupted. 'I think Kate's got the picture.'

'I don't want Katie to think it's her fault, Lionel. It's an act of God and maybe He's trying to tell you something, ja? Come live with us. Take pity on a couple of poor old people? You can still do your bit of gardening...'

At that moment Nomatuli arrived. She had borrowed the bakkie to go to the *Cash and Carry* in Hermanus to stock up her store and get some provisions for me. She dumped my shopping on the table and smiled broadly at everyone.

'...As I was saying, Katie.' Ma continued, totally blanking

Nomatuli. 'You can still do your bit of gardening and just think how convenient it would be for the children to get to school from our house. Jeth could even ride his bicycle.'

Nomatuli was busy separating her shopping from mine and Ma was forced to comment on what was going on. The Afrikaaner smiled patronisingly. 'Ah, this is so kind of you. We all know how Katie hates shopping but she really should have asked me. We know how busy you are with your little store.'

Nomatuli smiled graciously at the woman and sat down close to her. Ma moved her chair ever so slightly. Nomatuli poured herself a cup of tea and took a long noisy slurp. 'It okay, mame. My cousin is in the store today. I have to go to town to do my business at the bank. I am opening a new account for our "little store".'

She stressed the "our".

I hoped that Nomatuli hadn't seen Ma edging away from her, but Nomatuli caught my eye and deliberately moved her chair closer still.

Ma would not be defeated. 'We're so glad you're doing so well, aren't we, Lionel? I do hope this means you'll soon be sleeping somewhere more comfortable than a box room.'

I don't know where Ma gets her information from but I hadn't told her about Nomatuli's sleeping arrangements.

Nomatuli managed to keep the smile on her face. 'No problem. My new house is nearly ready thank you, mame.'

'Good.' Ma said. 'I'm sure some of the little…houses on the RDP can be made very comfortable.'

'My house is not up there, mame. It is in Kleinsdorp. You know it, I think? Beside the Bougainvillaea Cafe? It is white with a veranda all around and climbing roses up the wall?'

Yes, Ma did know where it was. We all did. It was a really pretty little bungalow with pink shutters.

Nomatuli was still talking. 'You must come for tea when I am moving in.'

Shortly after this Ma remembered a pressing engagement, the reason for her visit forgotten in her hurry to get away from my friend's triumph.

Lionel gave me a sympathetic look as he went out. 'You've still got your trees and the veggie plot, Kate. Don't forget, we're there if you need anything.'

'Thanks, Lionel.'

He looked at Ma. 'There you are then, Hannah. No one's going to starve.'

I could hear her grumbling all the way out to the car.

'Have you really bought that house?' I asked Nomatuli, as soon as they were gone.

'Not yet. But I am thinking about it.'

'She's such a pig to you.'

Nomatuli wagged a finger at me. 'No. She is so nice. She gives me such happiness.' Nomatuli's eyes were bright with mischief.

'I'll never understand why you didn't murder all us whites while you had the chance.'

You see *Zulu?* The film? Michael Caine?' she asked. 'We fought like lions with our backs to the veldt fire but...' and she shrugged her strong shoulders. 'Not enough guns and too many bastard whites. Do you know?' she said. 'My Mame tell me that our great great great Aunty – who was Aunty to the great Shaka and had her own Kraal, with many warriors – she believed white babies came from a great white flower that grew under the cold, grey sea. And the babies were half plant, half human, like a mealie cob.'

She saw my expression and slapped her thighs in delight. 'One more important news before I rescue my store from that good-for-nothing Nandhi.' She laid out a piece of paper in front of me. It was her bank statement. 'See. I repay the loan to the farm - with interest,' she added proudly.

I glanced at the figures. They were surprisingly good. She kept her prices low and it certainly seemed to be paying off. The only other shop in the area was in Kleinsdorp - the Spar, a supermarket with supermarket prices - and most black people didn't have transport to get into Hermanus.

'This weekend Purple shebeen is in business, Kate. My beer delivery arrives today.'

'You've done so well.'

'You help too, Kate. My business is not so good if you don't come to help and soon we will have big profits. That Nandhi? Pah!' and she screwed up her face in disgust. 'She is like a broody chicken. Always crying for her man. 'Why?' I ask. 'He buggar off to the mountains and leaves you with many babies – your always-ill babies. Do you think he cries for you? With all those bad women for company? And soon as he comes back you have more babies.'

Lilah's Party

In the end I did have a party for Lilah. I wasn't sure how I'd cope but I wanted her to have a lovely day and at last it had stopped raining.

Her friends from nursery were coming, plus their parents. There would be the Vantonde bunch, me, the kids, Miriam, Rob and Nomatuli – if Nandhi turned up on time for work. Nomatuli had promised to ring if there was a change of plan.

Nomatuli's mobile was the latest model – another gift from the marvellous Thembo. Most people on the RDP had mobiles. It had surprised me at first until I discovered that there were no landlines on the settlement. So, if the people were after a job, they needed a means of contact for prospective employers.

Ma arrived early with plates of food and grazed my cheek with her lips. She was in a good mood and even managed to keep the smile on her face when Lilah told her that Nommy was coming. Lilah was getting under everybody's feet so I took her with me when I went to pick up Nomatuli. On the way to the car I found Jeth and Jo Jo in the garden, shaking up bottles of Pepsi, so I took them with me too. We left everyone else hard at work. Gloria was laying a treasure hunt around the farm with angels holding the clues. Miriam was blowing up balloons. Ma and assorted Vantonde were making mountains of sandwiches. Antoinette was turning serviettes into 'swans' and Lionel, Maarten and Rob were getting the brais going.

As usual Jeth refused to get out of the car at the RDP and sat with his arms folded, glaring at anyone who came too close. Jo Jo came with me but he was a stranger there too and he kept his eyes down and walked close beside me.

Lilah had a wonderful time. Several of the women slipped sweeties and little gifts into her hands. They knew it was her birthday. This was Pete Vantonde's little girl and they all remembered Pete. The generosity of these people amazed me. When I saw how they lived I was ashamed. That they still had time for us was a minor miracle to me - *this rich white woman, with her big house and land*.

Nomatuli was waiting for us outside her store, parading in a stunning red dress and black straw hat. She twirled a purple parasol over her head.

Lilah hadn't seen Nomatuli since the store opened and she shrieked and ran straight into her arms, nearly knocking her flat. Nomatuli swung the child high in the air, giving her three smacking kisses. 'One for each year, angel child.'

When she put her down Lilah spotted the umbrella shaped parcel in Nomatuli's carrier bag. She was allowed to open it and we all crowded around and pretended to be astonished when she revealed a beautiful see-through umbrella, with fishes on it. She put it up and clasped it over her head, her grin appearing between a shark and an octopus. We all clapped. She wouldn't put it down even on the way home, with Jeth complaining bitterly because she kept poking him in the eye with it.

Nomatuli and I jabbered away happily like two best friends who hadn't seen each other for the long summer holidays. Her eyes were bright with excitement. Apparently Thembo was coming to stay with her in his next vacation. 'You will like him,' she promised me. 'Everyone loves my Thembo. He is a charming boy.'

'Like you?'

'Not like his bastard daddy, for sure.'

I couldn't wait to meet this perfect son.

Back at the house people were arriving and I had no time to worry about how I felt. Very soon the garden was full of excited, running children. We'd borrowed Miriam and Rob's swimming pool. The smell of barbecuing meat filled the air. Rob, Maarten, Lionel and some of the dads were cooking steak and drinking beer. Ma was partial to an expensive glass of sherry and she and some of her cronies sat sipping schooners of the sweet amber liquid on the veranda. Miriam and Antoinette took drinks around. Miriam looked fantastic in white trousers and black top. Antoinette was a great admirer of Miriam's style but somehow it never quite worked for her. She was wearing white trousers too - but they weren't made in such good material and looked like a badly wrinkled dishcloth. Her top was also white. But it was tight and her flesh bulged at the waistline and under her arms. Her black hair was piled up on her head like an ever-diminishing tower of blackcurrant jellies.

Nomatuli joined Ma and her cronies and accepted a large glass of sherry from Miriam. The women stopped talking the moment she sat down but if she noticed she didn't show it. She relaxed back into her seat and drank the sherry, smacking her lips appreciatively after each sip. I stood with her for a few minutes, noting with satisfaction that she was the best dressed of them all. She caught my eye and inclined her head graciously, her straw hat taking a bow.

Miriam brought the ladies a plate of assorted barbecued meats and some cucumber sandwiches. The ladies, conscious of their glasses of sherry and best dresses, chose the sandwiches. Nomatuli took a substantial piece of steak and tucked in with obvious enjoyment. The other women dabbed at their mouths with dainty serviettes and watched the black woman with badly-disguised amusement. Nomatuli finished her piece of meat, wiped her mouth, downed her sherry in one and got to her feet.

'When a dog prefers grass to meat at a party,' she announced majestically, slowly turning to include everyone, 'it is time to leave.' Then she smoothed down her dress and went off to watch Lilah cutting her birthday cake.

I was about to follow her, when I noticed Ma. Her face was flushed to a deep purple, almost black colour, and she was clutching the edge of her chair. I thought she was having an asthma attack and I shouted for Lionel. He came running, but when he tried to help her out of the chair, she knocked his hands away and struggled up on her own.

'What's the matter, Hannah,' Lionel asked. 'Is it your chest?'

'Take me home.'

'But why? What's happened?'

But Ma was already marching out of the garden.

Her women friends clustered around each other, whispering and staring accusingly at me.

Shortly after this Nomatuli had to get back to the store. I was glad of the excuse to escape. My friend fell asleep on the way home. She wouldn't be much use to Nandhi that afternoon. When I dropped her off, she tottered down the track, hat at a saucy angle – mission accomplished.

Back at Blue Gum everything seemed to be going well. I drifted from group to group pretending to be looking for someone – who was always somewhere else. The perfect alibi. Antoinette had taken over as games supervisor with two young dads to help her. When I asked her where Gloria was she said, 'Who knows?' annoyed at the interruption. 'Doing Gloria-things I guess.'

I tracked my sister-in-law down to the kitchen where she was making yet more sandwiches. It was stifling hot inside and Gloria's thick, golden hair, hung in a slab across her flushed sweating face.

'Hey, Gloria. I'm sure we've got enough sandwiches now. Come outside and cool off. Have a beer.'

She shook her head and continued buttering.

'The kids are going to do your treasure hunt in a minute, Gloria...'

'...Angel hunt.' She mumbled into the tub of margarine.

'Sorry?'

She raised her head slightly. 'It's an angel hunt, Kate, not a treasure hunt.'

'Of course. The angels are holding all the clues aren't they? And they're so sweet. Lilah thinks they're wonderful. Please come and see...'

But she shook her head. I watched her helplessly. I never knew what to say to Gloria. But Lilah loves her Auntie. The woman's bag is always full of angel things, little bits of gossamer material and shiny glass beads.

'We all have angels to look after us, Lilah.' I heard Gloria telling Lilah one day. 'They're called our guardian angels.'

'And my angel is called Tinkerbelle,' Lilah answered promptly.

It was Gloria's angels that got us all together the first Christmas we were at Blue Gum. I was five months pregnant by then and I'd stopped being sick. This seemed a good opportunity to make our peace with Ma. I felt sorry for the woman. I'm sure I wasn't what she had in mind for her beloved son, 'Peer'. Anyway, we had to tell her about the baby.

All those months and amazingly I hadn't bumped into any of them. I went into Kleinsdorp regularly to do the shopping. Pete was too busy to shop he said, but we both knew why he didn't go to town. Anyway, a week or so before Christmas I spotted Gloria in the Spar. She saw me, blushed furiously, and ducked down an aisle. We locked trolleys as she was rushing to get to the checkout ahead of me.

I smiled. 'Sorry, I'm hopeless at steering these things. Did I hurt you?'

She shook her head. 'No, it was my fault. Wasn't looking where I was going.' She stumbled clumsily against me and gave me a hug. 'It's lovely to see you,' she gushed.

'And you.'

'How's Pete?' She asked.

'He's...you know. It's difficult.'

'Did Pete tell you?' She said suddenly, looking at me directly for the first time. 'We used to play up there when we were kids? At your farm? Cowboys and Indians.'

I grinned. 'Nice. So? How's Lionel? And your mother?'

'Dad's good and Ma, well Ma's...Ma.'

'I don't expect she's too happy about me and Pete?'

She looked uncomfortable for a moment and then she took a deep breath. 'You could come for lunch on Sunday if you like, Kate. I'm

sure she'd...I'm cooking roast chicken and all the trimmings...
Please, come. This is all so...silly.'

I shook my head. 'That's really kind, Gloria, but Pete won't come.'
She sighed.

'I don't understand the problem, Gloria, but I have to go along
with what he wants.'

'I know.'

'But you could visit us, Gloria. I know Pete would love to see you.'
Her eyes were shining as she looked at me. 'Would he? Really?'

'Maarten comes.'

'I know, but he's braver than me. I'd like to, honestly Kate, but I
don't know what she'd say.' Then she looked at her watch, ducked
her head in a sort of goodbye, and scuttled off.

Gloria didn't come to the farm but she sent a message via Maarten,
inviting us to her Christmas angel display. Pete groaned but he was
smiling.

'Hey? Don't be horrible,' I lectured.

'You haven't seen Gloria's angels, Kate,' Pete said. 'They're
really scary.'

Maarten punched Pete on the arm. 'What d'you think, Pete?
More scary than the *Night of the living dead?*'

'Yup. Definitely.'

Apparently every Christmas Gloria decorated the Vantonde house
from top to bottom with hundreds of angels. The whole of
Kleinsdorp turned out for this spectacle. She charged a small
entrance fee and the money went to the Kleinsdorp Animal Rescue

- her other passion. Gloria was a volunteer helper there.

'One year,' Maarten said, not unkindly. 'The Kleinsdorp Trib did a special piece about the angels. It's on the wall in her bedroom, in a frame. I'm sure she'd show you if you asked.'

Angels weren't really my thing and I should have made up some excuse and given a donation but I didn't want to hurt Gloria's feelings. Anyway, she was trying to get us all together wasn't she? It was tough persuading Pete but he said as long as he didn't have to speak to anyone - 'anyone' being his mother- then he would come.

There were cars parked all down the street when we arrived. The front of the Vantonde house was decorated with twinkling lights. Gloria sat outside the door collecting money, dressed in something I can only assume was supposed to be angel-like. On either side of her crouched two grotesque winged harridans with droopy tutus. On closer inspection I saw they were garden statues. When she spotted us she waved delightedly. Pete went off to join the men drinking beer in the garden, leaving me to go inside on my own.

Every conceivable surface was covered with angels in all shapes and sizes - their tinsel and sequinned haloes sparkling in the candlelight. Even the garden had angel grottoes illuminated with Chinese lanterns.

I was doing okay, smiling at strangers, commenting on how pretty the display was. No sign of Ma yet. I'd got halfway around without disgracing myself but then I went into a room with angels sitting on toadstools and one had a beard. When I took a closer look, they all did, plus one was holding a fishing rod. At this point I totally lost the plot and dashed for the loo. It was only when I was inside and safely locked in that I saw the toilet had a see-thru seat with angels embedded in it. I staggered out in hysterics, laughing so much I wet myself. I was standing with my legs crossed when Gloria found me - her little squashed face, screwed up with concern. 'My God, Kate. What's the matter? Are you ill? Should I get Dr Coetee?'

Pete came in at that moment and led me away through the concerned citizens of Kleinsdorp. 'Sorry,' Pete kept saying as we stumbled through the crowd. 'Sorry, but she's pregnant,' he explained, as if this gave some credence to my bizarre behaviour. That was the first time I fully understood that you could get away with some seriously deranged stuff when you were pregnant.

I saw Ma's startled face appear from around the kitchen door as Pete hustled me out. She had a plate of mince pies in one hand and her mouth was open in a perfect "o".

A few days later Gloria arrived at the farm. Pete was out. I showed her around and made her a cup of tea in the van. She was very nervous. I guessed she hadn't told Ma where she was going. She only stayed for half an hour but when she got up to go she said, 'I'm so happy for you. About the baby? I've always wanted to be an Auntie.'

'What did Ma say?'

She looked away. 'She's pleased,' she lied.

'How about you providing a niece or nephew for us?'

She blushed. 'That's not going to happen.'

'You never know.'

'Oh I know,' she said.

'Never met anyone you really fancied?'

'Yes. But he...it didn't work out.'

'Shame.'

'He wanted me to go and live in Rhodesia, Zimbabwe now.'

'So?

'Ma was very ill - with her asthma, and dad was working away, so...'

'What was he called?'

'Lance,' she said forlornly. 'He was...lovely.'

After that visit she came to Blue Gum quite often.

The three Vantonde women were so different. Ma controlled, Antoinette seethed and Gloria sat quietly in the background, waiting to be noticed. She was always looking after people, second-guessing their needs. Pete had been very fond of her and worried about her future. We could see her staying in Kleinsdorp and looking after Ma for the rest of her life.

I watched her as she buttered the bread. There was something deeply disturbing about the way she was doggedly making sandwiches. In the end I prised the knife out of her hand and pushed her into a chair and gave her a glass of water. Her hand was trembling as she raised the glass to her lips and she spilt water all down her dress.

'My fault, Gloria, sorry. Here, let me mop you up.'

'It doesn't matter. No one will notice.' She sounded so defeated I wanted to hug her. She pushed the hair out of her eyes but it immediately swung back. It was lovely hair, luxuriant and glossy. I wondered why I'd never seen her with it loose before. It suited her. She usually wore an alice band, which took the hair severely away from her face and made her white forehead look long and horse-like. As she tucked the hair out of her eyes I saw her face. She looked so sad.

'Gloria? What on earth's the matter?'

She tried to smile but it ended up all twisted. 'You mustn't worry about me, Kate. It's you we have to worry about.'

'Has somebody upset you?'

She shook her head, then she leant forward, put her head on her arms and bawled - just like a kid.

I didn't know what to do. When she was finished she raised her blotchy, tear-stained face to me. 'I'm so sorry, Kate. I know I'm being terribly selfish, but I can't do this anymore...'

'...Of course you can't, Gloria. I told you. We don't need any more sandwiches...'

'...I'm not talking about the bloody sandwiches!' Her hand flew to her mouth. 'Sorry. I'm so sorry. I'm such a bad person. I've never said that word before. Never. And I've been tempted, Kate. My God how I've been tempted.'

I smiled. 'I can imagine.'

'What I meant was I can't do this anymore.' And she flung her arms wide. 'I miss him so much. You're his wife and it must be much worse for you but... but Pete was my best friend - my only real friend. And now he's gone and I won't ever see him again. And,' she drew a huge shuddering breath, 'I don't know if I can go on, without him.'

I put my arms around her and she rested her face on my shoulder. 'He was very fond of you too, Gloria. He often talked about you when he was in the UK. He missed you.'

181

She looked at me, hope in her eyes, wanting to believe me.

'I think you were the reason he came back to Kleinsdorp.' And suddenly I realised that this may have been true, because he'd never really explained why he wanted to return to the very place he had so desperately wanted to escape from.

'Did he say that? Honestly, Kate?' Gloria's smile was lovely.

I nodded. 'He wanted to be near you and the family and to make a difference to people's lives in this part of South Africa. Help redress the balance?'

'He was so kind to people, Kate. Always on their side - the blacks - even when we were little. It was difficult to be a liberal back then. I wasn't brave enough to do what he did. He nearly went to prison, twice. Asking too many questions about the Soweto riots. He went into the townships. I wanted to be like him but I was always too frightened of what …she'd say.' And she looked over her shoulder as if she half expected Ma to materialise. She sat up straighter and sniffed loudly. 'But I've got to get used to being on my own now, haven't I? I've got to make the best of it.'

That was when the black pit opened up in front of me again but Gloria didn't notice. She was busy peeling cling-film from a plate.

'Ma said to use this sparingly,' she said, as she slapped a more than generous amount of roast chicken between two slices of bread. 'But d'you know what I say, Kate? I say sod her.'

Antoinette

I needed to be somewhere on my own and I hurried out into the garden passing Miriam and Antoinette. Miriam mouthed *You okay?* at me and I nodded, blinking back the tears. Antoinette didn't notice me, she was too busy fascinating a group of young men, and handing out beer from the ice barrel. She pulled out a bottle of Pepsi for herself and I watched as she put her thumb under the cap.

'Oh my God, Antoinette, don't…' I shouted. Too late. Jeth's shaking had done the trick and my sister-in-law's white trousers were covered in brown gunk.

She froze as the liquid seeped into the blotting paper material, spreading out, making her trousers transparent. She was wearing a shocking pink G-string. Everybody stopped what they were doing and stared. Someone giggled and several of the men laughed. Miriam grabbed her friend's hand and hustled her indoors. I followed. Miriam took Antoinette straight upstairs past an astonished Gloria, who was still being lavish with the chicken.

Antoinette was sitting on my bed, her hands clasped in her lap. She was shivering. Miriam and I rummaged through my clothes and found her a long peasant skirt to wear. Miriam helped her out of her ruined trousers and I took them downstairs and put them in a bucket of water to soak, glad of the excuse to escape. I could hear Miriam talking to Antoinette as I filled the kettle. 'It's okay, really, no one noticed, I promise.'

Gloria was outside offering her chicken sandwiches to people.

When I went back upstairs Antoinette was curled up on the bed and Miriam had her arms around her. I put the coffee down and hung about, not knowing what to do. Antoinette's eyes were wide and staring and she was very pale. Her hair had collapsed and lay about her on the pillow in black heaps.

She was clutching Pete's old school photo against her chest. It was the one I had on my bedside table. I didn't have many photos of Pete but I'd always loved that one. He was so young and beautiful in it and he was grinning, as if he knew something that no one else did.

The party was breaking up and I had to say goodbye to people so I left the two women. When I popped back they were gone. My photo had disappeared too.

When the children were in bed and asleep I took a bottle of wine and the remains of the birthday cake out onto the *stoep*. Miriam was coming up the track so I got another glass for her.

She flopped down beside me, handing me the photo and skirt and then she raised her glass. 'God. I need this.'

'How is she?'

She screwed up her face. 'I think she's had better days, ja?

'Shame. But at least Ma wasn't there when it happened.'

'But her pals were, so she'll have been told all about it by now.'

'It must have been really embarrassing but …in the scale of things don't you think she over-reacted a bit?'

Miriam took another drink and watched me over the rim of her glass.

'Okay,' I said. 'She showed her knickers to a few people but, hey? "There's worse things happen at sea," as my granddad used to say. And what was the photo thing about?'

Miriam picked it up and pointed out a good-looking, dark-haired girl standing on the end of the bottom row, beside a well-built little blond girl. 'Recognise anyone?'

'Antoinette? And is that you?' I asked, pointing to the plump child.

She nodded. 'Only you're sworn to secrecy.' She moved her finger along the back row of boys and stopped at a young man. He was very blond and extremely handsome.

'That's Andrew Johnson - the heartthrob of 3B - and the love of Antoinette's life. He was from a British South African family, very liberal, very ...everything the Vantondes weren't. He and Antoinette went out with each other right through school and afterwards at Uni. They were madly in love, hey? I lost half a stone so that I could get into the bridesmaid's dress. They put down the deposit on a house in Cape Town and then suddenly Ma and Pappie Groos put a stop to it.'

'But why?'

'Andrew's father went to prison for breaking the race laws. He had an affair with a coloured woman. Sure, they left the country afterwards, lived in Malawi but the stain was on Andrew. The Groos clan kept on at Antoinette day and night. She was forbidden to see Andrew or contact him.'

'Why didn't she go off with him?'

Miriam looked very serious. 'You don't get it, do you, Kate? These people still have power, even now, but in those days... '

'...What happened to him?'

'He left South Africa. Went to the UK and married a Brit. Antoinette's life was over. She had her one chance of happiness and they took it away from her.'

'So why stay here? If it was me I'd...'

'...Where else is there for her to go? She knows she'll never find anyone like Andrew, so what's the point?'

Miriam finished her drink and got up. 'Time to get my head down. I'm on earlies this week.'

'Thanks so much for all you did today, Miriam. Lilah had a wonderful time. You and Rob were fantastic, as always.'

'It's our pleasure.'

I cut Miriam some cake to take back for her and Rob, avoiding the bit that Lilah had spat on when she blew out the candles.

She smiled her thanks. 'Glad it's all over?'

I nodded, my mouth full of cake.

'You did well.'

'Yeah, well luckily there were so many distractions I didn't have time to feel too sorry for myself.'

I sat on after Miriam went, enjoying the late evening sun. I was in that happy state between being really merry and drunk. That was when I heard Maarten's bike.

'Come, sit down,' I shouted, as he dismounted, patting the space beside me. He sat down, dislodging Spider, who sighed heavily and flopped down a few metres away from us.

'There's a glass on the table if you want some wine.'

Maarten shook his head. He'd brought some cans. He offered me one but I'd had enough alcohol to last me for several weeks.

'Lilah enjoy her day?'

I grinned, 'Are you kidding? She had an amazing time.'

'It's nice to see you happy.'

'Makes a change. I'm usually a miserable git aren't I?'

'I didn't mean that.'

'Just joking, Maarten.'

It was his turn to smile. 'So?'

'So what?' For some reason I found this incredibly funny.

Maarten took a long drink.

Suddenly I needed to lean up against something solid and I rested my head on his shoulder. I felt him freeze. 'Thanks for everything you did today.'

'I enjoyed it.' He said, moving imperceptibly away from me. 'You know I'd do anything for those kids of yours.'

'You're a nice man, Maarten.'

Was he blushing?

'They love you.' Why couldn't I shut up? I was embarrassing him.

He was watching a long line of ants marching up the wall. There were a lot of awkward silences tonight. He cleared his throat and flicked an imaginary speck of dirt from his sleeve. 'Ma was really upset this afternoon.'

That made me sit up straight.

He drained his can and opened another. Spider came and sat beside him and Maarten scratched him behind his ears. 'This animal's covered in ticks, Kate.'

'So? Why was she upset?'

He concentrated on his search for ticks. 'There's a lot of tick-bite fever in the area. When was the last time you got him front-lined?'

'What am I supposed to have done this time?'

'It wasn't you.'

'Who then? Nomatuli?' I laughed, remembering how Nomatuli had put all the old bitches in their place.

'Ma said the woman was bloody offensive to her.'

'No, Maarten, get your facts straight. Ma was bloody rude to Nomatuli.'

'She humiliated her in front of her friends, Kate.'

'So what? Ma patronises Nomatuli every chance she gets.'

'Okay, okay, no need to yell. I'm just telling you, okay?'

'Did she send you?'

He shook his head. 'Lionel told me. She was in bed with a bad attack when I got home, curtains drawn, Doc Coetee in attendance.'

If Maarten was waiting for me to be sympathetic he'd have a long wait.

'I wanted to warn you, that's all…'

'…"Warn" me? What for, for God's sake? Nothing happened.'

'You don't understand.'

'Oh, I think I do. Your mother's a manipulative, nasty old biddy, Maarten. She's never happier than when she's making trouble.'

'I don't want to fall out with you.'

'But that's exactly what she wants, don't you see? She uses emotional blackmail to keep you all in line. Anything goes wrong she gets ill. How very convenient.'

'You can't put on an asthma attack.'

'She can't bear it because you and Pete were mates, Maarten, and now you're my friend and she's jealous. She hates me…'

'…No, you're wrong…'

'…She controls you and Lionel and Gloria and even Antoinette. Can't you see what she's doing? When are you going to stand up to her?'

He couldn't look me in the eye. 'She's an old lady, Kate. She's had a hard time…'

'…So she keeps telling us,' I snapped.

'She can't help being what she is.' Maarten spoke very softly. 'It must have been very difficult bringing up two little kids on her own. You should understand that.'

'Yes, sure, but maybe she should move on? You've been in that squatter camp up the road, you've seen the conditions those people live in. Ma had it a damn sight better than they have.'

'Don't fight with me, Kate.'

I grabbed his hand. 'Hey, I'm not. You're my best friend.'

'You're pretty special to me, too.'

We held hands for fractionally longer than we needed and Maarten was blushing again.

I jumped in to save his embarrassment. 'Miriam told me about Antoinette's tragic love affair.'

'Pete was right about Pappie. He was a mean old bugger. Gloria and I stayed well clear. Luckily for us he wasn't interested in us. It was always Pete and Antoinette.'

'She's the one you should feel sorry for. Making a fool of herself in front of everyone.'

Maarten raised his eyes heavenwards. 'My sister's a drama queen, Kate. They'll forget all about it in a couple of day's time.'

'A bright pink thong? I don't think so.'

He caught my eye and grinned ruefully. 'God, what a gruesome family. Let's talk about something else, please.'

'Good idea.'

We both stared at the setting sun.

Maarten took another drink. 'D'you like it here, Kate?'

'What? On Blue Gum?'

'That but what I really meant was do you like it here, in Africa?'

'What I've seen of it. Yeah, it's stunning. That first year travelling with Pete was incredible.'

'I've been to the Ado Elephant Reserve but that's about it.'

'Why don't you go on safari? '

'It's a bit pointless on my own.'

'Surely there's some woman just waiting to be asked?'

'Not that I've noticed.'

'What about your childhood sweetheart? Pete told me about her. He said she was really nice.'

'She was. But now she's got three kids and a husband.'

'So? What happened?'

'We were incompatible. She was a vegetarian. Her breath stank of onions. And mine stank of meat.'

His mouth was smiling but his eyes were so sad. He had a nice mouth. I wondered what it would be like to kiss that mouth. All I had to do was lean ever so slightly towards him and if I closed my eyes, maybe I could pretend he was his brother. I tried to imagine his hand on mine, his breath on my skin.

'Does my breath smell, Maarten?' I whispered, my lips almost touching his cheek.

He stood up abruptly. 'Got to go. I'm on duty tonight.' He was searching for something in his pocket. 'I've got something for you.'

I tried to focus on the small shiny object he held in his hand. The dying sun bounced off the silver casing, blinding me. He pressed it into my hand. It was a mobile.

'Keep it with you. All the time, okay? Take it to bed with you. Promise? I've put in my number. Any problem you ring me, hey? Day or night.'

'I don't need a mobile.'

'You do.'

I shook my head and held it out to him 'I hate the things.'

'I don't give a shit what you hate. You're having one.'

'Don't you swear at me, Maarten Vantonde.'

'This is serious. Please. The kids might have an accident or anything. Humour me?'

'But it looks expensive.'

'I've got five for God's sake. I'm a techno geek, nothing better to spend my cash on. There's always something new with more bells and buttons. That one's basic but it will do the business. Oh and it's *Pay as you go,* Kate, so it won't cost you a fortune if Jeth gets on it.'

I looked at all the buttons – it seemed very complicated to me.

'Jeth will show you how to use it.'

'Thanks. It's very kind of you.' I tried to get up but I couldn't, so he held his hand out and pulled me to my feet.

'I think you should go to bed, Kate.

'Okay, Daddy.'

'And lock the doors.'

I stared at him. We never locked our door. There was nothing

191

worth stealing. I rested my hand on his shoulder. 'What are you trying to do? Frighten me?'

He moved sharply away from me. 'No, but I care about you, Kate. You and the kids.'

'You're very sweet, brother-in-law.'

He smiled grimly. Yeah, that's me, definitely "sweet".'

I waved the mobile over my head as he got onto his bike. 'Love you.'

The moment I said it I wished I hadn't. It was just a throwaway remark. It didn't mean anything, but I shouldn't have said it. Why on earth had I? Maarten's face was scarlet as he drove off. I went inside and flopped down on the nearest chair, dropping the mobile on the table.

Arson

At first I thought the pounding was part of my booze-induced dream but it went on and on until finally I woke and realised that the noise was real. Someone was hammering on the door. It was pitch black and the dog was going crazy. 'Okay, Spider, be quite.' I hissed, getting groggily to my feet and stumbling across the room, banging into things as I went.

'There's a police car outside, Mum.' Jeth was standing at the top of the stairs.

'Okay, everything's under control, Jeth, go back to bed.'

I found the light switch and opened the door.

Maarten was standing there, blinking in the light. He was carrying someone in his arms. 'I'm sorry, Kate' he said, pushing past me. 'But there was nowhere else to take her.'

As he laid the person gently down on the settee I caught sight of the woman's face. It was Nomatuli. She was still in her beautiful red dress but now it was torn and smeared with soot and one hand was wrapped in a dirty cloth. She was shivering and I knelt beside her and took her free hand in mine. 'My God, Nomatuli, are you okay?'

'There was a fire in the store.' Maarten said, punching numbers into his mobile. 'She tried to beat out the flames.'

Nomatuli's eyes flickered open, 'Sorry, Kate,' she croaked, 'So sorry. The bastards. They burn our beautiful Purple store.'

Then she started to cough.

'It doesn't matter, Nomatuli' I said, squeezing her hand. 'Nothing matters as long as you're okay.' I turned to Maarten. 'We should get Miriam.'

He was already talking to her on his mobile.

While we waited for her, Maarten liaised with his colleagues up on the RDP.

Jeth hadn't gone back to bed and was sitting on the bottom stair in the darkness, watching. At one point he ran upstairs and came down with his duvet and I helped him wrap it around Nomatuli's shoulders. She was shivering uncontrollably and her bloodshot eyes stared up at me. I poured her a large tumbler of whisky but she pushed it away.

'I am so sorry, Kate,' she muttered. 'So very sorry.'

When Miriam arrived she unwrapped Nomatuli's hand. The burns looked nasty. She cleaned them up and gave Nomatuli a shot. 'You've been very lucky,' she said, packing up her bag, 'the burns aren't serious.'

'"Lucky?" You say I am lucky?' Nomatuli clenched the fist on her good hand. 'I'll get those bastards if it kills me. Think they can steal from a Zulu? I'll kill them. All those Xhosa pigs.'

'You think someone did this on purpose?' I was horrified. 'It wasn't an accident?'

'Accident? Pah! All my stock, everything, gone, and then they kick over my stove and burn my Purple store. Accident?' She was shouting now, her voice cracking as she forced it. 'No, they want to see Nomatuli burn, that is the plan....' She ended in a paroxysm of coughing and Miriam sat her up and slapped her back until she spat up a huge black mess of saliva.

'Did you recognise anyone?' Maarten asked, when she'd got control of herself again.

Nomatuli shook her head. 'These are cowards, Mr Policeman, they have no faces.' Her voice was quiet now, sad. 'They wait till all is quiet, then they creep back like wild dogs in the night and steal my things. They want to kill Nomatuli, see?' she fingered a bruise on the side of her face. 'If I had not jumped up they would have stuck me like a pig and left me to roast.'

Maarten was talking to someone on his mobile. 'They've got the fire under control up there. '

'Let them burn. Let them all burn,' Nomatuli said, and closed her eyes.

After Miriam had gone I made up Nomatuli's old bed in the back room and Maarten helped me get her onto it. She was asleep before I turned off the light.

I lay awake for the rest of that night. The last of my savings were gone – gone up in smoke. This was it. The end. It was a relief in a strange way. This was as bad as it could get. At least, that's what I thought, back then.

I took the children to school as usual the next morning and when I got back Nomatuli was sitting in the kitchen. She was still in her red dress. I offered to lend her something to wear but she refused. We had to go to the police station to make a formal statement.

Maarten got her a coffee, sat her down and asked about her injuries. He was very kind to her. They had always got on well. They had a lot in common, sharing a good joke and a good meal, competing with each other to see who had the most sugar in coffee and how many rusks they could eat at one sitting. But there was nothing to laugh at today.

'Any luck up at the RDP?' I asked him.

Maarten shrugged, 'No one's talking, man. They say the men are shape changers. First they are a dog, then a rock.'

Nomatuli snorted. 'What do you expect from Xhosa cowards? They are frightened of everything. You say a thing, you get punished.'

When Maarten had finished with her she asked me to drive her up to the RDP.

'Are you sure that's a good idea?'

'You think I am frightened of these…worms? Have you forgotten who I am? '

The normally bustling lanes were deserted as we parked the car. There was a strong smell of burning still and tendrils of smoke oozed from between the shacks. But there was amazingly little fire damage, considering how closely packed the houses were. Only last week there had been a settlement fire, on the outskirts of Hermanus, where 135 makeshift homes were destroyed and two people had been killed.

A few women came and stood about us in a silent group. Women, who only yesterday had petted my daughter and clapped delightedly to see how amazing this Zulu woman looked in her red dress. These same women had taken their children to Auntie's store, shared food with her, swapped stories, laughed and cried with her. But today, not one of them could look her in the eye. Nomatuli swept past them, head held high, to what remained of the Purple Store.

There was nothing to mark where the building had been except a charred sign and the blackened shell of her stove. A pyramid of shiny tinned goods stood on the perimeter of the scorched earth.

An offering? Nomatuli took a wild kick at it, sending the tins spiralling away and then she spat on the ground. She spoke in a loud, clear voice. 'I will not live with these people again. They have disgraced the name of Xhosa.' Then, she turned her back on the women and marched back to the car, looking straight ahead, carrying the sign in front of her, like a shield.

Back at Blue Gum Nomatuli's courage failed her and she sat down heavily in a chair, clasping the sign to her. I made us some food but she wouldn't eat and we sat glumly together. She was slumped forward like a little old woman, her head resting on her hands. I'd lost my money but she'd lost her home, her livelihood, and her dreams.

'If there's anything I can do to help, Nomatuli.'

She shook her head.

'What will you do?'

She raised her head and looked at me mournfully.

'Will you go home?'

Her eyes blazed. 'What? To bastard husband? No. I die in jungle first. A lion eats me. That would be better for Nomatuli.'

'You can stay here, you know that. There will always be a bed for you with us but I can't afford to pay you to work for me. I haven't got any money...' I almost said 'now'. How my mother and Ma would enjoy this. They had been right. I'd done a stupid thing. True, it wasn't Nomatuli's fault but my savings were gone and the next bill that came would be the end for me.

Nomatuli must have read my thoughts because she took my hand and planted a huge wet kiss on it. 'No need to worry, Kate.' Was she grinning? She got up and spun around. 'I am a bad woman to tease you.' She patted her backside. 'Have you not seen how Nomatuli get fat lately? You English too polite to say, *Hey fat woman, Nomatuli, what you eating? Hippopotamus?* I have put on many pounds – rand pounds.'

She undid her skirt and loosened the waistband; then she pulled out a bulky money belt and flung it on the table. It was stuffed with notes. She took out a wad and waved it under my nose. 'Your money is safe with the Zulu woman.'

'But you said they stole everything.'

She patted her nose. 'Everything they could find, Kate. D'you think Nomatuli allow Xhosa dogs to steal her money? Even my cousin – my own blood, Nandhi? She also waits her chance. A Zulu woman from my own tribe. The shame will be on her head. No, they will never beat Nomatuli. They are jackals. But Nomatuli is too clever for them'

She tossed some money down in front of me. 'I am looking for a nice room to hire while I think what to do next?' She laughed. 'What? You want to catch bird in your mouth?'

'But why didn't you tell me?'

'Because, Kate, I want those people to think I have nothing. To believe they have beaten me.' She shook her head. 'But that will never happen, not while I live.'

As Nomatuli predicted the police never caught the culprits. People knew who was responsible but no one would speak – they were too scared. I didn't ask for my share of the money. I would manage for as long as I could. However, I insisted that Nomatuli opened a proper bank account this time.

And life returned to normal, or what passed for normal at that time.

Flits

Ever since she got home Maggie had been having the same dream. She woke with a start, a terrible feeling of dread in her. It was freezing cold but she was dripping with sweat. Reaching for the light switch she sat up. It was always the same – Jeth's nightmare - the one where the giant red snake was curled around the oak tree and the tree was screaming. It seemed ridiculous now in the friendly pinkish glow of her bedside lamp, but when Maggie was dreaming it was horribly real.

She knew she wouldn't go back to sleep so she picked up her book and flicked through the pages. Even as a child she'd been a bad sleeper. "Too vivid an imagination" her mother had accused. But the young Maggie had never worried about it because her favourite grandad was also a bad sleeper. She knew this because she'd overheard Granny saying that Grandad did "moonlight flits" "In fact…" her Granny continued, "…he is famous for it." It was only when Maggie was older that she realised that she might have confused "famous" with "infamous".

The child Maggie was proud of her grandfather's nocturnal jaunts. She loved to think of him flying through the midnight sky, conducting the stars with his silver-topped cane, a carnation in his buttonhole and his luxuriant white moustache shimmering in the frosted night air.

She only discovered the shameful truth by accident. Her granny was ill and Maggie had been told to be quiet and behave while her mum looked after Granny in the next room. That was when Maggie heard that moonlight flits were not the stuff of magic. They were something you must never talk about in front of people, especially Granny's friends and the bad-tempered woman, two doors down, who was Granny's landlady.

Maggie's grandad, Herman Morton, was the only surviving child of a love match between his father and a demure young girl from Hanover called Tilde, who died in childbirth at the age of twenty-two. As was often the case in those days the deceased's sister, Bertha, inherited the widower and his baby. Bertha and Herman's father subsequently had thirteen children.

Herman inherited two things from his mother, one - her beautiful blue eyes and two - his German name. How was she to know that, shortly after her death, Teutonic names would become very unpopular? 'Herman the German,' suffered ridicule, fear and finally hatred in the small Devonshire village where he grew up. Bertha used English names for her own children and changed her name to Bette – after her favourite film star, Bette Davis.

Herman left home as soon as he could and went to live in Newton Abbot, where he got a job in the local co-op coal yard. He wasn't cut out for manual labour but his dapper appearance and facility to sound as if he knew what he was talking about, soon had him behind a desk, where he rose rapidly to be, first the manager and then the area manager.

But the Co-op and Newton Abbot weren't big enough for Herman and he went into business with a friend, selling shares in a North Welsh gold mine. By now Herman was married to Eva, Maggie's granny, and had four children. The family moved into a posh town house in Exeter with live-in maid. Unfortunately for Herman, his friend was a crook. There was no gold mine and Herman lost everything, including his once trusting disposition. He vowed, from then on, to be the biter, not the bit.

His first 'flit' was from Exeter and thereafter the family roved the British Isles, staying while Herman built up contacts and started businesses and then 'flitting' to the next place. He changed his name to Harry and never spoke about his beautiful mother Tilde, or his German blood.

Maggie's mother didn't talk about her German ancestors either and Maggie never sat on her grandad's knee again. She'd begun to notice the bits of food glued to his yellowing, once-white, moustache and the flower he wore in his buttonhole was made from plastic and covered in sticky dust.

Maybe some inherited gene, preparing her for the next flit triggered Maggie's insomnia? Whatever the reason she couldn't sleep. She tried all the tricks, but nothing worked. She even attempted to write at night - her laptop propped on a pillow.

Maggie's one claim to fame had been a children's book, written twenty years ago. Her friends and acquaintances had been so impressed when 'My dad is a fireman' was published. 'Excuse me Mrs Dempsey? But are you the lady I saw in the paper? You've just written a story?' She was offered a three-book deal from the publishers, a series of 'My dad is...' but she couldn't deliver. Now she didn't tell anyone she was a writer.

Even Tom had been proud of her after that book. She'd spent a lot of time worrying about how he would cope with her fame. But when he eventually walked out on her it wasn't because he'd been sidelined by a successful authoress, it was a much more mundane and humiliating reason. It might have been bearable if he'd fallen for some young, anonymous bimbo. Then Maggie could have ridiculed this pathetic ageing male's frantic attempt to stay young. But Tom chose Ailsa Murray – Maggie's dog-walking companion, known for her sensible shoes and cheese scones. Maggie was the last to find out. She could have written the scenario herself, bored husband, mid-life crisis, turns to wife's best friend. It was insulting in its banality.

Ailsa was everything Maggie wasn't, plump, jolly with big breasts. The lovebirds had set up house in a village nearby, close enough for Maggie to catch glimpses of them at the theatre, or the music society, or once - to her mortification - in what had been Maggie and Tom's local. That was the only time Maggie truly lost her rag and she'd never set foot in the place since.

She e-mailed Tom when Pete died and he did what he always did, he'd thrown money at the situation. When Maggie asked Kate why she accepted money from her father but not from her Kate looked surprised.

'Because…he's not important in my life, Mum.'

Maggie put on her dressing gown and went downstairs.

She knew there was another reason she wasn't sleeping. She should have stayed with Kate and the children instead of running home like a spoilt brat. And why had she come home? Because she was jealous of Kate's relationship with a black woman? That's what it was, however much she dressed it up as something else. She'd thought about little else since she got back to the UK.

What had she expected? Her daughter to fall around her neck, pleading to be brought home? Kate was right; South Africa was Jeth and Lilah's country and hers... now. Maggie had wanted Kate to come back so that she could feel fulfilled again; to put some meaning in her otherwise sterile life.

She made a cup of rooibus and sat at the kitchen table sipping the scalding liquid. It didn't taste the same here in England. It was like all those gaudy foreign liqueurs, lurking at the back of the drink's cupboard, gathering dust. Maggie pulled back the curtains and stared out at the frosted, blue-tinged grass. It was 4.50 on a cold and frosty morning. It would be 5.50 at Blue Gum and getting light. The early morning mist would be clearing from the mountains behind the house and that raucous car-alarm bird would be hurling his bizarre call through the sky. It would be warm already. Maggie turned on the gas fire and sat down to wait.

She imagined Jeth and Lilah safely asleep – and the boy. She sent out pocket money for them all. No guesses what Lilah would buy with hers, and Jeth would get something scientific, but Jo Jo?

She glanced at the clock again. Was it too early to ring? She needed to hear Kate's voice. The nightmare was still there inside her head. She knew she was being irrational but she wouldn't be able to settle until she knew they were safe.

The children would be awake soon and she could have a chat before they went to school. Maggie shut her eyes and imagined the sunlight on the gum trees and the leaves sparkling and trembling in the early morning breeze.

She dialled their number and waited, willing Kate to pick it up, but it rang and rang. Maybe she'd dialled the wrong number? She tried again. Still no answer and this time the answer phone cut it. It was Pete's voice. She panicked and switched off. Why wasn't Kate answering? They must be awake by now. Maybe they were staying somewhere? Or camping in the garden? Yes, that would be it. So, she would leave a message and get Kate to ring her back.

When Pete's voice came on again she was prepared and launched into her rehearsed message. Maggie imagined her voice in that empty room and saw the toys on the floor and the remnants of food on the table and that marching line of ants.

Visitors

"Hi, you've reached Kate and Pete Vantonde. Sorry we're not here. Leave a message and we'll get back to you."

For a blessed moment I clung to the impossible. He wasn't dead. I'd been dreaming. My Pete wasn't dead. But the brain isn't emotional. *It's the answer phone you dummy. The stupid answer phone.*

Inexplicably, I was curled up on the floor behind a chair. I ached all over and, as I stretched my legs, my foot cramped. It was agony and I rolled onto my back, so that I could press my foot against the wall.

The phone rang again.

'Hi, Kate. It's Mum. Just thought I'd ring and see how you all were but you must be away. Hope you're having a lovely time wherever you are. Everything's fine here – freezing cold. Snow's forecast for the weekend. Give me a ring when you get back. Just for a chat. Hugs and kisses to Lilah and Jeth, oh and Jo Jo - and Nomatuli, and you too of course. Love you, Kate. Bye.'

Dawn was breaking and I could see the mobile on the table in front of the big window. I tried to get up but a hand grabbed me and pulled me back down again. Nomatuli was beside me, her expression grave, and her finger on her lips. That's when I remembered.

It had been Spider who woke me. He had an incredibly high-pitched whine, more like a bat's squeak than a dog noise, difficult to ignore. The moon was bright enough to read my watch – 2 a.m. 'Shut up,' I hissed, willing the dog to go back to sleep.

But then I heard it too. The African night is always loud and busy and has become as natural to me as my own rhythmic breathing but this noise was different - frightening. I lay rigid and sweating; straining my ears, hoping I'd imagined it. But no, there it was again - a sort of scuffling sound, not very loud but persistent. Animals often raided our dustbins at night but this wasn't like any animal noise I recognised. Once or twice I thought I heard words, but my imagination was running wild.

Slipping out of bed I went to where the children slept. Spider lay on the floor beside Jeth. He was on his haunches facing me and the moonlight lit up the crackling line of erect hairs, running down his back. His head rested on crossed paws but his eyes were on me. I motioned to him to keep quiet and crept to the window that overlooked the back garden. The swing creaked in the gentle night breeze and I saw the reassuring lights of Kleinsdorp in the distance. I shut the door that led onto the upstairs veranda, and turned the key in the lock.

Pete had collected African artefacts and we had an array of rusting trophies on the wall. I chose a spear and followed the dog downstairs. I stood by the front door, plucking up the courage to go outside. Suddenly Spider growled. The noise came from somewhere deep inside him and the ferocity of the sound gave me courage. 'Good boy, Spider,' I whispered. 'Let's go see what it is.' But before I could do anything a hand gripped my wrist. It was Nomatuli. She shook her head urgently, and leant across me, locking the door. She held her machete in her other hand.

'I have locked the back door also,' she whispered. 'And the windows are closed.'

My heart was thumping. 'What is it?'

'Bad men, Kate. I think they come for Jo Jo.'

At that moment something crashed against the front door and Nomatuli and I leapt back, clutching at each other. The dog launched himself at the door, barking furiously. Lilah screamed and Jeth and Jo Jo appeared at the top of the stairs, their frightened faces lit by the moonlight.

'Take Lilah to the bathroom, Jo Jo, and put a chair in front of the door. Quick. And don't come out till I tell you.'

Jeth was halfway down the stairs but Jo Jo grabbed him and hustled him back upstairs.

Spider was still going crazy but I grabbed his collar and quietened him. I needed to hear what was happening outside. There was silence for a few minutes but then we heard footsteps walking slowly around the house. There was a short burst of laughter. That scared me more than anything else. Nomatuli pulled me down behind a chair. We crouched there, hand in hand, until there was another furious hammering on the door and a shrill inhuman shriek. Lilah screamed again and Spider went berserk, leaping and tearing at the woodwork.

'My God, Nomatuli. What are we going to do?'

She pressed down hard on my hand, her nails digging into my flesh. 'We wait.'

I don't know how long we crouched there; ears straining for the slightest sound but at some point Spider left the door and came to lie beside us. We stayed where we were, cramped and uncomfortable, dozing on and off, until morning light filled the sky and Mum rang.

I must have gone back to sleep after that because the next thing I knew I was on my own and the front door was wide open. I got painfully to my feet and hobbled outside.

It was a bright shining morning and I had to shield my tired eyes against the piercing light. Spider was tracking backwards and forwards following scent trails. I patted his head as he came up to lick my hand. 'Good boy. You saw them off, didn't you?'

Nomatuli had a pot of paint and was painting over some words that had been scrawled in huge red letters across the front of the house. She didn't look at me. All her energy was concentrated on what she was doing.

'What does it say?'

Nomatuli continued to slosh on the paint.

'Please, Nomatuli. I need to know what this is about.'

Finally she threw the brush into the pot and rubbed at her hands with a rag. Then she stared at me, as if she were weighing something up. 'There is something else, Kate. Something very bad.'

I stood there blinking at her, my eyes smarting. But the pure, new day took the fear away and I was prepared for anything. My children were safe and we had survived the night. That was all that mattered.

That was when I noticed Mrs Stompy's chicks. Someone must have let the bantams out because they were pecking about, outside the open door. I bent down to pick one up but, as I did so, the door banged shut and I saw what was hanging there. I jammed my hand across my mouth, cutting off the scream. Nomatuli was beside me, her arms holding me.

Our beautiful black hen was impaled to the woodwork. A long nail had been hammered through her neck. Her eyes were glazed and milky and her beautiful black feathers were dull and flecked with blood. Stompy's chicks pecked on the ground beneath her, cheeping, as if expecting her to dig up some juicy grubs for them. Nomatuli took her down and we buried her.

When I knocked softly on the bathroom door, Jo Jo opened it cautiously, his red-rimmed eyes huge with tiredness. He was holding a curved knife – another of Pete's trophies. Lilah was curled up asleep on the floor beside Jeth, her head resting on his lap. I picked her up and we all trooped downstairs. The boys were subdued but Lilah seemed unperturbed, especially when Nomatuli asked, 'Who wants a fried egg on toast?'

'Me, me,' she yelled.

I watched as Nomatuli bustled about making breakfast. She saw my look and hissed at me as she passed. 'Only a chicken, Kate. Praise the Lord.'

I needn't have worried about how I'd break the news about Stompy, because Jeth had been outside having a nosy about and came running in, accusing his sister of leaving the chicken coop open last night. 'Stompy's gone and there are feathers everywhere, Mum. I told you there was a predator on the farm.'

Lilah rushed out to hunt for survivors. Mrs Stompy's chicks were rounded up and put in a special Lilah house, made from an old birdcage. The other hens would bully these chicks, without their mother to protect them, so Lilah would feed and water them and dig up bugs and worms for them. She would be their mummy.

Nomatuli winked at me. 'Lucky chickens, aye?'

While Lilah was busy with the orphans, the rest of us sat around the kitchen table. Jo Jo was very quiet, his eyes darting first to me and then to Nomatuli. I squeezed his hand and Nomatuli gave him an extra spoonful of brown sugar on his cereal. He didn't touch the food.

Jeth was manic. 'When shall we tell Uncle Maarten, Mum? About the bad men?'

'What bad men?'

Jeth gave me a pitying look. 'Last night.'

'Oh that,' I said. 'It was some boys from the village, Jeth, having a bit of fun. Nothing to worry about.'

'But we should tell Uncle Maarten,' he insisted. 'They shouldn't be allowed to do that - to frighten people. It's not fair.'

'Okay, Jeth, but not now. I think we should all go back to bed for a couple of hours, hey? It's still very early.'

But Jeth wanted to show Jo Jo the chicken feathers and maybe track the genet, and Lilah was on a rescue mission. Maybe it was best if we were all busy today. They'd only been gone a couple of moments when Jeth came bounding back in. He'd spotted Nomatuli's handiwork.

'Somebody's written a really ugly word on our house Mum. You know, that one…' he looked sideways at Nomatuli and whispered *Kaffir* into my ear.

I offered them R10 if they painted over all the words. I waited until they were all occupied and then I turned to Nomatuli. She looked very serious. 'D'you really think that this was about Jo Jo?'

She nodded. 'They want to frighten us. Make us give him back.'

I didn't know what to do. Maarten had ignored the fact that Jo Jo was an illegal up to now but if he thought the boy was endangering us and bringing bad outside influences into Kleinsdorp, he might have to do something. He was so wound up about our safety that I was worried he would insist I send Jo Jo away,

But Nomatuli was adamant. 'We must tell this to Maarten, Kate. These are very bad people. Too dangerous to keep quiet.'

'Tell me what they wrote, Nomatuli. Please.'

'No need,' she said. 'Ugly people, ugly words – not important.'

It was a school day but there was no way I was sending the children - especially Jo Jo. Jeth was delighted and when they'd finished painting they went off into the garden. They were making a new den somewhere. I heard my son's excited voice as they disappeared into the undergrowth.

'…and then if the bad men come, Jo Jo, we can hide.'

I couldn't reach Maarten on his mobile so I rang Ma and asked if she knew when he would be back.

'I'm not my son's keeper,' she said stiffly.

I explained briefly what had happened, keeping it low key, saying we thought it was some local kids messing about. After all, one dead chicken and some obscenities didn't amount to much. I don't know how I expected her to react but her long silence surprised me.

'"Obscenities" you say?'

'Yeah.'

'What exactly?'

'No idea. Nomatuli painted over them before I saw them. She didn't want the children upset.'

'I'm sure that was the correct thing to do - in the circumstances. We don't want Lilah and Jeth worrying.'

'Or Jo Jo?'

'I don't care what happens to that boy, Katie. I blame him for all this. I'm sorry you've had to learn the hard way but you should never have taken him in.' Her voice became businesslike. 'But he's not important. Lionel will come straight over to pick up Jeth and Lilah. They need to be somewhere safe until you can make other arrangements.'

'"Arrangements"?'

'The boy must be sent packing, of course.'

'Jo Jo isn't going anywhere.'

'Let me get this straight? You're willing to endanger my grandchildren for a …street boy? You've been lucky this time, Katie, no harm done, but what about the next time? Um?'

If she was trying to spook me she was doing an excellent job.

She softened her tone. 'All I'm saying is it would be safer for the children to stay with us, for a day or two.'

'That won't be necessary, thank you.'

Her voice went up an octave. 'Bear in mind, Katie, Jeth and Lilah are Peer's children and I know where my duty lies.'

I was determined not to lose my temper. 'There's nothing to worry about, Ma. It was just some kids from Kleinsdorp, looking for a bit of fun on a Saturday night…'

'…Rubbish It was the blacks.'

'Black or white, they're all the same at that age. All they want is to drive fast, play loud music and drink. It's the same in the UK.'

'No white boy from Kleinsdorp would do such a thing.'

'I've seen them, Ma. I've heard them. Hard not to. They drive through the farm at night tossing beer cans out of the window. Jeth collects them for target practice with his catapult.'

'This is not funny, Katie. Somebody could get hurt. I don't want to frighten you, but you've made enemies in this community. That woman and the boy don't belong with you...'

'...What d'you mean enemies? Who are you talking about?'

'The blacks don't like it when outsiders interfere. Believe me, I know how they think. They don't have the capacity to reason like us. They have smaller brains. It's been biologically proven. We are talking different levels of creation here. No one can blame them when they're violent. Is it a lion's fault he eats the antelope? This government can throw major money at the problem and it won't make any difference. Nothing will change the black and the sooner you realise that, the better.'

'All I've done is give them a home. What's so terrible about that?'

'Why d'you think that woman's drinking dive was destroyed?'

'That was nothing to do with me.'

'Wasn't it?'

'Of course not.'

'You invested your money in it, ja?'

'They were jealous of her. That's what Nomatuli said.'

Ma snorted. 'Oh well, if "Nomatuli said", what more can I say?' She allowed me time to think before she spoke again and this time her voice was soft and insidious. 'I hardly need remind you, Katie that you had a man to protect you before, but now you're all alone. A young woman, with two vulnerable children, living in the middle of nowhere...'

'...Five minutes drive from Kleinsdorp.'

'This isn't your nice little England, Katie. There are animals out there, and I don't mean just the four-legged variety. These …people have their own ways and you've meddled in their affairs. They don't like strangers coming here, taking over. That woman was lucky to escape with her life. And now they're knocking at your door…'

She was still talking as I switched off.

The Aftermath

All of us were on edge. Nomatuli had avoided me all day. Jo Jo flinched whenever there was a loud noise and Jeth was obsessing about the *bad men*. Thank God he wasn't with us when Maarten arrived.

I've never seen my brother-in-law so angry. He was shouting as he came through the door. 'What did I say, you stupid woman?' he yelled. 'Use the bloody phone.' The veins bulged in his neck. 'Why d'you think I gave it to you?'

'I'm sorry,' I stammered, 'but Lilah likes to play with it and I didn't know where she'd put it.'

Nomatuli frowned at Maarten. 'Do you want to frighten the children with all this yelling? Have they not been frightened enough for one day?'

Maarten took a deep breath and sat down, getting out his note pad. 'Okay, I want to know everything that happened. And I mean everything.' He pointed his pen at Nomatuli. 'You first.'

He sat with his back to me, jotting stuff down while she talked. He seemed especially interested when she mentioned the graffiti. When he asked her what the words said she rolled her eyes.

'Jeth said one of the words was *kaffir*,' I said.

Maarten was in the middle of writing something when I spoke and he stopped, pen in mid air, and swivelled around to face me. '"Kaffir"? Are you sure?'

I shrugged. 'You know what Jeth's like? He's got an active imagination. None of this makes sense, Maarten. Why would anyone want to target us? What've we done?'

'You mean, apart from stealing the boy from his minders?'

'But he was being beaten, Maarten. What could we do?'

'This is the real world, Kate, not some *happy-ever-after* fairy story. The boy was an important source of income to someone and maybe they're just not prepared to let him go?'

'Well they're not getting him'

Maarten snapped his notebook shut. 'I'll take a look outside.'

Within moments I heard the children shrieking with laughter. They'd obviously found their Uncle. Jo Jo loved the policeman now and I knew Maarten liked the boy.

Maarten had a long conversation with Nomatuli before he left. He took her outside and they spoke in Afrikaans. I saw his face fall at something Nomatuli said and she put her hand on his shoulder, as if she was comforting him. Maarten talked urgently to her and when he was finished she nodded and they came back inside. I went to the sink and stood with my back to them. Ma used Afrikaans as a weapon to put me in my place but I had thought better of these two. Maarten shouted out *goodbye* when he left but I ignored him. Nomatuli went out with him.

'You okay, Kate?' She asked, when she returned.

I shrugged.

'You're very...quiet.'

'It's time I got the kids in.' I brushed past her.

'Maarten asks Nomatuli how mummy is,' she explained.

I didn't say anything.

'He doesn't want to ask mummy in case it upsets her.'

'My name is Kate, Nomatuli. How would you like me to call you mummy?'

216

She chewed on her lip for a moment. 'He's a good man, this policeman. You should marry him. Give your babies a daddy.'

'What?'

'You need a man, Kate. You have protection with a good man. And this man? He cares for you. If the husband dies in our tribe, it is the duty of his brother to take the dead man's woman and children.'

'Thank God I'm not a Zulu then.'

'There will be other nights,' she hissed. 'Woman alone is not so good. White, black, any colour.'

I tried to push past her but she stood her ground.

'Everywhere there is talk of you, of Kate Vantonde. What Xhosa say about Nomatuli is …pah.' She flicked her fingers. 'But these Boers are your people and once they get the knife into you …'

'…They are not my people, Nomatuli.'

'Is this policeman not sexy?'

'I'm not interested. I'm never getting married again.'

'Why? Too much love for a dead man?'

'I'm not discussing it.'

'Okay, I understand. Mind your own business, black woman.' She went into her room banging the door shut. Moments later she came out with her bag. 'I go to the RDP tonight. I talk to my cousin, Nandhi. She says it is not her, who burns my store.'

'What? But you…can't…'

'…I have things to do.'

'Things?'

'It is arranged, Kate. Nandhi prepares for me.'

'But you don't trust her, you said so…'

'…She is my blood, Kate. I stay with her. Don't worry. You will be okay. You have, Spider and two Zulu warriors, and maybe more - who knows?'

'But what if they come back?' I tried to take the bag off her. 'Please, don't leave me.'

'I tell you. You will be safe.'

'How d'you know? I'm begging you, Nomatuli.' I took her hand. 'I'm so frightened.'

She removed my hand gently and picked up her bag.

'Tell me what was written on the walls, Nomatuli.'

She shook her head.

'Was it about me?'

'I go and say goodnight to the angel child.'

'It was, wasn't it? They hate me. Because of Jo Jo? But why? All I did was help a little boy. Is that so terrible? Please, Nomatuli. I have to know.'

She looked me straight in the eyes. 'Get big locks for your doors, aye?'

'You know who it was, don't you?'

'Remember the locks.'

At that moment a car drew up outside. It was Maarten again and this time he was carrying an overnight bag.

Nomatuli smiled at me and then went outside to look for Lilah.

'What d'you want?' I asked rudely, as my brother-in-law hesitated in the doorway.

'I'm giving Nomatuli a lift to the RDP. And then...'

Nomatuli came back with Lilah in tow. '...Then he comes back to sleep with Kate.'

'You need someone with you tonight, Kate, just in case.'

'I'll be fine,' I lied. I was so angry I was willing to make us all suffer.

Maarten was apologetic. 'This is official police protection, Kate. Don't worry; you won't know I'm here. I'll be back about seven. I have some things to see to before then. Okay if I leave my bag?'

He didn't wait for my answer.

Nomatuli gave me a cheery wave as they drove off.

The children were delighted that Maarten was coming to stay. Lilah hardly noticed that Nommy had gone again and bustled off to choose some special fairies to keep Uncle Maarten company. Then she brought Stompy's chicks inside, so that the nasty cat wouldn't eat them.

It had all happened so quickly, I wasn't sure how I felt. I tried to make sense of it while I changed the sheets on Nomatuli's bed. Why had she gone? Maybe she'd moved out to make room for Maarten? Why else would she go and stay with Nandhi again? Especially, after all she'd said about her cousin and the people up on the RDP?

But besides the questions there was another feeling nudging at me - a nice warm, comfortable feeling. Maarten would be here tonight. We would be safe.

It was dark before Maarten returned and I had locked the doors and windows and pulled the curtains. I knew the boys were watching me but Lilah was totally oblivious. She was in the kitchen hand-feeding the chicks and making a terrible mess. I turned the telly on and we watched some rubbish while we waited. I had it on so loud that none of us heard the motorbike and when Maarten banged on the door I nearly jumped out of my skin. Spider got to the door first, his tail wagging furiously.

I'd made some pasta. We had a lovely evening and the children went off to bed without a murmur. They slept well and so did I. Maarten had gone to work by the time we got up, leaving a note on the kitchen table. *See you tonight. I'll bring pizzas.*

And that was the routine while he stayed with us. We ate together, watched telly or went for a walk and then he'd carry the sleeping children upstairs to bed. He stayed for a week and there were no more visitors in the night. He and I were comfortable around each other and gradually my fear lessened. Life returned to normal except that now there were locks on all my doors and windows, and a patrol car came through the farm at least once a night. I was sad when Maarten told us he was leaving but I knew he couldn't stay forever. I would miss him – we all would - and not just because he was protecting us.

'Delicious, hey?' Maarten said, battling his way through my latest culinary disaster. It was his last night with us. 'You're a great cook, Kate.'

'Liar.' I smiled. He knew how to make me laugh – just like this brother.

He'd been on a late shift and the children were in bed asleep.

'I couldn't cook like this.' Maarten continued.

'It takes years of practise.'

'At least it's healthier than steak every night.' He patted his stomach. 'I can nearly see my feet when I stand up now.'

'I bet Ma's got something to say about that. She likes her men to be …chunky.' I was only teasing him but he looked upset. 'Hey?

Sorry, Maarten. I was only joking.'

'What? Oh no, I was thinking about something else. Didn't I tell you? I've got a place of my own now?'

'That's amazing, Maarten. Congratulations.'

'It's about time.'

'So? What made you take the plunge?'

He shrugged.

'Where is it?'

'A couple of doors down from our house. It's only an annexe, in a mate's back garden, but,' he added, grinning, 'I've got my own entrance. It's small but it's…mine. Maybe you'd like to come visit some time?'

I didn't know what to say.

'No, bad idea, forget it.'

'Don't be silly.' I pretended I hadn't understood what he meant. 'Try and keep us away, Maarten. The children will insist on seeing where their favourite uncle lives. They may even decide to move in with you.'

He laughed. 'Yeah, come over some time soon, bring the kids. We'll have a brai, celebrate.'

'I'm so pleased for you, Maarten. Don't expect she was too happy though?'

'To tell the truth, Kate, I don't give a baboon's shit what my mother thinks.'

That surprised me. I changed the subject. 'It's been great having you here. I really appreciate it.'

He had his head down, eating, so I couldn't see his face. 'Been good for me, too.' He looked up. 'But you'll be all right now.

Nothing to worry about. Everything's sorted.'

'Really?'

'Yeah.'

This was good news. 'You've arrested someone?'

He shook his head.

'Then how do you know it won't happen again?'

'Because I've had a word and they know that I'm watching them.'

'You know who did it?'

He nodded.

'Then why can't you charge them?'

'Not enough evidence, Kate. Don't look so worried. It's okay. I promise.'

We both went quiet. I still didn't know why we'd been attacked. If it was about Jo Jo, he was still with us. And I still couldn't get my head around Nomatuli leaving so suddenly, but at least she and I were okay with each other. She breezed in the morning after she went to Nandhi's as if nothing had happened. I tried to talk to her but she wouldn't discuss it. Whatever, I was glad we were still friends. I had been so hurt when I thought she'd abandoned me.

I must have been looking serious because Maarten said, 'It really is okay. You won't have any more trouble.'

'How can you be so sure?'

He took my hand and squeezed it. 'D'you think I'd let anything bad happen to you guys?'

'No, but…'

'…You've got to trust me on this one, Kate.'

And I had to leave it like that. I knew Maarten wouldn't let me down.

Jeth had a couple of very disturbed nights after Maarten left. I had to leave the light on for him but he's fine now.

When I eventually returned mum's call I told her we'd been staying at Ma's for a couple of nights. I don't think she believed me. I didn't like lying to her but what could she do so far away? Except worry? I hadn't told her about Nomatuli's store either.

'I know it's stupid, Kate,' she said. 'But I had a terrible feeling that something bad had happened to you all. Are you sure you're okay?'

'Yeah, Mum, we're fine.'

My mother's always been a bit psychic.

Word got around the farm and several people asked me what was going to happen to the boy. I didn't blame them for not wanting trouble on the farm but Jo Jo wasn't going anywhere.

New Venture

My confidence was returning. And as long as no one asked me too many questions I was managing. I was becoming a regular trader again at the farmer's market in Kleinsdorp, selling herbs, plants and seasonal produce.

Every morning when I drove the kids to school I parked outside the same little house in Kleinsdorp. It had been up for sale for a long time and the little garden was overgrown and full of aliens. This was what had first drawn my attention to the place. It had obviously been very pretty once, full of hibiscus, bougainvillaea and oleanders. There were also several nice little specimen trees struggling to keep their heads above the Port Jackson willow. Everything was smothered in Patterson's Curse. I leant over the fence one morning and pulled some of the stuff out and now I do it every day. It's like unwrapping a beautiful present. Each new day I get to see a little bit more of what lies beneath the weeds.

The house itself was a white, Cape Dutch style house with a veranda all the way around. My fingers itch to get into that garden and sort it. Stupid really, when I had so much land at Blue Gum and couldn't keep that under control. But this was manageable and I could plant some of my special trees and shrubs here. It could be stunning.

Dad had sent me a cheque recently and this plus Mum's money might just be enough to buy this place. I decided to ring the estate agents and find out how much they wanted. It would make an ideal little nursery. There was a car park at the side, which could easily be converted into flowerbeds and poly tunnels. I could sell Blue Gum and live here. But what about my promise to Jeth? And did I really want to live so close to my mother-in-law?

Nomatuli was very busy at this time. She was working for me and also for a gardening co-op, up on the RDP. A group of women were growing vegetables to sell. Elizabeth, the old lady from the Spar, was involved. Also this weekend Thembo was coming. Nomatuli had been preparing for his visit for weeks.

I tried to discuss my idea of buying the property in Kleinsdorp with her but I don't think she was listening. There was only one thing on her mind.

'My Thembo is beautiful,' she informed me as she stuffed another carton of his favourite ice cream in my freezer. 'He is so handsome; he could be a film star.'

I caught sight of her hands as she worked. Those once beautiful purple nails were chipped and broken again. She saw me looking. 'You don't have enough to worry about, Kate?' she asked, hands on her hips. 'You cry for my beautiful nails?' She shook her head in disbelief. 'English.'

I rang the estate agents about the house while she was there. The asking price was out of my league and I was surprised at how disappointed I felt.

Nomatuli raised her eyebrows at me. 'So? How much?'

So, she had been listening to me. I shrugged. 'Way too expensive for me.'

'I have seen this house, Kate. It would not make a good place to sell plants.'

I sighed. 'You're probably right.'

'But a café? It would make a very nice café for you and me.'

'A café?'

She nodded.

'For us? The worst two cooks in Kleinsdorp? I don't think so.'   I waited for her to laugh.

'We would employ a chef, Kate. That is how we would run a superior café.'

'I told you, I can't afford it.'

'But I have money, Kate. We can be partners once again. I have been thinking about a business in Kleinsdorp. I could live in the café. It has rooms above. It is even nicer than the house I lost. You could make the garden beautiful and people would come from miles around. No more shebeens or stores for those bastards to burn down. We sell teas, coffee, juices, and cakes; make pizzas and small tasty snacks, use your home grown vegetables? There are many tourists visiting South Africa now from all over the world. Rate of exchange is good and this is the Garden Route. We have a tourist trap in Kleinsdorp.'

She was out of breath by the time she'd finished.

'Are you serious?'

'I never joke about business.'

Neither of us had any experience in catering and I doubted that the town needed yet another eating place. There were three already. It was true that more and more tourists were coming through this part of South Africa but would they come to a little café, in a quiet little town, off the main road? I desperately needed to make money – proper money - but was this the way? The coming school term meant uniforms and fees; I needed a secure regular income.

Ma's Birthday

The following Sunday was Ma's birthday. Maarten phoned the night before to ask if I was going.

'Is there an option?'

He laughed. 'See you then. Oh, and tell Jeth I'm gonna get the surf boards out. Maybe he and I can go to the beach? And the black kid too, if he wants to come.'

'That's great, Maarten, thanks. Oh, and I'm bringing Jo Jo. D'you think she'll have a fit?'

'Can't Nomatuli have him?'

'No, she's going to Hermanus to meet her son.'

'What about Miriam?'

'She's working this weekend.'

'She won't like it, Kate.'

'Tough. The deal is we all come, or we all stay away.'

'Okay, okay, no need to lose your temper. I'm just thinking about the boy.'

'So was I. See you on Sunday, Maarten.'

Ma's party was the usual huge extended-family spectacular. Double bakkies lined Kleinsdorp High Street. People, children and dogs crowded everywhere. Gloria had produced a mountain of food and several brais were on the go. Maarten waved to me as we went in. He pointed at his watch and held up three fingers. I was fairly confident I could last out until 3 o'clock.

Lilah, Jeth and Jo Jo had made cards and little gifts for Ma and I'd brought her some pickled garlic. Pete had loved it, so I thought his mother might. I was wrong.

Black and coloured women served food and drink but Jo Jo was the only black guest. Johannes Groos and his cronies were there and I was aware of them staring at us and muttering to each other. Jo Jo saw them too.

Lilah and Jeth stuck close to their friend, sensing his rising panic. His eyes darted everywhere, looking for a way out. He said something to Jeth and the three of them ran inside the house. I hurried after them and, as I pushed my way through the crowds, I saw Ma follow them inside. I heard her shrill voice before I got into the hallway. She was standing with her back to me. The children were facing her. Jo Jo looked terrified. Jeth was red-faced and cross and Lilah clutched her friend's hand. Gloria hovered in the kitchen doorway and several black faces peeped out from behind her and then quickly disappeared.

'But...' Jeth was yelling. 'He only wants to go to the toilet.'

Ma jabbed her finger behind her. 'He goes out there. In the garden toilet. Not inside.'

'But...'

'...No arguments, Jethro.'

Gloria took a step forward. 'Ma? This is silly.'

'Keep out of this, girl.'

Gloria gave her mother a despairing look and ducked back into the kitchen, closing the door.

Jeth wasn't so easily silenced. 'But why must he go outside, Ouma? It's not nice. It stinks of wee.'

Ma's voice was hard. 'He goes out there because he's got germs, Jethro. He's…dirty. D'you understand? Well? I asked you a question. Do you understand me, Jethro?'

'Yis, but he's not…'

Ma held up her hand. '…I don't want to hear any more. Now, do as you're told.' She stepped aside and waited for them to obey her. That's when she saw me.

I pushed past her and pulled Jo Jo into my arms. Jeth and Lilah came and stood beside me. I was the first to speak and I was proud of myself because I was so calm. 'Jo Jo is not "dirty" and if you say something like that to one of my children again it will be the last time you see them. Do you understand?'

Ma was shaken but she wasn't going to be silenced. Her words hammered into me as we hurried out of her house. 'Thank you for ruining my birthday. You always do it, don't you? Make trouble, just like your husband. D'you know something? I wish you'd never come to this country. You have brought nothing but sorrow to us all.'

Thank God Maarten was waiting for us as we came out. I was determined not to cry. I kept my children close beside me and we all held hands as Maarten swept us off in his bakkie.

It was only later that I fully understood the situation. Maarten told me Ma had assumed that Jo Jo had Aids and she thought it could be passed on from using the same toilet. Such ignorance! But wasn't I just as bad? I still felt horribly guilty about the 'snake' incident. I'd been willing to believe that Jo Jo might have sexually abused Lilah, just because he was black. How different was that from thinking that the Sotho boy had Aids and Ma and her family might catch it?

However, understanding the situation didn't lessen my anger. I refused to let her poison my children's minds with her bigotry. She was still their grandmother and that connection bound us but I made some rules. From now on the children would not visit the Vantonde house unless I was with them. This would be difficult because Ma and Lionel often had the children for me. But they would be back at school soon and I'd just have to fit my work in around them.

I also decided that Ma couldn't come to our house anymore. Blue Gum was Jo Jo's home. Lionel and the others could visit us as they pleased but not her. I knew it would be hard for the rest of the family but they had to do what they thought was right and if they couldn't come, then I had to live with that. I wasn't brave enough to tell Ma to her face, so I wrote her a letter. I didn't discuss it with anyone and the first thing they knew about it was when Ma opened the letter and had the worst asthma attack of her life.

'She wanted to die,' Gloria sobbed down the phone. 'Please, Kate, don't do this to her.'

I was sorry for Gloria but I was not going to give in. Pete had warned me seven years ago about his mother and I should have listened to him.

Greys

Thembo didn't come to stay with Nomatuli after all. She waited for his bus for three hours in the rain. 'He had an important meeting,' she told me, not looking me in the eyes. 'About his studies.'

'So? Why didn't he let you know?'

'His phone? It was out of juice.'

I could see she was terribly upset so I didn't make any comment. But it wasn't all bad. We ate very well from her stores of food. She hid her feelings by throwing herself into our café project. Her enthusiasm reached out and infected me. She was so convinced it was going to be a huge success that I was carried along on the wave of her excitement. At least we were buying property and even if the café failed we still had that. It took all our savings to do the deal and as soon as the papers were signed we started work on it. We would need extra capital for fixtures and fittings so I rang Mum. She was incredibly supportive about the whole project and offered to lend us R50,000. She was so delighted when I accepted her offer; anyone would think I was the one doing her a favour.

When she came to visit us after Christmas the café would be up and running. Things were much better between us now. I even told her about what had happened with Ma and it was great to have her support.

She said she was reconciled to the idea of us staying in Africa. It made talking to her so much easier. It was fantastic to chat away without any sub text. She sounded happier than I'd heard her for a long time, at least since Dad walked out. We talked every week and the children loved to chat to her.

Eventually Gloria brought a message from Ma asking the children to tea. I accepted and left Jo Jo with Nomatuli. I knew this first visit would be an ordeal but I needn't have worried. It was surprisingly easy. Ma had never been interested in me anyway and now she could give her undivided attention to the children. She didn't speak to me for the entire afternoon. Lionel and Gloria were embarrassed but I went out into the garden and read my book. It was lovely to have some time to myself.

That first time Jeth was still angry with Ma but Lilah was more easily corrupted - one bag of sweets and a new fairy doll was all it took.

I became another Antoinette in the Vantonde household, sitting on the periphery of the family. And I soon appreciated what an interesting perspective it gave you – this detachment. When Antoinette was there we sat on opposite sides the room. We didn't talk. She and I were the watchers. I wondered whether the revelations about her tragic romance might have helped our relationship but it didn't. Once or twice I tried to bring the subject up with her but she looked at me blankly and turned her back on me. I got the message.

Now Maarten had moved out we didn't see him on our visits but we saw more and more of him at Blue Gum. He never mentioned Ma and we never discussed what had happened. Lionel was in a more difficult position but he popped out to Blue Gum if Ma was busy elsewhere. The biggest surprise of all came from Gloria. We had advertised in the local rag for a chef for the café and she had applied for the job. I was thrilled. We hired two women, Anne Marie and Rosemary, who had worked in a café before, and we also took on three young girls from the RDP, to work in the kitchen and wait on tables.

We spent a long time choosing a name for the café. Jeth dreamt up *Shaka's shack*. Nomatuli thought it was a wonderful idea. We would paint the café black and white and have shields, knobkerries and assagais decorating the walls. I thought this was naff and suggested *Greys* - after all, the proprietors were black and white. It was simple yet elegant. There was a lot of tooth-sucking and muttering but Nomatuli finally agreed, especially when I said we could still use the same colour scheme. We painted the doors black with white swirls and had white marble-topped tables and a black tiled floor.

Our major disagreement came over what form the opening night should take. Nomatuli wanted to send out personal invitations to people but I was determined to invite the whole of the Kleinsdorp community, the squatter camp, RDP and outlying farms.

Nomatuli rolled her eyes at me. 'Very good joke.'

I shook my head. 'No joke.'

She put her hands on her hips and frowned. 'These people, who live at the squatter camp and the settlement? They have rand?'

'We're providing food, Nomatuli, we agreed that. Nothing elaborate - a slice of pizza and juice for the children, beer for the adults?'

She snorted.

'They're nice people, Nomatuli.'

'Oh yes, very "nice" people. They try to murder Nomatuli in her bed.'

'Not the women and children, not the old men, not Elizabeth and...'

'...They lay in their beds with their eyes and ears shut and left me to burn.'

'They were frightened, Nomatuli, you said so yourself. Anyway you've gone back there to live, so you must think they're okay now.'

'Nomatuli had her reasons. But they are cowards. Why should I give such people my food and drink?'

'Please,' I begged.

'They won't come.'

'Maybe. But...'

She shrugged, suddenly bored. '...Okay, okay. Do what you wish. Nomatuli owes you this.' Nomatuli had the ability to make me feel like some whining child. I tried to justify myself, explaining that this was what Pete would have wanted - a chance to bring the community together, to build bridges in the new integrated South Africa. I knew I sounded pompous.

Nomatuli patted my knee. 'Yes, Kate, but this takes many years, not one bite of pizza and drink of juice.'

I don't know why I was being so stubborn. It was going to be hard enough for me to get through the night as it was. A lot of people would be coming that I hadn't seen since Pete's death.

However, there was one thing I couldn't shift Nomatuli on. There was no way she was giving away free beer.

The End of the Line

One afternoon, while I was working in the Grey's garden, I saw Ma and Lionel coming towards me down the street. Ma and I avoided each other now and when Ma saw me she grabbed Lionel and tried to hustle him back the way they'd come but he kept on walking, pulling her along with him. When they came abreast of me he said *hello*. He sat on the wall and we chatted while I carried on working. Ma Vantonde stood a few paces away, pretending to be fascinated by something happening on the other side of the street. Lionel was genuinely interested in what we were doing and I asked him to come inside and take a look. Ma was standing with her back to us.

'Just popping inside for a minute, Hannah. See what Kate's done with the old place. Are you coming?'

Her back said *no*.

'Aw come on, woman,' he said. 'You know you want to.'

'I may not be welcome, Lionel,' she said, stiffly.

'Of course you're welcome,' I said, forcing myself to smile.

I was feeling slightly more charitable towards Ma at the moment. Gloria told me that her mother was filling her freezer with rusks, banana cake and the ubiquitous koeksisters for us to sell in *Greys*.

Nomatuli was inside painting the walls. When she saw who it was she thrust her paintbrush in the pot and stalked into the kitchen, muttering rude words under her breath. It would take more than a few cakes to buy my friend's tolerance.

While I made the coffee, Lionel admired our black and white décor and inspected our shiny new kitchen. Ma Vantonde perched on the edge of a chair, drinking her coffee, pretending not to be interested. We could hear Lionel in the kitchen cracking jokes with Rosemary and Anne Marie. When Lionel joined us he was full of praise for what we'd done. It was great. Lionel was actually able to finish a sentence without Ma butting in.

But it didn't last. Everything was going fine until Lionel asked what we were going to do on the opening night. I was in the middle of explaining when Ma started to hyperventilate. Lionel rushed to get her inhaler and when her breathing was under control again, he tried to get her to go home. But she wasn't going anywhere. She mopped at her face, taking huge gulps of air, and finally found her voice.

'I can promise you one thing, girl,' she said, pointing a trembling finger at me. 'If you insist on this…stupidity I shall not be coming to your opening and neither will any of my friends, relations or neighbours. Tell her, Lionel.'

Lionel rubbed his hands together as if he was cold. 'It's difficult, Kate, you know.'

'Oh yeah, Lionel, I know.'

'No!' Ma was on her feet. 'You come here with your …liberal British ideas and try to force them down our throats. Well, let me remind you of something. We have lived with these people all our lives: not you. We have cared for them, fed them, supported them, given them work - not you. But that doesn't mean we want to sit at table with them.'

It was my turn to be angry. 'I'm not asking you to shack up with them.'

Ma put her hand over her mouth as if she was going to be sick.

Lionel avoided my eyes. 'They won't like it anymore than we do, Kate.'

'How d'you know? When Pete and I worked in Cape Town everybody mixed okay.'

Lionel shrugged. 'That's Cape Town.'

'Pete would have wanted me to do this.'

Ma's fist crashed down on the table. 'I am so sick of hearing what "Pete" wanted. He was always a troublemaker. It hurts a mother to say such a thing but he was contaminated when he was a boy. A teacher, co-habited with a black, polluted his young mind. The teacher was put in prison but it was too late for my son. The damage was done.'

'Hannah. It was a long time ago. Times have changed.' Lionel put his arm around his wife. 'Let's go home.'

But Ma would not be silenced. 'Pappie tried everything to …correct this indoctrination but it was too late. My beautiful boy was lost to me and in his place was this stranger, this man called "Pete"- your husband.' She struggled to her feet and marched out of the café. Lionel looked despairingly at me before hurrying out after her.

When the phone rang, later that day, I thought it was a heavy breather. I was about to yell something rude down the phone when I recognised Gloria's soft voice. 'I'm so sorry, Kate,' she snuffled at me. 'But I can't do it.'

'What?'

'I don't want to let you down but …I can't be your chef.'

I was stunned.

'Please, forgive me.'

'But why, Gloria? I thought you wanted to work here?'

'I do,' she wailed. 'But she says my immortal soul will be damned if I cook for you.'

'That's absolute rubbish, Gloria. Take no notice…'

But the line had gone dead.

I was devastated but there was no time to worry about it now. We had Rosemary and Anne Marie and we would just have to manage. I would advertise for a chef after the opening.

First Night

On the opening night the kids were as high as kites, especially Lilah, who was determined to eat her weight in cake. The boys buzzed about the café, trying to be useful, but getting under everyone's feet. They all looked smart especially Jo Jo, who was dressed in a sparkling white shirt and pair of dark trousers. Nomatuli had persuaded him to sing for our guests and he had spent ages up a tree with Jeth, rehearsing. It was the only place they could get away from Lilah, who wanted to join in. She was like me, tone deaf, the difference being that I knew it. She and Spider sat forlornly at the bottom of the boys' tree.

We had no idea how many people to expect since Ma had been dripping her poison around Kleinsdorp. The definites were Miriam and Rob and the Blue Gum people plus some people from outlying farms who had confirmed, but for the rest we'd have to wait and see.

By six o'clock some black families were standing about outside. We had three tables on the veranda and two in the garden. I was so pleased with the garden. It was beautiful. The men stood together talking loudly while their women sat quietly in their best dresses, keeping a critical eye on their immaculately-dressed and well-mannered children. Nomatuli tried to get them to come inside but they wouldn't. The clay ovens were at the right temperature and our two cooks waited for the orders to roll in. In the end we took the orders and served the pizza outside. It was probably the best place to be anyway. The ovens made it very hot inside. The children played chase in the garden and waved and shouted to friends walking and driving by.

At about seven o'clock bakkies arrived – Rob and Miriam's in the lead. Miriam put her arms around me and hugged me. It was such a relief to see a friendly face.

'It all looks amazing, Kate. Well done, hey?'

Rob pressed my hand and grinned sheepishly. 'Yeah, good one, Kate.'

I'd long since got over any embarrassment with Rob and I smiled back. 'Thanks for coming, Rob.' I knew this wasn't his idea of a good night out. He preferred a few beers in the local pub with his pals.

Antoinette came with them. I smiled gratefully at her but she didn't look at me. I guessed that her motives for being here were more about defying Ma than supporting me, but either way it was good. She'd only recently returned after the end of another disastrous relationship. Ma always forgave her oldest daughter's indiscretions but they were never forgotten. I felt genuinely sorry for the woman but why did she keep coming back for more? *Nowhere else to go*, Miriam had said, but anywhere would be better than here. She sat beside Miriam staring stonily ahead, only becoming animated when a man spoke to her, or when she and Miriam shared a joke.

Ma had done a good job with her friends and family. Only a handful turned up, probably planted by Ma to report back to her afterwards. I recognised this was paranoia but I knew she was capable of anything. I was disappointed that Maarten hadn't come, I expected more of him. Some English people arrived and there were a few coloured families but there was no atmosphere. If someone spoke everyone turned to look, as if they'd done something wrong. I made myself chat to the people I knew and I sat with Miriam and Rob and Antoinette for longer than I should have. Nomatuli turned up her music but it didn't help. In the midst of it all Lilah was behaving abominably, showing off to everyone, and being petted and spoilt. Eventually, Nomatuli bullied some men from the RDP to come inside and have a beer. They propped up the bar, drinking, smoking and moving to the music. They were cheerful and loud and one of them danced with Nomatuli. She was amazing and toured the tables, laughing and chatting away in whichever language was applicable. At least now there were some smiling, relaxed faces.

Jo Jo did his first song then, and, although there was a lot of background noise, most people listened. The black families crowded the doorway. Some of the children came inside and made a circle around the Sotho boy, clapping and swaying in time to the music.

Shortly after this Maarten and a group of off-duty policemen and their wives dropped by. They'd been to the pub first and were loud and jolly. I went to Maarten, threw my arms around his neck, and kissed him. I saw a couple of his mates raise their eyebrows at each other but I didn't mind. I was so grateful that he was here. Maarten knew most of the people, black, white and coloured, and there was a lot of good-natured banter. All at once the café was full of laughter and noise.

The rest of the evening went by in a flash and just before we closed Jo Jo sang again. When he finished everybody clapped wildly and then it was time to go home. Miriam was having the kids for me and I helped her scoop up the sleeping Lilah and put her in the bakkie with the boys. Jeth wanted to stay but Jo Jo was almost asleep on his feet. Inside the café everybody was preparing to leave and total strangers kept coming up to me and Nomatuli and saying how much they'd enjoyed the evening. Miriam said that *Greys* was just what Kleinsdorp needed.

Maarten gave me a hug before he left. 'Any chance of you coming back to my place when you're finished here? We're having a few beers.'

'I don't know Maarten. I've got to help clear up and sort things, you know.'

'Yeah, of course. It was just a thought…'

'…A nice thought.' I patted his cheek. 'Another time, hey? '

'Yeah, sure, another time. Night, Kate.' He turned to go. 'And cheers, hey? You're going to be a success, no question.'

'Maarten?' I called, as he walked to the door. 'Did anyone tell you? You're a lovely man.'

That made his mates laugh a lot and they clapped him on his back as he went out.

Finally the café was empty except for the girls in the kitchen and Nomatuli and me. Suddenly it was very quiet. Kleinsdorp was like a ghost town after 10pm.

I was still on a high and looking forward to having a drink with Nomatuli and talking about how everything had gone. But just as we were about to lock up three young black men came in and ordered beers. It wasn't quite closing time so I served them and then we stood about, waiting for them to drink up and go. They asked why there wasn't any music. They'd been told to expect entertainment. Then they demanded food but the ovens had been shut down for the night, so they lounged against the bar and talked loudly to each other, flashing their expensive jewellery and latest mobiles. It was well past closing time by now but they showed no signs of leaving.

Nomatuli was stacking chairs on the table nearest to them when one of them spat some words at her in Xhosa. She swung round to face the youth, her fist raised. I grabbed her arm.

'What is it? What did he say?'

Nomatuli yanked herself away from me and jabbed a finger at the culprit. She wanted him to hear. 'He asks me why I not burn with my shebeen?'

'He's winding you up.' I stuttered, fear grabbing at me.

But Nomatuli wasn't frightened and when she spoke again it was even louder. 'I recognise that one.' She pointed at the man nearest to her. 'He was there that night, I promise you. I know the stink of a Xhosa coward.'

I put my hand on her arm. 'Please, Nomatuli…'

She slapped my hand away and glared. '…Do not make me quiet, woman. It was him I tell you and his jackal friends. See how they smile? Show their oh-so-perfect teeth? They have come to finish their dirty work.'

At that moment our young kitchen workers came out of the back, chattering away, calling out their *goodnights* to us. The men replied, mimicking their young voices, making obscene gestures to them. Nomatuli escorted the terrified girls to the door and waved them off, telling them to hurry home. Then she turned the notice to *Closed,* put the key in the lock and looked at the men. 'We close now. Go now and don't call again. You are banned from our café.'

They obviously understood some English because they jumped

up angrily and one of them grabbed her arm.

'Get Maarten, Kate,' Nomatuli urged. 'We have trouble here. Go.'

I hesitated, not wanting to leave her, and then one of the youths crossed to the door, blocking my exit. Nomatuli thumped the man who was holding her, and, as he toppled backwards onto the floor his friends went to help him. In that instant I was out of the door and running.

The street was deserted. I kicked off my shoes as I ran. Maarten's place was only ten minutes away but it seemed to take forever. The Vantonde house was in darkness as I tore past, but there was a police car parked outside Maarten's and the comforting lights from his windows spooled down the path and out onto the road.

Maarten threw the door open wide to my hammering, the delight in his welcoming smile fading fast. I was bent double, getting my breath back. He tried to make me sit down but I grabbed his arm and pulled him towards the road. 'Quick, you must come, Maarten. She's on her own.' He shouted something in Afrikaans and two policemen followed us out to his car.

When we got to *Greys* the front door was swinging backwards and forwards on broken hinges. The interior was in darkness. 'Nomatuli.' I yelled, stepping into the blackness, but Maarten pulled me back. He found the lights and I stared around at what had been once been our beautiful café. Broken chairs and upturned tables littered the floor and we crunched forwards over layers of broken glass and crockery.

'Nomatuli? Where are you?'

She stood framed in the kitchen doorway. 'Hi,' she said, grinning. 'Sorry you missed all the fun, fellas. We had a good party, aye?'

She swept her arms around the room.

Somehow I got to her and wrapped my arms around her. 'Did they hurt you?'

She shook her head. 'I am fine, Kate. They have more bruises than Nomatuli, I think.'

Maarten joined us. 'Strange how trouble follows you two around.'

Nomatuli winked at him. 'Is strange to me also, Mr Policeman.'

'Kate says you think these were the same boys who set fire to your store?' Maarten again.

Nomatuli shrugged. 'All Xhosa look the same to me.' She turned her face away from him, so that only I saw her put her finger to her lips.

'We'll need a description.' Maarten continued, getting out his notepad.

'Cowards hide their ugly faces. They have baseball caps pulled down.'

Maarten glanced at me.

I shook my head. 'Sorry, Maarten.' I didn't like lying to him.

He went off to help his friends search the premises.

'What are you up to, Nomatuli?' I whispered. 'You said they were the ones who attacked your store.'

'They are.'

'Then what are you playing at?'

She shrugged. 'More important things than Purple Store, Kate.'

'We've got to tell Maarten.'

'No.' She kept a wary eye on the kitchen as she fired words at me. 'We must be quick before the policeman returns. We have business with these boys, Kate. They want Jo Jo. Some bad men pay money to them to get the boy back. They say we have stolen him.'

'So? That proves they are the gang who attacked Blue Gum?' I was halfway to the kitchen when she grabbed me.

'If we talk to the police, Kate, they will take Jo Jo. And we will never see him again. Do you wish that?'

'Of course not, but...' I struggled to get away from her but she held fast.

'What is more important?' she hissed. 'What is finished or Jo Jo?' She released my arm, softening her tone. 'We buy the boy from these guys and this time tomorrow he belongs to us. But you must not tell your boyfriend. R5, 000. Cheap, aye? Boy with voice like angel, very cheap. Only shame we didn't have this deal before they smash our café.'

'R5,000, R100,000, it makes no difference, Nomatuli. We don't have the money. Every cent we've got is in this café.'

She shrugged. 'The Lord will provide.'

But I didn't have her faith. 'Maarten could frighten them off,' I insisted. 'Then Jo Jo would be safe.'

'No, these boys will never give up. They have been paid to do this job. It is a debt of honour, Kate, and they will get our boy, one way or ...another.'

'But they're criminals, for God's sake. We can't let them get away with it. Maybe you've forgotten the night they came to Blue Gum, but I haven't. I never will.'

She sighed heavily. 'It was not these boys who came to visit your farm, Kate.'

I stared at her. 'Of course it was.'

She shook her head.

'Then who? Nomatuli?'

She muttered something under her breath.

'What?'

'I will tell you when we get home.'

'No, now, Nomatuli…'

'…Shh, he's coming back. Say nothing. Please? For Jo Jo's sake?'

Somehow I managed to keep my mouth shut and there was nothing more to do but thank Maarten and his friends and go home. Maarten suggested that Nomatuli stayed with me for the night. It might be too dangerous, he said, for her to go back to the RDP. He insisted on coming back with us, to make sure that everything was okay at home and followed us in his car. After searching the house he joined us in the kitchen. Nomatuli had got the kettle on and I was slumped in a chair.

'You okay, Kate?' He asked.

'I'm tired…you know.'

'Bit of a shock, ja?'

'Umm.'

'You won't have any more problems with these boys. It's the booze,' he explained. 'They drink too much, and then they go looking for trouble. It isn't personal. It's always the same on Saturday nights.'

I nodded.

He went to the back door. 'I'll just check outside and then I'll be off.'

While he was outside Nomatuli kicked off her shoes and sat at the table. She hummed one of Jo Jo's songs, as if she didn't have a care in the world.

I had a stabbing headache and closed my eyes.

'Everything's okay out there.' Maarten said, coming back in. 'But if you're worried I could always bunk down here.'

'No, we're okay thanks, Maarten. I need some sleep that's all.'

'Yeah, good idea,' he said. But I knew he was disappointed.

'Like you say, Maarten. It wasn't personal.'

He was watching me closely.

'I'm fine, honestly. Thanks for everything. Sorry we messed up your evening.'

He waved away my apologies. 'I'll clear off. Let you two get some shut-eye. Got an important game of poker on the go.' He bent awkwardly as if he was going to kiss me but I stood up and went to the door to see him off.

'We'll have a chat tomorrow, hey?' he said, hesitating. 'You can make another statement? I've got more paperwork on you two than the rest of Kleinsdorp put together.' There was a long silence. 'I'll say goodnight, then? See you tomorrow?' I saw the confusion in his eyes.

I nodded, 'Night, Maarten.' I tried to smile but my mouth wouldn't work. I just wanted him to go.

Nomatuli raised her hand in farewell. 'Thank you, Mr Policeman. Drive carefully.'

The Truth

'Well?' I said, turning to Nomatuli the instant I heard Maarten's car start up.

She got up and moved to her bedroom door. 'We must sleep now, Kate,' she said. 'We will talk tomorrow.'

'No way. You said you'd tell me who attacked Blue Gum. You promised.'

She sighed. 'For sure. But I promise someone else I will not say.'

'Who?'

Leaning forward she cupped my face in her hands; her long fingers were cool on my hot cheeks. I could feel the pulse throbbing in her wrist. 'Oh, Kate Vantonde. So much trouble follows you.' She took a deep breath 'Maarten says to Nomatuli that it will never happen again, Kate. He is a good man. I believe him.'

I moved out of her grasp. 'Maarten? What are you talking about?'

She sat back and folded her arms. 'We know who comes to Blue Gum that night. We know from the beginning.'

'You knew? My, God, you knew and you didn't tell me?'

She hung her head. 'I did not tell because…because she is his mother, Kate. His blood.' My friend's voice was soft, almost pleading. 'And you have need of her. She helps with Jeth and Lilah and if we say, what will you do?'

'Ma? Are you talking about Ma?'

She nodded.

'Oh come on, Nomatuli, that's crap and you know it.'

'I do not lie.' She glared at me. 'It is she, Ma Vantonde, who does these bad things.'

'Oh yeah?' I laughed nervously.

'I swear to you on my mother's sacred bones, Kate. This woman nails a living chicken to your door. And, worse than this, I find out tonight that it is she also who destroys my beautiful store and leaves me to burn.'

Either she was mad or I was. 'Come on, Nomatuli. My mother-in-law? She can hardly shift that huge bottom of hers out of the chair without help, how could she possibly do such things?'

I waited for her to laugh but she stared stonily at me.

'It was men who came to Blue Gum.' I persisted. 'I heard them, so did you. And it was men who attacked your store.'

She frowned. 'Of course this woman does not do these things herself, Kate. But she tells her people what to do. She also pays these Xhosa boys to do the devil's work at my Purple Store. They tell me, Kate.' She jabbed her finger at me as she spoke. 'They are proud of their "good job." They say how much the white woman gives them to destroy my life.'

'But it's…ridiculous. Why would she do such a thing?'

Nomatuli kicked the side of the door as hard as she could. 'Because she hates. She hates me, she hates Jo Jo, and she hates…you. This white woman say, *frighten this Zulu, make her run away, leave this place* But these boys are clumsy. They knock over the stove. But she is to blame if Nomatuli is killed. It is the same, Kate. It is worse. To watch and wait like a hungry hyena.'

'Okay, okay, let's say that what you say is true. She's a racist and she hates us and wants you out of my life, but what about the attack on Blue Gum, where's the proof? Maarten said there was no evidence. That's why he couldn't arrest anyone.'

Nomatuli eyes were slits. 'Have you forgotten the words painted in red across your walls? You want to know what they said, Kate? Okay, I tell you. They are written here.' She smacked the side of her head and then, clenching her fists, she shouted the words at me. '*This is the house of a kaffir-loving white bitch. All who dwell here will perish in the burning fiery pit. This is Yahweh's commandment.*'

'Those are the exact words?'

'D'you think Nomatuli does not know the words of hate?' she spat at me. 'Since I was a child words like these have hung around my black neck, like a hangman's noose.'

'But black people would never write things like that...'

'...It was not black people,' she screeched, furious at my stupidity. 'This is the work of the white baas.'

And then I understood...everything. I remembered Johannes Groos and his cronies in Ma's back garden, their cold eyes fixed on me and Jo Jo. But most of all I remembered Pete's words. '*You must never trust this woman, Kate. I know she's my mother but I hate her.*'

As if reading my thoughts Nomatuli asked, 'You know this man Groos I think?'

I nodded.

'He follows the madman who rides his big black horse over my people. Even now, even in this time, he is baas with his sambok. He wants our land for his own people. But if he comes I shall slit him like a snake and if I die a million others will take my place and ten million theirs, until the job is done.' Sweat was running down Nomatuli's face now and into her eyes but she made no attempt to wipe it away.

I tried to touch her but she shook her head at me.

'And you moved out of Blue Gum to protect me? Nomatuli? To protect me and the children?'

She shrugged. 'Myself also. I know what these people can do. They want me and the boy out of your house, okay? But Jo Jo has nowhere to go so I swallow my pride and go to Nandhi, beg her and the hyena for a place to lay my head.'

'I wish you'd told me, Nomatuli. I could have...'

'...What? What could you have done? A white woman on her own? With no friends. Better you didn't know. And this policeman promises to say strong words to this Johannes Groos, tell him he must not come to Kleinsdorp again, or he will arrest him and the others. Send them to prison.'

'But what about her, his mother? Would he send her to prison?'

Nomatuli didn't speak but I knew the answer. When Maarten had moved in with us after the attack, it wasn't to protect us. It was to protect her. He didn't care that the children and I had been frightened to death; all that mattered was the Vantonde name and her – that evil woman. I couldn't believe it, I had thought better of Pete's brother.

We talked and talked until the words became a meaningless buzz in my head and then we dragged ourselves to bed. I had to sleep, to get some strength for the next day. Whatever happened we had to make Greys work. All our energy must go there. There would be time to think about this other thing – but not now.

Now I knew who the enemy was, it made me strong.

A New Day

I didn't expect to sleep that night but when I opened my eyes it was a beautiful golden morning and I could hear Nomatuli singing downstairs. I lay in bed and watched the newly arrived swallows soaring in the air. Summer was here.

The children were waiting for me when I got to Miriam's. I told Miriam what had happened but I played the whole thing down.

She was horrified. 'My God, Kate. Did the bastards hurt you?'

'No. But Nomatuli was amazing. They got more than they bargained for from her.'

Miriam pursed her lips. 'That woman asks for trouble, ja?'

I didn't want to fall out with Miriam, so I said nothing, especially as she had offered to keep Lilah for the morning. My daughter was thrilled, of course. There were Stompy's chicks to look after and Miriam had pretty, girly things to play with and clothes to dress up in.

Jeth couldn't wait to get to Greys to see how bad the damage was. He wasn't disappointed. 'Blinking heck,' he said, standing in the doorway, his eyes wide with excitement.

Blinking heck was one of my mum's favourite expressions and I surprised myself by smiling. 'Yeah it is, Jeth. Blinking, blinking heck.' I caught Jo Jo looking at me. I ruffled his hair. 'Hey, Jo Jo? You sang so beautifully last night. Did you enjoy yourself?'

He nodded, allowing himself the tiniest of smirks.

'We were so proud of you. Weren't we, Nomatuli?'

'Of course. He is a famous singing boy.' She was running her fingers along an undamaged tabletop and winked at me. 'See? The good Lord watches over us - His children. He will help us through these troubled times.'

We set to, shovelling broken glass and china into bins. While we worked I thought about Jo Jo's ransom. Whatever happened, we couldn't let those men take him. We could sell some of the kitchen equipment but if we did that how would we earn money in the café? Every day the café was closed was a day's money lost. I was so busy shovelling and thinking that I didn't notice the forlorn figure standing in the doorway.

'Can I come in?'

It was Gloria - tears threatening as usual. I got to her before the dam burst and sat her down on our one unbroken chair. She looked around at the damage and sniffed loudly. 'It's not fair, Kate. Why you? Don't you have enough to worry about?' And then, in a hard voice. 'If there is a God I hate Him.'

Nomatuli took Gloria's hand in hers. 'The Lord is not responsible for bad things, lady chef, men do bad things. And,' she added, 'women also.'

I couldn't think of anything religious or profound to say so I squeezed Gloria's free hand. 'It's okay. It's not as bad as it looks.'

'But I should have been here, Kate. I shouldn't have let her boss me about. I'm a grown woman. I can say what I think and do what I want. You offered me a job and I accepted. We had a deal.'

'It's okay, no worry, we'll find someone else.'

'No. Please. I want to work here - if you'll have me? And I promise I'll never let you down again.'

Nomatuli didn't wait for my answer. She pulled Gloria to her feet and gave her a gentle push towards the kitchen. 'No time for sitting around with a long face. Get into that kitchen and do your job.'

There's a second-hand store in Kleinsdorp. I was on my way there, to see if they'd let us have some chairs on tick, when I met Lionel hurrying towards me.

'We've only just heard about last night, Kate. Are you okay?'

I looked into his worried face. *Was it you who hammered a nail through a live chicken's neck and skewered it to my door?*

'Kate?'

'I'm fine, Lionel, truly. It was Nomatuli who they…'

'…Thank God. We've been sick with worry. Can you spare a moment? Come back with me - talk to Hannah? Set her mind at rest?'

'Sorry, no.'

'Please, Kate. She's working herself up into a state. Her asthma…it's bad today…'

'…D'you know what, Lionel?' I interrupted. 'I really don't care.'

He flinched, as if I'd punched him. 'I know you two haven't always hit it off, Kate, but deep down…'

'…She hates my guts, Lionel. You know that and I know that. Now, I've got a million things to do.'

He looked so dejected that I knew for sure he hadn't been at Blue Gum that night. I was so glad. I touched his arm. My voice was gentler. 'Ma would be extremely happy if she never saw me again, Lionel. And that's the truth. Now, go home and tell her the bad news.'

'Bad news?'

'Greys will be open for business by midday today and we have our chef back. We're going to make it a success and nothing Ma can do will stop us.'

'You've got her wrong, Kate. I know she's a bit …but her heart's in the right place. You've got to understand,' he pleaded. 'Hannah had a very difficult upbringing, ja? Her father was a cruel man – she's been…damaged. And then she lost Pete's dad when she was very young. Kate?' he was pleading with me now. 'She loves those children of yours. She'd never do anything to hurt them.'

'I think you really believe that, Lionel.'

'Of course I do…'

'…Then ask her what happened at Blue Gum that night.'

'I don't know what you mean,' he stuttered.

'She's blown it, Lionel. And if she ever comes near my children again I'm going straight to the police. Tell her that.'

He couldn't look me in the eyes.

'I'll never forgive her for what she did.' I walked quickly away from him then, but he ran after me.

'Kate? Please.' He had an envelope in his hand and pushed it into my pocket. 'Don't open it till later. It's from me. Nothing to do with…. Okay?' Then he kissed my cheek and waved me away. 'Good luck, Kate.'

And the Lord did provide.

Lionel's cheque covered the cost of Jo Jo's freedom and the breakages and repairs. I got a dozen chairs from the store and glasses and plates from the Co-op.

When I got back to Greys, the main area was clear of debris, the floor was washed and the tables put back. No one would have guessed what it had looked like only an hour ago. I sent the boys to get the chairs from the store.

'That Lionel. Next time we meet I will give him a big kiss.'

Nomatuli said, after I told her about the cheque.

'I think he knows what she did, Nomatuli. I should hate him.'

'But you don't?' She put her head on one side, 'Forget troubles, Kate, we have work to do and this afternoon I will go to the RDP, put on my best dress, and do some business.'

The menu board was out by lunchtime and by 12.30 we had several customers. Nomatuli put on some music and she joked and talked to everyone. If anyone came in with children she was there, making them laugh, helping them cut up their food. I went into the back to see how Gloria and the girls were coping. Gloria looked up and smiled, wiping the hair out of her eyes. She offered me a spoon from the cauldron that she'd been stirring. 'Have a taste Kate.'

I didn't feel much like eating but I had a small plateful. It was delicious.

At 1-30 Maarten and his partner came in for their lunch. I ducked into the kitchen, before he saw me. I couldn't speak to him. I accepted Nomatuli's explanation of why she'd hidden the truth from me. It was for our sakes, but Maarten's motives were different, suspect. True, he cared for us but how much had his loyalty to his mother clouded his judgement? I watched as he and his friend sampled Gloria's *potjie* pot. He looked the same – a nice, gentle, man: my friend. But would I ever be able to forget what he'd done?

Nomatuli swept by as they ate and planted a kiss on each of the men's heads. 'These brave boys do not pay,' she announced to the room. 'They save my life.'

Before he left Maarten poked his head around the kitchen door. 'Great potjie, Gloria,' he shouted. That's when he spotted me.

'So, this is where you've been hiding.' He tried to touch my arm but I stepped away, pretending to be busy, stacking the dishwasher. 'You must have been up really early getting this place sorted, Kate,' he said. 'It's amazing.'

'I had a bit of help.' I muttered into the dishes.

'Did you manage to grab some sleep?'

'A little.'

'You look washed out.'

'I'm fine,' I snapped. 'I don't want to talk about it, okay?'

At that moment Nomatuli came in with a pile of dirty dishes and rescued me. 'I need help out there, Kate.' She looked at Maarten. 'Caught the bastards yet, Mr Policeman?'

He shook his head. 'We've spread the word, offered a reward, but hey, they're frightened, man. No one's talking.'

Nomatuli placed the dirty crockery on the side and went back into the café, calling over her shoulder as she went. 'You won't catch them, my friend. They have crawled back under the dung pile, where they live, for sure.'

I ducked behind Maarten and into the café trying not to see the hurt in his eyes.

After lunch Nomatuli went up to the RDP. When she returned she was smiling broadly and hugged Jo Jo and then me. 'Everything is fixed, Kate. No more worry.'

Later that night, when the children were in bed, Nomatuli and I sat out at the back of the house. It was hot and sticky and the outside lights were attracting moths the size of rats. Nomatuli was counting the day's takings and singing along to some music on her transistor. Handling money always made her happy. I watched as the pile of paper money grew and her smile widened but it would take a lot more than this before I could celebrate.

What did you say to Maarten?' She asked suddenly, not stopping her counting. 'Today? In the café?'

'Nothing.'

'You must not blame him. He thinks of you, all the time.'

I was silent.

'It's good we have paid those guys,' she said, changing the subject.

'Did they give you any trouble?'

'Why should they give me trouble? They get what they want. And we get what we want. All are happy.'

'And it's settled?'

'Sure, they go back to Cape Town now; make trouble for some other lucky people.'

'I don't understand you, Nomatuli. These are the people who nearly killed you and you don't mind them getting away with it.'

'Why should I blame the flea for making me scratch? Um? I save my anger for the big ugly she-cat.'

Music at Greys

The café did extremely well in those early days but I couldn't take much of the credit. Nomatuli was a huge power of energy, as was Gloria. I was only just appreciating what a multi-talented woman my sister-in-law was. Not only was she a great cook but she was brilliant at promoting the café. She got ads in all the local papers and on the radio. She produced leaflets for the local tourist agency and set up a Greys website. Gloria had found her confidence at last. She was even talking about finding a place of her own.

Her potjie pot, bobotie, pickled fish and Malay green curry brought in customers from as far away as Cape Town. Maarten and his police friends were daily customers and Miriam and Rob and their friends came at least twice a week. We were open every day and on Friday and Saturday evenings too. Friday nights became *Music at Greys*, when Jo Jo sang.

We were so busy I didn't have time to think about much else but it was weird how I was able to push the knowledge of what Ma had done to the back of my mind.

The children were on their long summer holiday now and I missed being able to leave them with the Vantondes. They got bored and difficult when they were at Greys all day but there was nothing I could do about it. Miriam occasionally had them for me and Maarten still took them to the beach on his day off.

At first Ma still sent invitations with Gloria for the children to go to tea but I tore them up. Gloria didn't ask why they weren't going but she must have been bewildered. Lionel was the only one who knew the score and he never mentioned Ma when he came to see us. No one did. It was as if they were all tiptoeing around her and me, waiting for something to happen.

During those first hectic weeks I only saw Maarten when he came to Greys to eat. I was civil but I avoided any conversation with him and pretty soon he got the message. I knew he was distressed but I really didn't have the emotional energy to deal with it. He'd betrayed me and I couldn't forgive him yet – maybe I never would.

What I really dreaded was his visiting Blue Gum again and when the inevitable happened I panicked. The children ran outside as soon as they heard his bike but I hid upstairs. He gave the boys their routine bike rides around the farm and then sat patiently, while Lilah showed him Stompy's chicks. Eventually I had to go down and he waited while I put the kids to bed. When we were alone he tried to talk to me but I answered in monosyllables and he soon made some excuse and left.

After that, when he visited, I always found an excuse to leave him alone with the children. Apparently, he wasn't the only one who noticed my behaviour because one day Lilah brought me one of Stompy's chicks. It was a handsome little cockerel, with the ragged beginnings of a beautiful, blood-red comb. My daughter placed the struggling bird on its back, stroking its shiny black feathers until it was hypnotised into stillness and then she put it gently in my lap.

'He's lovely, Lilah. What's he called?'

'Stompy baby,' she replied, her chubby fingers playing with the cockerel's comb. 'He is a Christmas present, for Uncle Maarten.'

I was amazed. Lilah didn't *do* presents. 'That's very kind, sweetheart, but I'm not sure it's such a good idea. Uncle Maarten is out all day and he might not have time to look after Stompy baby.'

Up till then any gardening I did was at Greys and Blue Gum was suffering badly. I managed basic watering in the poly tunnels but everything else had to survive as best it could. One morning I glanced out of the upstairs' window and our land was once more shrouded in the delicate violet blue of Patterson's Curse. Maybe I should get some beehives, make the first South African, *Patterson's Curse* honey? Perhaps then we could live in peace – this alien and me. That same morning I noticed a small figure moving about out there, swimming in the blue. It was Jeth, yanking out great fistfuls of the stuff just like his dad. He had a huge pile of it and the others were taking turns to jump in it.

Before I went to work I went down to the tree nursery and found several of my specimen trees dead or very sickly. I had been paying Lucky to do some watering down there but he was unreliable nowadays. He either over-watered or totally forgot. Nomatuli and he had split up so maybe he just didn't care.

I asked Nomatuli what had happened between them.

'Lucky, like all fellas,' she said, wrinkling her nose, as if she had a nasty smell under it. 'He wants something he smiles and is nice, but when he can't get what he wants he sulks and does bad things, like a child.'

Lucky had lost his job working for Rob. He was no use now he couldn't be trusted. Miriam told me she'd seen him punching Nomatuli. I found that hard to believe but then I remembered the unexplained bruise on Nomatuli's face, a few weeks back, when she said she'd fallen over something.

Holidays

It was to be our first Christmas without Pete and I was dreading it. Jeth dug up a small conifer and the children got out all our old decorations and put them up. There was none of the usual excitement.

Fortunately we were very busy so it hardly signified. We were only closed on Christmas Day itself and I decided to have our Christmas dinner in Greys. I couldn't face Blue Gum without Pete. Nomatuli was with us and Gloria joined us for dinner. I don't know how she managed it. I didn't ask. She brought presents from Ma and Lionel. Maarten popped in briefly with things for the kids.

That's when Lilah gave Maarten his present. She was so excited and hopped about from one foot to the other. She had found a little cage to put Stompy baby in and there were two paper bags, one filled with grain, and the other with strawberries. Maarten glanced at me over her head. We both knew he couldn't refuse.

Nomatuli gave me the best Christmas present ever. 'It is time to take your long face away, Kate Vantonde,' she lectured. 'Our customers need happy faces before they spend rand. One look at you and they are not so hungry.'

I hadn't said anything to Nomatuli but I hated being a waitress. It was my idea of hell. So, Anne Marie took my place in the café and I became the general dogsbody. I picked up the stores, went to the bank, did the garden, helped in the kitchen, and cleaned the café: whatever needed doing.

I didn't begrudge the time I spent at Greys but when Gloria and Nomatuli said they could manage without me for a week or two, I was thrilled. We all missed being at Blue Gum and the children were as excited as I was. There was someone else who would be extremely happy.

Since Greys had opened Spider spent his lonely days lying under the gum tree waiting for his family to return and worrying about why he was being punished. 'Back soon,' Jeth used to yell out of the car window, as he trotted alongside us - eyebrows raised - waiting for permission to jump in with us. Someone told me that dogs don't measure time like we do, and to a dog five minutes away from their family is the same as five months. All I know is Spider suffered every minute he was away from us, especially from Jeth.

When the children tumbled out of the car on that first day home Spider ran around and around in circles, barking and leaping up at everyone. Finally, when he was exhausted he took Jeth's wrist gently in his mouth and *carried* him to their favourite spot under the oak tree, where boy and dog lay down together - Jeth with his arms wound about the animal's neck. It was lovely to see them.

I hadn't looked at my son properly for weeks and he had put on some weight. His face was changing too. He nearly had cheekbones and the beginnings of an Adam's apple. .

It was great to be in the garden again. I dressed in my tatty, comfortable jeans and old T-shirts and got digging. While I got stuck into the garden, the children claimed back their territory. I'd forgotten how lucky we were having all this space. Lilah got her chicks back from Miriam. They had all grown into pretty little birds and were able to fend for themselves.

Miriam and I even managed a few evenings together. She and Rob came regularly to the café but it wasn't the same as sitting out on the *stoep* together as the sun went down and sharing a bottle of wine and a gossip.

The children had made new friends while we'd been in Kleinsdorp and our garden was often full of running, laughing and sometimes crying children. Jeth could still be quite manic at times and had this habit of showing off in front of the older boys. He would climb to the top of the highest tree and leap from branches way too high for him.

Jo Jo was flourishing too. Friday nights became a special time for us all. We all went to Greys for our meal on that night. These musical evenings became so popular that customers brought their own instruments along. There were guitars, marimbas, drums, and kalimba – those tiny finger pianos that Pete had loved to play. Jo Jo sang unaccompanied but then the musicians would join in. Blacks, whites and coloured people drove out from nearby towns but the local blacks still stayed away.

Nomatuli explained. 'No money is the answer, Kate. It's life, hey?'

'But it's not fair.'

'No worry, Kate. One day black people will have café, too expensive for the whites.' Then she would laugh, showing her teeth. 'What does it matter? Life is over too quick for long face. These Xhosa', she said. 'They maybe too stupid to make money. They happy to work for nothing, owe the loan shark, owe the storekeeper, get credit. This is life in this place.'

Mr Clever Stick

The new school term was nearly upon us and Jeth was very excited about going to big school with Jo Jo. He couldn't wait to wear his new uniform and be grown up. The Kleinsdorp school wasn't what Pete and I would have wished for our children. It was 90% Afrikaans-speaking but I couldn't afford to send them anywhere else.

Children start proper school when they're seven here, and Jeth had long since outgrown nursery. He needed constant stimulation. That's where he most missed his dad. They used to explore the farm together collecting insects and plants. Afterwards, they'd spend hours looking them up in Pete's books. Pete had inherited an amazing natural history library from his father. He'd been a baby when his father died of cancer. But when Pete's paternal grandfather had died Pete received a tea chest full of books that had belonged to his dad. Pete had treasured them and brought Jeth up to love them too. Jeth longed to be able to read all those long Latin names.

As the new school term got closer so Jeth got louder and wilder. Jo Jo, on the other hand, became quiet and withdrawn. I could hardly get a word out of him. It had to be something to do with school and I racked my brain for a clue. But he never complained and when I asked him if he liked school he always replied, "Yes, Auntie."

Things came to a head one morning when we were all outside in the garden. I was planting up some herbs and Jeth was burning holes in a piece of paper with his magnifying glass. I was working near him when he suddenly spoke to me in his angry voice. 'I'm not going to that smelly school. You can't make me.'

'So, why's that Jeth?' I asked calmly, determined not to show any surprise. 'I thought you were looking forward to it.'

He wouldn't look at me.

Maybe it was just first day nerves. I had always hated going back to school after the long summer holiday. I watched as a thin line of flame licked up from his piece of paper. 'Be careful with that Jeth, or…'

'…Or I'll burn the stupid farm down.'

'Don't you dare say that. You've seen what fire can do in this country.'

He glared at me. 'My dad said it was good.'

'Yes, so long as it's under control. But not set off by some silly little boy.' I grabbed the paper and smothered the flame.

He flung down the magnifying glass and marched off.

'Don't walk away from me when I'm talking to you. Jeth!'

I thrust my trowel into the soil and sat back on my heels, watching my son disappearing up the path to the oak tree. I had begun to hope that everything was okay between us now but I only had to look into his eyes to know there was still a huge gulf between us. I wanted to believe that he'd forgotten the day Pete died but I know he remembered that last terrible morning as vividly as I did.

Jeth was sprawled full length across the swing. His feet were on the ground and he was winding the swing around and around. I flopped down, beside him.

Looking up into the tree I remembered the day Pete climbed this oak and fixed the swing. He had taken ages getting it to hang straight.   Jeth was two and had waited patiently underneath, pointing at Pete and saying 'Dad, dad. ' When it was all done, Pete got the poker and burnt some words underneath the seat.

'What does it say, Jeth.' I asked. 'I've forgotten.'

Jeth stopped his winding and stood up; tipping the seat so that we could both read what was written. *This swing belongs to Jethro! Keep off*. He ran his fingers along the scorch marks. 'My daddy did this for me.'

He hadn't called Pete 'daddy', since he was about five. I blinked hard. 'Yeah, it's lovely isn't it?'

He resumed his winding.

'D'you know what, Jeth?' I said. 'Sometimes we say things we don't mean when we're angry.' He didn't stop the winding. 'I loved your daddy very much. You do know that, don't you? I never hated him. Jeth?'

The boy took his feet off the ground and I had to jump backwards, away from his flying feet.

I tracked Jo Jo down to the jungle gym, where he was playing with Lilah.   Jeth followed me and hung upside down from a rope, watching, while Spider jumped up and licked his face.

Jo Jo was standing with his arms open wide, waiting to catch Lilah, who was preparing to jump from a log.

'Can we have a little talk, Jo Jo? Jeth tells me he doesn't want to go to big school.'

The boy turned a startled face to me just as Lilah jumped. He fell backwards onto the grass with the little girl safely in his arms. Lilah thought this was very entertaining and wanted to do it again. I sat down on an upturned log and patted the space beside me. Jo Jo came and sat beside me.

'Has something happened at school, Jo Jo? Something...not nice?'

The boy looked away but I raised his head so that I could look into his eyes. He has very expressive eyes. Jeth dropped down from the rope and he and Lilah and Spider came and stood in front of us.

'I'm not cross, Jo Jo. Has someone been nasty to you?'

He shook his head.

'Are you worried about the work?'

'No, Auntie, I am a good student.'

'What then?'

He was silent.

Jeth took a step forward. 'The teacher's ugly.'

The older boy shot Jeth a warning look but Jeth ignored him...'

'...She beats him.'

'What? Why did she? Did you do something bad, Jo Jo?'

'No he didn't.' Jeth was full of indignation. 'She's a smelly ugly woman and I hate her.'

'Will you be quiet, Jeth. You don't even know her.'

'I do,' he shouted, his lip jutting out. 'Mrs Smelly Arrison is Ouma's friend. I've seen her - loads of times. She gets bits of food stuck in her teeth and leaves them there. It's yuck.'

'Mrs Arrison? Are you sure?'

He nodded. 'Smelly old...'

'...Okay, enough, Jeth. Can you tell me what happened, Jo Jo?'

Lilah wiggled her little bottom in between me and her friend and leant up against him, her head on his arm.

The boy hung his head. 'I deserved to be punished, Auntie. I was disrespectful to teacher.'

I couldn't imagine him being rude to anyone.

He took a deep breath. 'Some boys misbehaved in class and teacher was very angry, so she took out her stick. "See", she said, "This is my Mr Clever Stick. He can speak Afrikaans, English, Xhosa, he can even speak French. He knows all languages and he punishes all who are naughty and…" But then, I don't know why, I shouted out. "But Mr Clever Stick does not know Sotho." So, she took me and caned me and said, "Now my stick knows Sotho." And since that time I meet Mr Clever Stick very often.'

'Where does she cane you?'

He opened his hand and I saw the fading marks of parallel stripes across the palm. The gouges were quite deep and although the wounds had healed I knew how painful they must have been.'

'Why didn't you tell me when it happened?'

'I thought you would be angry with me and send me away.'

'I would never do that, Jo Jo. Would you like me to take you away from the school?'

'No, Auntie, education is important, especially…' and he took a deep breath. '…Especially when you are…alone. I have to learn fast, get a good job, make a new family and return to Lesotho – to be with my people.' He sighed. 'Auntie? I am sorry to be a disgrace to you and Nomatuli.'

Leaning across Lilah I kissed his worried face. 'You could never be a disgrace to us.'

There was no way I could prove the connection between the treatment of Jo Jo and Ma. But I didn't need proof. My loathing for Ma squatted inside me like some poisonous toad and I knew I had to do something about it.

Mrs Arrison

Maarten's rugby club was booked into Greys for lunch the following Sunday; so I offered to help out. It was an incredibly humid day and the heat bounced off the white road and pavements and made everyone irritable. Even the placid Gloria yelled at Anne Marie about not washing the salad properly. You could cut the atmosphere with a knife.

The children were in the garden going wild and I was just thinking that I'd have to take them home when Miriam came by and asked if they wanted to go to the beach with her. They didn't need asking twice.

After lunch things calmed down and Gloria, Anne Marie, Nomatuli and me sat outside under the shade of a tree, cooling off. We could hear the girls in the kitchen singing and laughing as they finished their work.

After a while I stood up. 'I'm just popping over the road for a minute. Okay?'

Gloria stared. 'Is something wrong, Kate? You've been very quiet today.'

I smiled at the worried woman. 'I'm fine, Gloria. See you.'

I knew they were all watching me as I crossed the street and walked towards the Vantonde house.

When I opened their garden gate I saw Lionel swimming leisurely up and down in their pool. He didn't see me. Ma was sitting on the veranda, her back to me. Her feet rested on a chair and an old electric fan chugged away in front of her, its flex snaking back into the kitchen. She had a cup halfway to her mouth when I said *hello*. She turned, saw me, and spilt coffee all down her dress.

'Katie? What a lovely surprise,' she trilled, as she mopped herself up.

The sun was behind me and she had to shield her eyes to see me.

'I wasn't expecting you... Please, sit down; I'll make some more coffee.'

'Do you know Mrs Arrison?'

'Arrison?' She sucked at the name and shook her head. 'No. Sorry, Katie. Never heard of her. Who is she?'

'She was Jo Jo's teacher last term.' I was watching her closely but her face gave nothing away.

Pushing down on the arms of her chair she levered herself up to standing.

'Strange,' I said. 'Because Jeth says she comes here, often. That you're friends.'

'Really?' She thought for a moment and then smiled. 'Did you say Arrison, Katie? Of course. You mean Desiree. I always think of her as Desiree du Plessis – her maiden name? We went to school together. We were in the same class, right up until I left.'

I had to give it to Ma, she was one hell of an actress.

'Have I met her?'

'Possibly, but she's a busy woman, ja? What with her family and her teaching. She's such a nice lady - loves the kiddies.'

'Yeah, that's what Jo Jo said.'

At that moment Lionel came dripping towards us. He was

grinning but his eyes were wary. 'Kate? Lovely to see you. Maarten still over there filling his belly?'

I shook my head. 'No, they were heading for the pub when I left.'

He turned to his wife. 'Any chance of a coffee, Hannah?'

Ma went off obediently and I asked Lionel about Mrs Arrison.

He pulled a face. 'My God. That's one terrible woman.'

'She's Jeth's teacher this term.'

'Poor kid.'

'I'll be keeping an eye on her.'

'Do that.'

Ma returned with Lionel's coffee.

'Ah, Hannah, thank you. No cake? ' And he took the cup off his flustered wife and settled back in the best garden chair - the one she always sat in.

I followed Ma inside. She was standing in front of the table with her back to me. I watched the fat under her arms trembling as she cut a slice of cake, and then she reached up into the cupboard for a plate. She wheezed as she worked.

When she turned and saw me she stumbled backwards, her hands fluttering to her chest. 'My God, Katie. You gave me such a shock.'

I waited.

'Would you like some cake? It's good. I can make some fresh coffee if you... Look, Katie,' two bright spots burned on her cheeks and she blinked the sweat out of her eyes. 'If this is about Desiree I'm sure I can get her to...' Her voice trailed off and she picked up the plate. 'Let's go outside, ja? Join Lionel.'

I took a step towards her. 'Pete begged me to keep away from you. Called you a manipulative, racist, bigot. Said he hated you.

274

Yeah, I found that hard to believe too. You were his mother, the children's grandmother; you wouldn't do anything to harm us. Would you?'

I stared into Ma's innocent blue eyes.

'And d'you know something really sad? I stuck up for you back then. Pete and I had some terrible rows over you. He didn't want you to see the children at all but that would have been too cruel. He gave in to me finally but I wish to God he hadn't...'

Ma tried to elbow her way past but I shoved her back.

'...Because now I know what you're really capable of. It was you who got that fanatic Groos and his cronies to attack Blue Gum. And you paid that gang of thugs to destroy Nomatuli's store. Did you want her dead? Is that what you wanted? To murder someone? Would that have satisfied you? Or was the plan to scare us half to death, so that we came running to you for protection?'

'How dare you accuse me of such things,' her voice was full of righteous indignation. 'I was at home on both occasions, ask Lionel, ask anyone.'

But I wasn't listening. I was watching her little rose-bud mouth as it spewed out her lies. I took another step towards her. 'But then you turned your attention on a pathetic little boy and unleashed that vile woman Arrison on him. And for what? For the sheer pleasure of hurting him?'

She gave a nervous laugh. 'You're mad. Everyone knows you've been ...unstable since my son died. But I've made allowances. They all thought we should have put you in the psychiatric hospital, but I stuck by you. You would never have managed without me and now you come her accusing me of this nonsense...And, as to this black?' Her lip curled. 'That is nothing to do with me.'

At that moment Lionel poked his head around the door. 'Everything all right in here?'

'Thank God, Lionel. Ring for Dr Coetee. She's paranoid. I think she needs sedating.' Her voice was shrill. 'Quick, don't just stand there.'

Lionel stepped inside the kitchen, closing the door behind him, and pressed Ma back into the chair. 'Be quiet, Hannah. Haven't you done enough harm already?'

Ma stared at her angry husband in horror. 'But, Lionel,' she whined. 'She says I...'

He looked at me. '...Go home, Kate.'

Ma was wheezing badly now, her face a puttyish grey colour. I felt no pity. 'I'm warning you, Ma. If you try to see my children again I'll go straight to the police and tell them everything. I swear.'

'Bitch,' she shrieked. 'They're my grandchildren. My blood. You can't stop me from seeing them.'

She struggled to stand up but Lionel caught her and pinned her flailing arms to her sides.

'I think you'll find that I can.'

'Everybody's talking about you. One of my sons not cold in his grave and you're already setting your cap at his brother.'

'Go, Kate.' Lionel urged.

'Those children are mine,' she screamed as I went out of the door. 'They belong to me, not some dirty, British whore. I read those disgusting letters. I know what sort of woman you are.'

Somehow I got outside.

A Criminal Offence

One evening, shortly after this, I was watching telly on my own when a vehicle stopped outside. The children were in bed and Nomatuli was at the café. Spider padded downstairs and waited by the front door, his tail swaying. I still didn't like unexpected visitors, especially at night, and I peered out from behind the curtains. It was a police car.

I unlocked the door.

Maarten stood there clutching an egg box. 'I was on my way home and I thought you might like these, Kate? Some banty eggs?'

'Thanks, Maarten. That's kind.' I took the eggs and waited for him to go.

He stood there awkwardly. 'Can I come in for a minute?'

I stood aside

'Can't be long,' he said. 'Watching rugby with the fellas. Big game. Springboks versus the Aussies. We're gonna murder them.' He took off his hat and stepped into the room, shifting uneasily from one foot to the other.

'Sit down, Maarten.'

He went and perched on the edge of a kitchen chair.

I sat down opposite him. 'So? How's Stompy Baby?'

'Bloody noisy.'

I smiled. 'Had any complaints yet?'

'Not yet, but it won't be long.'

Stompy baby had a harem now. He was the sleekest, fattest

rooster in Kleinsdorp and Lilah had given him two of her hens in case he got lonely. Maarten had made them a spacious run and smart hen house. Lilah kept a watchful eye on her chickens. Sometimes, when we were at the café, I let the boys take Lilah over to Maarten's house, so that she could check up on her uncle's animal husbandry. I wouldn't have liked to be in his shoes if he hadn't come up to scratch.

He cleared his throat. 'How are the kids?'

'Fine. School on Monday.'

'Good, good,' he said.

'Are you okay, Maarten?'

'Yeah…look, Kate, there's something I have to say. You may not like it but…there's been a lot of talk lately…'

He waited for me to say something but when I didn't he hurried on.

'… People are saying that you paid those guys for Jo Jo. The gang who trashed Greys?'

'What 'people'?'

'It's simple, Kate,' he said. 'Either you did or you didn't.'

'If I say I did are you going to arrest me or something?'

'This isn't a joke. You pay off these guys; they always come back for more. That's how it works. And they're dangerous. You're asking for trouble, ja?'

'It's got nothing to do with you, Maarten.'

'Why didn't you tell me what was going on?'

I looked away.

'The government is coming down hard on blackmail and ransom demands, Kate. These gangs are out of control. It's a criminal offence to deal with them.'

My mouth must have dropped open. He was accusing me of a criminal offence?

'We'll say no more about it this time, Kate, but if they come back I must be the first to know. Got that?' He went to the door, jamming his hat back on – mission accomplished.

'Just one minute.' I jumped up and ran after him. 'Don't I get a say?' I was so angry. How dare he? 'What would you call it?' I yelled. 'If you knew that a person had committed a crime and didn't report it? Isn't that aiding and abetting? That's a criminal offence in the UK. People go to prison for that.'

It was Maarten's turn to stare.

'You knew who attacked Blue Gum that night but you didn't tell me. All that pretence. How sorry you were for me. How you stayed with us and looked after us, made everything okay for us. But it wasn't for us, was it? It was for her wasn't it? For your bloody mother?'

He couldn't look at me. 'Who told you?'

'My friend told me. The only friend I have in this God forsaken country.'

'Nomatuli?' He sighed. 'You've got to believe me, Kate I never wanted any of this to happen. You and the children mean everything to me but…what could I do?'

'I dunno. Be a policeman? Do your duty?'

'She's not a criminal, Kate…'

'…No? So what would you call her?'

'She didn't mean it to happen. It got out of hand. Her cousin - that crazy Groos - got carried away, man. He's a bloody maniac. She wanted to scare you, that's all, so that you'd get rid of them.'

'"Them?"' I asked.

279

'The boy and Nomatuli. I know she was wrong, Kate, I told her, but they think like that – these people. She swore she'd never do anything like it again and I sorted out Groos. It was over, finished. Sure, I know what she did was wrong but we all make mistakes. Kate?' His eyes were pleading. 'And there wasn't any real harm done, hey? Just one dead chicken and some nasty words…'

'…Stop right there. There were three little children in this house that night. I was petrified, so God knows what it did to them.'

'It will never happen again, Kate. Ma swore on the bible. She's just a harmless old woman.'

'Maybe there's something else you should know about your "harmless" old mother. When Nomatuli did the deal with those guys to buy Jo Jo? They boasted that they were the same gang who destroyed her store…'

Maarten tried to interrupt but I wouldn't let him.

'…They said that an old white woman had paid them a lot of money to do the job. And that woman was called Vantonde.'

'They're lying. Those bastards are always lying.'

'Why, Maarten? What would be the point? They were so pleased with themselves. They wanted to show Nomatuli how clever they'd been. Ask your mother, Maarten; make her swear on the bible. Is attempted murder a criminal offence, Mr Policeman?'

Maarten slumped onto the settee and put his head in his hands. I felt sorry for him but it made no difference.

'She's sick, Kate.' He moaned. 'I'll make sure she sees someone, gets treatment. I promise.'

'Sorry. Not good enough.'

'What else can I do?'

'You came here to lecture me because I helped a defenceless little kid, but all the time you've been protecting a would-be murderess. And you're supposed to be the law around here?'

'I told you, Kate, it's finished.'

'No, it isn't, because now she knows she can do whatever she wants and get away with it.'

He looked up. 'You mean the boy and this teacher thing? She swore it wasn't her, Kate. And there's no proof.'

'Just like there wasn't in the Blue Gum attack? Remember? No proof, that's what you said, and I believed you – more fool me. You were Pete's brother and I...trusted you, Maarten. I would have trusted you with my life.'

He got up and stumbled towards me. 'You know how I feel about you, Kate? But please, I'm begging you, don't make me send my mother to prison. Shc's had the worst punishment anyone can give her. She's lost her grandchildren. She's a broken woman.'

'Goodbye, Maarten' I said, going to the door and opening it. He gave me one last despairing look before stumbling out into the darkness.

Back to School

On the first day back to school the children were up very early. When I got downstairs Jeth was strutting about in his new uniform and Jo Jo was helping Lilah select what she was going to wear to nursery. There was a pile of discarded clothes on the floor. She was determined to look as smart as the boys. Jo Jo looked happy enough. I think I'd managed to persuade him that everything would be okay. He was a trusting child; even after all the terrible things that had happened to him. Anyway, I had a secret weapon – Jeth. I knew he would tell me if anything went wrong.

Before we left for Kleinsdorp Miriam popped in to give Jeth a pencil case. Maarten met us at the school gates. He shook both boys by the hand and kissed Lilah, and then gave them R10 each to spend at break time. He didn't look at me. Gloria was there also, on her way to work. She'd made them some cakes with their names in icing on them.

As we walked into the schoolyard there was that same indefinable smell I remembered from my own school days. Maybe that's what fear smells like.

I hadn't been inside the school for a year. Nomatuli must have seen my panic because she took my hand and squeezed it. I managed a few *hellos* to the parents I knew and then we stood against the playground wall and waited. Some older children were showing off, while several big girls had adopted whole gaggles of little ones, who trailed after them like baby chicks. Most of the boys jumped and fought and yelled, until some adult shouted at them.

I pitied all those little kids in their unfamiliar scratchy uniforms. Jeth and Jo Jo stood close to us and I was glad when a couple of Jo Jo's classmates came up and talked to him and Jeth. That was when the school secretary found me and led the way to the Head's office.

Mrs Frivovalt was a small woman in her fifties with short-cropped, blond hair. She had a pleasant enough face but her mouth was beginning to drag down at the corners, forming *puppet* lines to her jaw. She shook my hand as I sat down, taking a quick peek at her watch, and I apologised for taking up her time.

'I'm never too busy to talk to my parents, Mrs Vantonde. This is a family school, and,' she added, patting my hand. 'We were all so terribly sorry about your sad loss.'

I took a quick gulp of air; then I launched into my complaints about Mrs Arrison. Mrs Frivovalt was quiet while I spoke. When I was finished she smiled. 'I'd like to thank you for being so…frank, Mrs Vantonde, or may I call you Kate? However, I'm sure there's been some silly misunderstanding here. Desiree…Mrs Arrison is the gentlest teacher we have and would never deliberately hurt any of her pupils. We don't believe in corporal punishment in this school, however, a quick tap can sometimes keep an unruly child in check.'

I was fighting to stay calm. 'Firstly, I have seen the scars on Jo Jo, Mrs Frivovalt, and they were not made by a "gentle," person, and secondly Jo Jo is not an "unruly" boy. Go out there now and I can guarantee he will be standing quietly waiting for the bell, while most of your other pupils are running wild.'

'Be that as it may…'

But I wouldn't let her speak. I explained about Jo Jo's tragic circumstances and the supposedly Christian ethos of her school. Then I told her that if Jo Jo was ever beaten again I would take him and Jeth away from her school and I would make sure that everyone in the town knew why.

When I was finished she stood up and walked to the door. I followed. She smiled at me and shook my hand. 'I can assure you that I shall have a word, Mrs Vantonde. However,' she opened the door. 'There is one matter that troubles us, about the boy. You run the new café in Kleinsdorp don't you? And by all accounts it is very successful? However, we wonder how ethical it is to allow a young child to sing in an establishment that serves alcohol? To an outsider it might look as though you were using this unfortunate child for personal gain.'

'Jo Jo sings because he wants to, Mrs Frivovalt. No one makes him. Have you ever heard him sing? He will be famous one day and d'you know what is really "unfortunate"? Your school will have had nothing to do with his success.'

Later, when I told Nomatuli what had happened she frowned. 'This headmistress is very powerful in Kleinsdorp. She runs the school, her brother the Spar, another brother the garage. They are big in the church. Her uncle is Pastor Billy - big shot churchman. Everywhere you look you fall over these Frivovalts. Be careful with these people is all I say.'

'Like you are?'

She snorted.

I went back to the farm to work for the morning while Nomatuli did her shift at the cafe. At lunchtime I popped in to have a sandwich with her before picking up the kids. In South Africa the children finish school at lunchtime. I was taking them to the beach this afternoon.

As soon as I walked into Greys I knew something was wrong. Nomatuli was hunched at one of the tables with an untouched cup of coffee in front of her and, even more telling, an uneaten piece of banana cake. The flies were gathering. Rosemary popped out of the kitchen as I came in and I mimed something to eat. She nodded and disappeared, coming back after a few moments with a sandwich and juice. She looked at Nomatuli and raised her eyebrows at me before hurrying back into the kitchen.

There was a letter spread out in front of Nomatuli.

I sat down opposite her and sipped my drink.

She pushed the piece of paper towards me. 'He's been failed, Kate. No more chances. Law school has ditched him.'

'Thembo?' Why wasn't I surprised?

'Bloody stupid boy. What I tell him all these years, Kate? I say "Work hard, be diligent. Then, one day you will be lawyer, earn big money, have good wife, big family and look after your old mame." And now? On the scrap heap like his bastard daddy. Get some poor stupid girl pregnant; make her life a misery. Then leave her for some new girl. Someone younger, more beautiful, pretty smile, white teeth, who shake her booty at him…' She drank back her coffee in one defiant gulp and took a huge bite of her cake. The flies retreated. 'But,' she said, spraying cake everywhere. 'No more money from Nomatuli. It is…finished.'

Thembo

The boys settled into school and there were no problems. Jeth was up first every morning waiting impatiently for the rest of us - his bag crammed full with homework and things to show teacher. Mrs Arrison had been given another class this year and Jeth loved his young teacher. He was like a sponge absorbing everything he was taught. Lilah met the boys at playtime but they were all making friends in their own age groups. I was glad. Jeth and Lilah's life had been very restricted since Pete's death.

Business was good and I was getting my life back together. Now Ma was out of our lives I could cope. And Mum would be with us in a few weeks time. I was so looking forward to seeing her and showing her what we'd done with Greys. I wanted her to be proud of me.

We'd begun work on the living area above the cafe. There were two bedrooms, a bathroom and a living area/kitchen. Nomatuli still had her eye on it but at the moment she couldn't think of anything but Thembo's disgrace. All her old sparkle had gone. She did her job but there was none of the usual banter and fun. She dragged around a ball and chain of misery and nothing any of us could do or say helped.

But then, a few weeks later, she received another letter from Thembo, asking if he could come to stay and work in Greys. And in the time it took for her to read this letter all his shortcomings had been forgiven and forgotten. All that mattered was that she was going to see her wonderful boy again.

From the moment that boy stuck his handsome face around the door Nomatuli changed. She trailed after him, wearing a perpetually dazed expression, touching and kissing him until he pushed her away. 'No more, woman. You will spoil my hair.'

She laughed but I don't think he was joking.

I recognised the look in his eyes - the predatory arrogance of a very young and beautiful male. He barely deigned to acknowledge the kids - or me - and I knew what he was thinking when he looked at the house. I didn't have the money for luxuries and I wasn't house-proud. What was the point when you opened the door and half the vegetation in South Africa blew in?

He started work in Greys the next day and took over the late evening shifts at the weekends, which suited us perfectly. Thembo was supposed to be working for his keep but I knew his mother was slipping him money. I kept my mouth shut. It was nothing to do with me.

The girls in the café thought he was fantastic and the teenage hormones flying about our kitchen were palpable. Anne Marie and Rosemary were both married with families but even they giggled a lot when the boy was on the prowl. Even Gloria started to take more care with her appearance.

'He's so good looking, isn't he?' She gushed one day, after he'd slipped his arms around her and waltzed her around the kitchen.

'If you like that sort of thing,' I said, noticing how shiny her hair looked lately. And she was wearing lipstick. She saw me looking at her and blushed. I prayed she wasn't succumbing to Thembo's charms.

When he wasn't making up to every female in sight he was quite a good worker and it was nice to have a man about the place. He had the same easy charm with our customers that Nomatuli had. There were drawbacks of course. He hung out with a group of young men and their girls from the RDP and went out partying with them most nights after work, waking the whole household when he came back in the early hours. Then he'd crash out until midday and expect Nomatuli to be there to feed him when he woke. She wore herself out rushing around, second-guessing what he would like to eat, and there was never a 'please' or a 'thank you.'

He could certainly turn on the charm when he needed to, like when he needed money. He'd grab Nomatuli and tickle her until she begged for mercy and then he'd sit on her lap and pretend to be her little boy. It made me want to throw up, watching this normally astute, intelligent woman being manipulated by this egotistical boy.

Jeth and Jo Jo thought Thembo was cool. They wore their baseball caps back to front and did a lot of *high-fiving*. Lilah was too young to be impressed by male beauty and Thembo didn't give her sweets or play with her so she soon lost interest. Lilah and Thembo were very similar.

After a week or two Nomatuli began to look really tired. She fell asleep, whenever she sat down. Normally she had massive stores of energy but not now and it worried me. I nagged her to go to the doctor.

I usually went to bed before she came home from her evening shift but one particular night I had fallen asleep in front of the telly, when suddenly the front door opened. I'd forgotten to lock it and, for a moment, I was really scared. But it was Nomatuli. She dropped her bag, collapsed into the nearest chair, kicking off her shoes and massaged her toes.

'Busy night?'

She managed a smile. 'I need new feet. These are no good. Too old.'

I put the kettle on for her. 'I didn't hear the car. Did Thembo drop you off?'

She didn't answer. Nomatuli had bought an old VW. Our bakkie had finally given up the ghost and so we only had the Renault, which I used for the kids and me.

'Did you walk, Nomatuli?'

'Thembo works hard for us, Katie, he deserves some fun'.

'He took your car? And left you to walk home in the pitch dark, at this time of night?'

She sighed.

'You can't go on like this.'

'No need to worry. Nomatuli will be fresh for work in morning.'

'I didn't mean that and you know it. I'm worried about you.'

She stared at me, daring me to say the words. 'He's all I have in the world, Kate. Why do you think I work like a dog? For him. No one makes me. My choice, Kate. I never interfere with you and your children. There are things that are not right here, but that is your business, you are mummy.' And with that she limped away to bed, her tea untouched.

Thembo stayed out all that night. The next day was his day off so he stayed in bed. I worked until teatime and when we got home he was just getting up. Nomatuli was doing the evening shift.

I had no intention of feeding him. He bribed the boys to make him a sandwich and then he lolled about, watching telly with the kids. I answered him if he asked me a question but I made no attempt to talk to him. I washed up and put the children to bed and when I came down he was on the computer, playing games. I went to get the washing in and when I got back he was putting on his jacket - another new one, expensive looking. He preened in front of me, turning slowly so that I could see him in all his glory. 'Tell me, Kate Vantonde. What d'you think? Is this okay? I would value the opinion of such a stylish woman.'

It was hard not to smile. 'You're such a liar, Thembo.'

He winked at me. 'Shame you can't come out with me, Kate. A woman like you, and a man like me, we could have a lot of fun.'

'I don't think so.' I replied.

He was gyrating to some beat in his head and snapping his fingers to the rhythm, and then he did a Michael Jackson moonwalk towards me. It should have been totally ridiculous; I wanted to laugh but he really was very good. He oozed right up to me and stopped, so that we were staring into each other's eyes. 'I think Kate Vantonde can boogie.' He swayed like some huge snake in front of me and then he caressed my cheek slowly with the back of his hand. 'Pretty woman,' he said softly. His hand was cool on my warm skin. I turned away and busied myself with the washing, sorting, smoothing, folding, allowing the familiar comforting smell of clean sun-dried clothes to fill my nostrils, blotting out that other smell – a man's smell.

At last I heard the door close quietly behind him.

I laid my hands flat on the table and saw they were trembling. That crass, arrogant little boy had moved me. I needed Pete so much but he was never coming back. I was on my own. I was always going to be on my own. I rested my head on my hands and wept.

Later as I was tidying away things I noticed my open purse lying beside the sugar jar. I couldn't remember leaving it there but I was always forgetting things lately. As I snapped it shut it felt light and I opened up the coin compartment. I always kept a supply of R5 coins to tip the parking and petrol attendants but there were none there. I looked where I kept the notes. There was one R200 note. I had been to the bank today and had drawn out R800. There were three R200 notes missing.

I bit my lip. Thembo had stolen the money. There was no other explanation. He had the opportunity while I was out of the room. Did he imagine I wouldn't notice, or maybe he didn't care? Perhaps he thought he'd earned it for that bit of flirting?

I made myself stay awake until I heard Nomatuli's car. At least Thembo had brought her home tonight.

She limped in and fell in a chair. 'We're going to have to get some more help, Kate,' she said, kicking off her shoes. 'Heaven help us tomorrow.'

Tomorrow was *Music at the Greys*.

She filled a bowl with water and soaked her feet. 'Ahhh. That is so good,' she said massaging her toes.

I decided to come straight to the point. 'Did you see Lilah playing with my purse today, Nomatuli? Before you went to work? I've lost some money.'

She froze.

'Maybe,' she said. 'Maybe not...' She lifted her feet out of the water and went to the sink. Her back was to me as she emptied the bowl.

I hurried on. 'Only you know how she loves shinies. Hides them all over the garden for the fairies to find?'

'So you've lost a few coins, Kate? No need to call out Mr Policeman then?' Her voice was hard.

'I've lost R400,' I explained. 'I'm sure it wasn't Jo Jo or Jeth so... '

'...So you think, who is the bad boy in this house?'

'I'm not saying it was him, Nomatuli...'

'...I cannot stay in a house where my son is accused,' she said, angrily wiping at her face.

'Nomatuli, please...'

She picked up her bag and marched into her bedroom.

To say there was an icy atmosphere at breakfast was a huge understatement. Even Spider tiptoed around the kitchen while he waited for Lilah to christen him with his daily anointing of soggy rice crispies.

Thembo wasn't home yet and from the look of the black bags under Nomatuli's eyes she hadn't slept. Neither had I. She answered if I spoke to her but apart from that said nothing. She looked so sad I wanted to throw my arms around her and tell her it didn't matter. I didn't care if he'd stolen the money. I would give him the money gladly, if it would make her happy again.

It was Nomatuli who brought up the subject. 'Mummy has lost some money, Lilah. Did you see her purse yesterday?'

Lilah shook her head and continued to eat.

'Are you sure, Lilah?' I asked. 'I won't be cross.'

She nodded as she measured out spoonfuls of brown sugar onto her cereal.

There was no more time to talk about it now. I had to take the kids to school and I was on the morning shift at Greys. It was Nomatuli's day off.

I thought about it as I drove. I was always leaving my purse lying about. Someone else could have stolen the money. Just because I didn't like Thembo didn't mean he was a thief. And even if it was him there was no way I wanted Nomatuli and me to fall out over it. I'd rather lose the money than lose my friend. I had to apologise to her before it was too late.

So, after I dropped the kids off at school, I turned the car around and headed back to Blue Gum. I saw Gloria as I drove back up the High Street and told her I'd forgotten something and would be a bit late for work.

I found Nomatuli slumped in the same chair I'd left her in, her hands covering her face. Her shoulders were heaving. I perched on the edge of the chair and put my arms around her.

'I'm so sorry, Nomatuli. I have no proof it was Thembo. Please, forget it.'

She looked up at me and shook her head sadly. 'My life is over, Kate.'

'Don't say that.'

'What am I going to do? I raise him the best I can, tell him right from wrong, give him everything he want, but he bad, like his daddy. He's a drinking, lustful pretty boy with no thoughts of kindness or pride. What I do wrong, Kate?'

'Nothing, you've been a brilliant mum. But really, it might not have been him.'

She sighed. 'Oh yes, he take it. I know. Because he take my money too and God knows how many other women's money.'

'It's not your fault.'

'Then who? He steal off me, he steal off you. I work my fingers to the bone, for what? So that this lazy boy can gamble, drink and whore my money away. And he is a Zulu. He has the blood of great warriors in his veins.' She got to her feet and picked up a stick that Jeth had been playing with that morning. 'I'll beat this boy when he returns. I'll kill the ungrateful wretch. I tell him this time for sure, Kate. No more money from Nomatuli, let him ask his bastard daddy – see how far he get.'

She was muttering to herself and slapping her thighs working herself up into a state. I wouldn't like to be in Thembo's shoes when he came home.

'Even this Nandhi make ten of the ungrateful boy. He will eat dung.'

I left her to planning Thembo's public disembowelment and went back to Greys. I had no wish to be there when her son returned.

When I got home with the children at midday, Nomatuli's car was parked outside. The prodigal son had returned. There was no sign of either of them in the house so, while the children went outside to play, I did some watering. I could see two figures inside the poly tunnel, one the unmistakable shape of Nomatuli, the other a tall but slighter figure - Thembo. I pushed the plastic barrier aside and stepped inside. Nomatuli was transplanting seedlings and Thembo was filling pots with compost. His immaculate white T-shirt was streaked with dirt and his gelled hair had wilted in the humidity.

Nomatuli turned a stony face to me. 'Have you met your new gardener, Kate? '

Thembo flicked an embarrassed glance in my direction.

'Hey, you've done loads. Thanks.'

'This boy has many more to do before he stops. Very cheap worker, Kate. He do this for nothing. Kind aye?'

I left them to it. Mother and son, working side by side, in perfect animosity.

Thembo left for Jo'burg the next day. 'To re-sit his exams before the new term start,' Nomatuli told me, 'And,' she said, before leaving for work. 'It is official. Nomatuli Izhaki is free woman now. No more running around after bastard husbands or bastard sons. I am looking after number one from now on.'

And I almost believed her.

Kippie Makusi

I noticed the man during Jo Jo's first spot on the following Friday night. His face was round and pleasant and when he smiled there was a dimple in one cheek. His skin was a light, almost olive colour and his black hair was streaked with grey and cropped close to his scalp. He wore a white silk scarf loosely knotted about his neck and a white shirt, jeans and well-cut black jacket. But it wasn't so much to do with what he looked like, it was his confidence. He was so at ease in his own body. I envied him. He must have sensed me staring at him because he looked up and smiled lazily at me.

He was part of a group that had *city folk* written all over it. The women were dressed in gorgeous clothes and one in particular stood out. Her black hair shimmered in the soft light, her skin glowed, and she wore a stunning plain white sheath dress.

Maarten and his pals occupied a table nearby and I couldn't help making comparisons. The policemen and their wives were loud and large and drank beer straight from the bottle, while the other group drank wine – our most expensive from a local vineyard - and talked in soft, educated voices.

The woman in white sat close to the man, her long fingers curling proprietarily around his wrist. She obviously didn't like it when Jo Jo sang because the man angled his chair away from her in order to listen. She talked loudly throughout the songs. Even Nomatuli's scowl didn't shut her up.

Gloria had taken the night off for some special meeting at the church and we always did pizzas when she wasn't cooking.

'Pizzas? My God. How exciting,' the woman sneered when Anne Marie showed her the menu, raising one beautifully plucked eyebrow at her friends. Anne Marie was flustered so I took over. If the woman wanted to be difficult then so could I. Greys was doing well enough without having to kow-tow to awkward customers. If they didn't like what was on offer, then they knew what they could do. I wasn't rude exactly but I was definitely brusque. I don't think the woman even noticed, she was far too busy giggling with her pals. But when I glanced up I looked straight into the man's deep brown eyes and he winked at me.

In the end they ordered two lots of pizzas and were the last to leave, so it couldn't have been all that bad. It was closing time and we were all glad when they finally settled the bill and got up to leave. It wasn't just their rudeness and arrogance that annoyed me it was something else, something I didn't want to acknowledge. I was jealous.

I stood by the door as they all trooped out, talking animatedly to each other and totally blanking me. I had this terrible urge to stick my foot out as the woman in white sauntered past and I didn't notice the man, standing beside me.

He grinned, as if he knew what I was thinking. 'I'm sorry we've kept you.'

'That's okay,' I said, turning the sign to *closed*.

He held out his hand, 'I'd like to introduce myself. Kippie Makusi.'

'Hi,' I said, ignoring the hand. Was I supposed to know him?

'The boy sings well.'

'I think so, considering the competition.'

The man's smile didn't waver. 'Might it be possible to speak to his parents? I'm very interested in talented youngsters and I'd like to set up a meeting with them.'

'Jo Jo hasn't any parents.' I stammered. 'I'm…we're looking after him.'

'I see,' he took a card out of his wallet. 'Could you give me a ring tomorrow and we'll have a chat, Mrs…?'

'Vantonde. Kate Vantonde.'

'He has a remarkable talent, Mrs Vantonde.'

'Yes, yes, he does.'

'Jo Jo you say?'

I nodded furiously. 'His real name's Johnny Zono but my daughter called him Jo Jo, when he first came to live with us and we've called him that ever since…' Oh God, I was babbling.

'Johnny 'Jo Jo' Zono?' The man smiled. 'A great stage name.'

This time I returned his smile.

He pressed the card into my hand. 'Till tomorrow then.'

I stood in the doorway and watched as their sleek cars disappeared up the main street.

Nomatuli came and nudged me in the ribs. 'Hey? One sexy man.'

'This mean anything to you, Nomatuli?' I handed over his card. 'He wants to talk about Jo Jo…'

Nomatuli took one look and let out a scream so loud she almost burst my ear-drums. Then she pranced about waving the card above her head. 'Do you know who has been sitting in my café, on my chair?' She picked up the chair, kissed it and then danced around the room with it. 'His bottom on my chair?' She ran her fingers over the seat. 'Eating my pizza with extra salami and mozzarella?'

'Who is he? '

'"Who is he?" Your education is so bad, Kate Vantonde. Everyone knows Kippie Makusi? Radio DJ for SAFM? Kippie Makusi? The great Kippie Makusi?'

'Never heard of him.'

She shook her head sadly. 'The whole universe has heard of this man except Kate Vantonde.' Her eyes were bright with excitement.

'So he's famous?'

'Famous?' My ignorance astounded her. 'He is such a famous man, Kate, he is bigger than…Nelson Mandela and …David Beckham and …' she searched about for the ultimate superlative…'My God, Kate, Kippie Makusi is more famous than Shaka. I promise you. He is one amazing guy.'

She turned to the astonished Jo Jo and pulled him into her arms, planting kisses all over his face. 'You are going to be a star, my child.' Then she went crazy, clapping her hands, doing a wild, hip-swinging dance and ululating. Lilah watched in delight as Nomatuli went round and round in circles, until she was so dizzy she had to sit down on Kippie's chair. She mopped at her face with a serviette. 'Kippie Makusi's backside has been on this chair. No one but Nomatuli must sit here ever again.' She glared at us. 'Do you understand?'

No one got much sleep that night and the next morning they all clustered around me while I rang the number on the card. I spoke to Kippie's secretary and she arranged for him to visit us that morning. It was Saturday so the children were off school and they were scrubbed and dressed in clean clothes. Nomatuli warned them, on pain of death - a Zulu death,' she insisted, and rolled her eyes. 'Sharpened stakes pushed into your ....' She saw my expression and stopped.

I'd never seen her so excited, not even when Thembo was coming. She must have changed her clothes five times before she was ready. And when the smart open-topped sports car purred to a stop outside she hid behind me, pushing me forwards, her bony knuckles digging into my backbone.

'Cut it out, Nomatuli.' I hissed. I didn't want to look like a prat in front of this man. I was determined to be cool and business-like after last night.

I thought Nomatuli was going to faint when it was her turn to be introduced to him. She was sweating and fanned herself furiously. After she'd composed herself she jabbed me in the back again. 'Ask Kippie if he'd like to try my speciality.'

"Speciality?" Nomatuli had always prided herself on being the only Zulu woman who couldn't cook.

Kippie accepted some coffee and cake from Nomatuli and then she stood behind him and watched every mouthful he took. When he added more milk to the coffee, she rushed to bring more. When he had almost finished the first cup she brought him another. I tried to catch her eye and make her leave him alone but it was impossible. He took it all in his stride. I warmed to him.

Kippie explained that he produced a radio programme for talented under-privileged youngsters. He thought Jo Jo's voice was exceptional and hoped to be able to help the boy's career. He wanted him to come to Cape Town and take part in his show. The man talked directly to Jo Jo and I could see the boy was terribly nervous. He was still very wary of men. At one point Kippie rested his hand lightly on the boy's shoulder and Jo Jo flinched. I drew the boy close to me and we sat facing the man, my arms around Jo Jo. This Kippie Makusi could be the boy's saviour but I was suspicious too – I had to be certain Jo Jo would be protected.

'Jo Jo can't come on his own Mr ...'

'...Kippie. Please. You are invited of course.'

'And Nomatuli. We are both Jo Jo's foster parents.'

He nodded. 'We want Jo Jo to be relaxed.' He smiled at the boy. 'Could you prepare a five-minute intro for the programme, Jo Jo? What you sang last night would be great.'

'I want to sing opera, Mr Makusi.' At last Jo Jo had found his voice.

'Opera, um?' Kippie was amused.

'You will not laugh when you hear me, sir.' Jo Jo said, before stalking out of the house. His back was ramrod straight. Lilah ran after him and Jeth scowled at the man before he too followed the others outside.

Nomatuli marched to the door. She was furious. 'This ungrateful boy will apologise'

The man grinned. 'No, no. I think I deserved that.'

Township Talent

The programme went out live at 7pm on Sunday, so I asked Gloria if she'd have Lilah for me. My sister-in-law had at last moved out of the Vantonde house and was renting part of a house with one of her friends from the animal rescue. This house was full of dogs and cats and Lilah loved it.

Miriam, Rob, Maarten and Gloria were there to see us off. Miriam had dragged me along to her hairdressers. I pretended she forced me into it but deep down I wanted to look good. I bought a new top and trousers and when I saw myself in the shop mirror the stranger who had been there since Pete's death had gone. It wasn't the old me but at least I recognised myself.

'You look wonderful, Kate,' Gloria said when she saw me.

'My mummy is pretty.' Lilah told everyone.

Maarten stood apart from us, talking to Rob, but his eyes were on me.

Even Miriam was impressed with how I looked. 'You look so sexy, Kate. Watch out for that Kip Makusi. He's a wild one, married three times, loads of celeb girlfriends.'

And suddenly everything was ruined. I felt cheap. I'd been tarting myself up for a man. But I didn't want another man – ever. I locked myself in the loo and sobbed my heart out. When Miriam knocked softly to tell me the car had arrived I didn't answer.

I could hear Jeth's excited voice. 'Hey, Jo Jo, look at the limo, its got AC <u>and</u> tinted windows.'

There was Nomatuli too.' Where are you, Kate Vantonde? Do you wish to keep Kippie Makusi waiting?'

And I knew I had to go. I sloshed some water on my eyes, grabbed Pete's old fleece and hurried out after them. Spider stood forlornly beside Miriam. She was going to shut him inside the house after we'd gone. We didn't want him following us all the way to Cape Town.

I bent down to hug Lilah and, as I did so, I saw her mouth curve downwards.

She clutched my legs. 'Come with.'

I hugged her to me. 'We're going to meet Grandma in Cape Town tomorrow. Would you like to come too?'

She nodded but she still clung to me. Maarten scooped her up and swung her up onto his shoulders. We got into the car and as we moved majestically down the track he galloped alongside us, with Lilah shrieking with laughter.

Nomatuli and the boys quickly discovered the free drinks and sandwiches, then the DVD's and iPods; so I didn't have to speak to anyone for the entire journey.

When we arrived at the studios I was composed. I still had the fleece draped across my shoulders. I had never liked new clothes, even as a child. There was something very comforting about things that had been worn before by someone else. It was something to do with the smell. I caught Nomatuli frowning at me.

'What?'

'That old thing,' she said, plucking at the fleece. 'Do you want to shame the boy?'

I slipped the coat off and left it in the car. She was right. We were shown into the viewing room and Jo Jo was taken straight into the recording studio. I was so proud of him. He looked so small and vulnerable, and yet he was incredibly calm. A technician fixed his head mic and sat him down, and then he saw us and waved and gave Jeth the thumbs up. I recognised the look on his face. It was like that first time I saw him singing in Hermanus. There was the same detachment and quiet confidence that made you trust in his ability. He could sing and he knew it. He didn't need to know anything else.

Although he couldn't read music he had widened his repertoire considerably. He sang spirituals and classical and light operatic works. He borrowed Nomatuli's transistor and sat for hours listening and learning the words to songs. Nomatuli had taught him some traditional Zulu music too.

Kippie had spent a lot of time with the boy in the last few days and gained his trust. I was beginning to trust him too and believed that he really did have the best interests of Jo Jo at heart. Kippie had grown up in a Jo'burg township, he told us, and was orphaned at a young age. He had struggled to better himself and said this programme was his way of paying back all the kindness people had shown him over the years. He had given Jo Jo an iPod, so that he could play back pieces and learn new ones. There would have to be formal singing lessons, but that would come later.

Tonight, the boy would sing live, unaccompanied. But that didn't bother Jo Jo. That was the way he'd always sung. And then it was time for Jo Jo to sing. Nomatuli and I held hands. Jeth sat forward in his seat watching his friend, his forehead pressed against the glass partition. Jo Jo sang beautifully and by the time he finished I don't think I was the only one who was crying. After the studio applause died down Jo Jo was taken to join the adults around the table. There was to be a discussion later and the panel consisted of a musical impresario from Jo'burg, the arts correspondent from The Cape Times and a government Minister for the Arts.

Jo Jo sat beside Kippie. 'Jo Jo Zono, everybody. A young man with an incredible gift.' There was more enthusiastic clapping.

The boy tried to smile but his lip quivered. Kippie bent down to hear what he was saying.

Kippie was amused. 'I'm afraid you're going to have to speak up just a little bit. What did you say?'

'I made mistakes.' The voice was sorrowful.

'Not from where I was sitting…'

'…But I did.' Jo Jo was not going to be silenced. 'I forget to breathe properly. I have to breathe or the note comes wrong.'

'Who told you that?'

'No one.'

'Did someone teach you to sing?'

'No.'

'And why do you sing?'

Jo Jo stared at Kippie as if he was stupid and shrugged.

Kippie smiled broadly at the boy and squeezed his shoulder. 'Thank you, Jo Jo, and now, with your permission I'd like to play the tape you made earlier? Is that okay? No nodding.'

'Yes,' Jo Jo replied firmly. 'That's okay.'

'Thank you once again, Jo Jo Zono.'

There was more applause and he was brought through to sit with us.

'I should explain,' Kippie continued, when there was silence again, 'that Jo Jo wanted to tell his story himself but he knew it would be hard for him to do it in public. So, here's a tape we made earlier.'

Nomatuli passed a bag of sweets along to the boys. Their heads were so close, as they picked out their favourites, black and blond hair blending together.

'My name is Johnny Zono and I live in Lesotho with my mummy and daddy...'

The boys exchanged glances and giggled.

'...We have a nice house. Some days Mummy works in the baby clinic and my Daddy is a gardener. One day he goes to pick apples in the mountains. He is away a long time and I am the man of the house. When he comes back I have a sister. She is Nella. We make a garden, Daddy and me. We grow mealies and tomatoes. I will be a gardener one day – just like my Daddy but then Nella is sick and my Mummy is ill and...'

His voice died away for a moment. I look to where he sits with Jeth, who has his arm around the older boy.

'...And... and soon there is only Daddy and me. He has tears on his face and he is angry when I see him. But the worst thing is one day he goes away to pick apples and never comes back. I wait and wait but what shall I do? I have no one. I am alone. So I hide on a lorry and it takes me to the big city'

At that point Kippie stopped the tape.

'Jo Jo didn't want to say out loud all the things that happened to him in the city, so let's just say he lived on the streets, got into trouble with the police. In jail someone heard him sing and brought him to Hermanus to make money for them. He sang to the tourists on the sea front and that's where he had the good luck to meet two very special women - Nomatuli Izhaki and Kate Vantonde.'

Kippie motioned to Nomatuli and me to stand up and take a bow, while the audience clapped. After this there was a discussion and then other children had their turn, but none was a patch on Jo Jo. When it was all over people crowded around the boy to congratulate him. He looked dazed; as if he was in some sort of dream and was frightened he'd wake up.

Afterwards Kippie took us to hospitality and while the boys gorged themselves Kippie talked to us. He said the station's phone lines and web site had been jammed with enthusiastic responses to Jo Jo's singing. Also that several producers from TV, radio and recording companies had already expressed an interest in him. He suggested we get the boy a good agent and wrote down a few names for us. Nomatuli was so excited she forgot her shyness and gave the great man a hug before we set off for home. Kippie shook my hand warmly. 'We'll be meeting again, soon I hope.'

Going Home

The drive home was a much quieter affair than the one going. It was late and after the first minutes of excited talk the boys fell asleep, wedged against each other. Even Nomatuli had her eyes closed, no doubt re-living her moments with the great man.

It had been stifling hot in the studios and I wound the window right down and felt the blissfully cool air on my face. As we climbed up the Sir Lowry Pass I saw the shimmering sea far below us - the huge moon giving the water an opalescent sheen.

Every stand of gum trees we passed had its own personal sound system, thumping out the bass beat of a million cicadas; bats swooped through the darkening sky and white owls sat politely on wire fences waiting for the signal to feed. I must have sighed because Nomatuli nudged me.

'Beautiful, aye? Our Africa?'

Nomatuli fell asleep soon after this. She snored with her mouth wide open, and her head resting on my shoulder. It was getting cooler now and I draped Pete's fleece over us. I held the soft, comforting material against my nose and breathed in. Could that still be his smell?

Somehow I'd survived losing him and we still had Blue Gum. I wasn't rich but I was managing. Greys was a success and the children were happier - even Jeth seemed less angry with me. Yes, things were definitely better. And to cap it all Mum was coming tomorrow. I was so looking forward to seeing her. I still didn't really know what my plans were. I wasn't sure I could continue to live in the same place as Ma Vantonde. Avoiding her for the rest of our lives seemed ridiculous. But I wasn't going to worry about that tonight. Tonight everything seemed possible. And Nomatuli was right, Africa was beautiful - *our Africa*.

It was pitch dark now and I leant across Nomatuli to wind up the window, but as I did so I noticed an orange glow at the horizon. The sun had set ages ago and I rubbed my eyes and looked again. It was still there. Leaning forward I knocked on the glass partition. I wanted to ask the driver what he thought it was but as I did so I dislodged Nomatuli and she woke with a start. I pointed up ahead. She was instantly awake and poked her head out of the window. 'Fire,' she said, as she came back inside. And I heard the fear in her voice.

Then I smelt it too, the unmistakable acrid stench of burning. As we travelled on, the fierce orangey-red line of fire became more substantial until there were individual pillars of flame, shooting high into the night sky.

'Where d'you think it is, Nomatuli?'

'We must pray it is not in Kleinsdorp.' Nomatuli took my hand.

I knew about these summer fires. I'd never experienced a bad one yet but I'd seen the swathes of blackened fynbos and burnt trees, stretching for miles on end.

Pete and I had watched a huge blaze on the mountain behind Blue Gum a few years back. 'The wind's blowing it away from us Kate.' He'd reassured me. 'We're safe but it's going to kill a lot of creatures.' He must have seen my distress because he put his arms around me and hugged me. 'Yeah, I hate it too, but the fynbos needs this regeneration every few years. It's natural.'

And he was right because by the next summer all the vegetation had put out healthy bright green growth and the flowers, when they came, seemed brighter and bigger than ever. After a year, a few blackened tree stumps were the only reminders of the conflagration.

But that was then and this was different; this was close to home, scarily close as it turned out. Approaching the turn-off to Blue Gum there were lines of fire trucks and police cars parked on either side of the road. Fire fighters were unrolling long lengths of hose and helpers were running between the groups of haggard-looking men with food and drink. One man was lying on the grass with an oxygen mask covering his face; several others were having their burns treated. A policeman waved us down.

'Where you headed?'

Our driver pointed to the entrance up ahead. There was a fire-wagon blocking the track. The policeman shook his head. 'No way, man. And we're closing the main road into Kleinsdorp in a few minutes. You'd better get moving.'

I put my head out of the window. 'I'm Kate Vantonde, officer, I live on the farm. Is everybody safe?' I was thanking God that Lilah was with Gloria.

The man nodded. 'Ja, everyone's accounted for. We knew you and the young ones were away.'

'Did Miriam and Rob Taylor get their horses out?'

He nodded and motioned us on.

As I was winding up the window I remembered Spider.

I was distracted after that when a helicopter swooped low overhead, so low we could see the men inside. The machine's searchlights lit up the ground and a red, water carrier swung beneath the fuselage, slopping water out in silver arcs all around us. The helicopter circled and headed for the farm.

I turned to reassure Jeth about Spider. I knew Miriam would have taken the dog with her. But the door on Jeth's side of the car was wide open and he was gone. Jo Jo had been watching the helicopter too and hadn't seen his friend go. I grabbed him before he could jump out after Jeth, slamming the door shut and locking it. Nomatuli held him tight.

I wrenched the door open on my side. 'Keep him with you.'

There was no time to argue.

'Be careful, Kate,' she yelled as I dodged across the road.

'See you in Kleinsdorp,' I shouted back and the driver accelerated away into the angry darkness. Someone called out as I ducked under the barrier and onto the farm track.

The fynbos was alight on both sides of the lane and I hadn't gone more than a few metres before a black fist of choking smoke rushed at me, robbing me of oxygen. I couldn't breathe and I covered my face, gasping for air. Then, just as suddenly as it came, the smoke cleared and I gulped in fresh air. There were pockets of untouched vegetation where the swirling wind had vaulted a space and veered in another direction. I tied the fleece across my nose and hurried on, head down, praying that I would catch up with Jeth soon. But my son was fast and he had a head start on me.

There were men outside Miriam's rondavel. The bakkie and horseboxes were gone and firemen were dousing the already smouldering thatched roof. The men saw me as I stumbled past and one of them broke away to follow me but the others called him back.

311

The helicopter was overhead again, bombing the fire with water. Most of the water missed the rondavel but some of it hit me and the force of it knocked me off my feet. I fell face down in a pool of water. I scrambled to my feet, spitting out bits of burnt vegetation; then I dropped the fleece into the water and draped the soaking coat over my head and across my nose. I could see Blue Gum now. Flames were galloping along our myrtle hedge and a tall pine, beside the house, suddenly exploded, showering me with scorched needles. The bakkie was in flames.

Our front door stood wide open and as I got to it the wind sprang up again and the blazing pine crashed onto our roof. The flames lit up the interior and I saw Jeth, standing in the middle of the room with Spider beside him. He had a heavy bag over his arm.

'For God's sake, Jeth. Run.'

He turned his shocked little face towards me. 'It's coming, Mum. The snake's coming for me.'

I dived in and scooped him up. Outside I tried to pull the bag off his shoulder but he clung to it, so I slung it across my shoulder, catching sight of his telescope and books. Taking his hand we ran back down the track to the road.

Miriam's house was engulfed now and the firemen had retreated. The fire on both sides of the track had joined hands, forming a sheet of flame. It was rushing towards us. There was no way through. We ran back towards our house. Maybe we could get out the other way, where the coral tree was? But this was blocked too. We stumbled around to the back of our house, towards the reservoir. The oak tree was alight. Jeth tripped and fell over and when I picked him up he was holding the swing seat against his chest. 'Leave the bloody thing,' I yelled. Jeth was coughing and choking and I put the damp fleece over his head and pulled him into my side, pressing his face into my clothes. All around us trees and bushes were bursting into flames.

I felt dizzy and nauseous and every breath I took hurt. I was totally disorientated. We were in the middle of a cauldron of fire. There was no way out. I sank to my knees, but Jeth kept pulling on my hand, trying to make me stand up. 'No,' he screamed at me. 'We have to keep running, Mum. The snake will get us if we stop. You mustn't lie down.'

But my legs crumpled beneath me and I was falling. Spider stood beside me whimpering and I put my hand on his muzzle and felt him licking me. Then the darkness came.

Lucky?

Nomatuli got the driver to take her straight to the RDP. She must check on Nandhi. Her cousin was a worthless woman but in times of trouble such things are forgotten. The frightened woman was very relieved to see Nomatuli and immediately agreed to be taken into Kleinsdorp with Jo Jo. She and her children could stay at Greys until Nomatuli returned. Jo Jo was to tell Gloria that Kate and Jeth were making their own way to Kleinsdorp.

'But where will you go, Auntie?' Jo Jo asked, his frightened eyes wide.

'To the squatter camp. The people there cannot speak Afrikaans. Maybe I will speak their language?'

'I could help too, Auntie.'

Nomatuli shook her head, 'No, you must wait in Kleinsdorp and help Kate when she comes. That is your job.'

'But when will she come?'

'Very soon. Okay? Now go.'

He nodded obediently and got into the car with the others. She felt his worried eyes on her as she hurried away.

Nomatuli recognised one of the fire-fighters and hitched a ride on his fire wagon to the camp. The fire was running like a mad dog and no one knew where it would strike next. It had jumped the highway once and could easily jump it again.

It had already engulfed the overspill camp, where hundreds of makeshift homes had been reduced to ashes. They drove past blackened shells of fridges and stoves, standing like sentinels along the razed ground.The sound of exploding gas bottles filled the air, while contorted sheets of corrugated iron lay on the side of the road.

The main squatter camp was in uproar. Firemen were attempting to lay hoses between the shacks but the people were piling their meagre possessions into the narrow alleyways, blocking the way. Two helicopters droned overhead carrying water bombs, but the galloping line of fire was getting nearer and nearer. There were outriders of brown smoke curling along the lanes, clutching at the shacks.

Nomatuli passed a young woman heaving a double mattress outside into the alley. She had a baby tied to her front and a toddler clinging to her legs. She spoke to the mother in Zulu and the girl understood. 'Don't worry, mummy. I will make sure no harm comes to your mattress.' The girl wanted to believe her and when a policeman came to take her to a waiting truck she went willingly.

A line of vehicles waited to take the squatters to safety but many inhabitants were refusing to leave, frightened that their meagre possessions would be looted while they were away. The situation was desperate. Men were losing their tempers and screaming abuse at each other. One young policeman was knocked to the ground as he tried to break up a fight. That was when Nomatuli saw Maarten. He was carrying a little girl towards a transport. Nomatuli waved and he saw her. When the child was safely inside the vehicle he turned a grey, soot-stained face to her. She explained the problem and within minutes he had organised several of the younger men to stay behind as vigilantes. They would only leave the camp if the fire took hold. This did the trick, and at last the evacuation began in earnest.

As they helped and encouraged people to leave the camp Maarten shouted at Nomatuli. 'Are Kate and the kids okay? '

Nomatuli nodded and began to tell him what had happened but her words were drowned out as a helicopter delivered another cache of water and sent it spiralling away over the camp.

'Miriam's been badly hurt.' Maarten shouted back to her. 'She was getting the horses out and a tree fell on the horsebox. She's in hospital. Broken arm and leg. Lucky she wasn't killed.'

But Nomatuli hadn't heard him. She was busy trying to persuade a frail old man to leave his oil stove behind.

At last everyone was evacuated except for the vigilantes. Nomatuli was climbing into the last bakkie when suddenly she remembered Elizabeth. 'Two minutes' she yelled at the impatient driver and ran back up the track. The old woman's shack was empty, so Nomatuli turned and plunged down a side alley – a short cut back to the bakkie. She was almost there when a hand shot out of the darkness and pulled her off her feet and into a shack.

She couldn't see the man but she smelt the beer on his breath. It was Lucky. He shoved her back against the wall, pressing his body against her, trying to kiss her. She twisted her head from side to side, but he placed one arm across her throat and pressed hard, choking her. 'Keep still, Zulu whore, or I will stick you, like the pig you are....' Then he tore at her skirt, trying to pull it up.

She heard someone calling her name but there was nothing she could do about it. Her knees were buckling and Lucky laughed, knowing that he had her at his mercy. . He pressed his face into hers and at that moment a pillar of flame shot high into the sky.

'You get Lucky the sack. Lose his good job with the horses. Think you're too good for Lucky, aye? But I am your master. Lucky teach you,' and she saw his mean little eyes gleaming with triumph

She didn't think, she opened her mouth and bit down. The man screamed and tried to pull away, removing his arm from her throat, but she held on grimly – tasting blood. He clawed at her and she felt a sharp pain on her face, but she wouldn't let go - she would die rather.

Twelve Hours

Every able-bodied man in Kleinsdorp was helping dig firebreaks around the perimeter of the town. The moving front of the fire was estimated to be 30km wide, with winds of up to 70km/h. At the moment the wind was blowing the fire towards the sea but if the wind changed direction, as it had been doing all night, then Kleinsdorp would be in serious danger.

All the cafes were open, providing food and drink for the weary rescue-workers. There were also reporters and television crews waiting for the next fatality. Two people had died already in the overspill camp but the numbers could be much higher. No-one really knew how many illegals lived in these temporary camps. The evacuees were on the town's sports field, where locals were putting up tents and feeding them.

There were rumours and counter rumours about how the fire had started. The favourite theory was that a farmer had been welding a broken irrigation pipe when a spark had ignited the surrounding vegetation. Others thought it had begun nearer to Kleinsdorp. Some suspected arson, while others blamed careless tourists for throwing cigarette butts out of car windows.

When Jo Jo and Nandhi and her family arrived at Greys it was open for business. Gloria, Anne Marie, Rosemary and the girls were all there. The café was packed out with people and when Jo Jo tried to tell the distracted Gloria about Jeth and Kate she was too busy to take it in.

When Nomatuli opened her eyes again she was in a moving vehicle, lying against Maarten, her head on his knee. He held a piece of cloth against her face and when he removed it she saw it was bright with blood.

'I thought you were dead, man.'

She tried to smile, but it hurt too much. 'Take more than that bastard to kill me, Mr Policeman.' She touched her cheek gently and winced. 'He tries to rape me. That little ungrateful bastard Lucky he…' She began to choke and splutter. There was something stuck in the back of her throat. Maarten hit her hard on the back and she spat something into his hand.

It was a round piece of bloody flesh.

'Not so Lucky after all?' Maarten said grimly.

Before passing out Nomatuli said something - something about a mattress?

Maarten took the injured woman to his house and the doctor stitched her wound and gave her a shot. Then Maarten sent for Gloria to look after Nomatuli, while he got on with organising the evacuees. But Gloria was too busy and she sent Jo Jo and Lilah to Maarten's house. They could look after Nomatuli until Maarten returned.

It was only later when the fire had safely by-passed Kleinsdorp that Gloria remembered what Jo Jo had told her about Kate and Jeth. But even then she wasn't unduly worried. The police and rescue services were everywhere so nothing bad could happen to them. But as time went by and there was no news she got more and more concerned. Finally it was she who raised the alarm. Jo Jo was at Maarten's, looking after Nomatuli and Lilah, so he didn't know what was happening. And Maarten was busy finding shelter for the homeless.

By now it was the middle of the night and the fire was still raging on Blue Gum. There was little to be done until the dirty post-apocalyptic dawn broke and Lionel and the rescue-teams could descend on the devastated farm. The fire had moved on by then, leaving behind a smoke-shrouded wasteland.

Nomatuli and Lilah slept soundly through that night, while Jo Jo kept watch.

Early the following morning, Maarten bumped into Gloria. He was on his way to yet another meeting with the town council, who were being difficult about providing more tents for the displaced people. Greys had been open all night and Gloria was buying bread and milk from the Spar when she saw her brother. She ran to him and threw her arms around his neck, weeping into his filthy shirt.

Maarten pushed her away. 'For God's sake, Gloria. Not now.'

His sister stared at him though red-rimmed eyes. 'What's happening, Maarten?'

'We've got a bloody emergency on our hands, Gloria,' Maarten snapped. 'That's what's happening.'

His sister's face flushed. 'Don't you dare shout at me, Maarten Vantonde. They're my family too.'

Maarten stared at her.

'Dear God,' she wailed. 'He's only seven years old.'

Maarten's family was in the kitchen when Maarten burst in. Lionel was slumped at the table. His clothes were black and his hands and face were streaked with soot. Ma sat in a chair opposite him, staring straight ahead. She was wheezing badly. Antoinette held the inhaler to her mother's mouth.

Lionel looked wearily up at his son. 'So? Got time for us now? Saved all of them up there, have you? Bit of a hero?'

'For Chrissake, Dad. Tell me.'

Lionel saw his son's pain and took pity on him. 'The fire came and …they were in it. I think they're… They must be. There's nothing left up there, man. Not a bloody thing.'

'No,' Maarten shook his head. He wouldn't believe it. 'Why didn't somebody help them?'

'Just the question I was going to ask you, Mr Policeman.'

Maarten towered over his father, his fists clenched.

Lionel shut his eyes, all the anger draining away. 'There's nothing to be done, Maarten. We've searched every inch of the place. They're…gone. We've got to face it.'

Maarten closed his eyes.

'God is punishing me,' Ma said suddenly.

'Please Hannah,' Lionel begged. 'No more.'

'I deserve to be punished,' she insisted, nodding her head up and down.

Maarten stared at his mother, missing the look that passed between Lionel and Antoinette. There was only one thought in his head. She was dead. His Kate was dead. He tasted ash in his mouth.

'Take her upstairs, Antoinette.' Lionel said. 'Give her a sedative.'

Antoinette took her mother's arm but the woman pulled away

from her. She tried to push herself up from the chair but she moaned with pain as her hands came into contact with the hard surface. Antoinette pulled her up and led her away. As she went through the door Ma muttered, 'God is punishing me.'

Both men watched her. It was impossible not to.

Maarten couldn't read the look on his sister's face as she shut the door behind them. To anyone else it would have looked like triumph.

Lilah was very happy to be with Jo Jo and help look after Nommy. She liked making Nommy's pillows nice and comfy and tucking her in. She ran out into the garden to pick flowers to make a special potion for sore faces. Stompy Baby came and allowed her to pick him up. She filled the bantam's water bowl then found the cockerel some grain and smoothed his beautiful shiny feathers.

Jo Jo was at the front door watching the activity in the main street. It was a mass of fire wagons, filling up with water from hydrants. There were police cars, civilian vehicles and ambulances everywhere. Exhausted firemen, volunteers and teams from *Work For Fire* clogged the pavements. Some men were lying asleep on the hard ground, oblivious to everything.

Jo Jo felt the town's panic. On either side of the road, inhabitants of Kleinsdorp were cutting down trees and bushes and those with thatched roofs were drenching them with water from the *leiwater* channels that ran alongside many of the houses. Just then Jo Jo heard Lilah coming back into the house and he closed the door quickly.

By the time Maarten got to the farm the fickle fire had taken what it wanted and moved on. The only thing left standing was the gum tree. Maarten parked just off the main road. Lines of exhausted, grim-faced rescue workers trudged past as he went in. Most of them didn't look at him but the one or two he knew shrugged helplessly. One man carried a fused lump of black plastic. He handed it to Maarten. It was the buckled remains of what had once been a telescope.

'Where was it?'

The man pointed to the tree.

'Any sign…any trace of a dog? This high…part ridgeback?'

The man shook his head. 'No dogs. Nothing, man. Look, come home with us, hey? Get some food in you, Maarten. Get some rest. You look God awful.'

Maarten shook his head. 'There has to be something. They can't just …disappear.'

'It was a bloody inferno in there. Everything's been incinerated. Come home.'

Waking Up

It was the smell of toast that woke Nomatuli that morning. The room was full of little pots of flowers that shone out at her. Lilah was perched on the end of the bed stroking the black cockerel.

When the child saw that her friend was awake she ran into the kitchen and came back with Jo Jo, who was carrying a plate of scrambled eggs on toast - Nomatuli's favourite. She was very hungry. When, she was finished she pushed the plate away and turned her attention on the children, who had been sitting, watching her eat.

'Is Auntie feeling better now?' Jo Jo asked.

She nodded and smiled. 'Who would not be better after such a feast? They were the best eggs I have ever tasted, for sure.'

'My hens made them, Nommy,' Lilah said proudly. 'They laid them for you.'

Now Nomatuli had eaten it was time to ask questions. Was the fire gone? Was the squatter camp safe? And the mattress? She'd had such a powerful dream about mattresses and noses. It took her a moment to remember the nose connection – but then she grinned and touched her cheek, tracing her finger down the stitched wound. It was still very sore. Her next question was where was Kate? Had she been here while Nomatuli slept?

Jo Jo didn't have any answers - he had been here all the time, he said. And Kate hadn't been to see them yet. Auntie would be at Blue Gum saving her belongings. That's why Lilah was here. Lilah leant against Nommy, fascinated by her wound.

'Is Maarten helping at Blue Gum?' Nomatuli asked.

The boy nodded.

'Poor Kate,' Nomatuli murmured. 'Now she loses her home. I am a lucky woman, Jo Jo Zono. In fact,' she struggled to sit up. 'I have so much luck I have some for others. But maybe this is my last warning, aye? Maybe it is time to shake the dust of this place off my feet? These people are not my people. They have lost their pride. They walk with their eyes on the dirt and a man who sees only the earth is a worm, aye?' She pushed herself up on her elbows. 'Maybe I shall sell my share in Greys to Kate – maybe become a money-lender, buy a big house in my homeland - near to my bastard husband? I would like that. I would like that very much.'

The boy sighed.

'What?'

He spoke softly, sorrowfully. 'Where do I belong, Auntie? I have no family. I am no one.'

Nomatuli pulled the boy down beside her. 'You, my child, are a star. Remember what Kippie say? He say everyone sends emails and texts and say they love you. Johnny Zono will belong everywhere. Wherever he lays his head.'

She stopped talking then and lay back, caught up in her thoughts.

Later that day she got dressed. She would go to Greys, see Kate, and talk about her plan.

Jo Jo was worried. 'No. You must stay in bed, Auntie. Uncle Maarten said…'

But Nomatuli needed to check that Nandhi wasn't stealing the takings and Gloria wasn't giving all their profits away. There was a limit to Nomatuli's generosity and she knew how soft-hearted their lady chef was.

As the three of them made their way up the main street Lilah skipped ahead. Nomatuli leant on Jo Jo. The town was still full of people and vehicles. When they got to the café it was standing room only. Nomatuli elbowed her way through to the counter, where Anne Marie was serving.

When the woman saw Nomatuli she came and threw her arms around the woman's neck. Then she saw her wound. 'My God, Nomatuli. Did he do that? And to think I liked that Lucky one time.'

'It will heal, Anne Marie. Skin will grow back. Nomatuli will be beautiful again?' And then with a chuckle, 'But noses don't grow back so quick, I think.'

'They have caught him, Nomatuli. That Lucky? It says on the news. He was at the hospital waiting for treatment. It is hard for a man to hide, with a piece missing out of his nose.'

Nomatuli smiled. 'Good, good.' And then she looked around the room. 'So? Where is she?'

'Who?'

'Kate, of course.'

Anne Marie's face fell. 'I...er...Look I have some orders to see to, Nomatuli. I'll get Gloria for you.' She turned and almost collided with Gloria, who was coming out of the kitchen.

The woman was very pale but in control of herself and went straight to Lilah. She kissed her and handed her over to Anne

Marie. 'You go see what Anne Marie's got for you in the kitchen, sweetheart. Auntie Gloria will be with you in a moment.'

Once the child was out of the way Gloria took Nomatuli's arm and led her to a quieter spot. The two women sat down facing each other. Jo Jo stood beside Nomatuli. 'Are you all right, Nomatuli? Your face, it's…'

'…My face is okay. Now tell me quickly. Where is Kate?'

Jo Jo began to sob. Nomatuli pulled him to her and rubbed his tears away with her thumbs. Then she raised his head gently. 'No crying, Jo Jo. Everything is fine.'

He shook his head despairingly 'No, Auntie. Everything is bad.'

Nomatuli looked at Gloria. 'Tell me.'

Gloria took a deep breath. 'On the night of the fire, when you came back from Cape Town?'

'Yes, yes.'

'You went up to the camp to help your people and Kate went after Jeth? Well…she never came back, Nomatuli …neither of them did.' That was where Gloria's courage failed her. 'Oh my God. That poor little boy…'

'…No.' Nomatuli crashed her fist down on the table. People stopped what they were doing and stared. Nomatuli glared at Gloria. 'It's a lie. Tell me it's a lie.'

Gloria shook her head in despair.

'Stupid woman,' Nomatuli raged. 'Stupid, stupid woman. They are not dead.' Then she crashed out of the café, knocking over chairs and colliding with people as she went.

Gloria dried her eyes and took a deep breath. Then she went back into the kitchen, to see Lilah. She had remembered something very important. She took the child on her knee and smoothed the fine curly hair out of the little girl's eyes. 'Who wants to come and meet Grandma at Cape Town airport?'

Lilah's little face lit up. 'Me, me,' she squealed, jumping down and pulling Gloria towards the door.

No one noticed Jo Jo slipping out of the café. He didn't follow the black woman. He ran in the opposite direction, out of Kleinsdorp, taking the track across the still-smouldering fields towards Blue Gum.

Nomatuli was looking for Maarten. He would know what to do. She'd been to the deserted police station and now she was at the Vantonde house. She walked straight in and found Lionel standing at the kitchen sink, his back to her.

'Where's Maarten?' she demanded.

Lionel was filling the kettle. There were several cups of tea on the table already, their surfaces wrinkled with scum.

Nomatuli touched his shoulder and he looked at her.

'She likes tea,' he said. 'We must be ready for her.'

'Please, Lionel.' Nomatuli shook him gently. 'I must find Maarten. D'you know where he is?'

'You've hurt yourself.'

Nomatuli's hand drifted to her face. 'I have to speak to Maarten. It's urgent.'

The man's forehead puckered as he tried to think. 'He was going…up there, last time I saw him. I told him it was no use.' Lionel took a shuddering breath. 'They're gone.'

'No. That is not possible. They are alive,' she said, challenging the man to disagree with her. 'And now you will drive me to Blue Gum,' she ordered, going to the door. 'Come. We must hurry.'

The Hole

Nomatuli stared about her. Everything was different. This fire-blasted landscape was as unfamiliar to her now as it had been the first time she walked onto Blue Gum, a year ago now. But back then the sun had been fierce and she was forced under her umbrella. Gaudy orange and red proteas had decorated each side of the track and Cape sugarbirds plunged from flower to flower drinking the nectar. The air had been full of the thrumming of cicadas, the muffled calls of collared doves and the droning of bees, while all around her the sweet smell of flowers, wild thyme and pine needles drifted in the air.

Now there was nothing. No colour but the funereal blacks, browns and greys of incineration. No sound, except for the wind shuffling the charred vegetation and the occasional *hiss* as moisture found a still burning pocket of foliage. No smells, but the stink of cooked cabbage hanging sickly in the air and the sulphurous stench of burning that stuck in the back of her throat, like a gag.

The mountains, the main road and the sky were cloaked in drifting dirty-brown smog. The track had dissolved into an amorphous mass of smouldering pulp. The woman's eyes watered and she took a sip of water, rinsed her mouth and spat it out. Then she moistened her bandanna and tied it across her nose and mouth, flinching as she caught the lip of the wound.

She took a tentative step forwards and saw the outline of the farm gate - miraculously intact - and beside it a small half-burnt tree.

Now she knew where she was and she plunged on, into the smog. The smoke whirled away for a moment and, in that space, she saw the gum tree directly ahead of her. It was still standing and one sound branch stuck out in desperate bravado. The scarred trunk was ghostly in the murky light. Oily frizzled leaves littered the scorched earth beneath it, like layers of dirty confetti.

She stared in disbelief at what remained of the house. The ground was strewn with blackened building debris, contorted corrugated iron, and twisted metal and charred paper. It was as if the fire had picked the books up to read and tossed them away, tearing pages out at random and scattering them. Something white shone up at her from the pile of embers and she picked up an abalone shell.

The myrtle hedge that had once surrounded the house was gone, except for a few random blackened twigs. The woman made her way into the back garden where fir-trees had exploded leaving blasted stumps, and the banana and bamboo groves were toasted into crisp roasted seaweed, giving off a strange exotic smell. The wind was erratic and squalls of blackened debris spiralled about her. The old oak tree had been totally engulfed and lay on its side - the huge tortured trunk split and still smouldering.

She was almost at the reservoir when she stopped and cupped her ears. After a moment she hurried on, kicking up clouds of hot cinders. Her hands were blistered, from where she'd beaten out glowing embers from her clothes, but she felt no pain. All her senses were concentrated on one thing. That sound.

Grasping the still smouldering bushes she climbed the reservoir bank. The water tower was destroyed and blackened timbers littered the top of the bank. Dead fish and frogs were strewn across the fire-baked reservoir and near the shoreline lay the pathetic feathered bundles of dead Blue cranes and Hadeda ibis.

But the woman wasn't looking at the birds. She was listening.

Tearing the cloth away from her mouth she tried to shout but she had no spit. 'Spider? Spider?' she croaked. 'Come. Come.' Then she clapped her hands repeatedly, louder and louder and waited. No response. She clapped again, bringing her hands together like the two sides of a coconut shell. The noise cracked across the landscape and this time there was something – a sound, very soft and faint but definitely there. The woman fell to her knees and tore at the burnt bushes. 'Good boy.' she urged. 'Come to Nomatuli, come.'

She began to scratch out a small hollow in the fired earth but it was set like concrete and her fingers were soon raw and bleeding. Every few minutes she sat back and shouted and at last there was the slightest of movements within the small excavation. A plug of blackened earth fell away exposing the soft inner red soil - like a raw wound. Now it was easier to dig she was able to widen the opening. When at last the entrance was big enough she lay down and pushed her arm into the hole, stretching her long fingers until they cracked. There was something there and it was moving. Withdrawing carefully she sat back on her haunches and waited.

'Good boy,' Nomatuli encouraged. 'Good boy.'

The earth-caked creature crawled slowly towards her on his belly, tail tucked between his legs, moaning with joy. When the dog was fully out of the hole he pulled himself unsteadily to his feet and retched and retched, bringing up gouts of red earth. His eyes were sealed shut with mud. Nomatuli moistened her cloth and cleared the muck away. Then she made a pouch in the material and poured some water into it, holding it to the dog's mouth.

He lapped the water slowly, swallowing painfully, and when at last he was ready she put her arms about his neck and whispered. 'Where are they? Show me, boy. Show me.' And he rested his heavy head on her hand and stared at her through sad, bloodshot eyes.

No One Here

Maarten had no idea how long he'd been asleep but when he opened his eyes it was almost dark. He had a painful delve on the side of his forehead, where he'd slumped forwards onto the steering wheel. Cursing himself he reached for his water bottle. His throat was raw and he drank and drank.

What was he doing in the bakkie anyway? He tried to remember. He'd come back to get a spade and some ropes. It was something to do – just in case - but he must have fallen asleep. He couldn't remember how many days had passed since he'd slept. Two? Three?

He sensed there was something different, something important, but his sleep-fuddled brain refused to work it out. Gazing out at the sky he saw the evening star. Of course, that was it. The pall of smoke had lifted. He could see lights from the town and car headlights moving steadily along the main road between Hermanus and Kleinsdorp. There was another light too, flashing red on his dashboard. Maarten had left his mobile charging. He picked it up. There was a message.

His big fingers were trembling so much he couldn't hit the buttons. 'Uncle Maarten? Uncle Maarten?' The voice was faint but it was unmistakably Jeth's. Maarten switched on the car's interior light and read the time on the message. 6 p.m. today. Only two hours ago. He almost dropped the phone as he dialled the number. He swore as he got the wrong one. *Please, please, please,* he prayed, as the right number finally rang. A metallic voice came back at him. *The person you are trying to ring is not available. Please leave your message after the tone.* He made himself stay calm, it didn't mean they were dead. Maybe the phone had run out of juice? Or there was no signal?

He grabbed the spade and ran back up the track towards Blue Gum. As he pounded along he saw someone moving up ahead of him. It was a slight figure – the figure of a child. He shouted but whoever it was kept running. He caught up with Jo Jo by the tree. The boy was very frightened until he recognised who it was.

'Jeth sent me a message, Jo Jo. On the mobile. They must be alive. Is there somewhere they could be? Somewhere they could have sheltered from the fire?'

'There is a place, uncle, up by the reservoir.'

'The den?'

Jo Jo was already running and Maarten crashed after him. He shouted into his mobile as he ran, calling for back-up.

Arrivals

Arrivals was almost deserted and Maggie checked her watch again. Maybe she'd given Kate the UK time? The hour difference always threw her. She'd give them a few more minutes and then she'd ring Kate's mobile.

She sat down on one of the chrome seats that looked so beautiful but were incredibly uncomfortable. A coloured woman and little girl sat beside her. The child spotted Maggie's handbag and immediately wanted it.

'No, Lavanne,' the child's mother scolded, pulling the struggling child away.

'It's okay,' Maggie smiled. Hitching the little girl up beside her. 'She can play with it. She's a sweetie. How old is she?'

'Nearly two,' the woman replied.

'It's a lovely age. If you've got the strength.'

The woman laughed. 'That's the truth.'

As soon as the child was up on the chair she wanted to get down again.

'Kids, hey?' The mother said putting her arms around her daughter's chubby legs and holding the squirming child firmly against her. 'You waiting for someone?'

Maggie nodded. 'My daughter and grandchildren.'

'Nice.'

'They live here. Near Hermanus.'

'Having a holiday?'

'An extended holiday. I'm thinking of selling up in the UK and coming out here to live.'

Maggie had no idea why was she was telling this woman her business. She hadn't mentioned it to anyone yet. She wasn't even sure it was a good idea. Kate might not want her for one thing.

'What about you?' Maggie asked.

'Lavanne's daddy. He's flight crew - British. We're thinking of going to the UK to live. Quite a coincidence, hey?'

'Won't you miss the climate?'

'No way. I hate the heat and that wind?' She made a face. 'It never stops. I've been to the UK loads of times. I'd move tomorrow.'

At that moment the doors whirred open and a short fair woman with a little blonde girl hurried inside.

'Gloria.' Maggie stood up and waved. 'Over here.'

'Good luck,' the woman said.

'You too.'

Lilah ran straight for her Grandma and Maggie bent down and lifted her up. Lilah clasped her arms tightly around her Grandma's neck, nearly throttling her. Maggie smiled at Gloria over the child's head.

'Lovely to see you. This is so kind of you. Was Kate too busy to come?'

Gloria put a warning finger to her lips and pointed at Lilah.

The women didn't speak again until they were well on their way to Hermanus. Gloria took the scenic coast road that hugged the base of the steep mountainside. The moon and stars were incredibly bright over the water.

Lilah talked for all of them. Maggie had never heard her granddaughter say so much. Words poured out of the little girl. Most of it was incomprehensible to Maggie but Lilah carried on regardless.

'…and Grandma, did you know?' The little girl's eyes were wide with excitement. 'Nommy has a cut right down her face. It's like this,' and she traced a zigzag pattern down Maggie's cheek. 'We did scrambled eggs for Nommy and I made a very special potion to make her better. And Uncle Maarten had dirt on his face. I saw three big fire engines, Granny. They had big tubes full of water and the puddles were this big.' And she made her arms go as wide as they could. 'And I helped Auntie Gloria. We made cakes and lots and lots and lots of people came and ate up all the food. They were all shouting. And then Jo Jo and Nommy went somewhere. That's when we came to find you.'

The sheer weight of those words exhausted the little girl and she sat back, snuggled into Maggie and closed her eyes. Within moments she was breathing deeply and rhythmically.

Maggie could bear it no longer. 'What's happened, Gloria?'

Gloria kept on driving. 'Hang on a minute, Maggie.' There were places to stop and admire the view all along this road and she steered into one of them and turned the engine off.

Maggie gently disengaged Lilah, lay her down on the back seat, and got in beside Gloria.

'We can't be long,' Gloria said, not looking at Maggie. 'But I couldn't drive and talk, I'd have crashed.' She attempted a smile but her face collapsed. 'Oh my God, Maggie. What are we going to do?' She tried to cry silently, she didn't want to wake Lilah, but she couldn't prevent the hiccupping sobs that escaped. 'I'm sorry, I'm so sorry.'

Maggie fought the impulse to shake the stupid hysterical woman till her teeth rattled but she put her hand on Gloria's shoulder instead and squeezed gently. 'Please, Gloria. Whatever's happened, I need to know.'

Gloria pushed the hair out of her eyes and clung onto Maggie's hand. 'There's been a terrible fire, Maggie. A real bad one. And, and… Kate and Jeth…we can't find them.'

The Den

Nomatuli took a gulp of clean, cool air and stared up at the stars, thanking God that the choking smoke had finally lifted. The moon was very bright now and she could see what she was doing. She was carefully scrapping earth from the tunnel entrance. Her brain screamed *hurry, hurry* but the soil was soft and she was frightened that the excavation might cave in at any moment. She had used timber from the water tower to shore up the sides of the hole but the wood had crumbled into charcoal.

The pile of excavated soil beside her was pitifully small. Sitting back on her haunches she wiped the sweat out of her eyes. Spider pawed her leg, reminding her he was still there. Nomatuli was light-headed from tiredness and her wound was throbbing horribly but she didn't stop digging. How long could they survive buried in soft earth? How long before they suffocated? Every few minutes she called out their names and then listened, but there was no response.

The rescue workers had all gone home. She'd heard them calling out to each other as they made their way back down the track to the road. She'd shouted but no one heard her. She needed help but if she walked back to Kleinsdorp now it might be too late for Kate and Jeth. How stupid to have come without her mobile. Now, all she could do was dig and pray.

If you save them Lord I will stay here and help Kate and never call my bastard husband a bastard any more. I swear.

Resuming work she leant into the hole and her fingers brushed against something hard. A rock maybe. She picked up the object. It was small and slippery to the touch - a mobile phone. She switched it on but it was dead.

At that moment Spider dragged himself to a sitting position. He was staring back towards the track and Nomatuli saw two shapes coming towards her through the gloom. One had a torch. The dog's tail lashed her leg.

'I am here,' she croaked. 'Come quickly. We must dig.'

Jo Jo dropped down beside her and she saw the large figure behind him.

'Spider was here and I think they are too.' She handed Maarten the phone. 'I found this. I have shouted and shouted but no one is answering.'

Maarten took her place beside the hole. He set to work with his spade. There was only room for one person to dig and Nomatuli sank back. .

'Give Nomatuli some water, Jo Jo. It's in the pack.'

Jo Jo did as he was told and then he disappeared over the lip of the reservoir. Spider went with him. After a few seconds the boy's voice came back to them. 'That is the backdoor, uncle. This is the front door. Come. I will show you.'

Maarten and Nomatuli scrambled up the bank. Jo Jo was amongst the burnt undergrowth on the edge of the reservoir. Maarten held the torch so that the boy could see what he was doing. After a few minutes Jo Jo turned his distressed face to them. 'It is changed. Everything has changed.'

Maarten slid down the bank to stand beside him. 'Okay, Jo Jo. Close your eyes. Now think, what was it like before, hey? Imagine that first day you found the hole. Tell me what it looked like.'

The boy's voice was strong and clear. 'We were looking for the great grand-daddy tortoise, uncle. Jeth said he lived in a hole in this bank. I told him, this is not possible. Tortoises do not live in holes but he said he would show me.'

With his eyes still tight shut Jo Jo pointed towards the bank. 'There is a big tree heather here, so huge it is like a proper tree and you can shelter from the sun beneath it. But when it rains the puff adder, which lives here, climbs to the top and lies out in the sun to dry. Here there is a pile of white stones and a little tortoise skull sits on the top. Jethro found that. Then between these two there is a giant aloe. It has big razor teeth down the edges and you must be careful, or it will cut your legs and arms into little pieces. Underneath this plant, just to one side there is an opening, big enough for us to wriggle through. It is a safe place. That is our den, uncle.' He opened his eyes again.

Maarten was swinging the torch backwards and forwards and they all saw something gleaming white in the spotlight. Nomatuli picked up a small tortoise skull.

Jo Jo kicked over some blackened stones, exposing their white underbellies. Spider was hoovering up the scent in the blackened vegetation. Maarten sliced through the skeletal bushes with his spade.

Nomatuli was on her knees again tearing at the scrub, when suddenly she let out a screech and held up her hand. Maarten turned his torch on her and illuminated the nasty gash on the side of her hand. Nomatuli's teeth flashed in the torchlight. 'I have found the aloe.'

'JETH?' Jo Jo's voice ripped through the darkness.

'KATE. KATE?' Nomatuli shrieked at the top of her voice.

And there was an answering sound. They held their breath and the hairs along Spider's back quivered. Then the noise came again. It was a voice, a child's voice. Maarten forced his bulky shoulders through the bush and into the opening but some of the surrounding earth gave way. Nomatuli and Jo Jo grabbed him and he backed out, breathing heavily. He shone the torch into the densest part of the twisted branches.

'There's something there.'

Nomatuli and Jo Jo crouched down beside him and they all peered inside. The torchlight picked out something white at the back of the hole. Jo Jo ducked down and wriggled into the space.

Within moments the boy crawled out again clutching a plank of wood. He turned it over. *This swing belongs to Jethro. Keep off!* Before they could stop him Jo Jo was back in the hole. 'Jeth is here,' he yelled after a moment. 'I can touch him.'

They heard the voice again, soft and pleading, and Jo Jo's response. 'You can do it. Please, give me your hand, Jeth. Uncle and auntie are here. We will pull you out. But you must give me your hand.'

Maarten lay full length on the ground and reached into the hole, grasping Jo Jo's ankles. 'When he gives you his hand, Jo Jo, hold onto him and I will pull you both out. But be very careful, okay? '

Nomatuli was on her knees beside Maarten muttering prayers.

Burnt Hands

'Stop here,' Maggie ordered as they approached the turn off to the farm. She was totally in control of herself again. No one was going to tell her that Kate and Jeth were dead.

'I can't, Maggie,' Gloria begged. 'It's dark, how would you find your way? All the paths are burnt out. Please, stay with me…'

'…Have you got a torch?'

'Yes but…'

Maggie was already searching in the glove compartment.

Gloria drove on doggedly but Maggie yanked open the door, preparing to jump.

'No, please,' Gloria screamed. 'I'll stop. Don't jump.' The car swerved off the road and skidded to a halt, throwing up a wave of gravel. Gloria was shaking. 'Oh my God, Maggie. You could have been killed.'

Maggie was out of the car and walking quickly away.

'I'll get someone to pick you up at the other exit.' Gloria shouted after her. 'The Kleinsdorp entrance? Please, Maggie. Be careful.' Gloria waited until the pinprick of light from Maggie's torch disappeared and then she reversed back onto the road. Amazingly, Lilah was still asleep.

By the time Gloria reached Kleinsdorp it was deserted. The fire had by-passed the town and the rescue services, ambulances, fire wagons and media had moved on. The squatter camp was safe and many of the people had returned to their homes. Gloria found Anne Marie and the others at Greys. She helped them to shut up the café. Nandhi and family had already gone back to their house. .

There was only one light on in the Vantonde house as Gloria parked outside. It was in her parent's bedroom. She carried the sleeping child indoors and laid her gently on the settee, covering her with a rug and kissing her on her forehead. She hoped her father was home, he'd know what to do. Someone had to go to Blue Gum and look for Maggie. She would stay here with Lilah. Suddenly she was so tired. It was as much as she could do to climb the stairs.

When she tapped softly on the door there was no answer. 'Dad, are you awake?' She knocked again, louder this time. 'Dad, please. I need to speak to you.'

The door opened a crack. 'For God's sake, keep your voice down,' Antoinette snapped

'Where's Dad?'

Antoinette attempted to close the door but Gloria jammed her foot in it and shoved. The door swung inwards and she fell into the room.

The first thing Gloria saw as she scrambled up was her mother. She was sitting on the edge of the bed in her nightdress. She cradled her hands against her chest. They were shiny and red and cracked. They must have hurt terribly. Gloria took a step towards her mother, 'Ma? What have you done?' The woman looked at Gloria but she didn't see her. Her head bobbed up and down, up and down. 'I must be punished,' she told her, attempting to stand up, but Antoinette pushed her back down.

'I told you, Ma, you're staying there. Now lie down.'

Ma did as she was told and Antoinette tucked her in. Now, all Gloria could see were Ma's small eyes peeping over the blankets and her claw-like hands resting on the counterpane.

'Close your eyes, Ma,' Antoinette ordered.

When Antoinette was sure that her mother was settled she grabbed her sister's arm and pushed the astonished woman outside.

'My God, Antoinette?' Gloria gasped, 'what happened to her hands?'

Antoinette shrugged. 'She had an accident.'

'What sort of accident?'

'It doesn't matter. What d'you want?'

And then Gloria remembered why she was there. 'Where's Dad? And have you seen Maarten? I've got Lilah downstairs and Maggie's on the farm searching for Jeth and Kate. I tried to stop her but…it's all such a horrible mess,' her courage failed her then and she was weeping again. 'What are we going to do, Antoinette?'

'For God's sake, Gloria. Don't you ever stop snivelling? This isn't pretty fluffy angel time. Welcome to shitty life. You want to know where Lionel is? Well? So do I? He walked out this evening and I don't know where he is. So, I'm in charge of her,' and she jabbed her thumb at the bedroom door.

'Poor Ma,' Gloria sobbed. 'She loves Jeth so much.'

'"Poor Ma?"' Antoinette snarled. 'You really want to know how she burnt her hands, little sister?'

'Was she up there? At Blue Gum? Searching for them?'

Antoinette smiled. 'She was at the farm for sure. But she wasn't there to help. Quite the reverse as it happens. She disappeared on Sunday night, soon as they all left for Cape Town with the black kid?

345

You could tell something was brewing. She had that look. You know? She ranted on about Kate and the black woman and the kid, and then suddenly she was gone. Lionel was thinking about organising a search party when in she staggers with her hands all burnt. She must have walked back from Blue Gum because Lionel found the bakkie up there with an upturned can of petrol on the track. The fire was already out of control. He was the one who raised the alarm.'

Gloria stared at her sister. 'What are you saying?'

'Our mummy is an arsonist and a murderess, Gloria. That's what I'm saying. Understand? Or shall I pack it up in a pretty little parcel for you? Stuck with sequins and glitter?'

'She started the fire? Our mother? '

'That's the one, Gloria. Our mumsy.'

'It's not true. You're making it up. You've always hated her.'

'True.'

'She wouldn't, she couldn't do anything like that. It's not possible. People have died Antoinette...and Jeth and Kate might be ...' She couldn't go on.

Antoinette touched her sister's arm briefly, almost gently. 'It's the truth, I promise you. Sorry. Shame you had to be born into this family, hey?' She opened the bedroom door and the pinkish glow from the bedside lamp warmed her white face, giving unnatural colour to her cheeks. She smiled at Gloria and said in a quiet, resigned voice, 'You do what you have to, Gloria, but don't involve me, ja? I don't care what happens to any of you...or me.'

'So why are you looking after her then?' Gloria managed, before the door shut. 'If you don't care? Um?'

'Oh I owe her this one, Gloria. I definitely owe her.' And then the door shut softly. .

346

Red Snake

The track had disappeared and Maggie had to fight her way through waist-high burnt vegetation. There were potholes, disguised beneath rafts of incinerated plants, and several times she fell headlong into the undergrowth. She was heading for what remained of the blue gum tree. Its pathetic blackened trunk was spotlighted in the bright moonlight. It shone like a beacon. If she could just get to it then maybe everything would be okay.

She stared at what remained of Kate's house. Mounds of smouldering blackened bricks littered the ground, interspersed with charred material and burnt paper that shifted and sighed in the light wind. The outline of the burnt-out stove and fridge stuck out from the debris and she saw the contorted skeletons of Kate's bakkie and Renault. She shivered. She was suddenly very cold. This was real; not some hysterical exaggeration from Gloria. And if this was possible maybe that other unspeakable thing was possible too? She looked frantically about her. Where could they be? Where could they hide from devastation like this?

That's when she heard voices and, scrambling through the remains of the house, she emerged in what was once the back garden. The voices were stronger here and she ran towards them.

'Kate? Is that you? Kate? Answer me.'

Nomatuli rose out of the darkness and grasped Maggie's hand. She showed no surprise at Maggie's sudden appearance and took her to where Maarten lay at the bottom of the bank. Maggie crouched beside him and he turned his anguished face towards her.

'We've found Jeth,' he said. 'We think Kate must be there too but Jeth won't come out. He's frightened - something about a snake. Jo Jo's talking to him but if Jeth panics, the whole bank might collapse.' He called softly, urgently. 'Jo Jo?' And the boy wriggled out.

'Let me try,' Maggie said, taking Jo Jo's place. 'Jeth? Can you hear me? It's Grandma. Come out, sweetheart.'

'Grandma?' Jeth's frightened voice rasped back painfully. 'The red snake's coming. It's going to get me, Grandma. It's going to eat me.'

'No, Jeth. It's dead, I promise you.'

'I can feel its hot breath on my neck.'

'We're all here. We won't let anything hurt you.'

'It crushed our oak tree, Grandma. I heard it screaming and now it wants me.'

'No, it's gone. I promise.'

'But...'

'I promise you Jeth. Now come out. Please. I need you.' She stretched her arm inside the hole and after, what felt like an eternity, she felt his small sweaty hand curl around hers, grasping her fingers. 'Good boy. Now, slowly, Jeth. I've got you.'

Maarten knelt beside her and when he was able to he took Jeth's other hand and they pulled the child out together.

Maggie gathered the boy against her. His clothes were burnt but he seemed unhurt. He gulped in great lungfuls of air, while his frightened eyes darted everywhere. 'It's really gone, Grandma?'

'Of course,' Maggie said. 'It's never coming back.'

Jo Jo brought water for his friend and held it to his lips.

Jeth had an old damp coat wrapped around his shoulders and Maggie untied it. It was Pete's fleece. 'Oh my God, Kate,' she whispered. 'Please.'

Maarten helped her and Jeth to a bank where Jo Jo and Nomatuli joined them. They sat close, their arms linked about each other. Maarten stood in front of them and smiled down at Jeth, his eyes bright with tenderness.

Maggie stroked the boy's spiky dirty hair. 'You are such a brave boy, Jeth.'

Spider came and Jeth rested his hand on the dog's head.

'Good boy, Spider,' he croaked. 'You told Nomatuli where we were.'

'This dog will have the biggest bone in Kleinsdorp,' Nomatuli promised.

The boy tried to smile. 'I heard you shouting, Nomatuli. It made me happy. Because you would find Spider and look after him.'

Maarten knelt beside Jeth. He tried to keep his voice steady. 'Is she in there? Jeth? Is your mum in there?'

Maggie held her breath

Jeth nodded but his lips were trembling and tears glistened on his cheeks. 'I hurt her, Grandma. She was so heavy for me to pull and there was fire and smoke everywhere. She got burnt. Her face...' He stopped, unable to go on.

Maggie held him closer.

He took a deep breath and continued. 'It's not too big in our den. Is it, Jo Jo? But she didn't cry. She was so brave. I talked to her all the time but I think she's sleeping now.'

Nomatuli sprang up and pointed back towards the house. Several vehicles were parking and their headlights lit up the gum tree. They could hear men's voices. 'Run, Jo Jo, go tell them we are here.'

Maarten was already back at the hole digging. He shouted over his shoulder. 'Tell them to bring spades and lights.'

There was an ambulance with the rescue workers and the Paramedics examined Jeth. They gave him some oxygen but they thought he was okay. They wanted to take him to hospital but he refused to leave. He got in such a state about it that they left him alone.

So, he and his Grandma, Nomatuli, Jo Jo and the dog sat with blankets wrapped around them, and watched while Maarten and the men did their job.

Arc lights were set up. The threat of a landslip meant it was too dangerous to use mechanical diggers, so they used spades and dug out from the front of the bank, putting in props as they advanced.

At last someone shouted. 'We've got her.' And they all ran to where Maarten stood holding Kate in his arms. Her head lolled to one side and her arms and legs were limp. Her eyes were closed and her face was blackened. One side of her face was covered in livid blistered burns. Maggie held her lifeless hands in hers as they hurried her to the ambulance. Maarten's eyes were bright with hope. 'You go in the ambulance with her, Maggie. I'll follow behind.'

But Maggie saw Jeth's face and knew she couldn't leave him. 'No, you go Maarten. I'll go with the others. Ring as soon as you have any news.'

He squeezed her hand and was gone.

The ambulance drove off and they heard the siren start up as the vehicle got out onto the main road and headed for Hermanus. The rescue workers took them back to Kleinsdorp and on the way they passed a man weaving about in the middle of the road.

'Bloody drunk,' the driver said, but he pulled up anyway, to see if the man needed help. It was Lionel.

Gloria sat downstairs by the telephone. She had only put on one small lamp and it lit up Lilah's blond hair as she lay fast asleep. Gloria had tried to ring Maarten and Lionel but neither was answering and now all she could do was wait. She tried not to think.

Every few minutes she went outside and looked up and down the street. She'd be able to see if Maarten came home, or if anyone was at Greys. After the frantic last few days Kleinsdorp's main street was eerily deserted. Paper bags and discarded hoses littered the pavements and feral cats foraged amongst the piles of food debris. All the houses were in darkness and the few street lights seemed dimmer than usual. One flickered on and off and made a buzzing sound.

At last several vehicles turned into the street and stopped outside the café. Gloria saw people get out and go inside. By the time the vehicles drove away she was bundling Lilah into the car.

The Paying of Debts

Kate was rushed into intensive care at the hospital. After an interminable wait Maarten was told that she was on a ventilator and that her condition was stable. The hospital was full of victims from the fire and the waiting areas were thronged with relatives. There were no chairs and he stood up against the wall and filled in forms. It was something to do. Kate didn't have med-care but he did.

When he was finished he handed the paperwork over to a young receptionist. 'This is my second double shift this week,' she complained, breathing her tired, stale breath in his face.

'Well. It's an emergency, hey?' He muttered, trying to keep his temper. 'People have died...'

'...You, next of kin?' she interrupted, talking to the wall behind him.

'I'm Kate's brother-in-law.'

She pointed at the place where he should sign. 'The patient's next of kin has to sign here.'

'Her name is Kate Vantonde.'

She waited.

He signed.

'You can go home now.' She said, dismissing him. 'Nothing's going to happen tonight. Ring the hospital tomorrow morning.'

He turned to go.

'Not before ten.'

Her voice followed him down the corridor and out into the cool night air. He could still smell burning.

They were all in the apartment above Greys. Lilah had been delighted to wake up and find her brother there. Maggie sat with her arms around them both. Jeth snuggled against her, eyelids drooping, fighting the urge to sleep. Jo Jo and Lilah were asleep already but Jeth had to know what Uncle Maarten said about his mum.

'But is she going to be okay?' Gloria had asked the same question over and over.

'She's on a ventilator, Gloria.' Maarten was fighting to keep control of himself.

'The good Lord will care for her.' Nomatuli's voice was strong.

Someone was crying. Maggie looked to where Lionel sat, hunched. His shoulders were heaving. Gloria sat beside him, her hands covering his. 'Shh, Dad, it's going to be all right. Why don't I take you home? Umm? Ma must be so worried about you. And she'll want to know about Jeth won't she? That's such good news. It will make her happy.' She had decided not to believe what Antoinette had told her.

Lionel looked at his daughter. There were tears running down his face.

No one should see their father cry. Gloria couldn't bear it.

Maggie heard a chair being scraped back.

'Come on, Dad.' Maarten again. 'I'll drop you off at home. I'm going back to the hospital.'

'But they told you not to ring until the morning.'

Maarten ignored his sister and helped his father to his feet. 'Come on, Dad.'

'I'm coming with you, Maarten.' Maggie rose carefully, not wanting to dislodge Jeth, who had finally given in to sleep.

'But you need to rest, Maggie, and so do you, Maarten.' Gloria sounded desperate.

Maarten rounded on her. 'For God's sake, Gloria. Stop bloody fussing.'

When they had gone Nomatuli squeezed Gloria's hand. 'They will watch over Kate and we will watch over the children, aye?'

The two women made up beds and settled the children. Gloria was glad to be doing something practical. When they'd finished, Nomatuli raided the café and made a meal for them.

Gloria couldn't eat. She felt sick. She didn't know what to do about Ma. Of course she thanked God that Jeth was saved and Kate was out of that hole but what was going to happen to Ma? Had she really done that dreadful thing? They thought the final death toll might be in the high teens. It wasn't real. It couldn't be. She wouldn't believe it. Her mother had deliberately started a fire? Impossible.

'You okay, Lady Chef?' Nomatuli asked suddenly, her fork halfway to her mouth. 'You look as if you carry the world on your shoulders. It is putting me off my food.'

'Sorry.'

'We are all worried, my friend.'

'But this is something terrible, Nomatuli. And I don't know what to do about it.'

There was a chink of light showing from his mother's bedroom as Maarten drew up outside the Vantonde house. He left the engine running and waited for Lionel to get out.

Lionel's hand was on the door handle but he didn't move.

'Dad?' Maarten urged him. 'I need to go.'

'Yes, son, I know, but...can you come in for a minute? See how she is? Please.'

Maarten sighed and turned off the engine. 'Won't be long, Maggie.'

He led the way quickly up the darkened stairs.

'If she's asleep we won't wake her,' Lionel whispered.

Maarten opened the bedroom door quietly. The small lamp made a pool of light in the darkened room and in the dim light it looked as if the two women were sleeping. Lionel was already backing out when Maarten rested a hand on his shoulder and pointed to an empty upturned bottle of pills on the bedside table.

Lionel groaned and lurched towards the bed. 'Hannah. What have you done?'

There was a bottle of sherry and an empty glass beside the pill bottle. Antoinette's hand hung over the side of the bed and a beer bottle lay just beyond the reach of her lifeless long fingers. The seeping brown liquid was forming a widening pool of beer on the carpet.

Ma lay exactly as Gloria had left her earlier that evening, her red, shiny, burnt hands lying on her chest and the covers drawn up to her chin. Antoinette was fully dressed. She lay with her back to her mother. Her long black hair had been brushed out and lay in a shiny arc about her on the pillow. Her skin was so white it shone out in the dark. Her eyes were open.

Coming Home

There is no wind noise here, no cicadas or frogs calling from the vlei; no Lilah snufflings or dog's claws *scrit scratching* on the floor circling in preparation for sleep. The only sound is a pulsing muffled beat.

The blackness, the taste of earth and smoke has gone and I am in a goldfish bowl of bright, white light. Red and blue threaded veins pulse jellyfish-like across my eyelids. My throat is raw, as if a red-hot poker has been rammed down it, and every breath I take is agony. I have no spit to swallow with and my lips form a crust against my swollen mouth. My cramped body stretches and spreads - a tree's roots searching for water. My arms lie crucified beside me, palms upwards.

There are voices there too - disembodied voices. 'There's a good girl, Kate. Take a deep breath.'

I obey and the coolness douses the fire in the back of my throat.

'Open your eyes.'

No.

'Please, open your eyes, Kate.' A man's voice, warm, deep and muffled like a funeral drum-beat. 'Please, Kate.'

Stop saying my name. I want to sleep. I must sleep.

'We are sitting you up now, Kate. Open your eyes.'

No.

'Don't let her sleep.'

'Kate? It's me. Mum. I love you.'

Mum?

'Please, Kate, look at me.'

I can't.

'There's someone to see you, someone very special.'

And a small, sticky hand explores my palm. My finger ends twitch and come to life but my other hand lays empty, forgotten, a block of flesh – ready to separate and drift away. But then I feel a fist resting on my flesh, like a cool round shell, and I close my hand about it.

Jeth?

'Everything's going to be fine, Mum.'

And that's when I open my eyes.

Beginnings

They were pleased with my progress in the hospital and it wasn't long before I was discharged. They're hoping the side of my face will heal without a skin graft. Miriam came to fetch me. She brought Mum, Nomatuli, Lilah, Jeth, Jo Jo and Spider, of course. I sat in the back with the children, clutching a pot plant and flowers, while they demolished two boxes of chocolates between them.

I forced myself to look as we passed Blue Gum but there was nothing to see, just blackness everywhere. We would be staying at Greys until I decided what to do.

No one mentioned the fire. At first all I wanted to do was sleep. Gloria and Nomatuli and the girls were always popping up with food and treats for the children. Mum helped out in the cafe too and it was the start of the new school term, so I was often on my own. It gave me space to think.

Maarten and Lionel hadn't been near me since I got home. Maybe they thought I needed time but I told Gloria I'd be happy to see them, any time. In the hospital my nurse told me that Maarten had sat by my bed every day, holding my hand and talking to me. It's strange because, even though I can't remember it, I'm sure I knew he was there. But once I recovered he stayed away. I wasn't the only one who missed him. 'Where's your lovely policeman?' the nurses asked. And, 'Don't know where your boyfriend is today but he wanted to give you this.' There were flowers and chocolates for me and one day, my beautiful little Coral tree - in a pot.

I needed to see him and thank him for everything and most importantly tell him I'd forgiven him. Nothing mattered now, now we were all safe. I had to let him know that I understood why he'd stood by his mother.

When I asked Gloria why Lionel and Maarten didn't come she couldn't look me in the face. 'They're busy, Kate.'

'Is Ma ill?'

Gloria shook her head furiously, suddenly very keen to be gone, 'But they send their love.' She was no good at lying.

I tried talking to Mum about it but she just changed the subject.

Finally I asked Nomatuli and she fixed me with one of her no-nonsense looks. 'I think that today maybe you are ready for the not so nice truth.'

I'm truly sorry that Antoinette died like that. But Ma? What she tried to do doesn't surprise me at all. My only reaction to her death is huge relief. Mum thinks that's terrible and perhaps she's right. All I know is that I don't have to be scared any more.

Nobody went to their funerals except Lionel, Gloria, Maarten and Miriam. None of the Groos clan showed up. It was held at the crematorium. Pastor Billy wasn't there. Suicide is a sin in this Christian community. Suicide. That was the official verdict and no one disputed it. It was well known that Antoinette was *a bit unstable* and Hannah Vantonde took her own life because she thought her beloved grandson was dead. *"Poor woman,"* I overheard Anne Marie say to Gloria. *"Too much grief for one woman to bear, ja?"*

I think that's what Gloria has decided to believe too. She's living at home again looking after Lionel. She clucks around him like one of Stompy's harem. Surprisingly she seems the strongest of us all. Maybe she has purpose in her life now and Nomatuli keeps her busy at Greys. Amazingly, Mum and Nomatuli are getting on well too. Of course I'm thrilled that Mum has decided to stay out here, I only hope it's really what she wants.

And Maarten? Each day that goes by I miss him more and more but what will I say when I see him? He loved his mother and she's dead and I'm glad.

The final death toll from the fire was nineteen and hundreds of poor people lost their homes and possessions. No one in the family has spoken about what Ma did. It is our secret. I will protect the name of the woman, who caused all that misery and almost destroyed me and Jeth, but it's not for her sake that I say nothing.

I don't know how long it will be before I can really believe we are safe. Sometimes, when I wake in the night I have such a terrible feeling of dread it takes my breath away. But then I open my eyes and they're all there, safely sleeping, my three children. I am close enough to touch them from where I lie. And the dog raises his head and looks at me, as if he too is surprised by our survival.

Jeth is silent as we bounce down the track in Lionel's bakkie. We haven't been back to Blue Gum since the fire. Jeth insisted on coming with me. Lilah and Jo Jo are in Hermanus with Mum and Nomatuli buying clothes. Jo Jo has his first solo spot on a charity TV show in a few weeks time. Kip Makusi has organised it and the money that's raised will go to the victims of the fire.

Miriam and Rob's bakkie is ahead of us on the track. They're checking to see if any of their trees survived the fire. It's amazing but there are still little pockets of untouched vegetation on the farm. Miriam's broken leg is healing well and she tells me they're moving to a smallholding just outside Cape Town. They're also thinking about adopting. I'm so pleased for them. I return their wave as we turn into what was once our home.

Jeth and I go in different directions.

All the back-breaking work Pete and I put into this place; all that love and all those tears, and for what? Absolutely nothing. I stare at the poor stricken gum tree. Surely it can never recover from this? Everywhere I look the ground is covered in a uniform shroud of sticky black soot. At least that's what I think until I get closer but there are other colours here. The patch of yellow daisies like a posy in the blackness; the solitary nerine, its beautiful pink petals shining out at me; the white and blue agapanthus, their flower heads dusted with black icing sugar.

I go up to where our tree nursery was. At least I don't have to be afraid of snakes today. Everything has been razed to the ground. All of Pete's special trees. I squeeze my eyes tight shut. *Regeneration. That's what the fynbos needs.*

Jeth is standing beside the excavation where his den was. He is kicking at the blackened earth and he bends down and picks up something. He holds the swing seat above his head. 'Look, Mum. It's still here.'

I join him. I can't bear to think about that time in the hole under the ground and I concentrate on the blackened piece of wood.

'How long does it take for an oak tree to grow big enough for a swing?' he asks.

'A long time, Jeth, hundreds of years maybe.' I take his free hand

and squeeze it. 'What d'you think your dad would want us to do now?'

'I dunno. What do you think?'

'I think he would want us to do whatever makes us happy.'

'We could stay at Greys,' he says, smiling. 'Lilah would love that because…'

'…It's close to the cakes,' I finish for him.

'Or we could go and live in England with Grandma.'

That surprises me. 'Um. But she says she wants to live here with us. Go into partnership with Nomatuli in Greys. Maybe I could start a proper plant nursery here on Blue Gum and we could build another house? Would you like that?'

'And we could all live together like one big happy family?'

I'm not expecting this. 'Well, it's not all that big.' I try not to think about Antoinette and Ma.

'Yes it is. There's Uncle Maarten. He's our family isn't he? Mum?'

Fortunately he doesn't wait for a reply.

'Then there's Grandma and you and…'

He counts off the people on his fingers, just like his dad would have done.

'…Lilah and Jo Jo, Lionel and Gloria and Nomatuli.' He's still counting. 'Oh and Spider of course.' He thinks for a minute. 'And then there's Anne Marie and Rosemary and …Nandhi, and Auntie Miriam and Uncle Rob and…'

When he starts on his school friends I ruffle his hair. 'We may need to build a whole town.'

I walk back to where the house once stood. Now is not the time to rummage through the remains. I look up as the evening sun kindles the

mountains into life and watch as the purple fingers of shadow probe
into the kloofs on the mountainside. I imagine a leopard standing there,
head raised, sniffing the air, ears pricked for the sound of encroaching
man. This is the leopard's home and one day he may come back. I
hope so. And Blue Gum was Pete's home. Where he belonged.
Suddenly I shiver but it's not the evening breeze that chills me.

'Kate?'

For a big man he moves very quietly.

'Maarten? Where've you been? I missed you.'

He stands there is his police uniform, twiddling his hat in one
hand, looking like a small child who's just put a brick through your
window. 'I didn't think you'd want to see me.

Not after...not after what she did.'

'Shh,' I say, holding out my hand. His large hand covers mine
and I feel the warmth of him and then I step into his arms. He
hesitates for just long enough to drop his hat and then he holds me,
and my face fits perfectly into the curve of his neck. I take a deep
breath and let it out slowly.

'Uncle Maarten, Uncle Maarten?' Jeth is waving and running
towards us. 'Can I have a go on your bike?'

As we wait for him to reach us two Hadeda ibis come bickering
through the sky and crash land on the remaining branch of the blue
gum. The branch bends crazily and threatens to catapult the birds
into the stratosphere. I catch Maarten's eye and we are both smiling
at the indignation on the bird's faces as they frantically flap their
wings to keep their balance. Then they hurl themselves upwards
and away, complaining bitterly into the distance.

I looked for Patterson's Curse that day. I didn't expect to find any. It's a clever little alien. It has survived the worst and now it is sleeping beneath the blackened earth waiting for the winter rains and the spring sun before showing its pretty little face above ground again.

A true survivor.